I o... "

Cairn blocked her path. Alysanna's startled eyes widened so she could feel her lashes against her brow. "I'm quite sure I don't know what you want with a governess." Alysanna knew exactly what he wanted; it was folly to hope his designs were honorable.

"Is that how you think I view you?"

"It is what I am." She cast her eyes sideways, afraid they could not veil the lie.

"What you are is . . ." Cairn stepped closer, lowering his arms like a gate around her. Alysanna felt she was turning liquid, nearly melting, as if Cairn were a white-hot blaze on her flesh. She closed her eyes, and her blood cried out for something nameless, sweet, and unspoken. She prayed he'd stop, but instead his lips brushed first gently against her own, then hungrily demanded them.

Cairn pulled her closer, leaving no doubt of his need for her. Unthinkingly, Alysanna lifted her hips wantonly to him, melding their bodies impossibly close. It was too much; if she didn't stop now, she never would.

"No!" she cried.

"Is that really what you want?"

Alysanna only wanted more of his hands on her face, his body crushed tight against her own, his mouth plumbing her soul with need . . .

—————————— ——————————

ALSO BY BLAINE ANDERSON

Love's Sweet Captive

Published by
POPULAR LIBRARY

Destiny's Kiss

Blaine Anderson

POPULAR LIBRARY

An Imprint of Warner Books, Inc.

A Warner Communications Company

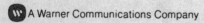

To my husband Mark, whose blue eyes and quick wit never fail to make my heart beat faster; to Alyce, whose loving care of Anna and Jill gave me the peace of mind to write; to my agent Sherry Robb, whose faith in me opened up a wonderful new world; and to my editor Jeanne Tiedge, whose keen judgement and guidance have made my work better.

CHAPTER
1

🌿

Briarhurst Downs, England, 1792

The pistol's silver barrel shook subtly, despite Alysanna Wilhaven's tight grip on its handle. Fear coursed like a current through her veins, but her voice spoke with calm assurance. "If you move one inch, I swear I'll fire."

She squinted to better gauge her target, fighting the urge to stare wide-eyed at the nightmare before her. Julia's body lay lifeless atop the carpet's thick warp, her raven hair blanketing its pattern as if loosened in some fierce struggle. Beneath her stepsister's satin waist sash, a rivulet of crimson seeped into the rug's pile, its path quickly lengthening and widening.

Alysanna shook her head to clear her vision, but her tears remained, lending the macabre scene an eerie soft focus as she drove her gaze up toward the ominous form towering over Julia. Looking more phantom than man, the murderer's black silhouette was relieved only by teasing shots of firelight.

He faced away from her, but his stillness encouraged her, allowed her the hope that he'd heeded her warning. Then, just as she took her first conscious breath since entering Briarhurst's library, the intruder turned toward her.

Had she more than the split second he gave her, Alysanna might have realized that, even head-on, the stranger could not challenge the pistol's threat. But confusion consumed her, and Alysanna sensed only that she must act quickly to avoid her stepsister's fate.

Reasoning fled in obeisance to instinct, and as surely as if she had committed the act a thousand times, Alysanna took a great breath and squeezed the pistol's stiff trigger. With an orange flash, its barrel exploded a leaden greeting into the stranger's twisting form.

If Alysanna's intent was marked by unwavering purpose, her aim was not. For though she could see her shot's bloody work on the murderer's thigh, she could also tell her quest had failed. The man lay prone on the thick carpet, but to Alysanna's horror, he again began to move. Fear sucked her breath from her as she realized she had only wounded him.

The pistol's spent missile stole her nerve. If she were to survive, Alysanna knew she had to run. The dueling weapon hit the parlor floor with a thud, its impact echoed by Alysanna's heels clicking across the marble foyer.

With frantic fingers she coaxed the lock free, then flew like a windstorm over the portico. She cursed her skirts, gathering them in wads as she jumped the porch's stairs, clinging close to the manor as she sped toward the southern wing.

With a tall hedgerow closer to the front door, Alysanna's choice of the more distant pavilion was not an obvious one.

At least she hoped so—she prayed with all her pounding heart that the silent, seemingly invincible stranger would not find her. She gasped with panic and exertion, yet struggled to still her loud breath, fearing any small noise would draw her pursuer like a hound to her lair.

She stood stiller than ever before in her twenty-one years. What she waited for she did not know; help was unlikely. Her stepmother Roberta was yet at the gala ball Alysanna had left early, and Alysanna suspected that the manor's full staff was filling their free night with the ribald pleasures of the nearby Bedford fair.

She tried to calm herself with assurances that someone would be home soon. But now, with no one near, she was quarry for a murderer who had not only killed her stepsister, but who was doubtless all the more bent on repeating the task in exchange for Alysanna's own botched attempt on his life.

Her fear made it hard to estimate time, but Alysanna leaned back against Briarhurst's cold stone for what seemed like a great while. There was no sound, no shadowy figure creeping around the pavilion's edge, and she nearly regained her composure when a crackle of close underbrush snapped her head in rediscovered terror.

The noise ended, then began again, beating out an insistent tattoo whose rhythm finally allowed her a sigh of relief—it was raining. But within moments the gentle patter ended, replaced by a torrent of watery misery that quickly soaked her dress's silk skirt and sent wretched trickles down her shivering, bare shoulders.

Alysanna's curly mane of cinnamon hair, undone by her swift canter home from the ball, stuck horridly to her wet flesh. Soon she was so uncomfortable she wished that if Julia's assailant were going to kill her, too, he would at least do it before she froze to death.

She had been flushed and hot from her argument with her stepsister at the Hamptons' soiree and had hardly noticed the unseasonable spring chill as she dismissed her carriage and rode home on a borrowed mare. But now, lacking even a light tippet, she was miserably aware of March's cold breath.

The audible dance of eager hooves in the courtyard's new mud abruptly ended her self-pity. Surely the whinnying animal awaited his murderous rider.

Alysanna's heart jumped to her throat, and she pushed her palms flat back against the building's slick wall, praying she had not been seen. Then, realizing the horseman might be friend, not foe, Alysanna leaned forward just enough to confirm her fears: she and the rider had already met.

She watched him mount with difficulty, the wounded leg's bloody flesh exposed by a fleeting pass of moonlight that forced its way through the burgeoning clouds. The stranger was obviously suffering, and he adjusted his seat on the animal several times, then dug the heel of his good leg into the sorrel's side. With a booming "Hoay!" horse and man flew like thunder down the Briarhurst road, then were swallowed by the darkness beyond.

Oblivious to the soaked earth beneath her, Alysanna collapsed, her head falling into her hands as a flood of teary relief surged in her eyes. "Julia!" Her stepsister's name, spoken aloud, quickly righted her as Alysanna remembered she still lay in the parlor.

When she had fired on the stranger, Alysanna had known Julia was dead. Yet now, her perceptions twisted by fear, she prayed by some miracle of fate that she had been mistaken.

Alysanna flew across Briarhurst's foyer, a wake of dark, grainy mud marking her path. Inside the parlor, just as before, was Julia. The crimson rivulet from her middle had slowed, though Alysanna guessed it was due more to the great wealth of blood already lost than any improvement in her state. Alysanna dropped to her knees, lifting Julia's bruised face into the cradle of her rain-soaked arms.

"Julia. Oh my God. I didn't mean it. I am so very sorry." Inexplicably, Alysanna spoke the words out loud, though her stepsister's horrifying appearance made it clear she couldn't hear.

While Julia's face was not beautiful, it had always been handsome enough to catch an occasional rake's eye. But its blush was now spent, faded to an ashen pallor. Alysanna stared at her, sobbing, then pressed her own warm cheek against Julia's cold flesh. Like a mother with a sleeping child, she rocked her gently, oblivious to the wash of red now turning her own aqua gown dark purple.

When Alysanna managed to open her eyes, she saw the cause of Julia's death—a pistol wound, raw and ragged, had torn through her stepsister's side. "Who was the man who did this to you?" Alysanna pleaded aloud, swearing silent justice for the savage killer.

Hoping for evidence against him, Alysanna laid Julia down and began to search the floor on her knees. But the distant slam of Briarhurst's front door made her spring to her feet, and she scrambled for cover inside a wall alcove.

"What's happened? Julia!" The voice, gratingly familiar, drew Alysanna from her makeshift den. She peeked cautiously out; it was Roberta. Her stepmother inspired small affection in her, but Alysanna knew now, of all times, Roberta certainly deserved her support. She rushed toward the doorway, and the stiff swoosh of her petticoats made the older woman jump. Alysanna reached to take her hands, but Roberta had already seen Julia and would suffer no distraction.

"Let me go!" Roberta pulled sharply back and raced toward

her daughter. Her eyes froze downward for a long moment, then wound their way back toward a teary Alysanna. "She is not . . . ?"

"Yes. She has been shot."

As if she too had been felled, Roberta crumpled, her hands flying to her face as she howled her anguish. She leaned across Julia's chest, her forehead pressed against her daughter's waist, her fingers tearing and scratching at her stained gown's ivory silk bodice. Roberta's sobs came in huge, racking swells, making her arch and heave with such force that Julia's body shook with each impact, looking eerily as though it still breathed.

Alysanna longed to comfort her but was shackled by her own horror. She stood back, allowing Roberta full rein for her grief.

Finally, when Roberta controlled her sobbing enough to speak, she rose to her knees, wiping the salt from her cheeks with the back of one shaking hand. She looked up slowly, as if she were ill, and locked her narrowed eyes on Alysanna. A strange realization flashed over her face.

"You!" Before Alysanna could digest her intent, Roberta sprung across the room, her hands waving wildly until satisfied with handfuls of Alysanna's loose hair. "How could you kill my Julia?" Roberta's voice was razored with fury, and her hazel eyes glistened with a feral glint. Alysanna was sure she had gone quite mad.

"I didn't," Alysanna blurted, wrestling with Roberta's fists and twisting her head sideways to loosen the woman's clutch. Roberta finally stopped her crazed assault.

"Then who?" Roberta demanded furiously, her face a tableau of anger and pain.

Alysanna sputtered her explanation as quickly as possible, hoping to stave off another attack. "There was a stranger. I came home early from the ball. After the fight with Julia, I went upstairs to find her when I heard a noise. I thought it a housebreaker and pulled the bell rope for help, but the servants had all left for the fair. I was alone, so I loaded father's pistol and went to see. This man—''

"Who was he?" No matter how quickly Alysanna dispatched her tale, Roberta wanted the account faster.

"I told you, a stranger. I came in and saw that Julia was dead. The intruder's back faced me, and I ordered him still. He moved and I shot. Then, when I realized I'd missed, I fled."

"You missed him?" It was not a question, but an accusation.

"Not entirely." Alysanna's sympathy was fading at Roberta's bullying. "I hit his leg. But it did not finish him, so I ran. This soaked state I'm in is the benefit of hiding outside in the rain."

"Is the man still about?" Roberta's features tangled in alarm as she turned her tightly coiffed head left, right and left again in quick little snaps.

"While I hid, he left. His horse was tethered in the drive, though I did not see it when I came home. That is all I know." Alysanna straightened her bloodstained skirt as she considered what to do next. "I suppose we should find the constable. Is he still at the ball?"

Roberta stumbled back to Julia, beyond hearing Alysanna's question. She stared down, her eyes glassy and distant, then knelt reverently beside her daughter. Her hand brushed across Julia's calm face, which lay in unnerving counterpoint to her mussed hair and gaping wound.

"Roberta?"

Her stepmother's head jerked sideways, and a look of annoyance flashed from her eyes. "Why are you bothering me?"

"The constable—we should let him know. Was he still at the Hamptons' when you left?"

Roberta shook her head as if something were buzzing about it. "He can't help. He's in his cups."

Alysanna let go a heavy sigh. If they set after the killer while his trail was still fresh, there was hope of capture. But a drunken search party might work more harm than good. It was raining and dark, anyway—hardly good weather for tracking.

More to the point, who would fetch help? Alysanna stared at Roberta, who rocked to and fro. There was no leaving her in this shaken state. They would have to wait until the morrow, then send a houseman to find Constable Fisk.

For now, there was the problem of Julia. They could not leave her here, though Alysanna didn't know what else to do. At the very least, Roberta needed calming. Alysanna poured a draught of brandy and bent close, extending the snifter. "Drink this. It will help." Roberta rocked on silently. "Roberta. You cannot stay here."

Her eyes narrowed, studying Alysanna. "Leave me alone with my Julia."

"*Roberta.*" Alysanna's tone implored her stepmother to reason, but the plea was useless. Roberta looked as unlikely as Julia to get up and leave. She intended to stay in the parlor, bent over the body; nothing short of dragging her out would shake her resolve.

With cross distaste, Alysanna resigned herself to sharing the vigil—to protect against the intruder's return, if nothing more. Her hands still shaking, she lifted the pistol back up from the floor and reloaded it with powder and lead.

With a weary plunk, Alysanna settled into a chair near the fire. She was tired—overwhelmingly, incredibly tired—as if a great weight were pressing her down. She felt drugged, yet knew it was vital she keep a keen watch.

Alysanna wrenched her spine to an awkward pose, hoping the discomfort would keep her awake. This was better. She rested the pistol's warm barrel in her palm. If he came back, she would be ready.

"Tell me again." The bantam rooster of a constable folded his stubby arms across his chest.

"I've told you all I know." It had been ghastly enough recounting last night's tumultuous happenings even once; Alysanna had no patience to repeat them again.

"Lady Alysanna, this is a serious matter. I need your cooperation." The constable squinted in irritation.

Alysanna had not slept at all last night, and she longed for a hot soak and bed. Why couldn't this nuisance of a man understand?

"You have my cooperation, but my story will not change simply for retelling. I have told you everything."

The constable's white brows drew together, giving him as stern a look as his cherub's face would allow. "Yet all you say is that some stranger killed your stepsister—a man you cannot even describe."

"His back was to me."

"Yet you say he turned before you shot. Surely you saw something of his face?"

"No. It was dark and . . ." Alysanna paused, suddenly realizing that the constable suspected she was withholding information. She had not considered her tale strange, but, on reflection, it did sound sketchy. She struggled through her memory, made cloudy by fatigue, for some overlooked fact that would make him believe her.

"The man was tall."

"And his hair color?"

Alysanna sighed. "It was too dark."

"There was enough firelight for you to shoot." Constable Fisk stepped closer, and Alysanna cringed at the stale smell of tobacco on his breath.

"As you'll recall, my shot failed. Perhaps if I had seen the man I would have killed him."

"Is it your habit to fire without asking questions?"

"She's always been an impulsive one. When her father, Lord Frederick, lived, even he stayed clear of her temper. It's her mother's Irish blood, you know."

Alysanna threw Roberta an arrow of a look. This was hard enough without her stepmother's prattle mucking it up more.

"So you said nothing to him." The constable made a note and pressed on.

"I told him not to move or else I'd shoot."

"And he didn't listen?"

"Obviously. Am I on trial? You seem to question my recital."

John Fisk grunted as he lowered himself into a nearby chair. "I am only trying to find the truth, so we must plumb your memory as best we can."

"You'd do better to find the killer than to waste your time here with me."

"Madame, I will choose how I spend my time. I will concede you seem to be of little further use. We'll mount a search for the man you accuse. Until he's found, please keep to the county."

"Am I being held?"

"Only a precaution—in case we need your witness. Have I your promise?"

Clearly there was no bargaining with the man; Alysanna sighed in resignation. "Yes." She spun away, staring out the window down the Briarhurst road. All she'd done was try to help Julia—and look what her altruism had wrought.

The constable nodded his respects to Roberta. "Your ladyship, I'll be going. I know you have matters of your own to attend to, with your poor daughter and all. I trust I can count on you to . . ." His voice trailed into a whisper, giving Alysanna the distinct sense he was talking about her.

"Good day, Lady Alysanna."

"Good day." Alysanna didn't bother to turn as she spoke her farewell. "I trust you will pursue this matter with all due speed."

"Assuredly."

She breathed a sigh of relief as the library door slammed shut. "How dare he! Imagine, implying my story is unsound."

Roberta straightened her skirt with a rustle. "I should think his search for the truth would be your cause as well."

Alysanna turned, ready to battle. "Why are my motives here suspect?"

Roberta's chin jutted forward as if her collar were too tight. "You must admit, the circumstances are unusual."

"And how is that?"

Roberta paused, cautious. The constable's questions had given her the idea, but she had to take great care how she phrased it. Her husband, Frederick, had distrusted her near the end—he had accused her of marrying him only to fatten her purse. To outwit her, he had written his will to make Alysanna sole mistress of Briarhurst, providing she resided there and left for no more than six months' time. It was a provision intended to keep Briarhurst safe from Roberta's greed—one Roberta doubted Alysanna was aware of. She had been so distraught the day of the will's reading that she barely heard anything. Briarhurst's rents could keep a fine style. If Alysanna could be forced away, Frederick's intentions might well be twisted to Roberta's advantage.

"Roberta, you look as though you didn't hear."

"Of course I did. I was thinking on your interests."

"That would be a change," Alysanna snapped tartly.

Roberta placed her hands on either side of Alysanna's slender shoulders and pressed her into a nearby chair. "It concerns me that this man, this murderer, is yet at large."

"I trust the constable will find him."

"Certainly he will try. But with no description, the hunt could take time—time I'm not sure you can afford."

"What is it you are implying?"

"You were a witness. You cannot think the murderer means to let you go."

Until now, Alysanna had considered little else but bringing Julia's killer to justice. It had not occurred to her that she might be a target. "You believe the man will follow me?"

"I think he would be a fool did he otherwise."

"But he has no reason to want me—I cannot describe him!"

"He does not know that."

Alysanna laced her fingers tensely as she considered Roberta's suggestion. No, the man had to be long gone by now. Whatever he wanted from Julia, he'd be mad to linger close by.

"I think your grief has you overconcerned. I am not worried for my safety."

Roberta could see this plan would not work; she must try another.

"Of course, you're right. But what of the constable? Your tale did not sit overly well with him. You claim a mystery man as Julia's killer—a man you cannot describe, wielding a weapon you cannot produce."

"Did you think the killer would leave the pistol here for our study?"

"I think your thin story may try the patience of some. And there is yet the matter of your argument with Julia. Of course I made no mention of it, but others at the ball overheard. It would be naive to think an inquest would not raise the tale."

"You know well what that was about. Julia wanted access to her marriage portion. I told her that I intended to keep control, but that she would not go lacking. I had no reason to wish her harm."

"I understand. Still, many heard your pitch more than your words. Then, to have both you and Julia leave so precipitously. . ."

"I came home to make amends with her. What's your twisted insinuation?"

"No notion that other's minds won't find. What's to stop our neighbors from thinking *you* Julia's killer?"

Alysanna's dark brows tangled in shock at Roberta's shameful suggestion. "Are you accusing me of the murder?"

"Your unfounded distrust has always done me a disservice, Alysanna. The notion of your involvement will not be mine, but others will come to it on their own."

Roberta's logic was transparent. No neighbor was likely to put the law on her scent—it was Roberta herself. "Do you plan to have me arrested?"

"You are so unfair with me . . ."

"I see your thinly disguised reasoning, stepmother. 'Tis to part me from Briarhurst so you can enjoy its wealth unhindered—wealth that you had no part in earning, save your pursuit of my poor, trusting father. Let me assure you, no scheme of yours will steal what is mine.''

"It would be quite out of my hands should the law find you guilty.''

Just now the full lengths to which Roberta was prepared to go became clear. She would see Alysanna on the gallows if Briarhurst could be made hers for the trade.

"If you have me arrested, I'll simply confess. Confessed criminals forfeit all their property to the Crown. You would lose everything—even Briarhurst. That would hardly serve your good fortune.''

Roberta's expression made it clear that she had not considered this possibility. Still, she continued the ruse.

"I would not want you to meet such an unfortunate fate, in any event. Yet, should it come to pass, sending Briarhurst to King George's coffers would be small solace if you swung from the gibbet. I trust you will come to see the wisdom of my plan. Between our friends' suspicions and the killer's need for protection, it is hardly safe for you here. Were I you, I'd flee—perhaps even pose as someone else—if you want to save your pretty neck.''

Alysanna stood frozen in frantic thought. Roberta's foul motives were shameful and clear; still, could it be she was right? Her argument with Julia had been loud and overheard. And the killer would have every reason to want her dead.

Yet, to abandon Briarhurst was unthinkable! Roberta's greed would find satisfaction, and giving up her home would force Alysanna to betray all Frederick had taught her to value.

"Heritage,'' her father had admonished, ''is the most precious gift of all. Your name and Briarhurst matter most.''

Briarhurst was less where Alysanna lived than who she was. Position was everything. Leaving, assuming a new identity. . . . No, Alysanna vowed silently, there must be another way. Hadley would know.

"The constable will speak with others who heard your fight. If you think to leave, my advice would be to do it soon."

Alysanna's eyes drifted, then snapped back to Roberta. "I'll go. But don't count the rents so quickly, stepmother. I am only off to see Hadley. His affections serve me better than yours."

Alysanna flew from the room, angrily crashing the front door closed.

"Hadley," laughed Roberta, tipping her face backwards as she cocked her hands on her hips. "Now, that should prove an interesting proposition."

CHAPTER 2

Alysanna blew past Lord Hadley Seaham's butler like a hurricane, knocking the wind from the gray-haired liveryman and making him leap to avoid being felled. Her urgent manner took Hadley by storm; though they were engaged to be married, such passionate displays were not what he'd come to expect.

Alysanna's speed was underscored by her wild appearance. Her rich cascade of sienna-colored hair, elaborately twisted with ribbons and flowers at last night's ball, now flew loose about her shoulders, its curly tendrils made even tighter by the morning rain. She still wore the aqua silk from the Hamptons' assembly, but last night's billowy skirt now hung limp and wilted.

She hurled herself into Hadley's outstretched arms, obviously overwrought. He pulled her close. Alysanna moaned in misery as she stood on tiptoe to press her wet cheek against his.

"Darling, you're half drowned! Where's your carriage? What's happened?" Hadley lifted her chilly face, then noticed that her emerald eyes glistened with a wash of tears. "Of course. It was the altercation with Julia, was it not? I saw you leave. I tried to catch you, but by the time I reached my carriage, you'd already gone. My poor love, I wish you'd waited. Were you up all night worrying?" He nodded toward her dress, noting how unlike her it was to look so disheveled. "I know how such things upset you."

"Oh, Hadley, it is more than you know." Alysanna pulled back slightly. With halting words, she recounted her odyssey with Julia and the constable. Finally, her chest heaving with sobs, she collapsed, exhausted, into a huge black wing chair facing the fire.

"So you see, Roberta thinks only to part me from Briarhurst. I can't leave. Yet, despite her vile motives, I can't deny that she does makes sense."

Hadley knelt next to her, taking one slender hand, reddened from its gloveless ride in the rain, in his own. "Are you sure the constable disbelieves you?"

"He is close enough. With a small push from Roberta, he'll have a warrant for me within the week. Damn that stupid argument! If I hadn't fought with Julia. . . . I should have just given her the money. I only refused because I thought it would end up in Roberta's purse."

"Perhaps if we could straighten matters out with the authorities . . ."

"It's hopeless. And anyway, that would hardly dissuade the killer's pursuit of me."

Hadley raised Alysanna's fingers to his lips, warming them with a kiss. "Are you sure he knows who you are?"

"At most he saw only my back as I fled."

"Then there's no reason for alarm."

"He knows I had business at Briarhurst. Unless he's a fool, he won't rest 'til he finds me. As galling as it is, Roberta is right—I have to go."

"But where? Can you stay nearby?"

"No point in that. A city—London, perhaps—though God knows who would harbor me there."

Alysanna's mind was clear but her chest jumped with erratic, frightened sobs. Hadley pulled her head close, trying to still her twitching breath. Suddenly she jerked upwards, her eyes brimming with an idea. "Beatrice!"

"Your old governess?"

"She is still in London—as of her last Michaelmas letter, at least. Perhaps she can find some place to stow me until the storm has passed."

Hadley's eyes reached out to her, but she had already decided. "Then there is nothing I can do to dissuade you?"

"No," Alysanna answered softly, pressing a kiss against his temple. "As much as I want to stay, I must go. It's the only way I can remain safe. I came hoping you would think of a way to keep me, but my only choice is all too clear."

"Is there anything I can do to help you?"

"You can find the real killer. It's the only way to clear my name."

"Of course."

"And Roberta—keep your eye on her. She is more dishonest than you know. Have I your promise?"

"Give me your trust. I'll not fail." Hadley clutched Alysanna tightly but could not restrain her as she rose.

"Then it is settled. If we hurry, we can still make the late-morning coach. I packed only a small bag, hoping I could stay with you and send for more later. As it is, my few dresses will have to serve more permanently, though it might be foolish to flee without disguise. Have you some things I can wear?"

Hadley raised his hands helplessly. "I do not keep a complement of lady's clothes here."

"Your chambermaids! Surely their closets hold something useful."

"If you think it will help."

"I think for now, we can consider that the Lady Alysanna Wilhaven exists no more."

"I suppose you expect my thanks." Hadley hurled his cloak halfway across the library, making Roberta jump as it landed next to her. From the fearful look on her face, she had thought herself alone.

"Is it your habit to enter like some madman? And what are you babbling about?"

"Alysanna's gone. Your handiwork has sent my future packing."

Roberta's face lit with hope. "Then, you didn't dissuade her?"

Hadley blew out a disgruntled snort and helped himself to Roberta's brandy. "I'd have tried, but you'd sewn it up too tight. I drove her to the coach house this morning. She's off to London, thanks to the vise you crafted, catching her between the constable and the killer."

"Her situation was not of my making. If you're implying I had anything to do with it, you're mistaken."

"Save your lies, Roberta. They've a familiar ring. You may not have sparked the constable's suspicions, but you did nothing to dampen them. And you've goaded Alysanna's fears of the killer himself. I'm sure you thought this would be a tidy escape from our deal—a way to keep Briarhurst all to yourself.''

Roberta twisted her fingers together. ''I won't deny it was a fortunate turn of events—one that may see me become Briarhurst's sole mistress, though I hardly feel jubilant. You'll recall this all began with Julia's death.''

Hadley could not contain a laugh. ''Yes, I see you have donned your mourning wear.'' He nodded toward Roberta's bright yellow dress—altogether unacceptable, considering her loss.

''I have lacked time to instruct my maid. How dare you imply. . . .''

''I imply nothing. I know you to be a liar and a cheat. You'll recall it was you who had the notion to steal part of Briarhurst to begin with. Surely you have not already forgotten our arrangement—that you would help me woo and wed Alysanna, in exchange for paying a portion of Briarhurst's rents back to you once I married her.''

''There was nothing unconscionable about our agreement. Alysanna was none the worse for it; she seemed happy enough with you.''

''If her happiness were paramount, you'd have let her choose her own mate. But then, that would have risked the estate slipping from your greedy grasp to a husband you could not control. How perfect that you knew of my gambling debts, my need for funds. Such timing—my return from abroad when Alysanna was vulnerable from her father's death.''

Roberta threw Hadley an indignant look. ''You're an odd one to suddenly take up her cause. You were all too happy to cooperate in luring her toward the marriage.''

''Indeed. But then, I had a fortune to gain. Now, with my fiancée forced off by your threats, what dim future can I look to?''

Roberta paced like a cat, uneasy with Hadley's agitation. "At least now you're free to chase any skirt you please. As I recall, you harbored no great passion for Alysanna."

"That's hardly the point."

"Then state it."

"I need funds. With Alysanna gone, I have only one place from which to get them."

"And where would that be?"

"Rather whom." Hadley stared back intensely.

Roberta tossed out a ribbon of a laugh. "Surely this is a jest. You think I'll pay you? I'm sorry for your misfortune, but 'twas not I who forced Alysanna's shot at some stranger. I have consequences of my own to deal with, not the least of which is Julia's death. Besides, I won't even own Briarhurst 'til Alysanna's been gone six months. It's written in the earl's will."

"A fact you have reason to believe she's unaware of. How convenient for you. And how inconvenient that I know. Do you think Alysanna's absence would bear up in a court of law if I revealed how you forced her off? And consider what would happen if I were to discuss our little arrangement with Alysanna—not only that she must return in half a year, but that you schemed to marry her to me in return for part of Briarhurst. If Alysanna knew the depths of your duplicity, she'd never keep her distance, no matter the cost. You know how impulsive her temper can be. You'd be lucky if she didn't shoot you."

"How dare you threaten me!"

A smug smile crept over Hadley's face. "Yes, if she knew you as the viper you are, I'm sure she'd risk anything to keep her precious inheritance safe. In your position, I'd not gamble on my silence."

Roberta squinted furiously at him. "You would have as much to lose as I."

"What? My fine reputation? Gone. My fiancée? Gone as well. The cost for my honesty would be all yours to pay."

Roberta slammed her palm with a bang on the desk. "All right! What do you want?"

"Five hundred pounds."

"Very well." Roberta opened the desk drawer and withdrew her ledger.

"A month. To start. We'll see where it goes from there."

"It is too much!"

"It is nothing compared to all you'd lose were Alysanna to return and cast you out. You and Julia were not faring too well until you mined the earl of Birkham's fat purse. And rest assured, if Alysanna comes back, I'll spend my every effort to clear her name—and her right to Briarhurst."

"If you think to still marry her, I swear I won't allow it."

"Don't trouble yourself. I'm glad to be free of her— particularly since I'll fare better with you as my banker. And I don't even have to keep to your bed. Thank God."

Roberta scribbled the note, her hand quivering with rage. She shoved the paper at Hadley's chest. "There's your blood money. It damn well better buy your silence."

Hadley smiled, then smacked a quick kiss on Roberta's cheek. "Thank you, love. It seems we are partners again."

Roberta wiped her face, feeling as if she'd just been soiled.

The morning swept over Alysanna like a feverish dream, leapfrogging from one nightmare to another. Despite her disguise of a maidservant's hat and oversized coat, she feared Hadley's carriage would give her away, so she'd asked to be dropped off a mile from the coach house. At the time it had seemed prudent; now, her skirts caked with the muddy aftermath of last night's storm, Alysanna didn't know what had driven her thinking.

The long march to the coach station had been hard enough; to make matters worse, the stage was full, and Alysanna was unable to find a spot. The final straw was the thieving driver, who had left with her bribe but failed to deliver the seat he promised. It had been over an hour since she'd seen the full carriage bounce off without her, yet the memory still brought a flush of heat to Alysanna's face.

With the next transport to London not due 'til the morrow, she had begun a discouraged walk back to Wodeby. Now, less than midway there, her soggy, tired feet ached with cold, and Alysanna fought against the overwhelming urge to stop altogether.

Alysanna sank her suitcase into the road's muddy slope and in discouraged exhaustion, she plopped down on it. She was almost too drained to be angry. So weary she could not bear to look at the winding turnpike, Alysanna doffed her oversized hat and dropped her head, her loosely pinned hair tumbling about her face. She spent a long, tired sigh and sought the memory of last night's lavish assembly.

Before the fight with Julia, the evening had been splendid. The lace-trimmed gown commissioned from the French mantua-maker, its embroidered fabric specially bespoken for her, had set envious tongues atwitter. To Alysanna's delight, Hadley had even allowed the minions of young men her beauty drew to dance their attentions on her.

A finely etched image of the candlelit gallery, its high walls awash with golden light and full to the brim with a contredanse's lilting strains, lifted Alysanna up from her cold, wet present. Absentmindedly, she began to hum softly. But a great splash of mud exploded her reverie, ending her song and jerking her suddenly filthy face upwards.

"Whoa, Solomon; there, Dante." Alysanna scraped a clammy dollop of mire from her eyelid, and looked up. A finely liveried driver atop the box of an elegant coach stared down at her. Gilded wheel hubs rocked the carriage's painted body forward and back with the horses' anxious movement, and Alysanna craned her neck sideways to see if she knew the madman traveling at such a dangerous pace. A handsome visage popped through the portal in the coach's door panel.

"Madame, my deepest regrets." Alysanna stiffened indignantly at the stranger's address, standing as she spat the grit from her lips. "I see our wheels have christened you with the road's debris."

It sounded like an apology, but there was an edge to the speaker's tone that rang wrong, and his mouth gave the slightest hint of a smile. His pleasant expression annoyed her, pushed her toward anger.

She knew she must look a sight, but this mess she wore was none of her doing and all of his. The least he could do was to sound sincere.

"Indeed," she snapped, trying to loosen the muddy globs that stuck to her skirt. "Had you not been speeding at a highwayman's pace, I daresay I would not have suffered this squalid bath."

Alysanna stared at the stranger; inexplicably, she felt the tension drain from her face. His slate-grey eyes danced with wicked promise, their mischief inconsistent with the patrician features in which they were set. The man looked much the aristocrat, yet the impression was shaken by his disheveled mop of sun-kissed hair, which tumbled just to the shoulders of his black velvet waistcoat.

The stranger sat intractably inside the coach, making no effort to step down and help her. Still, Alysanna could gauge him tall, and she imagined that he would easily tower over her own modest height.

"Of course. I gather from your expression that you await an introduction. I am Lord Cairn Chatham, duke of Lyddon. Madame, I am truly sorry for the distress I've caused. May I have the pleasure of knowing whom I've offended?"

"The Lady Alysanna W——" As she began the answer, Alysanna realized her real name would risk everything she sought to protect. Wilhaven was a moniker laden with power and prestige; to be safe, she would have to lie.

"Alysanna Walker. That is my name."

"My pleasure." Cairn Chatham dipped his head but his eyes clung to Alysanna, flattering her with their uneasy attention. Courtesy required that he stand, yet he made no effort.

"May I ask the purpose of your roadside vigil? Most on foot here are either beggar or rogue. Since you look neither, I can only assume you seek the coach house, but I must tell you it is quite some distance from here. 'Tis a dangerous proposition, even in daylight, to walk these wild roads unattended."

Alysanna's expression soured at the memory of the morning's disaster. "I hardly intended to walk. The coach to London was full, and, though the driver promised me a seat, his stage left with only my money."

Cairn nodded in commiseration. "A terrible turn of events. Perhaps you would accept my offer of transport. As it happens, I am en route to London, as well, though were I not, 'twould be the least I could do in light of the trouble I have caused."

Alysanna's first instinct was to agree, but she checked her

answer; it was wildly imprudent to travel alone with a complete stranger. The man looked like one of the Quality—he was certainly well-dressed, and the coach suggested a considerable station—still, it was not her custom to even address gentlemen to whom she had not been properly introduced. Now, to consider a full day with this man in the carriage's close confines. . . .

Alysanna decided it simply wouldn't do. She would be better off returning to Hadley's. But as she stared down the turnpike's twisting bends, she realized the distance home would take her more than a day on foot—a day that could well see her arrested, perhaps hanged for her silly propriety. She had no choice but to accept the stranger's offer.

"You are too kind. Are you sure my joining you would not be an inconvenience? I would be happy to pay you for your trouble."

"Madame, perish the thought. Consider the journey my apology for the mud you so attractively wear."

Alysanna stiffened at the comment, which cast further aspersions on the man's intentions. It was the second time in the few minutes they'd known each other that he'd commented on her person. Still, what other choice had she than to accept his offer?

"Very well, then. I believe my case will manage in the rumble-tumble."

"I should think so. Can you reach it?"

Alysanna froze at the reply. No gentleman would suggest she load her own luggage.

"You wish me to lift the baggage?"

"Only yours. I don't think you need move my valise to fit. Daniel could help, but, as you can see, Solomon needs his steady hand." Obligingly, one of the coach's pair of bays sounded a loud, eager whinny.

It was clear to Alysanna that, were she to achieve London today, it would only be by heaving her own suitcase aboard. With difficulty she managed, then returned, breathless, to the vehicle's open door. He extended his large hand toward her. Alysanna reluctantly accepted, but quickly recoiled once she was inside.

The coach was small but opulent, its buttery-soft leather a welcome change from her suitcase perch. Even the coach's interior walls and ceiling were richly upholstered. As she studied the carriage, Alysanna considered that this Cairn Chatham, duke of Lyddon, must be a very wealthy, if very rude, man.

Yet, despite the walls' padding, the spring chill set hard within, and Alysanna covetously eyed Cairn's thick woolen throw. It lay on his lap, and as the carriage lurched forward, he tightened it over his thighs, squelching her hopes of him offering it up.

Alysanna wrapped her hands around her elbows to lessen her cold misery, but the hint went unheeded, though not for lack of Cairn Chatham's attentions. He stared at her with an appreciative gleam. She had enjoyed men's attentions before, but not when she wore such ridiculous attire, and his scrutiny made her shift nervously.

Alysanna threw her gaze out the window to the hills beyond, hoping her distraction would discourage him. Instead, he reached toward her.

"May I?" He leaned so close she could smell the rich scent of leather on his gloves. He pulled one off and raised his hand to the edge of her face.

"Pardon me?" Alysanna wrenched as far sideways as the narrow seat would allow, her fears about her coach mate rekindled.

"There is a spot of mud on your cheek." His finger moved

toward her, and Alysanna snapped her head down, rubbing her face vigorously to preempt his efforts.

"Thank you. I can manage." She raised her chin, sure the matter was finished.

"Not quite." Before Alysanna could stop him, Cairn wet his finger and brushed a slow swipe over the crest of her cheekbone. Alysanna tipped her head back but the evasion failed. He softly smoothed off the smudge, and a shudder shot up her back at his touch. His eyes roamed over her face, devouring her with an indecent intensity.

There was something profoundly unsettling in his stare— a pull that made her feel she was being drawn close to him. Her response rattled her, and she sputtered a soft "thank you," as Cairn lowered his hand. He continued to stare, and Alysanna began to wonder if she looked suspicious.

On reflection, she imagined so. The oversized coat she had stolen from Hadley's maid was not only too large, but its worn, nubby cotton stood in stark contrast to the expensive wool dress she wore beneath.

Still, Cairn Chatham's eyes did not quite suggest distrust. Rather, they held a blend of delight and intrigue. The weight of it stirred her belly and made Alysanna want to wriggle.

Self-consciously, she tugged at the coat's closure, struggling to conceal the finely tailored wool beneath. Her elbow nudged the warped hat she had set on the seat beside her, and at once she realized that she was not only hatless, but that her nearly waist-length hair now tumbled improperly about her shoulders.

Alysanna guessed she must look terribly wanton, and she wondered that a man of Cairn Chatham's station would offer her a ride at all. Under other circumstances, she might have primped and paraded for a such a fine face; now, all she could hope for was that her appearance wouldn't draw his questions.

With forced calm, Alysanna gathered her tresses into a mass, then twisted them up into a chignon that she secured with the shabby millinery. The well-worn hat's interior felt unclean and awful, but at least it matched the coat. Alysanna raised her eyes to find herself still prisoner of Cairn Chatham's unrelenting stare.

"I liked it better down."

She did, too, and his comment pleased her. Still, it was quite improper to speak to her so, and Alysanna nearly rebuffed his interest until she reconsidered how far they had yet to travel. There was no point in provoking him. Hoping to draw Cairn's attention off her person, she struggled toward polite conversation.

"Tell me, Lord Chatham, what is your business near Bedford? I have not seen you in these parts before."

"I have no business here. My destination was farther north— the matter was of small consequence."

Alysanna bristled at his dismissal. She hardly cared what his purpose here was, but he could at least offer a civil reply.

"I see. But you are en route to London?"

"It is my home—at least during the season." Cairn's lap throw began to slip as he spoke, and in what seemed to Alysanna a strange hurry, he lunged to retrieve it.

Wrapping its thick folds around his breeches, he sighed raggedly. It sounded almost as if he were in pain, but his exhalation bore the unmistakable scent of whiskey. Good Lord, he was drunk!

"Sir . . . ." Alysanna again caught her tongue. Her escape to London was crucial, even if she must keep company with an ill-mannered souse to get there. Then, as if to bait her hard-won patience, Cairn pulled a small silver flask from his pocket and downed a long swig. This was too much. Alysanna's choler beat down her control.

"Lord Chatham, would it be possible to postpone your pleasures 'til we're no longer trapped in this coach together?"

"If we were traveling a shorter distance. As it is, the trip to London will take nearly the entire day. I fear my abstinence is impossible."

Alysanna sighed angrily, then snapped her head sideways, searching the rolling green hills speeding past the window as she tried to ignore his rude behavior. She refused to empower him with one more glance, but she could still hear. He took three or four more drinks, then finally, blessedly, fell into a deep, sonorous sleep.

Out from under his prying eyes, Alysanna now studied her companion. He had a fine appearance, to be sure. How strange to find such ill-breeding couched in such an attractive guise. The incongruous combination fascinated her, and Alysanna stared for a long while, gripped by the odd sense that he was somehow familiar. Was it possible they had met?

She thought of last night's legions of young sparks—could he have been among them? She concluded it was not likely. Lord Chatham said he had some business farther north. Likely he only reminded her of someone else, though Alysanna could not imagine that, with such dashing looks, she could not remember whom. She dismissed the thought, then closed her weary eyes.

She awoke to the sound of an apple's crisp crunch. For a moment she could not recall where she was, but the rough jostle of the carriage and the smiling visage of Cairn Chatham quickly grounded her.

"You must be tired. I doubt I could sleep without assistance." Cairn patted his upper pocket, and the metallic ding made it clear it was his flask.

"I'm fine," she answered, straightening her skirts as she inventoried what she was sure was her mussed appearance. She stared at the shiny green apple Cairn held in his hand.

"Is there a post house soon?"

"Yes, but we won't be stopping."

"Why not?"

"I am in somewhat of a hurry. I hope it poses no problem." In fact, the carriage's speed helped more than hindered Alysanna's cause, but it did nothing to assuage the hunger gnawing in her belly. She had often traveled the road to London before, but never without a meal stop.

"No, I just. . ."

"Of course. How thoughtless of me. You must be famished. Here—I'm afraid it's all I have. Poor planning." He extended the apple to her, but she made no move to reach for it.

Cairn saw her hesitation. "I'm sorry. I know I've already taken a bite. But as it is, this poor little fruit is the only sustenance. I did not plan on such a lovely—and hungry— companion."

Alysanna was embarrassed by his offer. He had been in the coach longer than she; he too must be famished.

"I couldn't. Really." She mustered a half smile and shook her head.

"I can hardly enjoy it in front of you."

Alysanna weighed her hunger against her guilt. "Are you sure?"

"After the inconvenience I've caused, 'tis the least I can do. I'm sorry we cannot stop. There are—extenuating reasons for my rush home. But you needn't starve." Again he offered her the fruit, and this time Alysanna took it.

"You are too kind." Alysanna dispatched the apple greedily. When she had finished, Cairn threw her a satisfied look.

"Better?"

"Much." Alysanna smiled, embarrassed by her gluttony.

"Tell me, Miss Walker, what is your business in London?"

Foolishly, Alysanna had not yet fashioned a tale. Ignoring his query would not work. Whatever came to mind would have to do.

"My family is from a northern county. My father . . . That is to say—"

"A northern county? From your comment earlier, I had thought you indigenous."

"No, I mean, formerly—yes, but of late I have lived elsewhere."

"And your father is still there?"

"Yes. No. He died. He recently died."

"You seem unsure."

Alysanna felt a rush of blood fire her ivory skin. "I would certainly know."

"Of course. I'm sorry." Cairn's gaze again struck its former intensity, and Alysanna felt as though he was branding her eyes.

"What is it you seek in London?"

"I am looking for an old friend of mine."

"Yes?" Damn his prying questions—was she under inquisition? She wanted to squelch his nosiness with a tart dismissal, but dared not rouse his suspicions. He knew she had come from Bedford. It was unlikely he would cross paths with anyone from there, but if he did, it would not serve her to have him telling tales of the strange, nervous woman he had found in the road.

"Pardon me, Lord Chatham, but you really needn't worry about my affairs. They are small matters. What difference could it make to you whom I seek?"

"None at all. It is only my natural curiosity. Though I

must admit, considering how I found you, I do feel somewhat your steward."

"That is not necessary," Alysanna snapped, then winced at the curt sound of her reply. "I'm sorry. My friend's name is Beatrice Doughton."

"Then you will allow me to take you to her?"

"Thank you, but I'm sure I can manage on my own."

"Miss Walker, you must see the nonsense of hiring another coach when you already have mine at your full disposal. I won't hear of anything other than delivering you straight there. Where does your friend Beatrice live?"

Alysanna realized that she didn't know. She had no address at all. All she knew was that Beatrice worked for a powerful viscount named Duncan Granville.

"I'm afraid . . ."

"Yes?"

"It sounds odd, I know, but I am unsure of exactly where she resides."

"Then how did you expect to find her?"

"It is difficult to explain, but—" Alysanna felt herself caught in a quagmire of lies.

"Does she live alone?"

"No, she is under the employ of a London lord—Viscount Duncan Granville. I'm sure once I reach the city I can find his home."

"I see. Will it serve then, to drop you near my own residence? I am close to St. James. You can make inquiries and hire a chair from there."

"Yes, thank you. That would be fine."

Cairn rapped his fist on the carriage wall, and the driver pulled the horses to a halt.

"Daniel, Miss Walker will be traveling back with me for the time being. Twenty-five Regent Street, please."

Alysanna paused. Surely, Cairn's driver knew his own address. Cairn caught the question in her eyes.

"He is new," he answered, smiling.

Alysanna nodded in agreement and settled back into her seat. If she had seen Daniel's quizzical response to Cairn's dictum, she would not have rested so easily.

CHAPTER
3

"Alysanna Walker, may I present my good friend, Viscount Duncan Granville." Alysanna's lips parted at the shocking introduction. When Cairn's carriage had screeched to a halt moments ago, she had thought the brick town home his own. Instead, Cairn Chatham had enjoyed his sport with her.

"You knew him?" Her eyes squinted in accusation, glowing hotter as she caught Cairn's irritating grin.

"Miss Walker, please forgive my ruse. It just seemed so remarkable that we should be thus connected."

Alysanna was struck dumb with rage. She snatched her small carryall, nearly tearing her skirt on the door's hinge as she bolted from the carriage.

She landed face-to-face with the blond, lanky man Cairn had just addressed. He looked older than Cairn—his hair was streaked with swaths of grey, and lined tracks framed his smile.

"You are Lord Granville?"

"I believe so." The man cocked a critical brow at Alysanna, making her remember she must look a strange sight.
"May I help you?"

"Yes. I mean, I hope so. I am seeking an old friend,
Beatrice Doughton. I understood her to be in your employ.
Is she still here?" Alysanna could feel the weight of Cairn
Chatham's stare, and it made her jaw tense uncomfortably.

"She is governess to my daughter Lily. If you wish to
speak with her, she is within, but make your visit brief. It is
nearly Lily's lesson time, and I should not wish her studies
to be importuned by your interruption."

The brusque dictum brought an angry flush to Alysanna's
face. By what right did this man order a Wilhaven about?
Alysanna then realized that as far as Duncan Granville was
concerned, she was no Wilhaven at all—only a rumpled
stranger. She swallowed hard; it felt like a large bite of pride
had gone down.

"I won't be long. Thank you." Alysanna began up the
stairs, but again Cairn Chatham thwarted her.

"Am I to keep your baggage, then?"

The suitcase! She had forgotten it in the rumble-tumble.
Alysanna rushed to the boot's canvas cover and struggled
clumsily with the heavy bag. Cairn, as she expected, made
no move to assist her.

"Madame, you look as though you require help."

"No need, Duncan. As you can see, my hearty coach mate
manages quite well by herself." Cairn's sarcasm boosted
Alysanna's resolve, and she freed the huge piece from its
compartment with a rough tug. Lugging the bag, she lurched
up the stairs.

"Thank you, sir. But, as Lord Chatham succinctly points

out, my journey has left me well accustomed to handling difficulty."

Alysanna rapped the brass knocker with such force that it made her wrist ache. But before she could escape him, Cairn volleyed a parting shot.

"It has been my pleasure, Miss Walker—truly. I trust we shall meet again."

"I do not think it likely," Alysanna fired, then reached to rap again as the door swung inward. A tailored butler, done to perfection in a gold waistcoat with matching breeches, stood at attention just beyond the threshold.

"Beatrice Doughton, please." The man made no effort to allow Alysanna entry. Even the butler seemed to appraise her worn appearance critically.

"And whom shall I say is calling, madame."

"Lady . . ." Alysanna caught herself. She certainly could not lay claim to her title in her current guise. She hoped Cairn had not heard her reply. "Miss Doughton will know me as her old friend Alysanna."

The butler paused in study, then stepped back, allowing Alysanna to enter a sconce-lined foyer. As he disappeared into a side chamber, she surveyed the opulent interior of the house.

Most town homes were quite a bit smaller than country estates, and Duncan Granville's was no exception. Still, the three-story structure compromised little space for its urban location. Directly in front of her a grey marble staircase, its path framed by a wrought-iron balustrade, led upwards, interrupted only by one broad, sunlit landing.

To the entry hall's side, she could see part of an enormous library, its walls paneled floor to ceiling with leather-bound books. Occasionally an oversized portrait broke the pattern, and two such paintings framed a massive door on the foyer's opposite side. Its size and grandness begged opening.

Alysanna reached for the door's black handle just as its bulk swung away from her, nearly causing her to lose her balance. She suddenly faced Beatrice, and the sight of her brought tears of relief to Alysanna's deep green eyes. The older woman's pink cheeks rose in a smile, and the lines edging her soft blue eyes multiplied as Beatrice grinned in response.

"Alysanna! Good grief, child! What piece of fortune brings you here?" Beatrice pulled Alysanna into the parlor, bombarding her with an endless stream of questions, but not allowing her time to answer even one.

"Why are you in London? Have you come for the season? And your father—is he well?" Beatrice paused, giving Alysanna the hope she could respond. But as she opened her mouth, a young blond girl, verging on womanhood, popped unexpectedly from around a huge winged armchair.

"Beatrice. . . might I?"

"Lily! Where are my manners? I want you to meet someone very special. This is—"

For lack of a better intervention, Alysanna leaned quickly forward and cupped her hand over Beatrice's jabbering mouth.

"Alysanna Walker. I am here to see Beatrice. I assume you are her charge?"

The girl nodded silently. "I am Lily."

"Alysanna?" Beatrice twisted her mouth free and registered her confusion at Alysanna's new last name.

"I must speak with you alone," Alysanna whispered. "Is it possible?"

"Come, Lily." Beatrice reached out her short, fat arms and drew the girl to her. From their close embrace, Alysanna could tell the two cared deeply for each other, and the loving image recalled times past at Briarhurst when Beatrice ruled her own youthful days. The governess whispered in Lily's ear, then snapped a kiss against her cheek. Lily smiled, then scampered toward the foyer, gently closing the parlor door.

"I have given her a reprieve on her Latin. Now," Beatrice continued, leading Alysanna to a chestnut-colored sofa near the large window, "what is all this secrecy?"

"Oh, Beatrice," Alysanna sighed, the exhaustion of the day's journey escaping her at last. "I've such a tale to tell."

Beatrice raised two plump fingers in a swipe at the tear trickling down one ruddy cheek. "Your father, gone to join your poor dead mother—it is too terrible to believe. And to have his last days vexed by a woman such as you describe. My heart aches to hear it."

Alysanna nodded, her hand patting Beatrice's plum-hued skirt. "Roberta made the end an even greater sadness that it should have been. I oft think the speedy consumption was a blessing, of sorts."

"My poor child. To lose first your fine father, and now Briarhurst itself. 'Tis a burden one so young should not be forced to suffer."

Alysanna's jaw set with familiar determination. "Roberta or no, Briarhurst will not slip from my hands. Hadley is working even now to clear my name. Before the frost is past, I'll be home again."

"But until? Is it your plan to stay in London?"

"It is the safest choice. Hadley has given me generous funds. I thought perhaps I could let a house."

"An unmarried lady of station, living alone? If you mean to hide in plain daylight, I'd think better of it."

Until just now, Alysanna had not considered her plan's

impropriety. Beatrice was right—such an arrangement would be most unusual. Ladies did not live alone, unless aged or widowed, and she was unlikely to convincingly plead either state. To set out on her own would call dangerous attention to herself.

"Surely some of our friends are left from my last visit here. The Crowleys, perhaps?"

"Child, 'twould not matter if they were. The more people know, the greater your risk." Beatrice rustled her way toward the arched window, staring pensively through its beveled panes. Her voice caught an edge of mischief Alysanna remembered well.

"There is a possibility."

"Yes?"

"My sister Lydia has been ill—nothing serious, but enough to require my attendance. I have spoken to Lord Granville about retiring. Of course, he must replace me until Lily is a little older. Until then, he will need a new governess."

"What has this to do with me?"

"Much, if you so choose." Beatrice scurried to the sofa and plopped down, bracing herself for Alysanna's reaction. "You could apply for the position."

Alysanna recoiled in surprise. "You cannot suggest that I work for a living?" A hot blush covered her face as she realized her insult. "It is an honorable calling, to be sure, but . . . I have hardly been raised to the task. And it's not as if I want for funds."

Beatrice took her response in stride. For all her fine points, Alysanna had always overvalued station—but to do so now would be at the expense of her own protection. "You may not lack for Crown's sterling, but when it comes to safe cover, you are indeed impoverished. Where better to hide than the last place you would be sought?"

Frighteningly, painfully, Alysanna felt herself succumbing to Beatrice's cold logic. As always, her former teacher was right. But to work? It was a matter she had never even considered. Surely things were dismal enough with her loss of both Briarhurst and her name; now, to sink further down, to earn her living!

"I know your mind on this, but you must overcome it." Beatrice shook Alysanna's chin gently. "You know I am right." Alysanna puffed out an audible breath that bespoke her accession; Beatrice smiled in response.

"But I have never done anything of this sort," she protested, still struggling against her conclusion.

"I'll be your teacher. For now, let's concentrate on getting you the job." Beatrice smoothed the folds of her lutestring dress as she always did when in serious thought. She jumped as the parlor door swung open, revealing Duncan Granville, who now held Alysanna's hopes in his hands.

"Beatrice. Surely that was not Lily I saw scampering upstairs? It is several minutes past the assigned time for her Latin."

"My apologies, your lordship. But there is a matter I would discuss with you."

"You may have a seat Miss Walker, though you must know I entertain no hope we can agree regarding your employment here. This senseless interview is a courtesy to Beatrice, nothing more. Although she assures me your previous position has left you with ample skills, it is quite against my principles to consider so young a woman for the post."

Alysanna had blanched at Beatrice's lies about her past governess work. The tale was not only untrue, it did not sway the intractable Lord Granville.

"I was not aware youth posed such an impediment."

"It is not youth, exactly, but marriageability. Prior to Beatrice, Lily was cared for by another governess—a woman about your age, to whom my daughter developed a strong attachment. It was a bond cruelly broken when the woman left to make a marriage.

"You see, Miss Walker, since Lily's mother died—when Lily was but a baby—my daughter has been my entire world. I'm sure you can understand that I have no wish to see her endure another wrenching departure."

"Lord Granville, permit me to assure you I have absolutely no intention of romantic involvement with anyone."

"Fine words, Miss Walker, but despite your worn appearance, I can see that you are still a woman some men might find appealing." The gall—how dare he question her attractiveness! It was all Alysanna could do not to stomp out of the room. She twisted her folded hands, turning her knuckles bloodless with rage. She would show this upstart she was no poorly raised county ward.

"*Je pense que si vous me connaissiez mieux, vous changeriez votre avis.*"

A look of impatience flashed across Duncan's face. "My French is somewhat lapsed. What is it you want?"

"I merely suggested that I might have a better chance with you if you were aware of my talents."

"I can see that your language skills compensate for your lack of modesty, Miss Walker. Still—"

"My Lord Granville, I implore your indulgence. I beg the courtesy of completing the interview. Beatrice will think me a great embarrassment if you dismiss me without so much as perfunctory questioning."

"It is pointless."

Alysanna knew she had nothing to lose by being bold. "Very well. If you will not inquire, I shall tell you. Not only do I speak fluent French, but my Italian is excellent. I know geography, have a quick mind for arithmetic, nimble fingers for needlework, and must in all candor tell you I am an excellent watercolorist and dancer, with a finely honed sense of deportment.''

Alysanna paused, suddenly awkward in her cocksure declarations. Such blatant vanity came hard to her yet she seemed to have Lord Granville's attention. Surprisingly, he tipped his head forward, seeming to direct her to continue.

Alysanna glanced about the paneled library. Her eyes came to rest on an oil portrait hung just over the wainscoting. ''The Latin motto beneath your painting is misspelled—the verb *ducere* should be future, not present indicative active—and, if you will permit me, I would be happy to play some Handel on your pianoforte for you. Unless you would prefer Bach or Mozart.'' Alysanna stopped, shocked by her own brashness. Her bravado spent, she bit her lower lip nervously.

Duncan's imperious look of moments ago now threatened to dissolve. Still, his words discouraged her. ''I confess, Miss Walker, that I am impressed by your many accomplishments—the breadth of which I find quite unusual, even in the finest of governesses—and by your efficient, if audacious, recounting of them. Yet I must repeat that no training, even in Latin verb tense, can overcome your youth.''

Alysanna released her hopes with a resigned sigh. ''I see. Thank you for your time.'' As she began to rise, the library door burst open. Lily, running and crying, rushed toward Duncan.

''Father!'' The girl bolted around the writing desk's corner and hurled herself into her father's arms, dissolving into loud, unrestrained sobs.

''Lily, what's happened? Are you hurt?'' Duncan tilted her small face upwards, hoping for some answer in her reddened eyes. Lily brushed back a strand of hair that stuck determinedly to her teary cheek, her answer escaping between broken, only half-stifled gasps.

"It was Mary Hamilton. I thought she was my friend. I showed her my new frock—the paduasoy with the Belgian lace—and Mary said . . ." Lily's tears overtook her voice. Duncan clutched his daughter tightly, stroking her soft blond curls with his large hand.

"Miss Walker, I think you can see yourself out."

"Certainly." Alysanna began again toward the door.

"Oh, Father, Mary said that it was lucky I was rich, that I could have such fine dresses, because I was so—plain!"

The words delivered a painful twist to Alysanna's heart. Lily's tender age was still within her own memory, as was the pain of other children's cruelty. Instinctively, Alysanna turned back to face Duncan and Lily.

"Miss Walker, we are finished." Duncan's tone was jagged and impatient.

"No, wait. Miss Walker, Father will lie because he loves me. You are beautiful. Tell me honestly, please—am I truly plain?"

Alysanna's heart sank on the question. Lily was not plain; in fact, Alysanna could see that she'd soon have men's heads turning. Still, what mattered more than how she looked was how she saw herself.

"No. Of course you're not plain." Alysanna extended her arms toward Lily, who rushed forward, locking herself about Alysanna's waist in tight, desperate gratitude.

"Truly? You would not say so just to please me?"

"Certainly not. This friend of yours, Mary—who does not sound much to me like the sort of friend you should keep company with—was only jealous of your pretty dress." Lily stared up with disbelief.

Alysanna smiled affectionately. "I see there must be no mirrors here. For if there were, surely you could not doubt my wisdom, though I understand. I had a friend once—a girl much like your Mary—who said the same to me."

"Truly? But you are so beautiful now."

"Swans grow. They are not born. A little patience and a kinder friend—that's all you need."

Lily pressed an exuberant kiss on Alysanna's cheek. "Thank you. Oh, Father, isn't Miss Walker kind? Shall we see more of her. Say yes!"

Duncan let go an exasperated sigh, then leaned his head against the spine of his chair. "I think we shall see much more of her. Miss Walker, should you want it, the position is yours. But I warn you, should I find you entangled, your employment here will terminate promptly."

"Thank you, Lord Granville. Rest assured, a man is absolutely the last thing I have in mind."

"Alysanna, this is Bridget, our cook. The tall, dark-haired man is John, the house steward. Next to John is Henry, Master's valet de chambre, and the gray-haired gentleman is Evan, our head butler. Of course, you already know our housekeeper, Mrs. Spooner, since she showed you your room, and the lady next to her in the cambric apron is Delia, Miss Lily's lady's maid.

"As governess, you will be seated according to rank, next to John at the table's head." Beatrice gestured toward a wooden seat butted against the pine's warped planks. Alysanna eyed her place disdainfully. It was a close call which was worse—the coarse dinner company she was expected to keep, or the dimly lit housekeeper's room in which she was expected to eat.

Nothing about the small chamber looked remotely like the

sort of place to enjoy a meal. In Briarhurst's luxury, Alysanna took dinner atop polished walnut laid with Irish linen. She ate from Wedgwood, her hand heavy with French sterling.

Now, simple pine planks bearing rough-hewn pewter hardly beckoned her. Her eye wandered up to a light fixture fashioned of old swords. It was a ridiculous piece, as silly as it was different from Briarhurst's crystal chandeliers. She had never felt farther from home than at this moment.

"I see why yer so slight, missy. Ye'll not get any meat on those tiny bones standin' starin' at the food." Bridget's ample Irish girth gave clear evidence of her enthusiasm for her own cooking. Her comment, along with Beatrice's guiding hand, dropped Alysanna onto the chair.

"Did Master find you through the register or the statute hall?" As he spoke, Henry, the valet, heaped his plate with a serving of venison, shoring its runny juice up with a glob of marrow pudding and a slice of wheaten loaf.

"I'm sorry?" Henry had the look of having asked a normal question, but Alysanna knew neither what he meant nor what she was expected to say.

Beatrice sensed her confusion, and fielded Henry's query. "Lord Granville placed no advertisement for the position. As it happened, Miss Walker, who is an old friend of mine, arrived seeking employment just in time for my departure." Alysanna managed a slight smile back at Henry, whose determined, noisy eating filled her with disgust.

"Then you have supervised a charge before?" Delia looked slightly older than Alysanna, and seemed much interested in gathering what information she could.

Again, Beatrice intervened. "Of course Miss Walker has had other charges. Lord Granville would tolerate no lack of experience in anyone to whom he entrusted Miss Lily."

"Might I ask your hire rate?" Delia's eyes widened with

anticipation, as Beatrice squinted distrustfully at her. The upstart shopkeeper's whelp was ever seeking to better her own lot.

"It is none of your concern, Delia." Alysanna was relieved. She not only had no response, but she was ravenous and much preferred eating to talking.

"'Twill be an interesting task to teach without a voice." Delia's comment drew the group's laughter, and her brows arched in such question that Alysanna knew she had to answer.

"I am quite in agreement with all Beatrice has told you."

"Well, if you won't tell your salary, then at least tell us what you got in your past position. Father said I would have done better as a governess than a lady's maid, but I think him wrong. Come, Alysanna, what's a little gossip cost?"

Alysanna suddenly realized she had no notion what she earned. She had not even thought to ask Lord Granville. She struggled to recall Beatrice's wages of years past but it was hopelessly long ago. All she could do was guess.

"Please, Alysanna, do tell."

"In my last position, I was hired for ninety pounds per annum. There, I hope your curiosity's sated."

Henry began to choke and clutched both hands around his thick throat, his fork and knife slamming onto his plate. Bridget slapped his back loudly, relieving his distress. "Ninety quid a year! Then you must get more than that now! 'Tis twice what I am paid. Can it be that Master values a schoolmarm over his first man?"

Alysanna wished she could sink straight into the floor. She had guessed terribly wrong. "Did I say ninety? The journey has taken its toll on me, to be sure. I meant nineteen. Yes. It was nineteen pounds a year."

The assembled staff breathed a collective "Oh," then returned to their frenzied feeding. Though the venison and pudding were both now nearly cold, Alysanna forced them down as eagerly as her dinner mates, hoping to avoid further attention.

Dinner was always served hot at Briarhurst, she recalled with longing. Then, remembering second table ate only once the family was finished, she realized she might as well get used to such chilly fare. At least she was spared third table. There she'd not only suffer the prattle of chambermaids and footmen, she'd probably get only cheese and bread, with meat a rare gift.

The syllabub and fruit came and went, and Alysanna cleared her own plate for the first time ever. With Beatrice in tow, she rushed upstairs to the small garret Mrs. Spooner had assigned her. Beatrice paused at the door before leaving.

"The Master wants to see me about Miss Lily. Will you be all right?"

Alysanna nodded, producing a weak smile.

"It is not an easy ruse, I know."

"No." Alysanna collapsed on her low, curtainless bed. "I am making a go at this, Beatrice, but I daresay it's more challenge than I'd thought. Already I am spent, and I've been here less than a day. And there is still the test of supper tonight!" She fell backwards on the feather mattress, noting how hard it felt compared to her swans-down four-poster at home.

"You must make this work. Your life depends on it." Beatrice planted a quick kiss on Alysanna's flushed cheek and scurried away.

Alysanna wandered to her tiny window and surveyed what darkness allowed of the broad square below. Phaetons and hackney coaches clattered noisily across the cobblestones, their paths lit by linkboys bearing wind-tossed torches.

Even in darkness the city seemed exciting, but Alysanna's enthusiasm fled as she realized how few pleasures her new life would allow. Her funds could buy what she wanted, yet she could hardly purchase a theater box and risk running into Duncan. Nor would there be any shopkeepers' wares—at least, none befitting her taste. Anything she bought would be hard, if not impossible, to hide in her garret, and would surely draw unwanted attention.

Her waking hours would be spent with teaching and lower-class rabble, and her nights confined to a room smaller than her closet at Briarhurst. A tear rolled over the crest of her cheekbone as she tallied all she had lost.

Without name and heritage, she was stripped of all that mattered to her. She remembered Duncan Granville's first prickly look of disdain, and fury bubbled up inside her.

And Cairn Chatham! How dare he deceive her, taking his rude sport with a highborn lady! She knew his connection to Duncan should frighten her. The same for the chance that her strange manners had caught Cairn's eye and would soon be confided to her new employer. Still, what nettled most were Cairn's teasing eyes, which seemed to mock and entice her all at once.

Alysanna resolved to banish him from her thoughts. Once Hadley set this right, Cairn Chatham would pay for his games. Until then, all Alysanna could do was hope he was finished with them.

CHAPTER
4

❧

"It seems, Miss Walker, that I am destined to find you in the most unusual circumstances." Cairn's piercing blue eyes peered quizzically through the tangled growth of Duncan's beech hedgerow, frightening Alysanna nearly to death.

It had been bad enough to see that damned carriage of his bearing down on her while she waited outside the house for Lily. Now, to be caught in her embarrassing attempt to elude Cairn Chatham was almost more than Alysanna could bear.

A minute ago the beech had looked her only option for escape; now it seemed a lamentably stupid choice. Instead of allowing her to avoid Cairn, Alysanna's frantic efforts had only bought her more of him.

"It's a most interesting manner of taking the air. Do you intend to stay in the bush?" Cairn arched his brow in bemusement as he reached out his hand. He leaned so far into the beech wood's branches that Alysanna could feel the heat of his breath on her face, and his closeness unnerved her almost as much as her ridiculously crouched pose.

Reluctantly, and only because she was unsure she could free herself of the twisted growth unaided, Alysanna accepted his offer of help. Cairn's fingers closed around her own more tightly than was necessary, and a small shudder, oddly pleasant, racked Alysanna as she stepped clear of the foliage.

"Thank you. The wind snatched my handkerchief and blew it into the beech. As you can see, I became too entangled for the want of a silly scrap of lace." Though now free from the dusty plant, Alysanna realized Cairn's hand still gripped her. She recoiled abruptly, leaving his palm extended, empty, in the air.

"You seemed very entangled, indeed. I trust you recovered the handkerchief." Alysanna's deep-set eyes widened perceptibly at her gaffe. She'd have to learn to lie better than this. Beatrice had been gone less than a week, and this was not the first time Alysanna's tongue had tripped her up.

"It was foolish of me to chase it. By the time I reached the hedgerow, the wind had routed the scarf far down the lane."

Cairn nodded in sympathy, the corners of his lips canting back in the promise of a smile. "I'm sorry your efforts were for naught, though you look none the worse for your dishevelment. Truly, I can't decide which of mud, dust, or velvet most becomes you."

Cairn's eyes ran a quick, delighted course down Alysanna's dress, turning her thoughts to the beech wood's damage. The gown's amber velvet had drawn a crackly blanket of leaves and twigs, and a spiderweb clung to the lace trimming of her morning coat. To worsen matters, Alysanna's thick chestnut hair had tumbled free of its pins, as it was often wont to do, and she could feel a long, curly strand spiraling down the side of her neck.

It seemed, to her unending vexation, that each time Cairn Chatham saw her she looked a terrible mess. Alysanna quashed the thought, annoyed that she cared. The ill-bred lout's opinion of her hardly mattered.

Cairn noted her pique and offered his arm in apology. "I'm sorry. I did not mean to cause you distress. Your retreat did make me wonder, though, if it was me you were avoiding."

Alysanna felt a hot blush fire her face, and she tucked her head down to conceal it. She straightened her skirt and began a fast clip back toward the house, hoping that Lily would appear to end Cairn's scrutiny. But his long gait easily outpaced her own, and, walking just in front of her, Cairn twisted his head back, earning a better view of her dirt-smudged stoicism.

"Why ever would I wish to avoid you?" Alysanna prayed her voice didn't betray her uneasiness.

"It is an interesting question." Cairn paused, then pressed on with his inquisition. "I must say, Miss Walker, that I was surprised to learn you had come into Duncan's employ, particularly since during our all-too-brief sojourn, you mentioned neither your past governess work nor your intention to seek a new position."

If she'd failed in evading Cairn Chatham, at least Alysanna felt vindicated for trying. As she'd dreaded, he did suspect her, though she was not yet fully sure of what. In any event, his interest was dangerous, and Alysanna knew she must do what she could to quell it.

"Lord Chatham, it confounds me to imagine why I should need to confide either the details of my past work or my future plans to you. Since you persist, I will grant you that I had not thought to take a position when I first came to London. But once I learned of Beatrice's plans to leave, the opportunity was too tempting to resist.

"I hope that satisfies you. I must say I am quite surprised to find a man of your station so concerned with someone you surely consider your social inferior." The words came hard, but Alysanna hoped the appeal to Cairn's upper-crust mores would end his interest in her.

Cairn spun on his boot heels, blocking Alysanna's path and nearly causing them to collide. Face-to-face with her handsome nemesis, Alysanna arched backwards beneath Cairn's height. His size was dramatic in contrast to her own petite stature. As when they had first met he was finely attired. His white satin waistcoat and tan leather breeches lent fine advantage to his lean, taut muscles. With his russet cocked hat, he was much the ton, though not in the manner of the French dogs Alysanna had often seen about town. Cairn Chatham looked almost accidentally attractive, and the unstudied appeal of it irritated her.

"You are most remarkable, Miss Walker. Such class snobbery is an unusual prejudice to be held by a governess. Can it be you consider yourself my inferior?"

Alysanna's jaw clenched at his question. "Only in brute strength. For it is clear that, unless you recover your manners and step aside, I shall not be able to move you on my own." Her curt, controlled reply was a triumph over her urge to slap him. Inferior—it was a preposterous notion! Once Hadley set the predicament with Julia straight, she'd give this scapegrace his due.

Cairn and Alysanna stared silently at each other, her fury

deflected by his teasing mirth. To Alysanna's relief, Lily's call parted them.

"Uncle Cairn! Alysanna! I'm sorry I'm late. Oh, good, you two have met." Lily skipped down the walk, the folds of her lavender camlet skirt bouncing with each hop. She jumped onto tiptoe, smacking a kiss on Cairn's cheek and interlocking her arm with Alysanna's. "Uncle Cairn is one of Father's oldest friends. He's not really my uncle, I just call him that. I always forget—how long since you and Daddy met?"

To Alysanna's relief, Cairn finally loosened his hold on her eyes. "Longer than you have memory, dear Lily."

"Father is older than Uncle Cairn, of course. But to think that Daddy has me and Uncle Cairn has not yet even made a match—though not for lack of interest by our London ladies."

"Indeed?" Alysanna's black brows rose with the question, and Cairn marked her interest.

"Oh, yes. Every year he's considered quite the season's catch." Lily raised her hand to Alysanna's ear and pretended a loud whisper, intended to be overheard. "Father and I plan to find him a wife before the year's out. He shan't have a chance."

Alysanna lifted her eyes to Cairn, who still towered close over her. "It seems your cause is hopeless, Lord Chatham."

"Perhaps. Depending on what my cause might be."

Lily tugged playfully on Alysanna's sleeve. "I know it's my fault we're late, but can we hurry, please? Amelia has promised to meet us at St. James, and I'm afraid she won't wait."

"Of course." Relieved, Alysanna struck a brisk pace toward the park.

"Miss Walker?"

Alysanna whirled around with angry resignation, making no attempt to disguise her irritation. "What is it now?"

"St. James has legions of beech woods. If I were you, I'd concede the battle before I engaged."

Alysanna drew her lip painfully between her teeth. With such force that Lily nearly lost her balance, Alysanna snatched her elbow and whooshed the two of them purposefully forward.

"Alysanna, do you understand what Uncle Cairn meant?"

"Pay it no mind, Lily," she answered distractedly, then swore to herself that she'd do the same.

"From the cut of that dress, Duncan Granville's parting with a pretty penny on your wages." Melissa Cavendish took in Alysanna's amber velvet frock with a more than critical and slightly envious eye.

Alysanna had hardly given the dress any thought when she'd donned it this morning; in fact, of the three dresses she'd stuffed in her small satchel, the golden morning gown was the least sumptuous. But now, as she noticed the humble, overworn garb of the two other governesses sharing her bench, Alysanna's embroidered fabric, with its lace trim, seemed painfully out of place.

"The dress was a casting from my former employer. It was foolish of me to wear it for work." It was clear that Alysanna needed more modest attire, but the resolution depressed her. It was less than a month past that the black bombazine she'd worn to mourn her father's death had been packed away, and Alysanna had much missed the bright colors and fanciful styles she preferred. Now, her tastes were checked less by propriety than misfortune. "The dress should have been saved for assembly. I don't know what I was thinking.''

"Assembly! If you think to find yourself a guest at Almack's, think better of it. Invitations to such balls hardly reach the likes of us. Surely you know?''

"Of course. It was a feeble jest.'' Alysanna trilled a small, nervous laugh and hoped her comment had sounded facetious. She must stop making these mistakes!

The vigilance needed to hold to her governess character exhausted her, and Alysanna longed for her small garret, where at least she could drop the pretense of belonging to a class she understood nothing of. But for now she was a prisoner—an unwilling intimate of women she would not even ask to tea.

"I came to London from a northern shire. What entertainment do you find here?'' Alysanna hardly cared, but hoped to shift the conversation away from its emphasis on her.

"There's a good time to be had at Drury Lane, if you can catch the play between dodging the fruit from the gallery. And Vauxhall, of course. The gardens are a fine place each Sunday to angle for a match.''

Vauxhall was populated by the middling ranks—hardly the sort of spot to amuse Alysanna. She hoped to heaven her note telling her whereabouts had reached Hadley, and that he would soon contact her with word that she could return home—before she was forced to suffer such tedious diversions.

"Deirdre and I are going Saturday next. Will the viscount allow you a free day?'' Melissa seemed eager to initiate Alysanna into her own social rites.

"It is not likely. Even if he did, it was a clear condition

of my employment that I was to undertake no romantic involvement.''

''You're teasing?''

''Not at all. Lord Granville is most adamant on the point.'' Alysanna was pleased to have an excuse for not going; she hoped Melissa and Deirdre would drop the matter.

''These high and mighty Quality—who do they style themselves, trying to manipulate us so? You'd think that Crown's sterling bestowed divinity for the power they dare to wield. If you ask me, their children are usually their betters, though even the little ones can make you long for the workhouse.'' Melissa tossed a glance toward Amelia, who giggled as she huddled with Lily on a nearby bench.

''Melissa, if you find the work so objectionable, why not leave?''

Melissa fired back an incredulous look. ''As if I had a choice! What else is there for a cleric's daughter, and a second born one, at that? Too educated for my own good, and too impoverished to be much good to any match I'd care to make. It's the worst of the world—to live in their fine homes but never quite be let into their lives. The least they can allow is our freedom to find what love we can. Vauxhall is none of Lord Granville's business. Come, say you'll go. Let's plan on it.''

''Melissa, I can't.'' Alysanna considered her own tangled present, which seemed both better and worse than her new friend's. For all the breeding Melissa lacked, at least she was free to pursue her desires. Her life had clear, well-laid rules; if she respected their boundaries, Melissa could expect some modicum of happiness, unlike Alysanna, who was parted by fear and some faceless murderer from the only world she understood. What grim luck to be tossed into one that she lacked both the desire and the aptitude to join.

"Suit yourself. But I think you'll find your days long and lonely under a spinster's cap."

"Perhaps." Alysanna knew Melissa was right—her days were already exactly that.

It was as if he had some devil's ken of her timing. There, inside his carriage, just as when she had fled the hedgerow two hours ago, was Cairn Chatham. She and Lily were some distance away, but Alysanna still slowed her pace, not wishing to repeat their earlier encounter.

"Must we take on geography now?" Lily stopped her distracted chatter about Amelia's new hat and made a dour face as the house came into view. She clutched Alysanna's arm pleadingly as they entered the foyer, her twinkling blue eyes begging an unlikely answer.

"Lily, Italy will be more pleasurable if you know where it is."

"I already know—it's somewhere south of France. Besides, it's not as if I have to ride there."

Alysanna shot her an admonishing glance. "Your father will be furious to find you anywhere but the library for the next full hour. Change quickly and meet me there."

"Very well. But you'd think I needed to work for a living, with all you and father make me learn."

The comment's irony made Alysanna smile. Duncan's insistence on Lily's schooling sprang from love, not ambition. Still, as Alysanna herself had painfully learned, it was altogether possible that Lily's studies might one day fill her belly as well as her head.

As Alysanna stepped onto the library's Persian carpet, she scanned the wall stacks for the lesson's maps. Every volume except one was nearby, and she soon spotted the missing tome on a high shelf. It was too far to reach, so Alysanna pulled the book ladder from the opposite wall and climbed to the top of its wooden stairs.

But even the ladder's additional height was not quite enough. Thinking if she could hook the spine, she could tip the book toward her, Alysanna began to hop, stretching her arm up with each jump.

"You seem to have a propensity for dangerous situations."

Alysanna didn't even need to turn to know the voice was Cairn Chatham's.

"And you seem to have one for bothering me. I thought you had gone." She twisted her head over her shoulder, catching another glimpse of that damnable smile.

"So you did slow down when you saw my carriage. I thought so. I must say, Miss Walker—may I call you Alysanna?"

"You may not." Alysanna turned back to the stacks, continuing her attack on the book.

"Very well—Miss Walker. It pains me to see you take such trouble to avoid me. Is it something I've done?"

"Why would you think that? Should it bother me that you were in your cups when you offered me a ride here, that you continued your drinking en route, that I was forced to load my own baggage, then deceived about your relationship to Duncan Granville?" With each accusation, Alysanna's low voice grew higher and louder.

"I apologize for whatever improprieties you believe me guilty of. It was true I had imbibed when we first met, but I was ill, a fact which also accounted for my failure to assist with your luggage. Had I known our paths would so intertwine, I swear I would have found my manners. Yet I must say that I still cannot wholly ascribe your anger to my indiscretions."

"Then what?"

"My answer will displease you."

"Then it would be in keeping with all you have done thus far."

"I think you dislike me because I see your new role wears a little rough." It was that damn velvet dress again! Alysanna scolded herself; why hadn't she changed? Fortunately, she needed both hands to keep her balance. If not, she would have fingered her skirt's fabric nervously.

To her misery, Cairn continued. "You do not seem quite the governess somehow—though I can appreciate that you've mounted a great effort toward that end. Still, there is a bit too much spirit in you. Frankly, I find it quite appealing."

"Thank you for your insight. But why bother? As Lily tells me, there are countless other ladies to fill your time."

"I am pleased the competition concerns you."

"It does not!" Alysanna stamped her foot so hard on the ladder she nearly fell. Fearing her choler would send her tumbling, she backed down the stairs and abandoned her efforts to get the book.

"The others needn't concern you. Our London ladies all look and live much the same. They are, if you will excuse the expression, much like sheep. They would lay proud claim to the philosophy, though perhaps not the appellation. But you, Miss Walker—you strike me as more of a . . . gazelle. You change your direction with little warning and most appealing speed. Like me, I think you have trouble following rules."

Cairn Chatham was so maddening that Alysanna vowed to speak no more to him after today. "It is flattering to be likened to a wild animal. But I must beg your leave since Lily will be here soon." Alysanna rushed toward the lesson papers she'd stacked on Duncan's desk, but Cairn blocked her path.

"Do you really want me to go?"

A moment ago Alysanna was sure she wanted him gone, and promptly. But now, so close she could tell he smelled of spice and tobacco, words fled. There was something magnetic about him—some force that froze her resolve and stole her will.

She stared up, wide-eyed and helpless, as his hands closed gently around her face. Quick little sparks fired off inside her, and Alysanna's flesh grew too warm for such a cold day.

Hadley had held her in his arms before, but his embrace had not made her head spin like this—as if she were ill. Confusion coursed through her, but before Alysanna could move, Cairn tipped up her face, lowering his mouth until it rested but a breath above her own.

"I've wanted this since I first saw you." He feathered his warm mouth across hers, and the brush of his wet lips made her gasp softly. Cairn pulled back and breathed her name, so close she could feel more than hear the word, then pressed his lips to hers again in promise of sweeter torment.

His arms melded her to him, and Alysanna's head rolled back as her arching body betrayed her. Vertigo caught her like the crest of a wave, and, though she stood safe in Cairn's embrace, she had the sense she was falling, the room and world swirling around her like a blurry whirlpool.

She moaned softly, only to have her breath snap like a trap at a noise down the hall. It was not the fear of discovery but what she'd allowed that horrified her. Alysanna's wits flew back in an outrage, and she wrenched her mouth free, pulling as far back as Cairn's tight hold would allow.

For a second she stood dumbfounded, her coral lips and unblinking eyes both wide with shock. Then, as Cairn's mouth lowered again toward her, Alysanna wound back her hand and landed a stinging slap on his cheek.

For once, Cairn responded as she expected—he stopped. But not before answering with a look of bemusement in what more rightfully should have been angry eyes.

"A change of heart? Or merely a concession to your conscience?"

"A proper response to your rude liberties." Cairn lowered his arms from her back, but trailed his fingers across her spine before he backed away.

Alysanna knew she should be relieved at his unhanding. But something that could not be and yet felt like disappointment tugged at her heart.

"Don't think that because I'm a governess . . ."

"I assure you, Alysanna—" Her indignant look flew at him, bringing a quick correction. "Miss Walker—that I attribute no low morals to your position as Lily's governess. Something much more significant overruled my self-restraint. I thought I had—an invitation."

Alysanna was outraged. Was he implying she'd asked for his aggressions? "I hardly call stopping when my path is blocked a bid for assault."

"It was your look, not your lack of momentum, that encouraged me. As a kindred spirit, I felt you would understand my indulging the impulse."

"Kindred spirit? I hardly think so. I ask you to leave me alone, and what I get for my trouble is your crude assault. Don't ever touch me again. Do you understand?"

Cairn nodded, adopting an unconvincing look of contrition. "I await your bidding, madame."

"It will be a long wait." The sound from the foyer grew louder, and a rap on the library door cut short her next salvo. Alysanna expected Lily, but instead a tall, beautiful blond woman entered.

She burst into the room in a bounce of rose taffeta, not even acknowledging Alysanna until after she'd planted a gushy kiss on Cairn's cheek. "Cairn, darling, what a delightful surprise! I come expecting to transact some dreary business with Duncan and am treated instead to the sight of your carriage." The woman cocked a golden brow toward Alysanna, leaning into Cairn as she spoke.

"And who is this? Has Delia been replaced as lady-in-waiting?" She nodded toward Alysanna, and her haughty look set Alysanna's teeth grinding.

"Maude, may I present Miss Alysanna Walker, Lily's new governess. Miss Walker, this is the Lady Maude Delamere."

"So pleased." Maude extended a lily-white hand just far enough back to make clear she had no intention of allowing Alysanna to take it. Determined to avoid another faux pas, Alysanna managed the obligatory curtsy.

Whoever this Delamere woman was, it was clear to Alysanna that she was Quality. Her cool pink taffeta, hemmed with a like-colored ruche, was topped by a blue half-redingote that pulled her small waist into a tight stomacher. A festoon of lace draped from both her elbows and bosom, making the latter look quite elevated. Alysanna guessed the result less genuine than the magic of some mantua-maker's wirework.

Curls of her fine flaxen hair trickled down beneath a broad-brimmed hat with ostrich feathers that rose stylishly high.

The look was similar to Lily's new fashion doll from France and was obviously quite costly. With Maude Delamere's fine face and violet eyes, the impression was breathtaking, and Alysanna felt a nip of jealousy as she realized how her amber velvet paled in comparison.

"Is something wrong?" Maude threw Alysanna an inquisitive glance.

"Not at all." Alysanna smiled politely. "I was only admiring your lovely dress."

Maude beamed as if she were quite accustomed to compliments. "Yes. Father had it brought back specially from his last trip abroad. It is Cairn's favorite color. What good fortune to run into him the day I am wearing it."

Maude glowed and shot Cairn a tantalizing smile. Whatever their business, Alysanna wished they'd transact it out of her sight.

"Perhaps when I am finished with the dress, you can have it."

The impudent comment made Alysanna's blood boil. "You are too kind."

Cairn freed Maude's arm from his own and clucked disapprovingly. "Maude, dear, if you choose to be generous, it would be better handled privately. I'm sure Miss Walker does not appreciate your public charity."

Maude pretended sudden understanding. "Of course. I'm so very sorry. I did not mean to be a . . ."

"Snob." Cairn finished the sentence, throwing her a chastising glance.

"Cairn, please! An appreciation of class hardly makes me terrible." Maude looked embarrassed by Cairn's indictment, and Alysanna was surprised to see a small blush fleet across her alabaster skin.

"Nor does it make you easy to endure, my dear," Cairn

added. Maude fashioned her lips into a pout, then eased them into a besotted smile.

"My apologies, Miss Wilkins . . ."

"Walker," Alysanna clipped tartly.

"Yes, of course. I'm sure it isn't easy being a governess, and I hardly meant to insult. It must be trying enough teaching all those dreary lessons."

"I do not consider knowledge dreary. Nor do I find it trying." Though it was Maude she addressed, Alysanna was not unaware of Cairn's merry interest.

"Oh, dear, let me try once more." Maude took a breath as if she were mustering patience for a cranky child. "Tell me, Miss Walker, what is it you study today?" Maude's feigned interest was transparent, but she looked to Cairn in expectation of his kudos.

"Today we read geography. Italy."

"How lovely. It is a truly beautiful country. A great deal of statuary. Of course, I don't suppose you have gone?"

In fact, Alysanna had been there often and in a better class of travel, she guessed, than this impudent blond dilettante. Still, it would seem odd for a governess to be so well-versed.

"No, I have not been, but I am a great reader. Today we study the northern part. It is an agricultural region. They raise sheep." Alysanna had not meant to say it, but Maude had pushed her past self-restraint. Cairn tried but failed to stifle a low laugh.

"Cairn, dear, whatever is so funny about Italy?"

Lily popped through the door, her disinterested expression lighting up as she saw the assembled group. "Uncle Cairn —you're back. Whatever for?"

"Some business too complicated to explain, Lily.

Maude?'' Cairn offered his arm, then brushed a kiss on Lily's cheek and squired Maude from the room. Lily looked to Alysanna for the day's lesson, but her governess stood adrift, unsure if she were angry or pleased that Cairn Chatham had left.

CHAPTER
5

The wicked image of a flock of Maudes grazing compla-
cently on the Italian landscape made Alysanna grin. Yet, if
Maude Delamere fit Cairn's sheepish description, she managed to do so quite attractively, and apparently with enough
appeal to woo him. Despite his indictment of her sort of
woman, they had left together, arms entwined.

"Lago di Como." Lily yielded the answer with tortured
slowness.

"I'm sorry?" Alysanna had lost the question.

"The largest Italian lake is Lago di Como."

"Di Gardo, Lily. But the two are close." Alysanna lashed
her thoughts to the day's lesson plan as Lily plopped with a
thump onto the japanned settee. "It must disappoint you to
have such a dense pupil."

"Certainly not. No such thing is true."

"Father thinks so."

Alysanna frowned solicitously. "Has he told you that?"

"No, but he puts such emphasis on my study. He must be convinced I'm daft to need such constant drilling."

"Perhaps he stresses your lessons precisely because he knows your mind is sharp. I think your father wants you to have a better lot than that of a foolish ninny disposed to naught but babble of assemblies and millinery."

"Such a lot would not be so terrible."

Alysanna stared at Lily with a reprimand. "You will disappoint me, Lily, if Maude Delamere is all you aspire to be." The instant the words flew out, Alysanna longed to recall them. Governesses did not question their social betters, and Alysanna's faux pas glared brightly. Yet her opinion spoke to a more dangerous matter: did Maude vex her so because of her affection for Cairn—a sentiment he seemed to return?

Despite herself, Alysanna knew it was that which nettled her. Yet why Maude and Cairn's relationship should bother her at all made no sense. It was not as if she had any interest in the man. She was engaged to Hadley. What matter if Cairn Chatham had his own entanglements?

Alysanna struggled to conjure Hadley's dark visage in her mind, yet each time, Cairn's sun-burnished face and teasing smile supplanted it. Why couldn't the rake just leave her alone? His rude deceit and shocking advances must have driven her mad. Alysanna repeated the litany of Cairn's crimes, hoping to marshal sufficient anger to exile him from her mind. Yet he returned in the most damningly pleasant ways, not the least of which was her still-warm memory of his lips moving languorously across her own.

Alysanna had only been kissed by Hadley before this, and nothing of his cold affection even came close to Cairn's volcanic touch. Was it that Hadley so lacked skill or that

Cairn so commanded it? Alysanna cringed with shame as she considered the question.

"Alysanna, are you ill?"

"No, Lily, of course not."

"You looked for an instant as if you did not feel well."

"I am fine." Alysanna forced a smile to hide her embarrassment. "We were speaking of?"

"Maude Delamere."

"I think it was Italy."

"But Maude is so much more interesting. Father says gossip's sinful, but did you know that Maude has been madly in love with Uncle Cairn for ages? You saw them—surely you could tell?"

"I wouldn't know, Lily." Alysanna knew she should put a quick and proper end to Lily's talebearing, but it was too fascinating.

"They were children together in Lincolnshire when their fathers launched an overseas trading venture. Uncle Cairn is exceedingly rich, you know. His father is dead, and since his mother now lives abroad, he manages all their holdings. He'll make a very wealthy catch."

"Lily, this does not interest me." Alysanna longed to trust her own protest. "If Maude and Cairn are to be married . . ." The words caught in her throat.

"Oh, no! Maude is lovely, but her interest in Uncle Cairn is altogether unrequited. It's sad, really. She has even dared refuse two of her father's proposed matches in the hope that she can win Cairn's heart. Imagine such faith to gamble against spinsterhood! Uncle Cairn seems fond of her, but father says he has made it clear that Maude is no more than a friend. It's a notion that still sets rough with Maude. So if we are to marry off Uncle Cairn this season, we will have to look beyond Maude Delamere."

Alysanna felt a bizarre relief at Lily's pronouncement, then bit her lip in punishment for the response. "Well, I should not think that too difficult. If everyone finds Cairn Chatham as charming as you say . . ."

"Oh, it isn't the ladies—it's Uncle Cairn who's the obstacle. He can chase a skirt as fast as any, but when it comes to marriage, he's just so—slippery!"

"Much like your attention today, Lily. We still have considerable ground to cover. Now, enough chatter about your Uncle Cairn. Tell me the countries on Italy's northern border."

Alysanna was relieved to have their conversation about Cairn Chatham end, and she studied her notes on geography as if they could deliver her from the temptation of his memory. But still, her mind strayed from the Italian foothills.

So, Cairn was a social legend. Alysanna loved a challenge, whether a headstrong horse or a fast game of quoits. Now, to her chagrin, Cairn Chatham had taken that form. He was so different from Hadley. Alysanna began to imagine her life as Cairn's wife. The thought drew first a shy smile, then a mortified blush.

Hadley! How could she think so lightly of her pledge to him? But for Julia's death, she would be scheduling fittings for her wedding trousseau even now. Instead, to think wishfully of someone else, and that galling Chatham man, yet— it was anathema!

No one had forced her to the match she'd made, as was the case with many girls of breeding. It was not unusual to find caring parents spoon their hapless daughters into loveless pairings. But Alysanna herself had chosen Hadley, and she had done so wisely, using her head, not her heart. Hadley possessed position, stability, a history of family—attributes of importance. Yet Alysanna could not deny that Hadley's dull predictability sometimes grated. Perhaps this was why Cairn's danger so enticed her.

Cairn was like a high cliff, ever drawing her toward his edge. For all his light banter, his eyes promised a deep, dark core. His carefree manner was like a shield, hiding some secret, powerful weapon. Worst of all, Cairn seemed to sense that Alysanna was drawn to him, and, unconscionably, he took advantage of her weakness. Why else would he have dared his burning kiss?

But this was pure lunacy! Even if she were not betrothed to Hadley, she could hardly consider another entanglement. As a governess, she could only seek out the coachmen and shopocrats of Melissa's ilk. And to confess her true identity, particularly to the already suspicious Cairn, would threaten her safety. There was no choice. The truth was too dangerous and her deceit too shrewd; together, they imprisoned Alysanna in her silence.

Still, she was unbalanced by his interest in a woman he thought only a governess. From the very start, his attentions had stretched beyond politeness. Alysanna struggled to understand, but tripped over the memory of his arms crushing her to him. The thought made her breath jag in her throat, and she coughed to disguise it from Lily, who still agonized over Italy's topography.

Suddenly, Alysanna realized what Cairn wanted from her. Men of his position were not interested in the likes of governesses, unless. . . . Her fury perked to a quick boil at the thought—Cairn Chatham sought some lower-class dolly to sate his flesh, all the while scouting a proper match elsewhere. That explained his too-eager interest.

A lord and a governess, indeed! She would waste no more thought on so vulgar a man.

"Yugoslavia, France, Switzerland, and Austria." Lily sat back proudly, pleased with her hard-won list.

"Liechtenstein."

"Oh, drats! I still say Maude Delamere's better off for not having to memorize all this silliness."

"That, Lily, is unlikely," Alysanna replied, considering that in many ways, Maude now seemed better off than both of them.

"Oh, Jenny, I shall be such a grown-up lady in so fine a gown!" Lily squealed and danced a spritely jig as she clutched the small poupee Jenny had brought from the milliner. "I have never had a polonaise skirt before. Can you make it exactly as on the doll, just as the ton wear in France?"

Jenny smiled with a nod and stroked Lily's cheek with her freckled hand. "I have made more than a costume or two in my time. I think we can fashion the skirt just right for a Russian princess. But first you must choose the color and fabric. Now, come see. I have already been to Aldgate for mercers' samples."

Jenny unwound several wide bolts of polished silk and bombazine until their widths tumbled in a pastel cataract across the sofa's back. None of the delicate hues suited Jenny's brilliant red hair and dark-flecked hazel eyes, but each complemented Lily's fair coloring exquisitely.

Jenny O'Malley's own grey lutestring made her look older than her twenty-eight years, though on second pass, her trim figure corrected the impression. As she spun the expensive weaves free of their spools, she turned toward a beaming Lily, who raised her hands in imploring confusion at the delicious choices.

"Must I pick just one? The blue is exquisite. But then,

perhaps the yellow. Yes, I wish the yellow. Unless. . . .''
Lily trailed her fingers across a shining swath of amethyst
silk, then threw Jenny a look of happy indecision.

"Then there is the ivory, of course. It would be a
most proper ball costume if we are to make you a Russian
girl.''

"Woman!'' Lily corrected with hopeful defiance, knowing
the assertion not quite true. "I will soon be fifteen, and I am
more than old enough for an allemande with father's rakish
friends.''

"Which is exactly why I have brought something very
special from the milliner.'' Jenny plumbed the depths of a
huge leather satchel she had dragged from her hired hackney
and withdrew a roll of turquoise silk fringe. Next came a
pleated ivory ruche, and finally, a diaphanous gauze handkerchief edged with delicate flowers of Flanders' lace. Lily's
eyes widened like huge blue saucers at the rich display.

"I thought these might do nicely on the ivory silk. Of
course, if you prefer the amethyst or the yellow. . . .''

"No, no! Please, it's the ivory I want! Mary Hamilton will
perish from envy when she spies my finery. Did you order
these just for me?''

"Your father sent me to Paternoster Row the month past
—as soon as he decided to hold the soiree. He thought it
only fitting that you should be costumed as the princess he
knows you to be.'' Lily rushed Jenny, nearly toppling her
with a tight, effusive hug of gratitude.

"You are not only London's best mantua-maker, you are
my best friend, as well. If I had my way, I should order
dresses every day to see you more often.'' Lily pressed her
cheek into Jenny's closely fitted bodice and squeezed her
even tighter than her corset's stays.

"I wish that, too. But I doubt that your father could afford such indulgence. Even his great wealth could not keep pace with your fine taste. Now, it appears to me you are a bit more the woman than at my last visit. Spin around and I'll measure to make the ivory a fine fit.'' Jenny playfully smacked Lily's backside, then rummaged through her bag for a tape. A light knock rattled the door.

"Yes?" Lily cocked her head around the wood-trimmed mirror. "Alysanna! I thought Father gave you a free afternoon."

"I came for the needlepoint I left here. I didn't realize you had a guest." Alysanna backed toward the hallway, but Lily hurried after her, pulling her into the room with both hands.

"Please, come in—I want you two to meet. Alysanna, this is Jenny O'Malley—she's my seamstress and my friend. And Jenny, this is Alysanna Walker. She has been my teacher since Beatrice left two weeks ago." Jenny bobbed a curtsy, and Alysanna dipped in return.

"I don't wish to interrupt your work." Alysanna looked enviously at the bolts of fabric and trim obscuring the sofa's birch frame.

"Not at all. I'm sure Lily would be happy to show you her choice." Jenny nodded toward the ruche and handkerchief Lily now twisted in curlicues about her neck.

"Look, Alysanna, Jenny has brought the most elegant silk. I chose the ivory, with the blue trim and lace everywhere, and a polonaise skirt, and oh! I shall be London's finest lady—young lady—in such a dress!"

Jenny and Alysanna laughed in unison, and the synchrony brought forth another giggle.

"It seems Lily is more fond of your business with her than she is of mine," Alysanna teased as Jenny guided Lily toward a footstool to measure the skirt's length.

"It is not your company, Alysanna," Lily protested, worrying she had offended her friend. "It is only geography I find loathsome. And Latin. And sometimes arithmetic. I confess I would rather tax my toes than my mind!" Lily whirled in a circle on the small silk hassock, the movement swelling her skirt into a shining cylinder and nearly unfooting Jenny's balance. With a loving but stern hand, Jenny caught Lily's hips and righted her.

"If we are to have the costume for the ball, you must hold still, please." With practiced efficiency, Jenny measured and made notes, pinning and scribbling as she talked to Alysanna.

"You've worked in London before?"

"I was in the employ of a northern shire family. In fact, I came to the city only to visit Beatrice—she is an old friend. But once I met Lily, my fate was sealed." Alysanna took pride that her lies, now oft told, were getting easier and, she hoped, more convincing.

"Lily catches us all, does she not?" Jenny said. Lily brushed a quick kiss against Jenny's creamy check, then restruck her statuesque pose. "Of all my ladies, Lily is my favorite."

The girl beamed at the compliment. "Jenny began as an abigail, you know. Fortunately, Lady Garfield staked her funds for a shop. Had she not, I should lack both her silk finery and her good company."

"I was most fortunate," Jenny continued. "Though my family was humble, I secured work as a lady's maid. After several years with Lady Garfield, God rest her soul, her bequest allowed me to begin on my own. The likes of my kind are rarely so lucky."

Alysanna watched Jenny's flying hands drape trim and hang yardage with bumblebee speed; her talents clearly were formidable. It was wrong that Jenny could turn a living only because of her former employer's grace. Alysanna could not have imagined having her fortunes bound to another's charity—until now. Perhaps she and the mantua-maker shared a strange kinship.

Jenny closed her notebook and dropped in mock exhaustion onto her heels, her glossy skirt puffing out like a dumpling around her. She nodded toward Alysanna's green camlet dress, expertly wadded to brace against the spring chill. "It appears that your own talents have earned you a good keep."

Alysanna blushed. She should have arranged for something less elegant by now, but Lily's twice-daily lessons and Duncan's sharp eye kept her much the prisoner in the Granvilles' gilded cage.

"It was a casting from an employer."

"Fine taste then, your lady. The embroidery is gold thread."

Alysanna feigned ignorance. "Yes, I do believe it is, though I have seen little enough of such luxury to know for sure."

"I should say she was close to your size, as well."

"My sister was skilled with a needle. 'Twas she who cut and tucked it for me."

Jenny nodded her approval. Unlike Alysanna's governess friends, Jenny seemed more pleased than covetous. Alysanna suddenly realized that Jenny could help fix her overdone wardrobe.

"Though my funds are limited, I do need proper clothes. Perhaps you could offer a suggestion. . . ."

Jenny's eyes lit with the entreaty.

"The mercer I frequent has serge and fustian, both quite

proper and easily had for a few shillings. Of course there is also lutestring or Yorkshire cloth, if either strikes your fancy.'' Jenny paused, remembering that even she couldn't afford the purchase. Surely Alysanna's means were as limited.

"If you can manage the cloth, I'll be happy to set you with some new gowns. As a favor, of course."

Alysanna was stunned by Jenny's kindness; it had been so long since she'd experienced such charity. She had imagined her social inferiors full of envy and avarice—but Jenny was not so.

"It is most generous of you, but I couldn't . . ."

"Nonsense!" Jenny interrupted. "It would be my pleasure. As soon as I finish Lily's silk, we'll find some fustian and fit you out."

Alysanna knew refusing Jenny would insult her more than the dressmaking would inconvenience her. "Thank you. I shall eagerly look forward to it." A deep cough turned their eyes to the hallway.

"Come in, Father," Lily called. "We are all quite respectable." The mahogany door opened, revealing Duncan, who stood red-faced from Lily's jest.

"I wish a moment with Miss Walker. I had forgotten your appointment, Jenny."

"Your lordship." Jenny sprang to her feet, then dipped a nervous curtsy. The ease Alysanna had seen her wear moments ago was chased off by flustered agitation.

"I trust you are making progress on the gown."

"We have chosen a silk; I will begin today." Jenny proffered a quick little smile, hardly returned by Duncan's somber stare.

"I had thought you to have begun long ago."

"The fabric you requested was slow in its shipping. I understood that you would wish to wait, rather than suffer inferior material."

Duncan locked his hands behind his back and shook his head brusquely. "You quite misunderstood me. The dress must be ready in a fortnight, no less. If you cannot manage, perhaps we must secure services elsewhere. Need I remind you there are countless other mantua-makers eager to draw my wages?"

Jenny's shoulders hunched forward, as if Duncan's threat pressed them down. Instead of the anger Alysanna would have expected, Jenny conceded, looking accustomed to such arrogant insults.

"The dress will be finished on time. I should not wish to lose your business, my lord."

"Very well." Duncan strutted toward the door, then recalled the errand that had sent him to Lily's room in the first place. "Miss Walker, I would see you on a related matter. Meet me in my study at once."

"Papa, it is Alysanna's day off!" Lily begged, hoping to spare Alysanna her father's bad spirits. Duncan shot back a silent reprimand that did not escape the governess's notice. Alysanna had no wish to share Jenny's fate, and knew she'd fare better to surrender her time if it would keep Duncan's black mood at bay.

He sped so fast down the hallway that Alysanna heard the tails of his frock coat snap as he made the stairway turn. She dashed after him, but Jenny hooked her hand before she could go, whispering loudly. "Next week we'll work on your dress. Don't look so glum! I'm more than used to this. He's all wirework, that one. Rigid outside, but a true heart underneath."

Alysanna couldn't imagine why Jenny would excuse Duncan's vulgar conduct. Had she grown so used to his indignities that she no longer saw them? It was a sobering thought; Alysanna vowed to avoid such a fate.

Whatever Duncan's business with her, she prayed he would dispatch it quickly. He was a boor and a snob, and one month past she would not have suffered a single moment in his coarse company. But that was almost a lifetime ago.

For all his professed urgency, Duncan obviously considered Alysanna's time expendable, for when she reached the library, she found herself quite alone. Sinking into a thickly padded armchair, she tipped her head backward and stared at the colored oval frescoes that sectioned the coffered ceiling.

Expertly painted copies of Michelangelo's Annunciation and the crucifixion of John the Baptist hung like moral canopies over opposite ends of the long room. In the library's center, a large, more vibrantly colored inset showed God's divine touch of mankind. The subject made her smile; it was particularly fitting for the household of a man so convinced of his own divinity.

The door lock clicked as Duncan marched in, much the martinet. He seated himself with great noise and authority behind the bulwark of his writing desk.

"As you may have gathered from Jenny's prattling, I am giving a bal masque a fortnight hence. Though Lily will not attend the full evening, I would like her to make a brief appearance. It is the particulars of this which I wish to discuss with you."

A grand ball! Music, candlelight, and finely dressed lords

and ladies swirling in patterned perfection spun through Alysanna's mind. An ache for the life she had lost worked through
the pit of her stomach.

Duncan continued, oblivious to Alysanna's distraction. "I
doubt you are familiar with the elaborate sort of fete I've
planned, which is why I wish to outline the evening.
You will serve as Lily's counselor, Miss Walker. Are you
listening?"

Alysanna's eyes had wandered in wistful memory, so
obviously that even the unobservant Duncan saw her distance.

"Of course. What is it you wish?"

"Dancing will commence at seven o'clock At half past,
Lily may join our company, though she will retire before
supper at ten. I have engaged Charles Thornton, a well-known
dance master, to instruct my daughter on the allemande and
cotillion; she is already well familiar with the contredanse.
Her costume will be as Jenny and I agreed. Delia will see to
her hair and preparation, but you will be charged with over-
seeing her deportment. It is a mother's task, but since she
lacks one, the duty falls to you."

Poor Lily. Duncan had mapped her evening out like a
regimented campaign, and Alysanna pitied her charge.
What could have been a splendid affair was fast becoming
an exercise in filial obedience. Duncan's assumption that
Lily's sentiments were not worth polling saddened Alysanna.

"I understand."

"Then understand as well that I wish you to be mindful
of your capacity. In your own right, you have no place in
such society, and I expect you, as I do others in my employ,
to avoiding calling attention to yourself."

"Then there will be no costume for me?" Alysanna could

not resist the sarcasm, though the suggestion actually made sense. If Duncan wished her to blend in, she'd do better as a French shepherdess than in her mousy governess garb. To her surprise, he took her seriously.

"Miss Walker! I must say that although I have been well pleased with your instruction of Lily, there is something in your attitude that is most irritating. It is almost as if you feel you deserve treatment beyond that which your station allows. Surely you were accorded no different privileges in your last position?"

Alysanna could not imagine, even if she had held a thousand governessing positions, that her employers would not have offered her more charity and respect than the crumbs Duncan cast her. Still, she needed his safe harbor, and Alysanna reminded herself that she must do what she must to avoid jeopardizing it.

"I did forget myself. I was merely caught up in the excitement."

"Well, you and the other servants can look forward to dinner samplings at second table. But I warn you to entertain no foolish thoughts of further participation. You are paid for your services, Miss Walker, not your company. It would make me most unhappy to find my governess behaving as a guest. Are we clear?"

"Clear as the call bell next to my door."

"Then you may go." Alysanna bolted to her room. It was cramped and depressing, but at least once she was there, she could safely doff her false manners.

She collapsed wearily onto the hard-bottomed bed and stared at the small slice of sky framed by her narrow window. A gull swooped past with a plaintive cry. Alysanna watched it float on an updraft and ached to trade her tightly laced fate for its unbound freedom.

His lordship the Viscount Duncan Granville—the gran-
diose name rankled Alysanna almost as much as its owner.
Her father, the earl of Birkham, had been a notch above him,
and Alysanna longed to demand Duncan's proper address of
her, to hear "the Lady Alysanna Wilhaven" trip with proper
respect off his acid tongue.

If he knew who she was, surely he would not dare behave
so abominably. His treatment of her had been bad enough,
but then there was Jenny. She, poor thing, had no better
lot to dream on. Why did she endure Duncan's insults?
Perhaps her resignation was what happened to people who
lived at others' disposal. Like beaten dogs, they knew nothing else—concession, more than pride, was their daily
bread.

As daughter of a wealthy earl, Alysanna had been served
by many menials, and now she wondered if she had ever
behaved like Duncan. Indeed, she was not sure that she had
ever considered her servants' feelings. She recalled the times
she had snapped at the cook or chastised her groom with a
complaint about the handling of her gelding, and her face
blushed hot. Had all these people been Jennys, their agonies
buried in their masters' oversights?

"By your leave, sir!" The young boy's call drew Alysanna
to her window. A footman, still too young to razor his face,
dashed before an elaborate calash, trying to pass a sedan
chair.

The boy's white stockings were caked with mire from the
uncobbled streets, and his pasty brow shone with beads of
sweat, which had already soaked a tumbling forelock. Behind
him a gold-wheeled coach, drawn by two high-stepping bays
ruled by a liveried driver, pulled a well-dressed lord to some
likely game of hazard.

Here was privilege, all its costs and wonder, distilled in

the simple transport of a human body. Alysanna vowed that, once her own rights were restored, she would never again allow herself the vain impudence that filled Duncan Granville. Silently, she also swore that she would win back all she had lost—else she knew she could not continue.

CHAPTER
6

❦

"Tell your master that Roberta, countess of Birkham, is here." Roberta didn't bother to look at the butler as she spoke to him; her eyes were too busy devouring the opulent interior of Cairn Chatham's London home. Above her a massive crystal chandelier filtered glittering rainbows onto the plaster rosette from which it hung, and across the harlequin-patterned floor, a sideboard flanked by matching marble pedestals bore an enormous floral display with ripe blossoms that exploded their sweet, honeyed scent into the entry hall.

Roberta stepped tentatively toward the large saloon in which she had been instructed to wait. Considering the rich French furniture and oriental tapestries, she was surprised that Cairn Chatham had any interest at all in part of Briarhurst.

Certainly the parcel she had bartered to him was arable and had respectable rents. Still, a man of such means could purchase entire estates. What use did he have for her fifty acres? She hoped Cairn had reconsidered. Her finances were now much improved by Alysanna's opportune departure, and Roberta had thought better of her wish to carve up the property.

As she waited for Cairn, Roberta stared at the golden walls and like-hued carpets, which were bathed by the warm afternoon light. A nearby Florentine clock marked the time with its gentle ticking, but Roberta was in no hurry. Everything about the glorious room felt rich and full, and she reveled in its easy luxury as she sat back into a nearby sofa's puff of silk cushion.

"Your ladyship." Cairn had been watching her silently for some time. She was as he remembered; even copious lace and curls did little to soften her angular, disagreeable face, which he suspected owed a greater debt to mean-spiritedness than parentage.

Roberta was startled at his greeting. Her eyes widened, then danced with delight at his handsomeness. They had only met once before this, but the London assembly room had been packed to capacity that night, and the noisy throng must have distracted her. How else could she have failed to notice his special appeal?

Now he was completely done up in magnificent black velvet, breeches to waistcoat, and the outfit's sumptuous darkness was relieved only by a snow-white cravat. Even his knee-high boots were a midnight hue. The effect was more than striking, and it occurred to Roberta that she might not wish to conclude their dealings so quickly after all. Cairn caught the assessment in her squinting brown eyes, and it amused him. Most women worked hard to disguise their appetite for men; Roberta unabashedly reveled in hers.

"My Lord Chatham." Roberta dipped her head with sufficient leisure to allow full admiration of her Cherubino hat. Silently, she berated herself for having selected the olive lutestring suit for today's journey. It was practical, but much less becoming than she now wished. "It is a pleasure to see you again. I was concerned when you failed to appear, as we had agreed. I feared you had been press-ganged by some wicked highwayman."

"My apologies for any worry I caused. I had thought to return to Briarhurst, as planned, to complete our business, but some other—unfortunate matters intervened."

Roberta pursed her lips as if they were pulled by a drawstring. "Nothing too terrible, I hope."

"Nothing you need be concerned with." His gray eyes stared straight at her, yet Cairn seemed withdrawn, and his curt tone was one of dismissal. Clearly, he wished to proceed to what business had brought her here. He sat at the helm of a long mahogany desk and gestured Roberta toward a nearby chair.

"Though your letter did not say, I trust you have come to complete our transaction. I have in hand the funds we agreed upon." Cairn pulled a silver key from his watch pocket and fitted it into the metal plate of one of the desk's small side drawers. Roberta leaned awkwardly forward from her small perch and warbled a nervous laugh.

"Actually, it is precisely this matter that I wish to discuss. I know we had agreed upon the sale of the land, but since we last spoke, my circumstances have changed somewhat."

"Indeed? Well, I warn you, Lady Wilhaven, any effort to increase the parcel's price will not serve your interest to sell. Our contract, though only verbal, was more than fair and certainly binding. I have no intentions of paying you a shilling over the five thousand pounds we agreed upon."

"No, no, it's not that at all." Roberta's hands flew about her face in flustered agitation as she struggled to correct his impression. "I would not dream of such faithlessness. It is not that I wish more money for the land—it is that I no longer wish to sell it, after all.''

Cairn slapped the drawer key down loudly on the desktop and leaned into the cup of the chair's wooden back. ''This is an unexpected turn. I had gathered from our earlier meeting that you were—how shall I say—in need of liquid funds?''

''Yes, that was the case, but as I said, my circumstances have altered for the better.'' Roberta smiled gamely and lifted her dark brows until she looked clownish.

''It has been less than a month since we spoke. You must have enjoyed a speedy business recovery.''

Roberta shifted uneasily from one hip to the other, her short riding coat rubbing against the slick fabric of the silk sofa with an annoying chafe that drew Cairn's gaze.

''Of sorts. I hope it would not indispose you to dissolve our arrangement.''

Roberta's request surprised Cairn. One month ago, she had been desperate for funds—this according to their mutual friend, who had introduced them at Almack's. At the time the name Wilhaven had given Cairn pause. His mother had been friends with a Lord Wilhaven and, on further inquiry, Cairn had discovered the man to be Roberta's deceased husband.

Cairn's mother, the dowager duchess, had heard tales of Roberta's greed, though she had not met her. When she had been told that Lord Frederick's widow was slicing up the estate, Lady Chatham had instructed her son to purchase all he could for safekeeping. If Roberta intended to keep the property, so much the better. Still, Cairn was not about to free her easily from her flimsy lie.

''I would like to oblige you, but I have since acquired land adjoining yours, the purchase of which would prove quite a waste lacking the Briarhurst property. I'm afraid it would be most difficult to release you, Lady Wilhaven. Our mutual friend, Sir Tarleton, assured me you were a woman of your word. Is it your intention to make him a liar?''

Roberta could see that her efforts to withdraw the offer were failing, and she took a different tack.

"Indeed, I will abide by my promise, Lord Chatham. In fact, if you truly wish to continue, I would not consider doing otherwise, despite the pain I will be forced to suffer upon parting with the land.''

"The sum we settled on is more painful to me than you, I think.''

"Oh, no, it isn't the money. I hadn't wanted to burden you with my personal problems, but now I feel I must tell you that I only sought to sell the land to honor a debt my husband incurred just before his death. He succumbed to consumption, you know, and was quite bedridden—even his mind lost its usual acuity. I begged him against the investment, but he insisted.

"Then, only days after his passing, I received the horrible news of his business loss. I needed funds to operate the house and had no choice but to part with the land—acreage that was less valuable to us in pounds than in sentiment.

"Lord Frederick—my husband—always held Briarhurst in such high esteem. It is an old estate—one that has been in the family for generations. To relinquish a part of it— well, I. . . .''. Roberta sobbed and gripped her forehead in anguish, hoping to reflect the distress her lies, if true, would have brought.

"And yet you were willing to sell quite enthusiastically, as I recall.''

"Destitution can make for painful choices. Of course, when my—our—fortunes unexpectedly reversed, I was immensely relieved. I no longer had a pressing need to divest the parcel, and I hoped you could be persuaded. But. . . . forgive me." Roberta covered her eyes and gulped theatrically. "It's just that I have been a widow such a short time, and the thought of my poor, dear Frederick. I did tell you when we met I was a widow, did I not?" Roberta's eyes lit flirtatiously, in strange counterpoint to her purported distress.

"Yes. I am very sorry for your loss. I must confess that hearing the story of your decision to sell does cast a different light on your situation."

Cairn could see Roberta's hopes rise. She dropped her hands abruptly from her face, revealing neither the red nose nor wet cheeks her weeping should have wrought. "Perhaps we could dismiss our agreement . . ." Cairn strode toward a marble sideboard and poured a full glass of dark claret, then offered it to Roberta. "Madame?" She shook her hatted head in refusal, but her hand shot out in quick reconsideration.

"Well, perhaps—just to ease the pain of recounting the loss of my dear husband. Are you sure that your kindness in forgiving our agreement would not importune you? I should not wish to bring about your financial distress . . ." Roberta knew it strengthened her credibility to protest Cairn's generosity, but she prayed he would not renege on his offer.

"I can see now I should be distressed only to cause you further sadness. Please consider the matter finished."

Roberta beamed up at him, and it was all Cairn could do not to shake his head at the incongruity between her happy mien and the misery she wore but moments ago. She was made for the stage, this one.

The tension that had twisted Roberta since she has stepped into Cairn's foyer dissipated, and she dispatched the claret entirely too fast. Now Briarhurst was all hers. Perhaps, with the right dress and attitude, Lord Cairn Chatham might be, as well.

Roberta set down the heavy glass and bounced her curls with one gloved hand as she studied Cairn's face. He was younger and richer than she was; the magnetic combination brought a smile and an offer from her eyes.

"Will you join me?" She tapped her glass.

"Unfortunately, that is not possible. I was on my way out."

Roberta wondered if she could manage an invitation to wherever Cairn was going. She had promised to meet Hadley across town, but he'd keep. Opportunities like Cairn Chatham rarely came her way. "An evening at Almack's, perhaps? Or a grand assembly?"

"Neither. But thank you for inquiring." Cairn opened the saloon's main door and offered his arm for escort. Roberta downed the remaining claret in an unladylike gulp and eagerly grabbed on. "I thank you again for your kind understanding. If you should find yourself near Briarhurst. . . ."

"I think it unlikely," Cairn answered, walking her out, then pushing her hand from his forearm as he reached for the long black cape and half mask held by his valet. "My business is much in London these days."

"Ah! A masked affair! It seems forever since we have had such revelry at Briarhurst." Though it was clear Cairn had no intention of including Roberta, still she persevered.

"Then you must hurry home and arrange some of your own merriment." Cairn swung the front door open.

"Yes," Roberta answered, stalling as she leaned against the gilded balustrade. "Well, Lord Chatham, do have a lovely evening."

"I shall," Cairn answered. "I enjoy a good disguise."

* * *

Hadley shook the dice hard, as if vigor alone could bring about the desired result. They hit the table's moss felt with a padded click, and the crowd issued a collective gasp.

"It seems the odds have smiled on you again, Lord Marquess." Hadley's face betrayed no emotion as his gray-haired gaming partner drew in the note Hadley had placed in the table's center, and added it to the top of a high stack.

"It was a deep wager. Perhaps another throw will let you recover?" The elderly marquess raised his palm in question, but Roberta pressed angrily against Hadley's ear.

"Hadley, no! You are down five hundred pounds tonight alone. It's my money you're spending, and I won't have it!"

Hadley wiped the perspiration from his brow with a yellowed lace handkerchief, and answered Roberta through clenched teeth. "Enough of your bad mood! 'Twas I came to town to watch your spending, not you mine. Our Lord Marquess is a four-bottle man, and I tell you he can be beaten!" Hadley reached again for the dice, but Roberta clamped his wrist painfully.

"At piquet, perhaps. But hazard is a game of chance. The dice have been turning the old lord's way ever since you began." Hadley threw Roberta a look of indecision that spent her patience.

"Pffff!" she spat, then spun to leave, but not before Hadley pinched her arm with a final low plea. "If you could advance me next month's . . ."

Roberta snapped free of his hold. "I've done enough—don't expect any more relief from me!"

Hadley knew further wagers were sure to be disallowed by his own questionable credit, leaving him no choice but to follow the disgruntled Roberta.

"My lordship, I thank you, but as you can see, my com-

panion has grown impatient. Until next time.'' Hadley bowed
a polite farewell and dropped the dice, hurrying to keep pace
with Roberta's quick clip down the long, portrait-hung hallway that led from White's back gaming room.

He had passed through the club portals often before, though
rarely with so great a loss as he had suffered this evening.
Each throw had laid him deeper down. But instead of checking his damage and suspending wagers, Hadley had grown
more desperate to throw again, surer with each toss that the
dice could deny him no more. His hopes had exceeded his
luck, and, though Roberta's last payment covered tonight's
losses, he wondered how he could possibly continue supporting Wodeby, much less his appetite for hazard and cards.

''I hope you're pleased. The marquess was wagering high.
I could have caught him with one more toss.''

''Or caught a swift wagon to the workhouse. You should
be thankful I saved your foolish neck. You'd have had Wodeby itself on the block.''

''It might as well have been, for the little I've left after
tonight,'' he grumbled, following Roberta into the rocking
calash. ''If Alysanna were still slated to be my bride, I should
not have to worry about such pittances as went down this
evening.''

''Don't turn on me with your insults. Alysanna left of her
own accord. It was hardly my doing that she mismanaged
the pistol. If she'd been a better shot, you'd still be going to
the bank on your betrothal. Perhaps you should have improved her marksmanship.'' Roberta smiled smugly, pitching
Hadley's pique a notch higher.

''Well, it worked out nicely for you. Your coffers are fatter
with no stepdaughter to keep.''

Roberta stamped her foot angrily on the carriage floor,
accidentally signaling the driver and abruptly sending the

calash lurching forward. "Yes, but I've gained another leech in the bargain. Now, stop your whining. You'd have stood no chance at all with Alysanna were it not for my aid. She was hardly disposed to any match after Frederick's death. It was a credit to my counsel that you duped her into accepting your tainted proposal."

"Really?" Hadley snapped furiously. "And what makes you so sure I might not have won her on my own? I am earl of Hughdon—quite a catch in many eyes."

"At least spare me your lies! You're a high-toned wastrel with a taste for loose molls and fast gaming tables. Our dear Alysanna prizes stability. Do you think such a well-bred miss would have given you even a moment had she known that Wodeby was mortgaged to its roof? Or that you had, how shall we say, a somewhat checkered past with the ladies? Luckily, your debauchery was not as legend here as I heard abroad."

"I was foolish to trust you at all," Hadley slurred, the stale smell of gin on his breath bringing Roberta's hankie to her nose. "You seem much the lark tonight. What accounts for your insufferably good mood?"

"I paid a call to our duke, Lord Cairn Chatham. The gentleman's fine looks are as dapper as his fat accounts."

Hadley managed a surfeited smile. "Oh, then my Roberta has lost her girlish heart . . ."

"Don't be a fool. What I nearly lost was a piece of land I no longer wish to sell. But I charmed him off the notion. All of Briarhurst is once again mine."

"He released your contract?"

"Yes, and even after he had purchased an adjacent parcel to complete our acreage. It was a most agreeable resolution."

"A most odd one, if you ask me." Hadley's speech was

worsening by the moment, its decline accelerated by the small silver flask from which he swilled.

His words faltered, but his logic did not. " 'Tis rare to find such charity in business." He tried to snap his fingers but missed, instead producing only a fleshy rubbing sound. "Of course! How foolish of me—it was your blinding beauty!"

The insult was grating, but close enough to the mark to give Roberta pause. The circumstances of her meeting with Cairn Chatham did seem odd. At the start, he had been adamant on the transaction; yet, with scant persuasion, he had released her. And after he had already paid out precious pounds for the adjacent parcel—a waste, to hear him tell, without her property as complement. Something smelled wrong, but Roberta was too tired to fathom it tonight. She had Briarhurst all to herself—that was what mattered.

Hadley leaned his foul breath into her, and his lips pulled back in a satisfied smile.

"Well, however you did it, I am pleased. The more for you, the more for me."

Roberta squinted and shook her head subtly. "You have enough!"

"Not quite. My loss at the tables makes that clear. I'll need more."

"You'll rot in hell before I give you a shilling over what I've agreed."

Hadley rapped his knuckles on the carriage wall, and it lurched to a halt. He cracked the door and leaned out, yelling to the driver. "Not the post house. We wish to see Lord Duncan Granville. His address is . . ."

"Stop it!" Roberta snatched Hadley back in by his revers and her face hardened. "Are you mad?"

Hadley smiled smugly. "Mad enough to know you'll do anything to keep Briarhurst all to yourself."

Roberta slapped her gloves hard against the door, bellowing her own instruction. "Driver, ahead! To the post house."

"Well?" Hadley cocked one brow in question, and his irritating expression made Roberta shake with rage.

"Very well. You'll have what you need." Roberta paused, her flecked eyes narrowing. "But I warn you, bleed me dry and we'll both sink in this mire. Now, shut your mouth. I've had enough of your drunken babbling."

Hadley smiled before taking a final swig of the flask's gin, then descended into a loud, snoring sleep.

Roberta stared at the heap of him, jostling limp-jointed across the carriage seat from her. But for Hadley, Briarhurst would now be hers alone. He was greedy. Worse than that, he was stupid, though he'd certainly found enough wit to call her bluff. But his profligacy could easily outpace her funds. Yet what could she do? At all costs, she had to keep Alysanna away. The best way to ensure that was to buy Hadley's silence, whatever the price.

Roberta's head dropped like a stone into her hands. She felt tired and heavy. It was all too much to sort out tonight. Briarhurst was intact—that was what mattered now. Tomorrow, she'd think of a way to handle Hadley.

The distant strains of a Haydn suite wafted up from downstairs, stealing Alysanna from her dark, tallow-lit garret to the dream of a light-flooded hall. In her mind's eye, she danced with delicious abandon. With her eyes closed it was easy to see the glorious, effortless past—a time when her days were filled with no dilemma greater than what dress and wrap would suit the week's soiree.

Alone in her tiny room, Alysanna's thin slippers stepped

lightly in time to the orchestra's lilting melody. She turned with a curtsy and a smile to her imaginary partner, and could almost feel Hadley's arms encircle her narrow waist. Alysanna began to spin, her dark gray fustian skirt suddenly transformed into ballooning layers of rustling, indigo silk.

Alysanna was drunk on memory, and she tilted her head back with giddy delight, tossing out a ribbon of a laugh. But her eyes flew open, and she snapped her arms free of her imagined squire as she saw his face. It was not Hadley at all, but Cairn Chatham who held her! What misguided longing had replaced her fiancé with Cairn's coarse visage? Alysanna shook off the question; it was only Cairn's presence downstairs that had brought him to mind.

He was probably full in the midst of the ball's merriment. The ongoing clatter of carriage wheels and the echo of excited greetings from arriving guests had stopped some time ago, replaced by a distant din that, though muted, made clear the lively society downstairs.

Alysanna could easily envision it. She had walked through the great chamber earlier that day, when there was already an extravagance of flowers and fresh candles arranged for the evening's merriment. Now she imagined a mist of fragrance and light dusting legions of the ton, all fancifully dressed, like butterflies whose beautiful, short existences were breathtaking to behold.

Delia had likely finished Lily's hair and dress by now. Alysanna had seen the Russian princess costume two days past when Jenny had delivered it. Its ivory silk with aqua trim was even more stunning than Alysanna remembered, and Lily had been thrilled beyond words. Duncan had even granted his daughter the use of her mother's tiara for the evening, as well as the diamond drop earrings and bracelet that were specially fashioned in France as the coronet's companions. Alysanna's heart still raced at the memory of her own first ball, and she smiled as she imagined Lily's present state of mind.

"Alysanna? Will I do?" A properly flustered Lily peeked her head in, then stepped tentatively beyond the door. Even in the dim light, Alysanna could tell she was beautiful, and she stretched out her arms in silent approval. Alysanna had never actually seen any Russian peers, but she could not imagine that any could rival Lily's royal appearance. The girl rushed toward her, begging further assurance.

"Is the dress suitable?"

"You are more exquisite than I was—I mean, I have not seen any of my charges look as lovely as you do this moment. Turn about." Lily obliged with a rapid spin, the polonaise folds of her overskirt lifting softly.

"Have you your dance card?

Lily fumbled with the silk cord that suspended the tiny ledger from her wrist. "I am ready—if only anyone asks. A suitor is something even Jenny's fine trimmings cannot stitch." Lily drew her thumb between her teeth and winced hopefully.

"The evening will be more wonderful than you have dreamed. I am sure of it." Alysanna laughed playfully, taking Lily's small face in the cup of her hands. "Now, I imagine it's past time. Shall we?"

With a deep, nervous breath, Lily led the way to her social debut. As she and Alysanna dropped into the midst of the noisy gaiety, the serenade of strings and the hum of polite banter grew into a happy cacophony.

Now they could not only hear but also see the ball's lively revelers. Lily gasped with delight at the whimsical parade. A nunnery abbess, a jewel-encrusted sultana, even a shepherdess with a genuine lamb chatted blithely with nabobs and pilgrims. Literary figures abounded, as did artists, the best indisputably Duncan's Rubens. Some of the gentlemen looked uncostumed, but Alysanna pointed out that the more daring ladies often came as men.

The outrageous assortment produced an altogether magical effect, and, though Alysanna's father had often thrown such masked affairs when she was still at Briarhurst, even the most elaborate of their fetes could not rival this one. Both Alysanna and Lily stood in open-mouthed awe.

Duncan, who had been partnering a shepherdess through an allemande, applauded the music's end and hurried to greet his daughter. A broad smile spread across his face, and he swelled with pride.

"Lily, you are a dream to behold. Before these young sparks trample me trying to catch you, will you grant one dance to your aging father?"

Lily beamed at Duncan's teasing and threw Alysanna a pleased grin. The crowd parted as Duncan ushered his daughter toward the crush of the full floor, and as they reached center, the gray-haired maestro lifted his baton and struck a contredanse. With a whoosh and a girlish peal of laughter, Lily began the first of many pairings that would make her feet ache by evening's end.

In line with Duncan's pointed instructions, Alysanna tried to disappear. But amid the burst of silks and satins, the gold-trimmed lace and the silver fringe, Alysanna felt as obvious as a brown hen in a covey of peacocks.

Everywhere she looked the guests laughed and raised their sparkling crystal in champagne toasts she heard only half of. When they looked at her, which was rare, their eyes skipped over, or shot straight through, as if she were some gauzy thing lacking flesh. Was this what being an outsider felt like? Alysanna cared little for it.

When Lily's confident smile made clear she no longer needed her, Alysanna backed out of the gaiety, receding to the servants' stairs. There she collapsed in exhausted depression, dropping her chin to her hands with a heavy sigh. The pose was unladylike and unbecoming, but no one could see her anyway. The crowd was so tightly packed that Alysanna had managed only an occasional slitted glimpse of her charge.

Ironically, about the only person Alysanna *could* see well was Maude, done to perfect excess in a gypsy's guise. Her tall frame was hung with yards of scarlet silk, the hem and sleeve ends torn to imitate the wear Alysanna knew none of Maude's gowns had ever seen. A thick twist of gold rope wound a lusty serpentine across her cantilevered breasts, cinching in her tiny waist and finishing in an explosion of tassels that made her narrow hips seem wider when she moved.

Alysanna had to admit that the effect was quite becoming, though, had she herself commissioned the gown, she would have omitted the matching gold coins with which Maude had liberally peppered her straining bosom. Maude's mask, also scarlet but trimmed with a black ostrich, was entirely unnecessary, Maude having ensured with the lack of a headdress on her thick blond curls that no one could mistake her for a lesser being. Alysanna hated her for her grandness and longed with all her heart, for tonight at least, to be just like Maude Delamere.

As the evening bloomed, Lily left her father's side, his role deeded to a line of dashing suitors. Committed to the stairs, Alysanna resolved to forget Maude, and she resettled her skirts for a long wait.

The orchestra's tune was one she knew, a cotillion she had danced herself but a few months past, and Alysanna began to hum along softly. By now, she had abandoned watching the crowd; witnessing their happy revelry only scooped out what little hope was left in her heart. Save Duncan and Lily and the insufferable Maude, she knew none of them anyway. Surprisingly, even Cairn Chatham had made no appearance, an absence Alysanna mused briefly on, then thanked fate for.

Wishing only escape, Alysanna closed her tired eyes, then began to sway softly to the music's rich swells. She drifted with the melody and, when it ended, capped with a burst of the dancers' applause, Alysanna looked up. There, resolutely in front of her like some frightening dare, was a pair of shining black leather boots.

Her startled look volleyed up the wearer to see who had discovered her sprawled pose, but it was no use. The man was covered, nearly head to toe, in midnight black, his head concealed by a terrifying executioner's mask. Alysanna jumped to her feet, expecting some outraged lord's reprimand for her servant's indolence.

"No need to rise. I was enjoying just watching you."

The deep timbre of the voice was unmistakable—who else but Cairn Chatham would have found her here!

"For a moment I was thrown by your disguise, though the impression does suit you." The dark, nearly floor-length black cape, with its companion mask, gave Cairn much the appearance of night. Still, Alysanna could see a small slice of mouth, and now that she was looking, that galling grin of his, threatening to crack.

Cairn bowed in response, laughing low as he grabbed the hood's nape and pulled it forward, revealing his thick mop of sun-brown hair. "I thought it better than a sultan suit. Too many Persians scouting harems here." Cairn nodded toward the bustling dance floor, where Alysanna counted at least three sultans. She knew she should be annoyed at Cairn's attentions, but her boredom made her grateful for any diversion.

"Are you lost? The servants' quarters seem an unlikely place for Lord Granville's guests. Didn't I see Miss Delamere gypsying about?"

"It's heartening to know that your difficult circumstances haven't compromised your spirit." Cairn leaned against the paneled wall and crossed his arms, as if he intended to stay. Unnerved, Alysanna gathered her skirts and retreated first one, then two stairs toward the upper rooms' safety.

"And what 'difficult circumstances' would those be?"

"Why, your governess position, of course."

Cairn Chatham seemed to suspect her of some crime, and Alysanna grew increasingly concerned at his interest. If he thought her guilty, she wished he'd just accuse her. But instead, Cairn baited her with the subtle suggestion that he knew secrets he was not about to tell.

"I can't fathom what it is about me that makes you so certain my lot is not of my choosing. Surely you don't question the pleasure of Lily's company?"

"We both know Lily is hardly the issue here. It is more that . . ." Cairn paused, raising a gloved hand to his chin as if he wished to choose his words carefully. "It is that something about you is ill-suited to the back stairs." He smiled wryly.

Alysanna was hard-pressed for a reply. He was right—the back stairwell was far from her accustomed milieu. Cairn caught the accession in her silence.

"You'd rather be dancing."

Of course I would, Alysanna mused angrily. Cairn's stupid comment and strange attitude were edging her toward outright rage. "What servant would not wish to be master?"

"Many. But few have the spine. May I?" Cairn stretched out his hand in invitation.

"What?"

"I would have the pleasure of a dance." He spoke as if the request were entirely logical, but Alysanna's mouth gaped in shock at his audacity. Surely he was having his sport with her. Even a lord deep in his cups wouldn't publicly partner a governess.

"Don't tease me."

"Don't be so quick to think my interest spurious. The allemande is just beginning. Wouldn't you rather dance than watch it?"

"Well, of course, but . . ." Alysanna realized he meant the offer, then had trouble gathering her thoughts. How she'd love to dance! But with Cairn Chatham? After all his insults and duplicity, how could she consider it? Still, it was only a dance. But even if she wanted to, it was an unspeakable impropriety. Such a pleasure could cost her greatly. "Duncan—er—Lord Granville would have my head. I was expressly instructed to disappear."

"Then you shall." Cairn looked around quickly, then called a summons to an elderly Scheherazade. "Lady Garton!" The woman turned, took in the call's speaker, and smiled at Cairn's beckoning. She approached, straightening her bodice and beaming as if she expected him to ask for a dance.

"Would it be possible to borrow your mask?" Lady Garton's heavily lined lips parted in protest, but Cairn pressed on. "It is gilding the lily, you know, to disguise your beauty."

She sputtered with an awkward laugh. "What do you want with my mask? It is not yet time to reveal, and the gold hardly suits your costume."

"I know it is an improper request, but I would consider the temporary loan a great favor. I'll return it personally when we dance the next allemande." Cairn winked slyly. The promise of a spin on his arm apparently was deemed worth the strange request. Lady Garton sighed her accession and unknotted the mask's golden ties from her gray powdered head.

"Lady Garton, you are, as always, my very favorite." Cairn bowed deeply. "Now, if you will excuse me." He snatched Alysanna's hand, yanking her around the balustrade and stopping only long enough to tie the mask's velvet strings.

"Perfect! Though a shameful blight of beauty." Cairn donned his black hood and lurched forward, still clutching Alysanna's hand as they sped toward the sweet-smelling floor's warm center. At first Alysanna's feet dragged indecisively, then, acknowledging the futility of resisting both her own and Cairn's inclinations, she scampered behind the thump of his boots like a kitten toward cream.

They reached what Cairn had deemed their place, and the violins, as if waiting only for their arrival, struck out in a climbing crescendo. Cairn and Alysanna bowed, and, as they bent down, he leaned his cheek close, his mouth pressing warmly against her ear.

"Courage, Alysanna," he whispered. "I think you already know much of it."

CHAPTER
7

The heavenly swell of violins and flutes issued a clarion call to part of Alysanna too long buried. Their climbing strains set her feet in happy surrender to the allemande's lively pace, driving all misgivings on the imprudence of her actions from her mind.

Moments ago she had stood a dejected outsider, peering into a privileged life no longer hers. Now, she jetéd triumphantly in her rightful world, its fine pleasures suddenly existing only for her bidding.

Though her modest gray dress was like a dark eddy in the swirling midst of bright silks and satins, Alysanna danced as if she were the soiree's centerpiece, snapping her fustian skirt with each step and turn to fully display it to all who watched.

She was much observed, at first because of her stark dress. But then, as she swayed to the music's aching theme, the guests' critical appraisals changed to admiration of the mysterious, confident beauty on Cairn Chatham's arm.

Alysanna dipped and twirled, oblivious to their stares. Her eyes traveled no farther than Cairn's own, which held her more compellingly than his embrace might have, had the patterns of the allemande not parted them.

She had agreed only to dance; yet she had unwittingly struck a more dangerous deal. Each time Alysanna spun toward him, the heat of his stare burned through her. She tried to dismiss it, not wishing to encourage whatever misinterpretation he had undoubtedly assigned her decision to partner him. Still, she could not shake off his too-keen attention, and, even more surprisingly, Alysanna found herself almost pleased with the appreciative smile that threatened to part his lips.

Cairn's entire face now beamed its approval of her, as if he understood the deliverance her feet gave her heart. He could not know that this Alysanna was more quintessential, more true than the governess she played; still, his look lacked the haughtiness she would have expected in the face of a man who had lifted her misery with such a gift.

Odder still was the heady feeling that washed through Alysanna each time they touched. As they wound through the dance's swift pas de bourrées, Cairn did not so much hold as possess her hand, his fingers wrapping her own with a gentle force. They reached overhead for what should have been a perfunctory turn, but Cairn brushed improperly close, the warm impression of his taut muscles still palpable even after he left.

She had danced the allemande with a thousand different suitors, but it had never before felt like this—so breathless, so intimate. Alysanna's heart thumped in her ears each time Cairn's hand brushed the back of her waist, and she told herself the surge of excitement welling up in her was because of the dance's rigors, no more. But why, then, did it end each time he withdrew?

The music climbed higher in rapturous flight, and Alysanna tapped her feet in happy time until the strings tumbled and slowed. As the allemande required, Cairn pulled Alysanna close at the music's end, drawing her into a loose embrace. It was all quite proper, yet a luscious wickedness filled her up as she stood unmoving, making no effort to back free of his hold.

His grip was not so tight that she was prisoner; rather, some mutinous part of Alysanna chose not to move away. Cairn gazed at her with a silent request, and his mouth opened as if he would speak, but there were no words.

Only then did she hear the room's heavy silence. It fell all around like a wet, cold curtain, crushing the lively din that moments ago vied with the leaping strings. The sudden weight of eyes bore down on her, and their press made Alysanna feel smaller than she already was. She cringed fearfully— was this some unspoken outrage for her bold impropriety? Alysanna searched Cairn's eyes for instruction.

"Help me."

"You've crashed their tight little clique. They mean you no harm—they are only intrigued."

Alysanna surveyed the room with a slow, circling turn. She hardly believed their stares benign, but it was true that she could see more question than anger in the guests' half-masked faces.

"What shall I do?" she whispered.

"Smile and take my arm. You are still masked. Everyone wonders—but no one knows." Cairn's confidence buoyed her hope.

She followed obediently as they began from the floor. But just past the orchestra's head, a drum roll and trumpet herald nailed their feet. The dance master stepped forward, raising his palms to signal for silence.

"Lords and ladies, the time has come to unmask. Please remove your disguises now."

Panic coursed through Alysanna as she turned toward Cairn. Even the almond slits of her borrowed mask could not disguise the terror in her eyes.

Yet her panicked look was a weak reflection of her thoughts, which flew through her head like a covey of flushed birds. Dancing with Cairn, even in disguise, had been crime enough. Now, dance master's dictum or not, she would not worsen her sins by revealing herself. She had to escape.

"Take a breath." Cairn yanked Alysanna toward the parlor door, but Duncan popped out, seemingly from nowhere, rising like an angry pillar before them.

"Cairn." Duncan nodded slowly, and his eyes stuck on Alysanna, who threw her own to the floor and lowered her head in a useless effort to hide.

"Duncan. If you're looking for Lady Halsham, I think she slipped out with a Chinese rake." Cairn hoped the red herring would draw off Duncan's scent.

The rest of the room had unmasked and, though few were surprised at their partners' identities, the merrymakers' chatter had hit its earlier pitch. But as the guests saw the tense scene unfolding at the room's head, silence fell again.

"I should like an introduction." Duncan nodded toward Alysanna, who canted her head so far toward the floor that her chin touched her chest.

"This one is mine, Duncan. I won't have you stealing her." Cairn smiled wickedly, hoping his jest would dismiss Duncan's interest.

"I must disagree." Duncan already knew who hid behind the mask. "Miss Walker!" He hissed more than spoke, and, as he pulled her mask free, Alysanna saw Duncan's gloved fist clench against his thigh, frightening her with the expectation that he might strike her.

"Lord Granville." For lack of a better notion, she smiled gamely. It was clear that Duncan expected an apology. Why couldn't Alysanna's tongue find one?

"Have you nothing to say for yourself?"

"I . . . no, sir. Nothing." Even as her impertinence continued, Alysanna vowed to stop. If she wanted to keep this governess position, she'd better muster some quick contrition. Yet the indomitable pride her father had sired caught her obeisance deep in her throat, and nothing at all came from her lips.

All she'd done was dance. It was no crime, though to look at Duncan's nearly bursting face, one would think it a capital offense.

"I am shocked both by your outrageous behavior and by your insolent lack of apology. I thought I had made clear my expectations."

"Indeed, sir, you did. It was just . . ." Alysanna's eyes drifted across the floor, as if she expected to find some answer there.

Mercifully, Cairn intervened. "Entirely my fault, Duncan. Miss Walker protested, but I would hear nothing of it. Come, man, where's your humor? You must admit, the governess costume was a good disguise."

Duncan's boot thumped against the parqueted floor, the echo of its heavy heel parting the expectant silence. "Your foolish decision, Miss Walker, may well cost you your position here. We'll discuss this later. Now, to your room at once!"

The tyrannical cut of Duncan's tone made Alysanna nearly shake with rage. He ordered her as if she were some naughty child! Still, there was nothing to be done unless she sought a rude toss into the street's rough fortune. She nodded her accession and, eyes still downcast, turned to go. Just before she passed his reach, Cairn caught her hand.

"Alysanna." The depths of his eyes softened into a smile. "It was my pleasure. Truly."

She paused, trying to decipher his coded message, then, wanting nothing so much as to vanish from the earth, bolted in near explosion. Fury cut like a knife through her scattered focus, summoning a wave of tears. She shielded her eyes and fled, skirts in hand, up the long stretch of stairs.

Alysanna took them two at once, breathless by the time she reached the top landing. Finally safe from witnesses, she leaned back in despair against the wall, covering her face with her hands as she dissolved into loud, anguished sobs. Duncan's blunderbuss reaction had been disproportionate. Still, that would be small solace if he cast her out.

"It really was none of her doing." Cairn hoped that, in assuming responsibility for Alysanna's behavior, he could lessen Duncan's wrath.

"Will you tell me you forced her onto the floor?"

"I did. Now, does that ice your choler over this silly imbroglio?" Cairn's patronizing manner pushed Duncan too hard. He was a cherished friend, but his iconoclasm now wore thin.

"Silly? An employee passing as a guest at my ball?"

"Come, man, what harm was done?"

"It was an insult to my authority."

"So you will dismiss Miss Walker and make Lily pay for my indiscretion? Duncan, snobbery is a nasty trait."

"You have mentioned it before. Now, next time you have a taste for the help, you'll find they're mostly in the housekeeper's room, where they belong. Please keep your ballroom partners to a better class of company."

Cairn shook his head in dismay. "Then I can do nothing to ease your anger with her?"

Duncan was obviously surprised at Cairn's response. "You've taken this cause quite to heart, I see. What's my governess to you?"

"I find her—intriguing."

"Bread and water are so when you're used to fancier fare. To which end. . . ." Duncan nodded toward Maude, who stood, head cocked and eyebrow lifted, just within earshot.

Duncan swept over the floor, calling loudly enough for the whole room to hear. "Maestro, a contredanse, if you please!" Hoping he'd restored the festivities, Duncan strode toward the library, but not before Lily caught his sleeve.

"Father, please, Alysanna is so special to me. I beg you not to dismiss her."

"What she did, Lily, was unthinkable."

"She only wished a small pleasure. And she has given me so very much of just that. Please. . . ." Duncan's hardened face gave Lily little hope his heart would change. Before she could plead again, a dark-haired swain dressed as a Greek peasant snatched her hand. Thinking her father might do better if left to sort his thoughts, Lily accepted, but not before throwing him a final beseeching glance.

Duncan collapsed wearily into the chair, downing a stiff swig of cognac without so much as bothering his usual pass of its snifter under his nose. The click of the study's ebony door handle preempted what he intended to be a speedy dispatch of the entire shot.

"Maude? What are you doing here? Last I looked you hardly lacked for suitors."

"I would speak with you, Duncan. Might I? And some

claret, if you please?'' She pointed toward a ruby decanter next to the cognac.

Duncan poured her a draught, marking the match of the scarlet liquid to Maude's red gypsy guise. He sauntered toward a small settee, indicating she should join him. ''Now, tell me, what's knotted your pretty face?''

''Your governess.''

Duncan let go a displeased sigh and shot his eyes toward the parlor. ''The result of my bad judgment. I should have trusted my instincts on that one, though I confess my fear at the onset was that she'd abandon Lily for some lovesick match. It hardly crossed my mind the woman would repay my kindness with such disobedience.''

''You know what must be done.'' Maude leaned toward him, laying her hand beseechingly on Duncan's breeches and searching his eyes for the answer she yearned for.

''I shall rebuke her again.''

''Your heart's as soft as a chocolate cream. You must do more than that—she must be dismissed! Surely you cannot be considering another course?'' A look of genuine alarm puckered Maude's patrician features.

''I'm so furious, I've hardly considered where to go from here. Such impertinence from a servant—and before my friends, yet!''

''Unforgivable.'' Maude bobbed her blond curls in quick sympathy. ''Which is exactly why she must not have a chance to repeat such impropriety.''

''If it were my decision, she'd certainly be packing now. But Lily is so fond of her—she has already pled Miss Walker's case.''

''Lily's judgment, though advanced for her age, is still that of a child.'' Maude's great passion in this matter did not escape him. Management of staff was not an issue friends oft bothered to raise.

"You seem much interested in what I would guess is of little consequence to you. Or is it?" For some time, Duncan had known of Maude's interest in Cairn. But until this moment, he had failed to appreciate the depth of her sentiments. "Cairn finds her little more than a curiosity. Surely you perceive no threat from such a mouse?"

"Of course not!" Maude laughed, thinking Alysanna was a bold mouse, if one at all. "My relationship with Cairn could hardly be damaged by such a woman. Still, I should not wish to see his curiosity cause undue strain between us. We have been quite close of late. In fact, if I can trust you to keep the secret, I think we might be on the verge of a betrothal."

Duncan was stunned by Maude's assertion; this was the first he'd heard of it. If Cairn were considering this grave step, surely he'd have confided his intentions. "Cairn said he wishes to make you his wife?"

"Not exactly," she answered equivocally. "But as you know, we have kept close company since childhood. The match would be perfect." Maude perched the glass on the walnut card table and rubbed her hands nervously, as if even she could not quite trust her assertion.

"I agree that you would suit him well. Still, Cairn has been slick with other clutches. Ever since Elizabeth—"

"That is past," Maude interrupted. "What matters is our mutual affection—which I should not like to see daunted by a low-class distraction." Maude stopped, fearing she had overdisplayed her interest. "I'm sorry, I didn't mean to speak so frankly. It's only that, if you truly have Cairn's interests at heart, as I know you do, you'll send that Walker woman elsewhere. Any involvement between them would be most unfortunate. Have I your word?''

"You have my promise to think on it. But I still must consider Lily's feelings. Trust that at least I'll deliver some harsh justice in return for her audacity." Maude still looked hungry, but Duncan's stern stare made clear he would not sate her. "Now, if you want to advance your cause with Cairn, you should make yourself seen. Who knows where an allemande can lead?''

Maude smiled coquettishly, hooking her fingers just beneath her bodice's neckline and tugging so as to display a touch more cleavage. With a smile and a giggle, she bounced determinedly toward the parlor.

There, in the midst of the merriment, was the target of her intentions. She rushed toward Cairn and pressed close, batting her lashes as if they'd caught an ash.

"Cairn, darling, an allemande! Oh, please, it's so much more wonderful than those stuffy contredanses where I suffer other partners. Please, take me to the floor!"

She vaulted onto tiptoe and touched her rosebud mouth to his ear in a high whisper. "I hate all these clumsy fops. I should have my turn with a man who can truly handle a woman.''

Cairn knew Maude well enough to concede it too troublesome to resist her petition. Her interest in him exceeded the bounds of his in her. Still, she had always been a steadfast friend, and he wished no breach of the closeness the years and their families' mutual interests had forged. Her infatuation would play itself out soon enough. Cairn raised his arm obligingly, and Maude gifted it with her ring-laden hand, curling her fingers around its crook and stroking his black velvet jacket in a way that would have pleased him, had the hand belonged to Alysanna.

As they found their niche in the bowing assemblage, the violins again took flight, and Cairn moved with practiced grace to the lacy strains. But his thoughts drifted far from the rote steps of his feet. He had been selfish to draw Alysanna toward such a danger. Had he correctly gauged the depths of Duncan's snobbery, he would not have pressed her. He doubted Duncan would dismiss Alysanna, but his friend's hot temper would seek further satisfaction. Cairn would raise the matter again with Duncan, but he would wait—better to let his heat cool for now.

Maude's svelte figure and fair coloring were more than appealing, but they were wasted on Cairn. His mind over-flowed with Alysanna. Even as a drably dressed governess, she outshone all the glittering sultanas and gypsies. Her magic was beyond mercers and milliners. It was a rare wildness—something fierce he could not quite touch, but knew he must possess. She was a locked door, and Cairn would not rest 'til he found the key.

Alysanna put a match to the solitary taper at the back of her bureau, but its scant light barely even lit the adjacent bed, much less her small room. The tallow's fatty smell was ran-cid, compared to the beeswax to which she was accustomed, and the light's tiny halo looked lonely and desolate, nearly forced from existence by the darkness that surrounded it. It was a feeling much like that creeping through Alysanna's heart.

It was not only Duncan's fury that had wrought her misery, though his dressing down was reason enough for the flow of her tears. It was the gnarly tangle of fate that had sent her to this miserable ruse.

Her father's death, Roberta's treachery, then the loss of both Julia and Briarhurst—each taken singly was a felling blow. Yet their sum seemed less than the total of their parts, as if together they were so totally crushing that Alysanna could not allow herself to fully experience the pain, lest she be hopelessly overwhelmed. Like the cold that filled her tiny garret, fate had numbed her.

She collapsed dejectedly onto the bed, her eyes glazing with tears as she freed her thick swath of auburn hair from the discipline of its pins and allowed it to tumble onto her aching shoulders. Alysanna wished she could as easily shake off her fears that Hadley would fail to find the dark-faced murderer before she too met Julia's black fate.

Why hadn't he written back? He knew where she was—the letter she had sent the day she was hired had made it clear. Her message had been guarded, for fear of discovery, but perhaps she should have been more explicit. If Hadley knew how she rotted under Duncan's gloomy aegis, surely he would hurry her rescue.

In her heart, Alysanna knew it was not Hadley who earned her anger; it was rather her own impotence that sent her soul screaming. Certainly her fiancé was trying to bring her home. Such matters just took more time than she had patience. It had only been a month since she'd left Briarhurst. Alysanna assured herself that one month more would see her home, her birthright and proper name restored.

In the meantime, there was still the thorny mess with Duncan. She had seen his rage lit before, but not with the force he'd displayed tonight.

Strangely, Alysanna almost empathized. No servant of hers at Briarhurst would have dared such impropriety. If so, what punishment would she have meted out? The answer fired like a lethal shot through her mind—she was to be dismissed.

She saw herself wandering disconsolately through the London streets, begging her fate, and the image racked Alysanna with an icy shudder, summoning a fresh sting of tears. She reached for her linen mantelet, wrapping herself in its flimsy warp, but the fabric hardly diminished the wintry misery that gripped her bones.

Alysanna hunched on the small bed, too tired to kindle a fire and too chilled to sacrifice the pitiful comfort her huddled form had trapped. At least the lit taper's flame looked warm, and Alysanna stared hypnotically at its luminous jumps and licks as she remembered what had led her to tonight's debacle.

If she found no fault in her failure to apologize, at least she admitted the stupidity of accepting Cairn's offer. Why had she agreed? Alysanna wanted desperately to believe it was only that she longed to dance, but her heart mocked her, knowing it was not so much the allemande as Cairn that she wanted.

She'd struggled against admitting her feelings for him ever since his bold and provocative kiss in the library. It was then that her body had begun to betray her with the river of heat his touch coursed through her veins.

Alysanna had every reason to loathe and distrust Cairn Chatham, yet she couldn't. In fact. . . . She snapped her head hard sideways as if something had struck her.

What was she thinking? She was engaged to Hadley— pledged as wife to another man's bed! Her problem with Cairn was not his roguish manner—he was the wrong man! Alysanna stiffened in her chair, chastening herself for such wanton thoughts, yet still prey to them.

She had never experienced such swelling excitement when Hadley came near. Surely it was only that Cairn was forbidden—why else would she be so breathless and flustered when he stood close, so ready to abandon all she held dear?

Her misfortune was to blame for her mad thinking, she was sure. That would explain her behavior, but what was it Cairn had wanted with her? Last week's quick kiss could be hung on mere lust. But to partner a governess before his peers—he had taken even more risk than she.

Just then Alysanna's logic found its shocking conclusion: perhaps it was her social station that drew him to her. At Briarhurst, she had oft worried that some wastrel suitor would woo her fortune in the guise of her person. Did Cairn only want her for her lack of the same? If his passion was meant for a penurious governess, would she lose him by confessing the truth?

Again Alysanna lost hold of her resolution to dismiss all thoughts of Cairn, and she slammed her fist on the bed, exasperated. Enough! Her future was promised to Hadley. His predictable image paled depressingly against Cairn's fire, but she was pledged, by law and conscience, to her fiancé's bed.

Whatever she wanted from Cairn Chatham would have to be sorted out later. As long as she was a fugitive, she belonged to Hadley. Nothing would change until she could reclaim Briarhurst. But something had to be done.

21 March, 1792
Dear Hadley,

   The ruse as governess grows harder each day. Honestly, I am unsure how much longer I can or will be allowed to continue. I long desperately to hear news of your search—how else could I risk my life with the delivery of this missive? I ache so to come home. Please hurry. Godspeed.

Your loving fiancée,
Alysanna

Alysanna scratched out the words "loving fiancée," along with her signature, telling herself that a signed note, if intercepted, would endanger both of them. In her heart, she knew better.

CHAPTER
8

"Have care!" The running footman's warning sent Alysanna scrambling for cover behind the closest path post, but
not before she had painfully twisted her ankle. It was the
third time in as many blocks that a sedan chair had whizzed
past her on the narrow sidewalk, each vehicle nearly knocking
her flat, despite her frantic attempts to heed the bearers' calls.
To worsen matters, last night's rain had only added to the
already offensive street mire, and a clattering hackney had
splashed the resulting slop more than once from the cobbled
street pools onto her skirt.

If Alysanna had not been pretending the role of impoverished governess, she would have hired her own sedan chair
directly outside Duncan's door. But such an extravagance
was risky. With her salary so limited, Duncan would have
been more than suspect to see his governess hailing transport
clearly beyond her means. So comfort bowed to safety, and
an annoyed Alysanna walked nearly the full five blocks from

St. James to Charing Cross before hiring one of several sedans waiting in a small garden circle.

Once inside the chair, she pulled her lace handkerchief from her reticule, not wishing to touch the street's ordure with her one pair of good kid gloves, and used the linen square to brush off as much of the brown glop as would part from the hem of her serge skirt. Alysanna studied the mottled hankie, then, deciding that carrying it was worse than relinquishing it, cracked the sedan's wooden door and dropped the lace into the decaying moistness of the street below.

She had told the bearers she wished transport to Houndsditch, for that was where Beatrice and her sister Lydia let a small flat. But as Alysanna peered through the chair's smudged window at the passing city, she realized that in her two free days since she had entered Duncan's employ a month past, she had seen nothing at all of London's sights.

She hoped that a detour might give her a sense of a real outing and lift her flagging spirits. She certainly needed cheering—her pride still stung from Duncan's further pummeling that morning. Alysanna pounded her fist on the sedan's front wall, but the street din swallowed her request. It took a second, more vigorous rap before the chair reached a full halt.

"What ye be wantin', milady? We's headin' down the Strand, jest like ye told us. Ye promised a full fare to Houndsditch. Ye ain't changin' yer mind now?"

"No, but I wish a more circuitous route."

"Ain't no circus here since two months past." The balding bearer leaned his shiny head too far inside the sedan for Alysanna's comfort, giving her a strong whiff of his thick breath, made so objectionable, she guessed, from the same lack of hygiene that had probably taken his front teeth.

"I still wish Houndsditch. But take me past the Royal

Opera House en route." Alysanna had heard Handel's "Water Music" performed there when she had traveled to London with her father four years past, and the memory brought a warm glow to her heart. Their opulent box, her father's quick wit, the swell of strings—they seemed to lift her from her silken seat. It had been a time of bounty. She longed for a taste of it and hoped a turn past the theater's face would buoy her up.

"It's outta me way. I'll run ye where ye want, but it'll cost ye some shillings more."

Alysanna pulled five shiny coins from her purse and held them out in the flat of her glove's palm. The bearer's eyes glistened, then, so quickly he made Alysanna jump, the man snatched the money eagerly and stuffed it into the uppermost pocket of his dirty woolen jacket.

"Opera 'ouse 'tis, milady!" Mercifully, the sedan door closed quickly, allowing Alysanna some unfouled air. With a rough start, the chair began at a jog to turn off the Strand toward the bohemian enclave of Drury Lane.

Alysanna took in a deep breath and tried to calm herself, but the truth was that the bouncing chair and the loud clatter of iron carriage wheels in the adjacent roadway perfectly mirrored her jangled nerves. She had set out for Beatrice's not knowing where else to go, not even sure she would return to Duncan's at all, and hoping somehow that her friend could impart the wisdom that would inspire her endurance of her tense situation at the Granvilles'. But in her heart, Alysanna sensed it all was lost.

Miraculously, in light of Duncan's pitched rage, he had not yet dismissed her. Alysanna half wished he had—then the decision would not have been hers to make. As it was, she was not sure that she could continue her ruse with the obeisance Duncan's starched propriety demanded.

"You must remember who you are!" he had thumped at her, his hands locked rigidly behind the tucks of his waistcoat as he paced up and down the library carpet, like a schoolmaster deciding whether to wield the rod. "You are in my employ and you will abide by my rules!"

Employ! Alysanna commanded enough money as mistress of Briarhurst to employ Duncan five times over. She had heard rumors his grandfather had married beneath his class— the daughter of a shopocrat, according to Mrs. Spooner's tale. To think a man descended from such rabble stock dared abuse her with his snobbery! Alysanna stamped her foot in fury, then, as the sedan began to slow, she called a "Go forward!" loudly enough to correct her inadvertent command.

She straightened the tilted brim of her warped felt hat and rested her chin in the cup of one glove, gazing wistfully at the street sights blurring past. The route from St. James to Houndsditch was a pastiche of the city's wealth and misery. Through the brick-lined squares where the ton hid from London's unpleasantries behind their thick walls, past dark warrens where cylinders of smoke-spitting chimneys drew desperate human clusters to their tiny hearths, and along row after row of open bulkhead shops bartering everything from linen to fish, Alysanna saw London's glory and shame.

The sights alone surfeited the senses, to say nothing of the deafening sounds. Even through the glazed sedan window's muffling, Alysanna could hear the hawking cries of beggars and link boys, the milkwomen's lusty yodel, and the warbling ballad singers who laid their caps for coins at street corners. Above it all a heavy mantle of sea coal smoke hung like mourning, lending London a melancholy that, at this moment, perfectly matched Alysanna's aching heart.

Out here, somewhere amid all this life, were amenities that, a short time past, could easily have pleased her. But

ow she was a ghost at the feast, her true self acknowledged
y no one save Beatrice.

The entire ride, though it covered several street miles, took
ess than half an hour, the bearers' quick pace due more to
heir greed for another fat fare than any need to please Aly-
anna.

"We's here, milady." Alysanna waited for the sedan door
o open, then, realizing that she must open it herself, she
tepped out and inquired if there was change from the honest
noney she had paid at the start. The toothless bearer shook
is head vigorously, and Alysanna realized she had been
oolish to give him the full fare, that the ride would likely
ave cost less if he'd not known the extent of her means to
ay.

Hadley's traveling money was more than half gone, but
Alysanna reminded herself that she still had her governess
vages. If she found the strength to continue her ruse, it would
e good practice to live on the small sum. Clearly it was
seless to quibble over the ride's steep price.

Houndsditch was far removed from Duncan's rarefied
vorld, full of smaller, squatter structures that shared the noise
nd odor of a huge thoroughfare full not only of thick traffic
ut equally abundant refuse. Still, as Alysanna took in the
nodest homes lining the footpath, the impression softened
omewhat. Despite the obvious discomforts of the swarming
ub, the houses had an honest, if not freshly scrubbed look
bout them, and the cant of their crooked grins suggested that
ecent folk lived inside.

Alysanna studied the scrap of paper on which she had
vritten Beatrice's address and walked the half block to the
loor, tapping the brass knocker gently against a scratched
ortal only half the height of the Granvilles' royal entry. At
irst no one answered, giving Alysanna the fear that Beatrice

might be out, but a second knock brought a familiar call from within.

"Yes?"

"Beatrice? It's Alysanna."

Alysanna could hear Beatrice's stiff fingers inefficiently working the lock. Finally, the door revealed her familiar face.

"Alysanna! What good fortune brings you here?"

Alysanna closed her eyes and spent a discouraged sigh that answered more eloquently than any complaint. Beatrice snatched Alysanna's hand and pulled her silently into a small parlor.

"Sit," she instructed with great authority. "I'll get you some tea and then we'll talk."

Alysanna felt more at ease than she had since she'd left Briarhurst, and she leaned with relief into the threadbare sill of the modest settee. The furnishings were more worn than any to which she was accustomed, but their comfort surpassed the rigid propriety of either Duncan's town home or, she had to admit, her own Briarhurst.

The flat was small but cozy, and looked, as it should, much as if two spinster ladies occupied it. The parlor was filled with an overabundance of needlework, and its low walls were papered with a floral explosion Alysanna was sure no man could abide.

Beatrice scurried back, bearing a cup brimming with fragrant, steaming tea. From her reverential handling of the bone china, Alysanna guessed it little used, likely selected only for special guests. Alysanna's slight frame was chilled from the ride, and she took a deep drink, then coughed violently as she realized the tea was laced with more than sugar.

"Brandy?" she sputtered, thumping the heel of her hand against her bosom, as if to bring back up what had already gone down.

"I knew that look at the door well. I thought this would help."

The tea was too alcoholic for Alysanna's taste, but she knew Beatrice was right about her disposition, so Alysanna sipped away on the spine-stiffening concoction, albeit in smaller swallows.

"Now," Beatrice announced, snuggling close and tilting up Alysanna's cold-reddened face. "Tell me what has happened."

"Oh, Beatrice," Alysanna moaned, loath to confess her failure. "I can't go on."

"What did he do?" Beatrice knew Duncan and Alysanna well enough to fathom they had made for some angry chemistry.

"Nothing, exactly. I danced at his silly ball."

Beatrice's soft features hardened into a mask.

"I wish it weren't true. It's just—well, it's difficult to explain. Cairn Chatham . . ."

"Lord Cairn Chatham?"

"I suppose you know him?"

"I know him well enough to tell he's trouble for you."

Beatrice's distrust of the man set Alysanna on edge. She'd come for advice on Duncan, not Cairn.

"I'll admit he can be galling."

"Oh, Missy, that one's a roué if ever there was one. More ladies than he has pounds in the bank, and he has plenty of those, to hear tell. 'Twas bad enough you managed such an impropriety. But you couldn't have picked a worse accomplice."

Alysanna knew Beatrice was right. Yet some traitorous part of her heart rose to Cairn's defense. Her allegiance to him surprised her and undid her balance more than Beatrice's fervent assault. But Alysanna was too tired for more disagreement; instead she conceded the point.

"I suppose you're right. But my immediate problem is Duncan."

Beatrice's face sobered in sudden understanding, and she whispered her fear as if speaking it loudly would make it true. "He didn't dismiss you?"

"Nearly. I think it was only Lily's entreaty that saved me, though he's as twitchy as a hawk without a hood. Beatrice, I can't endure much more. Perhaps I should just give up and go home."

"You needn't trouble the journey. Our gallows here work just as well."

The word *gallows* drew Alysanna's hand to her throat. She had forced the horrible prospect of hanging from her conscious mind, but her dreams were not so circumspect. Now, with the chance that some future misbehavior would push her from Duncan's wardship, Alysanna had spent last night churning and moaning in a fitful dream of a noose about her neck.

"Well, then, what am I to do?"

"Did you apologize?"

"He didn't insist. I swore I wouldn't do it again."

"It's a fine line you're walking, my darling. Did you really come for my advice?"

"Of course."

"Duncan will let you off unscathed this once, but he'll look for any small excuse to dismiss you. You must apologize. Beg his forgiveness. Plead anything, but be contrite. I know he's surly and high-handed, but right now he's your hope to stay alive. And anyway, what would Lily do without you?"

Alysanna had to admit that however much she'd come to loathe Duncan, her love for Lily overmatched it. Mustering

an apology was hard, but perhaps she had come today knowing that was what she must hear.

"Can you make it right with him?" Beatrice's serious tone
made it clear that she expected Alysanna's compliance.

"If I must." Alysanna caught the doubt in Beatrice's
squinting eyes. "I'll apologize—though there are moments
I think I'd actually prefer the gallows to his stuffy company."

Beatrice clucked disapprovingly. "Well, it's not forever.
And not as if you need marry the man. Have you had word
from Hadley?"

Alysanna pulled out the lacquer-tipped pin that held her
hat and sighed at the sight of its unevenly worn felt. "Quite
frankly, I'd expected a letter by now, but I imagine he's been
too embroiled in finding Julia's killer. Though I did send him
a second note this morning."

"A second note? I can hardly believe you chanced a first.
A hired rider could disclose your whereabouts!"

"I sent it by stage mail. The envelope's clean of my hand;
I paid one of Duncan's young footmen to seal his lips when
he left it at the posting house. It didn't seem so wild a risk."

"Any contact risks too much."

Alysanna's distance from Briarhurst had dangerously mod-
erated her once-healthy fear. "I doubt Julia's murderer even
saw me. And to trace me here—there are times I think this
ruse is uncalled for."

Beatrice's plump features froze in shock. "Until you know
who killed Julia, you mustn't expose yourself. Not to mention
that shrewish stepmother of yours—her threats alone should
steer you off the notion of going home."

Alysanna slumped dejectedly into the settee. Once again,
Beatrice was right. Perhaps she was just too exhausted to
think straight. "Very well. But this guise is so galling. My

room is too small, the food is inedible, and these clothes!'' Alysanna spat the word *clothes* questioningly, as if her nubby serge gown didn't deserve the appellation. Then, to her embarrassment, she realized that she had reproved a life to which Beatrice, judging from her bleak surroundings, could no longer even hope to aspire. A shameful blush crept over Alysanna's face.

"I'm sorry. I must sound like a terrible snob. It's just . . .''

Beatrice patted her hand indulgently. "I know, child. The station is not rightfully yours. There is an order to the world, and it's like milk over the cream when it isn't kept. Which is another reason why your mention of Cairn Chatham distresses me.''

"What do you know about him?'' Despite her resolutions otherwise, Alysanna found Cairn on her mind often of late. Even more gallingly, her thoughts of him pleased her.

"I know he is Lord Granville's close friend. He's exceedingly handsome and wealthy—and off limits to the likes of our kind. No matter that you're promised to Hadley. Even were you not, the fastest route to Newgate Prison is an out-of-class entanglement that would draw attention to you. Now, promise me you'll spend no more thought on him. Alysanna?''

Alysanna snapped her drifting eyes back to Beatrice. She had not meant to give Cairn Chatham so much ground in her mind, much less disclose her preoccupation with him. But the truth was, since he'd held her at the end of last night's allemande, little else had filled her.

Alysanna clutched *Clarissa Harlowe* tightly. She had read the sad tale several times. It was the saga of a young woman whose family's greedy ambitions had forced her to an unhappy match. Fleeing her miserable circumstances, she was seduced by a rapscallion who eventually led her to death.

The tale plucked sympathetically at Alysanna's heart. Like Clarissa, Alysanna longed for the reins of her own galloping fate; she only hoped she too would not meet Clarissa's end.

At a price of three shillings, the book was an indulgence Alysanna could ill afford. Yet the luxurious feel of its un-scarred leather resting in her hand far outweighed the impru-dence of the expense, and Alysanna in no way regretted her stop at a small bookstore on her way home from Beatrice's. With her novel and the apple she had purchased from the fruit vendors near Houndsditch, Alysanna paid her sedan fare and disembarked.

She started a brisk walk down St. James's length. Then, remembering that Duncan had banished her from the house for the whole day, she reconsidered, deciding she had time to sit and read. With unaccustomed leisure, Alysanna settled onto one of several wrought-iron benches lining the park and cracked *Clarissa Harlowe*'s spine.

From her own little perch, there was an expansive view of the lacy aviaries lining Birdcage Walk, though the cages' bright fowl were easily matched by the Quality's finery as they meandered along the park's paths. Alysanna turned back the book's first page and bit with a loud snap into the cold, crisp apple. But the murmur of the pedestrian river moving along the wide walkways proved too distracting, and Aly-sanna closed the novel, unable to resist such a fine parade.

The promenaders' slow pace, the pink blooms bursting with spring's license from acacia boughs, and the soft midday breeze lent the scene a transcendental feel. It was like a sweet confectioner's dream. Alysanna tilted her face skyward and breathed in the heady drift of the wind's creamy smell.

The landscape shifted from plume-hatted ladies squired by their mates to ducks gliding silently over the water's blue gloss to an occasional dog quenching its thirst at the canal's shallow end. Suddenly, Alysanna's gaze locked on a too-familiar sight: there, where her own sedan chair had stopped but moments ago, was Cairn Chatham's phaeton.

She squinted desperately at the carriage. Perhaps she was mistaken; she was not. She not only knew the phaeton, but she knew its occupant all too well. A hiccup caught in her windpipe as Cairn stepped down, dismissing his driver and starting at a clip toward where she sat.

From the set of his look, he hadn't yet spotted her. Most likely, he only sought some afternoon air. Yet, as if fate had fashioned it, here he was, quite alone and bearing down hard on her fear-frozen form.

Her thoughts skidded like a cat on ice. For reasons more lasting and compelling than she had time to list, Alysanna knew she should avoid Cairn Chatham at all costs.

She still could. If she hurried, she could bolt before Cairn caught sight of her. At the very least, she could shield her face with *Clarissa*. She'd promised Duncan to forswear further contact. She'd promised Beatrice. More than that, she'd promised herself.

Every vow crumbled. Cairn's gait beat toward her, and Alysanna's resolve easily melted. He looked too handsome in his buff breeches and tan waistcoat, his mouth cocked in that promise of a smile, his grey eyes inviting her somewhere unspoken, uncharted. Whether it was these temptations or mere madness that held her still, Alysanna surrendered. Driven by some lunacy she knew she must later account for, Alysanna closed her book, swallowed her last bite of apple, and smiled.

Cairn's eyes searched the park's masses for a familiar face, then, as if he heard her silent call, he turned toward her. He stopped, then closed the few yards separating them, halting again as his boots reached her hem. He was silent, then bowed gallantly.

"Miss Walker."

"Lord Chatham."

"I see you are unaccompanied. 'Tis a pity to enjoy such a bright day alone." Cairn nodded toward the space next to her. Alysanna feared but yet hoped he would sit down.

"Yes. Duncan—Lord Granville—has given me a free day." Cairn's face darkened at the mention of Duncan's name. "I am pleased to hear it was not more than that. From his mood, I feared your holiday would be permanent. I would speak with you, though I think it would be better if we walked—moving targets, as it were."

Cairn's lips drew back in a teasing smile, and Alysanna's circumspection fell under the entreaty. Moved by some sorcery she could not control, Alysanna rose and walked, her gaze trained forward but her every fiber focused in sharp awareness on Cairn's presence alongside her.

"I apologize for last night. Your terrible fate was entirely my fault. Had I thought it through, I would not have forced the dance."

"There is no need for regret. It was my choice." Alysanna was sure that was true enough. Whether she had wanted the allemande or wanted Cairn Chatham, only her own desires had driven her to the floor.

"I would hope it was your choice." Cairn threw Alysanna a look of such intensity that she was sure her pulse lurched visibly from her skin. She feared she'd have to speak, when she could barely manage to breathe. "I want you to know how deeply I regret the repercussions of our imprudent, though delightful, pairing."

"It is of no consequence. I survived the reprimand—though barely." Despite the dire results of her behavior, even Alysanna could not ignore Duncan's ridiculous overreaction, and the image of his face, puffed red with rage, brought a smile to her lips.

Cairn laughed. "I suspect that Duncan has more than met his match in you. Still, I spoke with him this morning. Not, unfortunately, in time to spare you his wrath, but I made him promise to blame me, not you, next time."

Alysanna slowed, confused. Was Cairn suggesting they'd meet like this again? She could no longer trust her self-restraint, and she prayed he had some of his own. "I should not think there will be another opportunity."

Cairn spun about, blocking her path. "Do you think I only wanted a dance?" Alysanna's startled eyes widened so she could feel her lashes against her brow, and she stood mute, uncertain and embarrassed at her transparent reaction.

"I'm quite sure I don't know what you want with a governess." Alysanna knew exactly what he wanted; it was folly to hope his designs were honorable.

"Is that how you think I view you?"

"It is what I am." She cast her eyes sideways, afraid they could not veil the lie.

"What you are is . . ." Cairn stepped closer. Alysanna knew she could think clearer with more distance between them, and she tried to retreat, but backed with a thump into a tree. Cairn leaned forward, lowering his arms like a gate around her. Alysanna knew no one body could fire such heat, but she felt she was turning liquid, nearly melting, as if Cairn were a white-hot blaze on her flesh.

To stand so intimately in public was madness. Alysanna's eyes darted sideways only long enough to see that, without realizing it, she and Cairn had wandered from the main path into a secluded grove. But even without witnesses, such an intimacy was very dangerous. Yet she was helpless against him, weak and without volition. He stole her breath, and in its stead filled her up with a storm's eye of desire.

Cairn's hand broke over the crest of her cheekbone, his thumb tracing her face's contours until it settled on her chin. He tilted her parted lips toward him, and everything spun away into a dark void. It was as if Alysanna could now only see and feel as filtered through his wildfire touch.

She closed her eyes, and her blood cried out for something nameless, sweet, and unspoken. She prayed he'd stop, but instead his warm breath came closer, until his lips brushed first gently against her own, then hungrily demanded them.

This was nothing like the gentle tease of his kiss in the library. Cairn's mouth consumed her, levying her very soul in response. Alysanna's resolve turned to spindrift, blown off by a hurricane of sensations. A wellspring of abandon bubbled through her, soaking each inch of her raw, tingling flesh.

Cairn pulled her closer, and she could feel his hard muscles through her skirt, leaving no doubt of his need for her. Unthinkingly, Alysanna lifted her hips wantonly to him, melding their bodies impossibly close. It was too much; if she didn't stop now, she never would.

"No!" Gathering her will in a tight little ball, Alysanna pushed away furiously. Cairn didn't even try to stop her; his questioning eyes only searched her own.

"Is that really what you want?"

Alysanna only wanted more of his hands on her face, his body crushed tight against her own, his mouth plumbing her soul with need. But these were rash, outlawed pleasures that would damn her when reason returned.

"Leave me alone!" Alysanna's conscience bridled her desire, breaking her free of his loose embrace. Her lips still stinging with the heat of Cairn's kiss, she exploded like a chased hare down the path toward the safe haven of Duncan's door.

Jenny's full weight slammed with breathtaking force into Duncan Granville. He stood so rigid, and the impact was so great, that her heavy satchel was knocked from her arms, disgorging its full contents in a colorful jumble on the foyer floor.

"I'm sorry," she sputtered nervously, amazed that she had not seen him before the collision, and unsure who had bumped into whom. Then, fearing his gruff manner of late would reappear, Jenny apologized properly. "It was my fault, your lordship. Entirely."

Duncan's cheeks flushed crimson, Jenny guessed in rage, but in fact in embarrassment that his interception of her had been so obvious. When he'd heard her footsteps padding down the staircase, he'd thought only to catch her before she left. He did not mean to injure her.

"Are you harmed?"

"No. And you?"

Duncan's knee had been badly torqued by the bag's wild flight, but he bit down hard to suppress his pain. "It was nothing. Your samples, however . . ." He gestured toward the ruche and lace explosion that twisted in a serpentine toward the library door.

"I can manage." Jenny hurried to refill her satchel with the bright assortment. She reached toward a tangle of satin ribbons just as Duncan did the same, and their fingers touched gently, causing a quick recoil in jittery tandem.

"Please, allow me." Duncan began restuffing. Jenny could not tell if it was an offer or a command. Either way, he seemed determined, and she stood in silent embarrassment as her employer scrambled kneeling across the hall's marble.

She had rarely seen Duncan dispense a favor, and his willingness to help fix a mess she guessed more of her own than his making took her aback. In the long moment as he finished with the frilly debris, Jenny studied him.

Duncan Granville was an attractive man, though his physical attributes hardly drew a lady's eye in a crowd. His lithe build and grey-blond hair were not notable, nor were his angular features, which looked so narrow as to be almost wolfish. He was no dandy, to be sure. It was something else that tweaked Jenny's heart and knotted her head each time he came near—some kindness that even his pinched view of life couldn't cloak.

Jenny had admitted her attraction to him long ago, yet why she was drawn to a man with such rough, snobbish ways still baffled her. There were days when his rudeness was so plain, so bold and undisguised, that she shook with rage once she was out the front door, still stinging with the burn of his sharp rebuke.

Yet she always forgave him, perhaps because she suspected his discourtesies only masked his fear—fear that, lacking his well-heeled propriety, he would find himself as unacceptable as he dreaded others would. It was a trait she had seen much of in her high-toned clients, and one that ran deep in Duncan Granville.

Duncan tugged at the satchel's clasp, trying to make a seam of its sides. When he had gotten them as close as they would go, he pushed the bag toward Jenny, though he still clutched its handle.

"If you've a moment, I would settle our accounts."

"Of course." Duncan hoisted the case from the floor, and

Jenny followed obediently into the sunlit library. Pulling his account ledger from a bottom desk drawer, Duncan cracked the book's spine and brushed his quill through a dark inkwell. With practiced speed, he dispatched a note and extended it toward her.

Jenny bobbed a curtsy for the payment and began to fold the paper. But before she tucked it into her reticule, she gasped at the check's large amount.

"Lord Granville, this is far too much. The cost of the fabric and labor was considerably less than . . ."

"I understand. But your work has been more than acceptable. Lily is most pleased, and I wish to include a small bonus for my appreciation."

Jenny's huge eyes stared incredulously. The payment he had offered was substantially more than a small bonus—it nearly doubled the agreed-upon sum.

"Sir, your generosity embarrasses me." It was apparent from her crimson face that Jenny was quite unsettled. Duncan's jaw clenched at her response. He had not meant to bring on her distress.

"Nonsense!" he snapped, then smiled, struggling to correct his sudden rebuke. "It is only right to reward your hard work. And, to hear tell, I am not the only employer who finds your talents so worthy."

Jenny grinned shyly, her eyes hooded with modesty. Her handiwork was skilled, and she knew it had gained her a reputation. Still, she had not considered that a man such as Duncan would waste a moment's thought on her fortunes.

"Thank you. It's true I have had an auspicious year. Lady Throckmorton alone has ordered ten gowns. In fact, I am considering hiring an assistant to keep to my schedule."

Duncan suddenly seemed more at ease. Unlocking his

arms, he strolled close to her. "It pleases me to hear it. When the lady's usual seamstress left for Lincolnshire, she asked my recommendation. I was happy to give her your name."

Jenny's lips parted at this revelation. Such lucrative work a gift from him? Referrals often gained her business. Still, Duncan seemed unlikely to argue a mantua-maker's merits.

"Then I am even more in your debt." Her chestnut eyes widened further in gratitude, then held fast to Duncan's face, giving him full appreciation of their childlike innocence. There was a softness about her that most women lacked—a vulnerability that could not be learned. Her creamy cheeks and freckled face only added to the effect, making her look as though she would be smooth and easy to the touch, much like the velvet ruches that fell from her bag.

Duncan had such disconcerting thoughts of Jenny too often for his liking. Each time they arose, he diligently expunged them, like dark little sins.

She was his employee, likely to have risen no higher than scullery maid but for her former mistress's kindness. Whatever vile attraction drew him to her was a defect that must be burned out.

Duncan's grandfather had suffered greatly for his choice of a middling wife. It was a burden that weighed on Duncan's father, and likely would have tainted the grandson, too, had he not spent his life assiduously pursuing the ton's hard-won blessing. Duncan had worked unflaggingly on the Granville standing; he would not now gamble it for the sake of mere lust.

"Lord Granville, the Lady Maude Delamere." Duncan's butler stepped aside. Maude posed like a Gainsborough portrait in the doorway.

Judging from the pink flush of her cheeks, she had been

outside, though she had already doffed her cape, revealing a
floral gown ablaze with petals of saffron and teal. Her blond
hair, which usually tumbled suggestively down one side of
her long neck, was bound in a loose bun just barely visible
beneath the brim of her yellow silk hat—restrained, Jenny
guessed, only to better display the like-colored ribbon encircling her throat. Maude raised one gloved hand to the pearl
pin that glowed in the necklace's center and reached the other
toward Duncan.

"Am I early?"

Jenny had seen Maude often before when she'd come to
fit Lily. She knew she was a great beauty, but until now, had
never been forced to stand in direct opposition to her. Jenny
knew her own dull looks failed embarrassingly against
Maude's saucy silks, and she felt her shoulders hunch.

It was not only Maude's fine dress, which Jenny knew to
be a costly affair; it was her delicate face, her stature, her
title. If Jenny entertained any notions of a relationship with
Duncan Granville, this paradigm of femininity made clear
that her master was accustomed to finer fare.

"Jenny, you may go." Jenny had thought their dealings
unfinished, and Duncan's curt dismissal stung more than
Maude's haughty stare. Dejected, Jenny hoisted the satchel
onto her arm and began to leave.

"Don't tell me you forgot our appointment?" Maude trilled
a laugh. "You promised I could have that stallion for the last
hunt. My purse is full, and I'm aching to empty it into your
greedy little hands. You're not busy?"

"Could I forget you?" Duncan motioned Maude toward
the settee, and she breezed past Jenny like a perfumed zephyr.
"Jenny was just leaving. She sews for Lily, you know. Hardly
a guest."

Jenny rushed out as fast as the bag's weight would allow, and Duncan's words cleaved painfully into her heart as they had done so many times before. Mercifully, the butler considered her exit unworthy of his attention and was not there to witness her flight. It was fine with Jenny; she didn't want anyone to see her tears.

CHAPTER
9

❧

"I hope you don't mind a mouthful of turf. Duncan, you're a fool to sell Dauphin to me—with that horseflesh, I'll ride even you into Donegal's ground." Maude tossed off a sliver of a laugh, then hurled a thick packet of pounds at him. Her manner suggested the sum was trivial, but the thud of the paper's weight on the desktop denied it. "Now, you won't renege? You promised I could have him in time for the final hunt."

Duncan raised his palms in mock surrender. "I swear. But be forewarned, he's a great deal of animal. You might well find yourself bottom up in one of Donegal's ditches."

"He needs a strong hand, that's all." Maude popped one eye in a playful wink and tugged daintily at her gloves, a finger at a time. "And I'm the lady to do it."

"You know, you might as well keep your money 'til next season. With only one more hunt, you'll not get much out of him this year. And you'd hardly find such quality horseflesh of use for draught around London.''

"How tactless you are, Duncan. Making such an obvious comment when you know all I really wanted was an excuse to see you. Besides, I am tired of riding so far back in the pack. I get to hunt little enough as it is. With Dauphin, I'll match even the huntsman's pace.''

"You need no excuse to see me, dear Maude." Duncan had never entertained any romantic notions about Maude; she had always made it clear that her hopes hung on Cairn. Still, he was flattered by her bubbling presence.

Maude's father, the duke of Malvern, commanded high repute in the House of Lords, and the family's great fortune, ever swelled by pursuits ranging from cooperage to coal, was legendary. The Delameres were suns of the social world, and when Maude danced her bright attendance on Duncan's household, a habit which he knew hung more on Cairn's friendship than the charms of his own company, it was a fine feather in his cap.

"I think it is not me you wish to see. Cairn has gone north on business—some tedious matter with labor at a mine.'' Maude's surprised look made clear she hadn't known, and Duncan rued his imprudent disclosure. "I'm sorry. I thought you knew.''

Maude sighed blithely, affecting disinterest. "Well, if he chooses not to confide his plans to me, I can hardly go chasing after him. Though perhaps, with the advantage of Dauphin's speed . . .'' Maude gave him an impish smile and shrugged. Her persistence was amazing. If she was hurt, she was hardly discouraged.

"Despite your jest, I sense that your hope for a future as duchess of Lyddon has dampened since our last discussion. Was there some breach between you and Cairn?''

"Nothing like that." Maude brushed her gloves across the lap of her skirt as if removing invisible fluff. "In fact, nothing at all. Cairn, as always, accords me the utmost respect and kindness. He says I am his dear friend—Lord, how I've come to loathe those words! I can only hope we are headed for something more combustible than friendship.

"If not, Father will have his smug vindication. He has yet to forgive me for shelving all those foppish suitors that came through our parlor last season. I began to think he'd make nearly any match just to be rid of me. French dogs and fools—every one of them! The memory still makes my head ache." Maude quivered her shoulders in disgust, pertly bouncing her kerchief's ruche.

"Your father only wants what's best for you."

"As if he knew!" Maude shot Duncan an irritated look. "It seems of late only you and I, and frankly only you when you're in a decent mood, can see my suitability for Cairn. I'm counting on your clout with him. Everyone else has abandoned my cause. You, Duncan, are my only ally. I'll even trust you with my secret—I plan to give this chase only six months more. After that, I'll fully surrender. First, I'll offer up my virtue with no hope of marriage, and, if Cairn is still heartless enough to refuse me, I'll toss my creaking form into the Thames." Maude drew her hand across her curl-topped brow.

Duncan could see how she forced her light manner. "Maude, you needn't pretend with me." For all her flipness, Maude loved Cairn. Duncan knew that her failing hopes hurt more than her pride would allow her to confess.

"Well, what's a lady to do?" She hummed a sigh of resignation. "Now, enough of my sad fate. I trust the tempest of last fortnight's ball has been calmed."

"Lily is still afloat on her triumph, if that's what you mean."

"Actually, I was referring to the incident with your governess, Miss . . ." Maude paused as if she could not recall Alysanna's name; in fact, she remembered everything about her overly well.

"Alysanna Walker. Thankfully, we're past that debacle. I called her to account again the next morning, extracting a full promise of no such future impropriety. And Cairn—"

Maude arched one brow quizzically. Cairn had refused to discuss the matter with her; perhaps Duncan would prove more pliable. "Yes?"

Duncan had no need to rouse Maude's ire with an account of Cairn's plea for Alysanna. "Suffice it to say that I do not expect any further misbehavior."

"Well, our unpredictable Cairn notwithstanding, it was certainly bold behavior for a governess. Had you no inkling of her flaws?"

"None at all. She came to me through Beatrice, who praised her with a mother's zeal. It did not occur to me to press further, though hindsight makes clear I should have. No matter now. Miss Walker has forsworn, on penalty of dismissal, any further breach. In her defense, I must say she is quite accomplished. She is well versed in everything Lily has need of, except, as we've painfully learned, deportment."

Maude smiled in quick sympathy, then waxed serious. "She seems quite young for such a wealth of talent. I'd say about . . ."

"Twenty-one. She had one four-year position prior to this."

Maude's brows rose in surprise. "It is a tender age for such a fine impression. Was she trained at governess school, or perhaps the unhappy result of a ruined father?"

"Her abilities were so impressive I did not ask." Maude drew her lower lip between her teeth and squinted like an angry kitten. Duncan could see he had upset her.

"Surely you do not think her a threat?"

Maude tweaked a blond curl against her brow as she tipped her head down, arranging the angle of her face to conceal its sudden blush. "Don't be a fop! I don't know what came over me at the ball. I was not myself. It was just that Cairn had all but ignored my fine costume, so I was in a snit to start. Then, with that ridiculous allemande, I jumped to a foolish conclusion. Your governess a threat—Duncan, you do make me laugh!"

Maude leaned close, pressing her hand on the velvet crease of Duncan's forearm. "But I must confide to you that I am surprised to find you know so little of a woman to whom you have entrusted your only child. It is, of course, your choice."

"You speak as if you mistrust her."

Maude paused as if reluctant, then continued anyway. "I would not presume. Who, better than you, could judge the integrity of a woman who spends nearly all her time with Lily? It is only that people of a lower class often do not understand proper values and morals. This is a failing we have already seen in Miss Walker. I would be saddened to have you discover anything, shall we say, unseemly, in your governess's past—particularly something that might influence Lily negatively."

Duncan appeared to think on the matter. Then, to Maude's chagrin, he looked unconcerned. "I shall keep my eye on her. But with Beatrice's recommendation, I am hard-pressed to suspect Miss Walker of anything beyond poor judgment. I am sure the problem has been handled."

Maude could tell that Duncan's patience was spent, and she brushed a perfunctory kiss against his cheek, then rose, tucking each finger into its glove's soft fold.

"Well, I'm off. I've fittings for a new hunt habit. I shall have the mantua-maker match colors to Dauphin's coat!" With a skip and a laugh, Maude flew from the library with the speed of a woman late and facing a long agenda.

Once outside, her light manner fled. Damn Duncan's assurances—Maude knew Cairn was succumbing to the governess's wiles. She wished she could have nipped his interest by banishing Alysanna altogether, but Duncan would not agree to dismiss her. Cairn's low-class siren still called to him, threatening Maude's future.

It was precisely because Maude knew Cairn so well that she worried. She had seen the forbidden draw him before, like a hound hard on a fox. God knew he loved a challenge. His horses were wild, his businesses chancy, though usually profitable, and now, it was beginning to look as though he'd gamble on this Walker woman whose surface begged scratching.

Maude shook her head in disgust; her own title and station were likely liabilities in her quest for Cairn. Perhaps were she more like the enigmatic Alysanna. . . . Maude's eyes flashed wide in disbelief—she would not emulate her, even if she could! Breeding and position would win out, awarding Maude the spoils of Cairn's love.

But wishing Alysanna gone would not make it so; Maude needed leverage. To hear Duncan tell, the little minx had no history at all—no characters written by her past employer, no family, and she was a surprisingly tender age to have such broad experience. Maude knew she alone must divine the truth—who Alysanna was, where she came from, and, most of all, what she wanted.

* * *

Maude's tall form was easy to spot in the foyer's soft shadows. Alysanna hurried toward the stairs, wadding the voluminous folds of her rustling skirt, trying uselessly to still the sound of her petticoats' swish. But even so, the heels of her shoes betrayed her intentions, clicking across the marble tiles and drawing Maude's unwanted stare.

"Miss Walker."

"Lady Delamere." Alysanna nodded, optimistically continuing forward. Perhaps Maude had somewhere else to go.

"How pleasant to see you again. I am glad you survived the ball." Maude edged toward her, like a lioness stalking prey.

Alysanna cringed, stifling a moan. Her shoulders tightened and a lightning bolt of pain forked through her neck. Lord, how she wished herself anywhere else.

"As you can see, I am in fact still here." Alysanna threw a gauntlet of a look at Maude's fire-filled eyes.

"I must applaud your . . . boldness in dancing with Lord Chatham. The allemande could have proved quite disastrous." Maude tipped her hat's satin bows toward the library.

"It had its repercussions." Alysanna raised her chin insolently, and Maude's lips set hard, a small twitch shooting up her flushed cheek.

"Whatever was it urged you toward such folly?"

"Perhaps I merely wished a dance."

"Surely there are footmen aplenty in the servants' quarters." Alysanna had never struck anyone, but now she felt her hand tightening into an unladylike fist, and wondered for an instant if it would fly of its own accord into Maude's petulant face. " 'Twas not a footman who asked."

"Indeed. I hope your maid's heart is not due for a fall. You mustn't dream of things you can't have."

Alysanna would settle for no less than full fire. "And what would those things be?"

"I think you know well. Things to which a governess is not entitled."

"If a simple dance is that to which you refer, then I suppose I am due to fall. Though it would be my tumble, not yours. But I do appreciate your care for my welfare."

"You're welcome. I am always happy to offer my wisdom."

"And at your age, I imagine wisdom comes easily."

Maude glowered at Alysanna, clearing her throat with an angry cough. "I am wise enough to find so many accomplishments quite odd in one so young. Duncan has been filling my head with tales of your skills."

"How kind."

"Indeed. Few fathers would hire a governess lacking characters."

"They were lost en route from my last position."

"How fortunate that he would take you on faith."

"Some souls are predisposed to trust."

"Some men are fools. In truth, Miss Walker, I find your story most suspect."

Alysanna's chest tightened like a stone was pressed to it. Maude's cocky impertinence had been too tempting to resist. But now Alysanna sensed she was cornered, and she feared that indulging her pride had been foolhardy. She tried to sound calm, but could not manage.

"If I may be so candid, Lady Delamere, your sentiments toward me matter little. Yet I must tell you that I am considered trustworthy. No one who has given me their faith has been disappointed."

"Yet you did leave your last post. I did not hear the exact circumstances. A dismissal, perhaps?"

"The services of a governess were no longer required. My charge left."

"I see. And where exactly was it you worked?"

"A small estate in a northern shire. I doubt you know the family."

"Come, give me a try. Perhaps we have more than one common friend?"

The reference to Cairn made Alysanna stiffen. She felt increasingly like a ripped hull on rough shoals. Maude stared back with unwavering determination.

"The Crowleys. I doubt you have crossed paths."

Maude's coral lips parted in satisfaction. "We most certainly have. How remarkable—they are both nearly three score years! I have heard of late children, but Mrs. Crowley must have been nigh fifty at the time of the birth. What a sight that must have been!"

Alysanna blanched at her error. It had been stupid to use a real name, but the Crowleys were all she could think of in her panic. Of course their children were far too old.

"My charge was their grandniece. Lady Celia's parents often traveled abroad. She was temporarily in the Crowleys' care."

"I see. And where are the Crowleys now? In London for the season?"

"No," Alysanna answered, sure they were, but praying, unconscionably, that they were infirm enough to be bedridden. "They are still in the north."

"Well, you'll have a chance to visit next month."

What did Maude mean? Was Duncan planning to dismiss her after all? "I don't understand."

"When Duncan moves to Donegal Manor. He goes each summer, as do all the Quality, when the season ends. Surely you knew?"

Of course—Alysanna knew the grandees traveled in

season between London and their country estates. Had her father not so loathed the city's noise, the Wilhavens would have done the same. But until now, she had never considered that Duncan would uproot her from the anonymity she had come to him seeking. Alysanna suppressed her panic, smiling lamely.

"Perhaps we can visit the Crowleys together. My family's home of Totten-Hoo is close to Donegal. I'm sure we'll be seeing much of each other."

Good lord. First the unwanted move, now Maude, too.

"Somehow I can't imagine you'd wish to keep my company," Alysanna demurred.

"Miss Walker, you do underestimate my interest in you."

Alysanna stared back blankly, afraid the mixture of shock and fury filling her would flash hot if she allowed any expression. Maude broke into a too-sweet smile and straightened her gown's folds as if they had been mussed. If Alysanna had been unwilling to admit it before, now she knew with certainty that she and Maude were adversaries—and the prize of their contest was Cairn Chatham. How far would Maude go to ensure that she won?

"Good day, Miss Walker. I'm sure you have your studies to attend to. I've some of my own." Maude dashed with a mission through the front door, vanishing into the clatter of the square outside.

She raised her hand to summon her coach, then closed her eyes in thought. At once the thundering carriage sounded all too loud. The driver was dead on her, and Maude jumped back quickly to avoid being hit. His miscalculation would normally have brought her sharp rebuke. As it was, Maude's mind was fully on Alysanna. That woman had secrets, and Maude was hell-bent on unearthing them.

* * *

Alysanna stood like a turtle baking beneath the radiance of the glorious spring sky. Its golden bath poured over her, and she hoped Duncan's carriage would never come. Her miserable meeting with Maude had left her raw and agitated, and this quiet moment was a welcome respite from the chaos that seemed so ubiquitous of late.

She knew she shouldn't complain; at least Duncan had lent her the coach for transport to the Strand district to purchase Lily's watercolors. The walk was long, though Alysanna would not have been surprised had Duncan insisted she manage it. Today, however, she felt overmatched by the task.

The governess ruse had not grown easier, as she had expected. Instead, its challenge increased, like a weight that grew heavier with the distance. And her burden had been worsened by Maude Delamere. Questions from *anyone* about her past jeopardized Alysanna's disguise; Maude's resolute determination promised even more danger.

Alysanna drew in a deep breath and tipped her face from the shadow of her hat's wide brim. The midday heat beat down on her cheeks like a thousand candles, and she thought with amusement that it was a pose Maude Delamere would likely not hazard for fear of darkening her porcelain skin.

How was it Maude had noticed her interest in Cairn even before Alysanna knew? Maude had only seen them together twice—once in the library, and again during that fateful allemande.

What tiny error had drawn Maude's eye? Alysanna felt her hold on reality slipping. Maybe she was so thoroughly rattled that she couldn't discern what behavior was normal and what screamed with suspicion.

It was clear that Maude meant to have Cairn, whatever the acquisition took. Even if Alysanna could forswear her growing feelings for him, Maude was not likely to stop. Through Beatrice, even through Cairn himself—there were too many perilous routes to the truth.

How stupid and overconfident she'd been. She had come to Duncan's to hide, but the debacle with Cairn had trained an even brighter light on her presence. Worse yet, she was soon to be spirited from London's safe sea of humanity to some provincial prison where she could easily be found. For all her trouble, she might as well have stayed at Briarhurst. The thought decayed her already sour mood even more, and Alysanna craned her neck toward the square's end, now hoping for the approaching silhouette of Duncan's coach.

Instead, a more familiar form drew her eye. It was Jenny, doubled half over and leaning against a black iron railing several town homes away. She looked ill, and Alysanna rushed forward to see what was the matter.

"Jenny? Are you all right?"

Jenny looked like a frightened, trapped animal, but her expression softened under Alysanna's stare.

"Oh, Alysanna." She reached out, drawing Alysanna into a tight embrace. Jenny clung desperately, spending her tears in a mounting crescendo.

"What's happened? Are you ill?"

"Can we walk? Away from here?" Jenny whispered, struggling to straighten the seams of her morning dress and using the back of one glove to wipe away the teary rivulets racing down her cheeks.

Alysanna knew Duncan would be furious with her if she missed the coach he'd taken such trouble to arrange; still, first things first. "Of course we'll walk."

Jenny tried to lift her satchel, but again dissolved. Thinking her friend could not manage the task in her present distress, Alysanna intervened.

"Let me." Alysanna looped her fingers around the bag's handle, but Jenny stopped her.

"You needn't. I am used to it."

"Jenny." Alysanna shot her a look, and Jenny gave up her hold, then followed Alysanna's lead.

"Now, tell me," Alysanna repeated, "are you ill?"

"Only if lovesick qualifies. And I swear, it's worse than the rheum."

"Someone broke your heart?" Alysanna could hardly imagine that any man Jenny chose wouldn't return her affections. Jenny was no great beauty, but what she lacked in physical charms was made up for by her generous heart.

"Don't pretend not to know—as if I could disguise my feelings." Alysanna stared at her quizzically, shrugging.

"It's Duncan." Jenny raised her hand to preempt Alysanna's protest. "I know, 'tis a folly that nothing can come of, but I can't stop it. I do love him." The confession burst like water from a dam, summoning a fresh wave of tears that overflowed Jenny's eyes and came even faster as Alysanna pulled her shaking shoulders close.

Jenny needed understanding, but Alysanna could think only of the rude treatment Duncan had offered this woman who now professed to love him. "But he has acted so abominably toward you. Really Jenny, of all men to choose!"

Jenny shot back an incredulous stare. "As if we choose —would that I could! I'd hardly pick a lofty lord to break my heart on—I'd much rather someone with some hope of returned affections."

"Then why pine for him? At best, he's mercurial. At worst . . ." Alysanna stopped, realizing how insensitive she must sound.

"I know, he's a terrible snob. But it's a paper wall he hides behind. He's insecure—afraid to gamble with the ton's high protocol. Alysanna, there is a kindness in him, too. I know you've no inkling of it, but in my three years with Lily, I've seen much of his decency.''

Alysanna shook her head in disbelief. ''I've seen precious little of this stock you trade on and enough of Duncan's insults to know there's no change due for that hardened heart. It saddens me to hear that you entertain such notions.''

''I know nothing can come of it,'' Jenny sighed, checking her tears just enough to speak. ''That's why I'm so unraveled.'' She massaged her puffy eyes as she spoke. ''There can be no future for us. I understand that. But would my head could tell my heart. I know I should leave. But how can I, loving both the father and the child? I wish I'd never had the luck to find them.''

''Jenny, I know this is hard, but giving your heart to Duncan Granville is only courting pain. You must let it go.''

Jenny stared back as if Alysanna were trying to catch water in a basket. ''How do you let go someone you love, even if you cannot have him?'' Her eyes pleaded for an answer.

Alysanna said nothing. She only wished she knew.

CHAPTER
10

"Bloody scold! She wants to know what progress I've made. What am I to tell her?" Hadley strode angrily across Briarhurst's library as he waved the letter. "It's been nigh two months since Julia's murder, and I've nothing to tell. Alysanna may think if I haven't found the man by now, I'm not likely to."

Hadley crumpled Alysanna's note into a crackling ball and tossed it with disdain onto a nearby table. He wished he could as easily dismiss its contents.

Roberta shuffled the thick red leather spines of her account ledgers in and out of the jam-packed bookcase like huge playing cards, trying to free slots for two volumes that rested precariously on the shelf's uppermost lip.

"Roberta!" Hadley barked impatiently. "You act as though this doesn't concern you."

Roberta's head snapped backward so hard it looked to fly

off. "Of course I'm concerned. But instead of mewling and whining, I've done something about it."

"Done something? You haven't jeopardized Briarhurst?"

Roberta pulled a paper from her desk drawer and sauntered casually toward him. She plopped onto the settee, pulling Hadley close and half-covering him with her skirt as she fluffed it out. A relaxed air surrounded her, and as she tipped her dark ringlets over the sofa's back, Roberta pushed the document toward him.

"Here. Read it."

Hadley's fingers fumbled, finally managing the paper's folds. "It's a warrant for Alysanna's arrest!"

Roberta smiled smugly. "Thanks to me."

"What did you have to do with this?"

"A word to the constable about her fight with Julia. I gave him the names of a few witnesses and some embroidery on the tale of their constant bickering."

Hadley threw the document to the floor, but Roberta scrambled after it, smoothing its furrows.

"Good God, be careful! It wasn't easy persuading that Fisk man to trust me. He has another warrant, of course. But after I noted that Alysanna might slip in and out of here in the dark of night, he authorized me to arrest her."

Hadley snorted in disbelief. "Have you gone mad? If she's arrested and judged guilty, she'll confess, sending all our sweet pounds to the Crown. She told you as much. What were you thinking?"

"That fiddle-faddle about her confession was just that. Whatever else she is, our missy's bright enough not to trade a little vengeance for her life. Besides, she won't get caught. From what you say, she's safe with some nursling in London. It's perfect—the warrant will keep her gone 'til Briarhurst's all mine. It's a bit of a balancing act, I'll admit, but more than worth the trouble.''

Hadley stood silent as he reasoned. ''All right. But what use is the warrant if she doesn't know?''

Roberta leaned back, squinting as if to see Hadley better. ''What a stupid coxcomb you are!'' Hadley hauled his fist back in threat, but Roberta seized it midair. ''Ah, ah. You still need me to sign your notes. I'd think twice about any unseemly behavior.'' Hadley lowered his hand slowly, leaning in resignation against the settee.

''You're so smart, tell me what to do.''

''I got the warrant for exactly this. Take the document— be careful not to lose it—to Alysanna. Once she sees it, she'll think twice about returning, no matter how slow your progress.''

''Why can't I just write her?''

''Because your charms—whatever they are worth—will work better in person. We can't chance a mistake. She must see the warrant, hold it, believe it enough to fire her fear. This paper, a kiss, and a smartly told tale should handle her nicely.''

Now that Alysanna lacked all access to her inheritance, Hadley had completely lost interest in her. He hated the notion of seeing her at all; seeking her out to mount a bold lie would be even more miserable. ''You're sure there's no other way?''

Roberta tipped her head down, glowering from beneath her brow.

''Very well. I'll go. But I'll need some gaming money. And the new calash—not that leaking mail coach of yours.''

A triumphant smile crept over Roberta's face. ''Tomorrow, then?''

''Tomorrow.'' If he had to go, Hadley would rather leave

sooner than later. But he relished the task like a man with a toothache en route to a bad barber.

Alysanna pressed her warm cheek against the cold pane, feeling the drum of the wind-thrown rain as its sheets shook the beveled glass. She stared emptily at the rain-swept swell of hills beyond. Their silhouettes were edgeless and soft, made dim and blurry by the storm's assault.

Even in the midst of the blow, the land looked strangely still. Elms and beeches twisted and bent, but the loden hills stood resolute, too far from her sight to acknowledge their siege. A tear edged over the crest of her cheek, and she prayed that she, too, could suffer as stoically.

At least the deluge had not come two days prior on the journey from London. The Great North Road had been pocked enough, even with the grace of a week's good weather. In such a tempest as now hurled itself against Donegal's stone, surely the Granville entourage would have slowed considerably, perhaps have been stuck outright in the turnpike's mire.

Even with good speed, the trip had been agonizing—a chatter-laden day in Duncan's tiny coach with only one meal stop at a shabby inn pretentiously named the King's Chamber. The turnpike's twists recalled Alysanna's last such journey, made with equally wretched impetus.

Not that Lily, Delia, and the cook, Bridget, had not done their best to entertain. Why shouldn't they have been cheery? Even the staff looked forward to glorious, fete-filled months in the cushion of the lush Northamptonshire hills. The promise of warm, dry weather and summer's sweet swell lured them easily from their memories of cold, wet London.

Even before she saw Donegal, Alysanna was sure it must be an impressive place. The sketch Duncan had framed on his library wall looked most imposing, and her memory of the drawing's charcoal outlines, coupled with the servants' self-possessed babble about the perquisites of employ in such lavish surroundings, prepared her for an estate of prodigious proportions.

What she saw, however, as the carriage lurched from the elm alley girdling the pool that lay at the base of the manor's facade, exceeded even her wildest dreams. If Duncan had less money than her father, he also had less reluctance to part with it.

Donegal was a Palladian leviathan, its multiple grey stories rearing in cloudward contrast to its horizontal sprawl. It was not, as were many of the shire's stately homes, an ancestral estate with walls that laid claim to Angevin cornerstones. Donegal Manor was a tribute to the will and wealth of Duncan's father, James Granville. Overeager to free the taint of his father's low-born wife and made bold with indignation at the grandees' snobbish memory, the elder Viscount Granville had wielded his wealth to commission a residence the grandeur of which had rarely been seen. If it would not reinstate the family's social standing, Donegal Manor would, at the very least, steal his detractors' breath.

Alysanna's own breath caught in her throat as the carriage pulled to the driveway's head, halting in front of the grit-stone and marble portico. She craned her neck upward, but still could not see the building's full height from the carriage window—its hugeness made her cringe with apprehension.

Whatever else it was, Donegal Manor was no tucked-away warren. But before Alysanna could lament her new fate, she was whooshed inside with the rest of the staff, followed by an unending stream of baggage disgorged by Duncan's hired post chaises.

At Donegal, Alysanna was no longer penned in by her

London garret's close-built walls. Now her room, more properly termed a chamber, seemed endless, its ebony spiderstone fireplace and Hepplewhite furnishings serving not so much to lift her spirits as to remind her of the luxuries she had so long done without.

Her eyes roamed over the cinnabar-colored pattern of the Persian carpet and widened in further wonder at the room's sumptuousness. She tried to be thankful that, if she were still a caged bird, at least she was prisoner in so fine a gaol. Yet nothing could buttress her faltering spirits. It was not even her safety she ached for; it was Cairn.

Now and then, as often as she failed to drive it from her mind, the memory of how alive she felt each time he came near stirred inside her. Ever since the morning after the bal masque, she had begun to know, and on some level had even admitted, the magnetic pull he worked on her. Yet to acknowledge it now, in Cairn's absence—to truly thirst for him—trained a frightening light on her need.

Alysanna blushed with shame; she was still engaged to Hadley. If not bound by passion or decency, she was at the least legally obligated. Certainly, she was wholly at Hadley's mercy to regain her birthright. Roberta was no help; who else would take up her cause?

Hadley was risking his life to restore her own. How could she brazenly long for another's embrace? Yet even her guilt could not deny Alysanna the balm of belief that lessened her pain. If the memory of Cairn's attentions made her misery easier to bear, so be it. There would be no future with him anyway. It was a wish on the moon, so what harm was done?

What harm, indeed? Alysanna collapsed into the mahogany arms of a writing chair nestled behind a small desk. It was not enough that she was forced from the life she knew. Now, she must distance herself from her heart's desire, as well.

* * *

Alysanna pulled the ties of her bed jacket tight, adding a wool shawl for the journey downstairs. The fire in her hearth burned ardently. Still, the two days she had spent at Donegal had reminded her that, while fine country manors offered more room than town homes, they were also harder to heat. The ceilings were high, and the wall seals lacked integrity. No matter how well-tended each room's blaze, Donegal's thick stone never banked enough warmth to chase off its chill.

If there had been any prayer of sleep, Alysanna would have pinched her candle's tallow wick and snuggled into the cocoon of her posted bed. But slumber was a taunt, just out of reach, beckoning, then dancing away, laughing at her gyroscopic thoughts. She rubbed her aching eyes and stared wearily into the promise of a long, dark night.

Alysanna wished she had gotten a book from the library earlier. As governess, she was encouraged to take her choice, a privilege hardly accorded other staff. But Duncan believed that her edification served Lily, as well, and Alysanna appreciated his generosity.

She had, however, spent the day unpacking. Then there was dinner in the housekeeper's room, and thereafter, one task after another, all of which postponed her trip downstairs.

Now, with no book to close her eyes on, sleep skittered away. Even watching the candle flames lick and leap had ceased to entertain. Alysanna longed to still the rattling in her head.

Had she been bred to a governess's low circumstances, Alysanna likely would have redressed for the journey two flights down. But, being who she was, the inconvenience outweighed the impropriety, and she opted for a quick dash over a late-night corset. She was unlikely to be witnessed anyway; the hall clock had chimed midnight some time ago.

Alysanna pulled on the creaking oak door to the hallway and stiffened at an updrafted blast of cold. She tightened her shawl and crossed her arms to contain the small heat she already owned. Her hair, loosened from its pins for bed, trapped a bit more warmth as it draped in a chestnut blanket of curls around her shoulders.

She scurried with cat feet down the wide, straight staircase, an avenue designed, Alysanna guessed, for grand entrances. A red runner cut a bloody swath through the stair's pristine marble, butting into a similarly patterned rug that met three more, forming a square around the foyer's open center.

If she had suspected it before, Alysanna now knew with certainty that the full house slept, no doubt still exhausted from yesterday's journey. The cavernous entry was totally black, save the single taper she carried, and the lonely effect unsettled her. As a child she had suffered no fear of the dark but as a full-grown woman, Alysanna was sadly wiser regarding its perils.

The library was just off the foyer's right. Cupping a crystal bulb of a handle, Alysanna freed the door with a click and a turn. As the heavy wood cracked, a burst of light flew out at her, firing her face with its midnight sun.

Several candelabra lined the library's length. Even though their beeswax tapers burned low, apparently lit some time prior, the effect was that of a room so bright that it should have been filled with a crowd.

''Hello?'' The silence swallowed Alysanna's question. The book-lined walls stretched threefold longer than Duncan's town home, but she had full view of the library's length, and, save a snow-white cockatiel in an ornate silver cage near the room's far end, there was no sign of life. Alysanna smiled, pleased for the solitude.

/

She could not even begin to guess how many books were in the tightly packed wall. She had heard tales that Duncan, hardly a man of literature, had purchased them sight unseen by weight alone. If that were true, it in no way diminished their worth, for Alysanna's quick review made clear some bibliophile had chosen well.

Goldsmith's *The Traveller*, *The Rivals*, even Johnson's *Lives of the English Poets*—all Alysanna's favorites begged taking. Greed beckoned, but she recalled that her duties left scant time to read. And if Duncan sensed she abused her privileges, he would withdraw them.

Alysanna stood the pewter-based taper on a nearby table and pulled *Evelina, or the History of a Young Lady's Entry into the World* from its niche in the leathery stacks. The book was an easy read, perfectly suited to her present mood. Alysanna smiled at the buttery feel of the skin in her hands. This, at least, was one pleasure still hers.

She was tempted to sit and read by the fire, but Alysanna knew it would be folly. Duncan would be furious to find her here, and the pleasure outweighed the risk.

She began toward the door, intending to snuff the candles, but, as Alysanna turned, she froze as if the whole room were ablaze.

"Cairn! I mean, Lord Chatham!" There, stretched out like a panther on the library sofa, lay Cairn.

"Alysanna." He rose to his elbows, then upright. "I didn't mean to frighten you. Had I known you were expected, I would have prepared a proper greeting."

"I should say the shock of you lurking in the shadows is greeting enough." Alysanna was breathy with surprise, unsure if she were frightened, angry, or pleased.

"No doubt. It has been nearly a month since the park."

The memory of their exquisite, shameful kiss ignited her cheeks with a crimson flush, and Alysanna tilted her head downward, uselessly trying to hide its fire.

"You've been much in my thoughts. I wanted to see you, but I had unavoidable business. My mines in the north . . ."

Alysanna nodded quickly. "Yes, so I was told."

An inviting smile crept over Cairn's suntanned features. "Then I am pleased that you asked of me—I feared you might be angry."

"Angry?" Alysanna could hardly imagine what for, then her conscience rallied indignantly at the memory of his brash behavior that day in St. James.

"I was angry. And I trust such an impropriety won't happen again."

"Alysanna, please." A look of impatience flashed from Cairn's smoldering eyes, and he stalked toward her. "We will not go on playing this silly game, I hope, pretending disinterest?"

"I . . ." Alysanna was unsure how she wished to answer. "What are you doing here?"

"My estate—Foxhall—is nearby. I thought you knew."

"No." Alysanna's brows rose in surprise. "I didn't." She paused, pleased to again have him close, but still frightened. "Duncan, I think, is upstairs. Surely, if he knew you were here, he would be most unhappy to find us alone."

"He knows. I was invited as his houseguest."

"But Foxhall. . . ."

"The wing I usually occupy suffered a fire late this winter. I had hoped the repairs would be complete in time for the final hunt. But building, like love, often proceeds too slowly. Until the rooms are finished, I plan to stay with Duncan."

"So you have been here ever since. . . ." Alysanna shuddered at the thought of Cairn lurking in dark hallways, observing her every move with his burning eyes.

"I only came late tonight. I'd guess that Duncan gave up on me. I had hoped to arrive earlier, but one of my horses threw a shoe."

"Oh," Alysanna breathed, still reeling with shock. Only moments ago she had ached to be near him. Then her longing had been safe, an impossible dream, like a little girl wishing to wake up a princess. Now it had come to pass.

Alysanna realized with discomfort that her indulgent craving had only increased her need for Cairn, and she wondered fleetingly if, in some unfathomable way, she had actually willed his presence here. However it had come about, she was thankful.

Her heart thudded loudly in her ears, and a rush of dizziness teased her equilibrium. Yet even such infirmities felt wonderful, welcome.

"I am pleased to see you. Though my memories were quite vivid, looking at you again makes them pale in comparison." Cairn smiled as he spoke, his eyes traveling Alysanna's slight stature with clear approval.

She averted her eyes, confused. She knew she wanted Cairn Chatham, but he wanted her back for all the wrong reasons. And there was still Hadley.

"May I see your choice?" Cairn stepped close—so near she thought she could actually feel heat radiate from his flesh onto her own. He reached toward the book and brushed his hand, perhaps unintentionally, across Alysanna's fingers.

Their touch was like an explosion that made them mute. Time warped and lifted, and a thread of light stretched between their eyes.

"Alysanna." Cairn spoke softly, then crept his hand

around the book's spine, interlacing his fingers with hers. Alysanna could feel his pulse through her flesh, and it beat fast, though it was no match for her own galloping blood.

"Miss Walker!" Duncan's sharp rebuke shot cannonlike down the room. In mirror imagery, Alysanna and Cairn snapped their heads toward him, her lips parting in horror and Cairn's closing in resignation.

"Need I even ask what you're doing?" Duncan marched toward them with military commitment, raising his hands as he would against two ruffians in a brawl. Cairn and Alysanna stepped away from each other. "And you Cairn! It was a condition of your stay here."

"Duncan, you are overreading this. Truly, nothing . . ."

"Yes," Duncan nodded angrily, "nothing but a repeat of the shameful scene at my bal masque! I tell you, Cairn, my home has always been open to you. But if you cannot abide by my wishes, I shall be forced to ask you to leave."

"Duncan, come, man." Cairn braced his friend with an arm and took him aside, just beyond Alysanna's hearing. "You're in a huff for nothing. I came in late and fell asleep. Miss Walker wandered in to select a book. As it happened, she chose the very volume I wanted. As was proper, she offered it to me." Cairn hardly relished his lies, but he was committed to every one of them if they kept him near Alysanna. She was still too frightened, unlikely to come to him on her own.

Duncan's doubts etched boldly over his tightly configured face, and he cocked one challenging brow. "A book, Cairn—really! I am not a fool."

"Find me a Bible—I'll swear an oath. What sort of ingrate would violate your trust the very night of his arrival?"

Duncan considered the question and chose not to answer.

"Very well. What was it you chose?"

"I'm sorry?"

"The book?" Cairn squinted at Alysanna's novel, trying to read its spine, but Duncan's demand preempted him. "Miss Walker, may I see the book's title?"

Alysanna shrugged, stretching the volume out as she stared straight ahead.

Duncan whirled toward Cairn, his dark eyes squinting with distrust. "*Evelina, or the History of a Young Lady's Entry into the World?* I had no idea you had a fondness for female melodrama."

"Perhaps you know me less well than you think." Cairn smiled gamely.

"I think I know you well enough. And I'll give your workmen two weeks to finish that wing. After that I'm sending you packing, fire damage or no."

Hadley stepped free of the opulent carriage and crept toward Duncan's door with the enthusiasm of a cold man facing an ice bath. He had promised Roberta he would talk to Alysanna, but now, faced with the real prospect, he was undergoing a change of heart. He'd always been good at slippery escapes—perhaps he should just answer this siren's call.

Pretending his affiance to Alysanna would be bad enough—she would expect a kiss or a hug to strengthen their promise. Hadley hardly felt up to such a display. But to launch such a grand lie on top of it—this was for more seasoned tricksters, and Hadley felt completely unsuited to it.

Just now, as he stood with his hand poised to ring the bell, it occurred to him that he could lie—assure Roberta he had handled the matter, even though he had not. But that ruse would solve nothing with Alysanna. She must see him—and the warrant. Hadley pushed the bell and swallowed hard.

No one answered. Again he rang. This time his request

was met with the wood's aching creak, and a squinty-eyed woman peered through its crack, looking to refuse whatever he begged.

"Madame." Hadley doffed his hat and crooked it over his chest in a small bow.

"What is it you want, man?"

"A little civility, perhaps?"

Mrs. Spooner was not amused, and she nearly caught Hadley's hand in the door as she tried to slam it.

"Please." He pressed his glove hard against the panel. "My apologies. I was expecting someone else."

"And who might that be?" Mrs. Spooner made her lips disappear into a seam.

"Miss Alysanna Wilhaven."

"Wilhaven? There's no one here by that name, though we did have an Alysanna Walker."

Of course! Alysanna would have changed her name for safe hiding. "Yes, Walker. I misspoke." Just now Mrs. Spooner's full answer dawned on him. "You say you did have? Has she gone?"

"Two weeks past."

Hadley's mind spun on what had become of her. Had Alysanna been discovered and dismissed? Worse yet, was she en route to Briarhurst, even as he came to prevent such a calamity?

"Did she leave an address?"

"Well, of course she did. The whole household's gone for the summer—Lord Granville's estate of Donegal. If it's important, I can contact our lordship."

Hadley knew he should have anticipated this. "No, that is not necessary."

"May I ask what your business is with Miss Walker? We understood her to have no family. If it is a matter of an unpaid account for Miss Lily's books, you can address it with the houseman—providing, of course, that it was an authorized expense.''

''No, nothing of that sort.'' Hadley could see that the plug of a woman wielding Duncan's door was not about to admit him for the scarce introduction he'd offered. ''I am Lord— Mr. Walker. A distant cousin of Alysanna's.''

''She did not mention you.''

''I'm not surprised. I've been abroad for some time. Only recently returned, with news to tell of our family's bettered fortune.''

Mrs. Spooner's face softened like sun-warmed butter. ''Well, you should have told me to start. Poor child thought herself without kin. I'm sure she'd be thrilled to see you. 'Tis a pity the household's already gone.''

''Indeed.''

''Will you be traveling to Donegal, then?''

Hadley had no intention of another miserable pilgrimage after Alysanna, but decided, since he was here, that he might as well garner what he could from the chatty Mrs. Spooner.

''Unfortunately, my schedule requires my presence in London. But I am eager to hear news of my cousin's condition. Might I come in?'' Hadley gestured toward the foyer Mrs. Spooner looked to be defending like a grey-haired bulldog.

''Well . . . it's somewhat improper, the master being gone and all. We usually don't admit staff's guests. Lord Granville likes tight reins, he does. But I suppose, since you're blood to Miss Walker. Very well.''

Having made the decision to admit him, Mrs. Spooner now seemed eager to do so, and she stepped back in quickly, relinquishing her doorpost and allowing Hadley a full view of the richly done foyer.

So this was where Alysanna sought refuge. The house was

smaller than Wodeby, but Hadley considered the dear price such a parcel must command in so crowded a city, and he almost felt jealous thinking Alysanna's fate an improvement over the penury her absence had bequeathed him. Then he recalled her new role and his envy fled.

"Have a seat in the parlor, and I'll tell you what I can, though Miss Walker kept much to her own. But you probably know that already."

"Yes, our Alysanna was a shy flower." Hadley suppressed his shock at the woman's strange comment. Alysanna was gregarious and chatty—how had she managed such an impression?

"Please." Mrs. Spooner pointed toward a small settee and Hadley obliged, slowing noticeably as he passed a satinwood table heavy with crystal decanters. He longed for a quick, stiff shot, but held his tongue. Mrs. Spooner, whom he had deemed the housekeeper, was an unlikely dispenser of such luxuries, particularly to a man she thought only the distant relation of another employee.

"What is it I can tell you?"

Hadley considered how best to balance what he wanted with what a cousin would logically ask. "Alysanna, she is well?"

"Oh, yes, young and robust, that one is, though I think her appetite could use a little boost. But then I prefer a slightly broader girth." Mrs. Spooner patted her own wide hips, which were significantly broader than Alysanna's.

"I am happy to hear she is in good health. How was it exactly that she came to Lord Granville? I had thought her friend Beatrice held the post."

Mrs. Spooner was thrilled to be the keeper of gossip, and she dispensed her information faster than Hadley could take it in.

"Oh, Beatrice was with Miss Lily for several years. But her sister took to her bed and needed nursing. And, as luck would have it, Miss Alysanna came to our door, and Lord Granville took her in."

"I see." At least Alysanna had propitious timing; her luck hadn't fled along with her fortune. "And is she happy with Lord Granville?" Things sounded so splendid that Hadley could not fathom the urgent tone of Alysanna's letter.

"Miss Lily is a joy. She and Miss Alysanna—well, they've become quite a pair. But Lord Granville. . . ." Mrs. Spooner's voice trailed off, drawing Hadley's quick fire.

"Yes?"

The plump housekeeper leaned forward and answered in a raspy whisper. "Don't repeat this or it'll be my head, but our lordship does have his gruff moods. Not that he doesn't have a good heart. But those of us in his employ do need our patience. Poor Miss Walker found that out at the ball."

"I beg your pardon?"

"Oh, 'twas a terrible scandal. Lord knows what madness she had in mind, but I heard—I was not there, but Tom the footman saw it firsthand—that she actually danced in public with Lord Chatham!"

Hadley's eyes popped wide with question. "Lord Chatham?" Hadley assumed Mrs. Spooner had more to tell; he was right.

"Cairn Chatham, duke of Lyddon. Oh, there's a catch to turn the ladies' heads. I can see why he caught Miss Walker's eye. Still, such imprudence if she wished to keep her job. And his lordship—well, who knows what he had in mind, spinning a governess across the floor for all to see!"

"He lives in London?"

"Yes, he's here every season. But like the Master, he summers in the shires. He's even staying at Donegal while some work is finished on Foxhall's main wing. Ohh!'' Mrs. Spooner covered her mouth with her fleshy hand, and her eyes danced with mischief. ''I hadn't thought until just now, but there's a powder keg in search of a match! Let's hope Miss Walker has better sense than before!''

''Yes,'' Hadley droned. Lord Cairn Chatham—surely there could not be two such names. Yet it was too incredible to think that Alysanna had stumbled on the one man who could divulge Roberta's scheme to sell part of Briarhurst.

Did Alysanna know? And did Cairn know Alysanna's true identity? The possibilities were serious.

Hadley's mind wobbled like a top. Even if he could get Alysanna out of the Granville household, he could hardly undo her acquaintance with Cairn Chatham. If she discovered Roberta's plan, Alysanna would rush home breakneck to defend her birthright. Strangely, it was safest for Alysanna to stay put. The best Hadley could do was frighten her sufficiently to keep her at bay.

''Mr. Walker?''

From her tone of address, Mrs. Spooner had been trying to rouse him for some time. ''Are you all right?''

''Yes, quite. Just recalling my fonder times with my cousin. Perhaps, after my business concludes, I'll pay her a visit. Could you direct me?''

Mrs. Spooner drew the quill from Duncan's desktop and chicken-scratched her instructions on a sheet of paper. ''This should get you there.''

''Thank you.''

''Now, if you visit Miss Walker, be sure and tell her Mrs. Spooner sends her best. She's a sweet child, that one. And she's had a rough time of it.''

Hadley smiled indifferently. He hoped he was not about to follow suit.

CHAPTER
11

Lily hoisted her pink skirts immodestly about her knees and ran giggling into the peached alley encircling Donegal's front grounds, then disappeared into a rhododendron thicket. Alysanna cupped her hands over her eyes as she sat on the reflecting pond's marbled edge, and Cairn could see her nod with each count she spoke out loud. He marked ten before she sprang to her feet and called her warning.

"Ready or not, here I come!"

To Cairn's delight, Alysanna also lifted her skirts, exposing a slender pair of sculpted calves. To his dismay, she also dashed off, vanishing from the green ellipse at the manor's feet.

Cairn smiled and leaned back into the stone bench that was tucked inside a pocket of hornbeam hedge. From the raised earthen tier just off the house's right wing, he had watched Alysanna, unnoticed, for some time. It was nearly an hour since she and Lily had decided there was more to be gained from the warm spring air than some arid text, and, surrendering the day's lesson, had begun a playful game of hide and seek.

This incarnation of Alysanna was not one Cairn had seen before. She was like a faceted diamond, shimmering brilliantly however she turned. One moment she was all decorum and dignity, the next, wild and unpredictable.

Perhaps because of this, it was Alysanna to whom Lily turned with her heart's secrets. Delia, as Lily's abigail, should rightly have been her confidante, but only Alysanna understood the needs of a girl at Lily's juncture in life. Cairn found their affinity for each other, especially with their age difference, remarkable, and he attributed it to Alysanna's chameleon knack of suiting herself to any circumstance she encountered.

Had Alysanna known that Cairn was studying her, no doubt she would have displayed considerably less of her nature. The few times they had crossed paths since they had been discovered in Donegal's library had been fleeting passes in the foyer or garden. And on those occasions, it was clear from Alysanna's terse conversation and nervous foot tapping that she had decided against inviting Duncan's choler.

Since the bal masque, Cairn's patience with Duncan's well-honed snobbery had waned, and, as he settled against the hard contours of the bench's warm marble, the stone's veins radiating back the heat of the cloudless sky, Cairn considered how perfectly the disciplined plantings and well-demarcated paths stretching across the garden mirrored Duncan's tidy soul.

The manor, built atop a much more modest dwelling when Duncan was still a child, was a tribute to the senior Lord Granville's vainglory. But Duncan alone claimed credit for the extensive, ostentatious landscaping, most of which was completed after his father's death.

Cairn smiled, recalling Duncan's struggle, at great expense, for the appearance of an estate much older than it was. The architect had been told to draw plans in keeping with those of the past century, and the result had been a mismatch of two hundred years of design.

Beyond the rhododendrons in the front hub lay a wide gravel path, its circumference so great that a carriage was needed to travel it in less than a full day. Its route led in turn to a Chinese pagoda; an obelisked memorial to Duncan's deceased grandfather; two separate rotundas, one sporting an imported Italian telescope; and a fishing pavilion with its own kitchen and a small but elaborate dining room.

Duncan had considered the further addition of an hermitage, complete with hermit, but his neighbors had successfully suppressed his strange inclination. Altogether the diversions were an overabundance, though Duncan insisted stalwartly that his highborn guests expected such extravagance.

Alysanna and Lily had vanished down the gravel roadway. If Cairn had thought he could follow unobserved, he would have summoned his phaeton and done so. He wished Alysanna had stayed. Watching her skip through the bursting blooms of Duncan's parterre, her arms full of pearl-hued kalmias, had filled him with a strange peace. It gave him the sense that, despite their strained circumstances, all was right with the world.

Alysanna had that talent with things she touched. She was a wellspring of love, so full and overflowing that kindness bubbled from her core, spilling onto anyone near. The thought wore comfortably, swelling a familiar feeling in Cairn's breast. He fleetingly indulged it, then remembered how close he'd come before to such harmony.

The black-haired visage of Elizabeth Shelstone reared in his thoughts, miserably snagging his good mood. How he had loved her, trusted her—enough even to confess, when he learned the truth, that it was he who had purchased her father's Durbrow Mill, laid on the auction block by John Shelstone's mismanagement and stacks of unpaid notes.

Cairn could not have known when he acquired the business that he would lose his heart to the daughter of Durbrow's former master. When he wrote out his payment, Cairn knew only that the mill was bankrupt. It was only later he learned that, the morning of the sale, Durbrow's distraught founder had driven his carriage at a wild man's pace off a cliff, no doubt in anguish for his lost fortunes.

The tale was tragic in its own right, but it came to have more elegiac results. Elizabeth Shelstone's satin manners at the season's assemblies belied her family's threadbare distress, though it would have mattered little to Cairn, even had he known the impoverished state that had thrown her on the goodwill of better-situated London relations.

Cairn had thought nothing of her name. Shelstone was common enough, and London was far from Durbrow's shire. But when he had asked for her hand, Elizabeth had told him of the loss of her father and her hatred for the scoundrel who had stolen his mill and wrought his passing.

Cairn had confessed, a disclosure made in love with the hope of forgiveness, but it had cost him his soul. Elizabeth could bear no future with a man she claimed had killed her father, and she had ignored Cairn's pleas of innocence. His trust in her had been misplaced, and the painful lesson had leveled him.

It was this tragedy that had brought on his fear of entanglement, a disposition that ironically made him legendary among the London ton, evoking incessant matchmaking by well-meaning friends. Cairn Chatham hardly fancied himself a catch, but the ladies took his independence as a personal challenge, and pursued him all the more for it. It was a legacy he would gladly have relinquished, if only he were able.

Each season Cairn grew more alone as the ranks of his bachelor confreres dwindled. Some happily succumbed; others found the altar to meet their familial duty. But among them all, not one could match Cairn's resolve to defend his heart. Elizabeth had cleaved it in two with her betrayal. How could he risk that again?

Just then, Alysanna's velvet rasp of a laugh lilted up from a yew cluster near where Cairn had last seen her, and it beckoned him like a siren's call. His chest flooded with emotions he had long since exiled, but still he could not ignore what he'd learned from his anguished tutelage. If he were to have Alysanna, his secrets must remain his alone.

Maude's milky fingers wound their way to the high octaves of the pianoforte's jet keys, finishing the Handel sonata with a lacy flourish.

"Bravissima!" Cairn's plaudit snapped her head in a spin about the rose parlor, and her eyes smiled as they found him. He clapped again in loud approval. "The keys are your slaves!"

"You devil, you scared me half to death! I'd no idea you were done with father."

"It went swifter than planned. Not that Jason isn't good company, but the market rates for Indian spice are a dull subject for a warm June day."

Maude fluffed her skirt's white flounces over the piano bench's brocade, and Cairn answered her invitation by approaching.

"Poor dear—is making money so toilsome? Your mother

would swim the Channel if she knew how the Chatham fortune threatened to languish with your indifference,'' Maude teased.

"I confess, the easy pounds bore me. There's small challenge in managing solid ventures. I much prefer a gamble.''

"Yes,'' Maude answered, "I have noticed. In fact,'' she continued, "there is a matter of some gravity I would discuss with you. Have you a moment?'' She gestured toward a music chair.

"For you Maude, always.''

Maude only wished it were true. At least she had his full attention now. "I wish to talk to you of Miss Walker—Alysanna.'' Maude had intended to investigate Duncan's governess before speaking with Cairn, but when she had learned he was staying at Donegal, so close to her, the situation had forced her hand.

Cairn sighed wearily. He'd anticipated that Maude would try to steer him off his interest and he'd have brusquely dismissed anyone else who dared raise it with him. But for all her misguided jealousy, Maude was a valued friend, and he would not choose to insult her.

"What about Miss Walker?''

Maude struggled for words, though, knowing her so well, Cairn was unsure if her hesitation were genuine. "I . . . find her troublesome. May I speak frankly?''

"I have rarely known you to speak otherwise.'' Cairn smiled, and Maude returned a nervous grin, then sobered.

"I am aware of your interest in her.''

"Surely we are not going to drag up all this business about you and me . . .''

"Cairn, please! My pride's been through enough mud with your kindness and pity. I'm painfully aware of your sentiments toward me.''

"I do love you, you know—in my own way."

"Yes, I know that quiet, filial way." She sighed. Then, taking a stiff breath, she said, "My interest in you has hardly been sisterly, but no matter. The issue with Miss Walker goes beyond my own dashed hopes. I believe, fully and with all my heart, that the woman is hiding something dangerous."

Cairn arched one brow, looking genuinely surprised, and Maude wondered fleetingly if his usual wits had waxed dull under Alysanna's spell. "What led you to such suspicions?"

"She is wrong for all she purports to be. According to Duncan, her talents are overabundant for a woman so young. And she has no characters—not even a note to show from her former employers. To cap it off, she claims to have worked for a family whose matron is too ancient to even consider . . ." Maude's tongue stuck on the words, ". . . having a child at such an advanced age. Then that allemande —I know, 'twas at your bidding, or so I have gathered, but she did agree. I'd say it was an odd choice for a woman wishing to keep her post. And since you didn't seem capable of noticing. . . ."

"What is it you're suggesting?"

"Even I'm not sure. But I know Alysanna Walker is counterfeit. Her skills, her manners, they are too highborn for—"

"For a lowly governess."

"Well, yes."

"Maude, will you ever cling to your narrow view of the world?"

"Cairn, stop! You know as well as I that there are codes of conduct, mores we are bound to. If you will not concede violating them wrong, then at least admit that Miss Walker has acted suspiciously."

"Perhaps she is simply different from the ilk of woman

you know." Cairn's tone smacked of insult, and Maude felt like she'd just taken a blow on her upraised chin.

"What, may I ask, is wrong with the sort of woman I know? The sort I am?"

Cairn leaned toward her and took her hands, giving Maude brief hope that he would recoup his affront with an apology.

"Absolutely nothing. But I think there are finer parts of you that would overrule your snobbery if given the chance. You needn't be concerned with Miss Walker's curious traits. Frankly, I find them refreshing." The tone of Cairn's voice made clear the depths of his interest in Alysanna.

"Cairn, you are frightening me. Tell me your purpose with Miss Walker is—a base one." Maude snatched her hands back as if the forthcoming confession would soil her.

"Maude!" They had always spoken openly, but Cairn could hardly believe her bold implication. "This is not a matter for a gentleman and a lady to discuss."

"If it is all that will rescue my chances with you, it is indeed." Her huge blue eyes filled with tears, and Cairn raised his thumb in a swipe at the overflow.

"So," she gasped haltingly, barely able to choke out the words, "if you must have her, then take her and be done with it. I will still be yours, even if you must lie with some lower-class . . ." Maude's composure dissolved before she could finish.

Cairn had not meant to cause her such pain, and his heart wrenched as he realized what his pursuit of Alysanna had cost her. He'd always known Maude wanted him as a husband, but he'd hoped she could settle for friendship. Now, he could see his optimism was folly.

"There," he soothed, gently stroking the top of her shaking head. "No need for tears over me."

"Was I so foolish to think there could be more?" Maude's

entire body shook, and the blond tendrils framing her face trembled with each ragged inhalation.

Cairn lowered his eyes in affirmation, and Maude's chest jumped with her failure to stifle another sob. "Very well. Somehow, I will accept that you do not want me. But even if you must have your way with Alysanna, promise me that, after you are done, you will free yourself of her. I tell you, all you see is veneer—there is something not right, not solid beneath."

Cairn's eyes searched Maude's incredulously. "Do you know me so little to think that all I wish from a woman is to bed her?"

Maude's lips parted in undisguised shock. "What is it you're saying?" Her alarm was audible. Until now, Maude had thought Alysanna only a tempting dalliance—she had never considered that Cairn might have serious designs on her. "Cairn, what is it you want with her?"

"Nothing." He knew the truth would distress her, and he prayed she would let it go.

"No, it is something, indeed. Surely you're not considering an entanglement?" Cairn's silence answered, and, at the horrifying realization, Maude sprang from her seat and flitted quickly around the pianoforte's length.

"My God," she gasped, her feet grinding to a sudden halt, "you're thinking of marrying her!"

"Maude, this is overhasty." Cairn wanted desperately to drop the matter. Whatever he said would be drowned by Maude's fears.

"Cairn, even if Alysanna Walker is what she claims, then she is but a governess! A man of your station and wealth cannot drag down his rank with such a woman. And if she is not what she pretends, what then? Will you commit your heart to a woman who would deceive you? She may seek only your fortune, or perhaps she is a woman turned out for just cause by her family—she could even be a criminal! I tell you, Cairn, my every instinct makes me shake with fear for you—Alysanna Walker has things to hide!''

Maude planted her arms akimbo on her hips, her best entreaties pled. Surely Cairn would not ignore her warning, yet he was silent.

''Cairn? I tell you she has secrets!''

Cairn stared immutably back. ''Who among us does not?''

It was only by the grace of God and the odd angle of Dauphin's fall that Maude was not killed instantly. Would that the poor horse had been, for though Cairn was quick to dispatch Dauphin's writhing misery—his snapped leg was clearly beyond repair—it had taken him long to reach the scene of the accident.

Moments before, Maude had pressed like a wild lark to the forefront of the pack, nearly catching the huntsman's heels. With Cairn having drawn the unenviable lot of day's gatekeeper, he followed a distance behind, riding pistoled in defense against some angry farmer's rage.

The day had begun much better. The fox had been unkenneled just after breakfast and, after a wait to allow the scent to mend, Duncan and the season's final party had set out. Hounds, huntsman, and whipper-in were hungry for the chase, poised for a crisp romp across the blanket of fields that lay beyond Donegal's manicured grounds.

The riders, whose number approached twenty, were largely gentleman neighbors—ladies were allowed only as irregular participants in such manly affairs. Today, however, Maude had been granted a place in the season's last ride.

At first the pace had been swift—the horses had devoured acres of alternately poached and grassy terrain at the hounds' loud bidding. With an open draw and a good cheek wind there was little to impede either horse or dog, and all sped with fiery blood toward their flame-haired quarry.

Then, for some reason, the scent had gone cold, and the frenzy had faded. The hounds checked, and, for what seemed like a great while, the horses drifted itinerantly through the thick gorse, their riders suddenly close enough to speak, not shout, their grumbling observations.

For at least a mile the party wandered, the belvoir tans dragging out the stale line in the hopes of a fresh find. Suddenly, as if hit with a great gust of scent, they feathered, then gave tongue and bolted, their nostrils hot with the fox's wind. Though by now far beyond the equestrian pack, the huntsman's "Holloa!" and whipper-in's horn were heard by all.

The riders' pulses quickened, and with heels and spurs dug hard in their animals' sides, the hunt party exploded forward, their mounts' rearing hooves and flared nostrils making them less like horses than smoke-breathing dragons. With dash that belied the morning's long ride, they thundered en masse over the flat terrain, the horses' banged tails snapping up and down with their gallop's beat.

Maude, who had been too eager all day to display her prowess with Dauphin's temper, now gave her bravado full vent, urging the already keen animal forward too fast until finally, she outpaced the hunt pack and rode first behind the huntsman.

Three fences lay between him and the dogs, each making Dauphin more eager for the next as his hooves sailed over. Like a great equine angel, Maude and the horse breezed effortlessly over the railing tops, the crimson ribbon on Maude's dark hat whipping in perfect synchrony with Dauphin's black swath of tail.

Even from his position at the rear, Cairn could see her reckless manner, and something about the forward cant of her seat frightened him. He knew she had been upset by their talk yesterday. Now, watching her race breakneck across the Northamptonshire fields, Cairn could not help but wonder if her daring was meant for him, and the thought brought a wash of shame to his suntanned face.

By now Maude had nearly caught the yelping hounds, and Cairn breathed a sigh of relief, knowing at least she'd not outrace the scent. A final timber fence shot up on the horizon. It did not look overly high, yet Cairn swore that even from his great distance back, he heard a "Ware" called in warning by the huntsman. But if Maude heard the caution, she paid it no heed. As she had done on each other barrier met that day, she urged Dauphin forward, then gathered him in some ten yards shy to allow him full strength for the jump.

He was a breathtaking animal—lean of neck, but with plenty of bone—and, though too headstrong for most gentle hands, Maude had ridden him admirably, if with a bit too much daring. When she had bought the horse, Cairn had thought them badly suited, but today she rode as if Dauphin's wild nature had filled her own soul.

Seeming to trust her bidding, the horse bowed his strength to the whims of her will. His snarling hooves bore down on the wooden beams, and, as though lifted by the wind, he took to the air, effortlessly clearing the fence's uppermost rail.

Then, as Cairn breathed his relief, both animal and rider fell from view. Soon all Cairn could see was the pitiful railing of the stallion's hooves as they thrust upward and tore at the air, barely visible above the fence's lower bars. As he finally reached them, Cairn saw the cause—Dauphin had faltered on a hidden combe.

Everyone's eyes riveted on Maude, who was thrown in a sprawl some ten yards downwind. From the look of the spill, she should have been badly injured; in fact, she had only suffered a sprained wrist.

Dauphin was another matter. He lay whinnying softly, as if pleading for someone to end his misery. When the foreleg was seen to be shattered and all agreed that nothing could be done, it was Cairn who had loaded his pistol and trained it in anguished mercy on the poor, suffering beast.

Such tragedies were not rare and did not always end what might otherwise be a successful day. Yet Duncan's heart had sunk on the stallion's destruction, and, with Maude nearly hysterical, Duncan had declared the hunt finished and marshaled the group homeward, allowing at least one small fox another season's grace.

The ride back had gone slowly, and when the entourage finally reached Donegal's gates, Cairn felt Maude relax against him, the tension that had strung her muscles taut now draining free.

Maude had ridden over early that morning from Totten-Hoo, but her return was impossible in her injured state. Duncan had decided she'd stay the night, and had ordered a hot bath and a stiff drink. Then, in grief and tribute to his fine lost animal, he'd retired alone to his room.

The other riders, most of whom lived far enough to have come by coach two days prior, retired to their own pursuits, and Cairn considered how to spend his own afternoon.

If Maude had needed him, he would have stayed nearby. But she'd taken a stiff dose of laudanum. Now she slept and looked likely to continue to for the remainder of the day.

Cairn longed to clear his own thoughts, and he returned to his own stallion, Nuit, planning to cool the animal with a walk through the forest skirting Donegal's grounds. The horse should have been tired from the day's fast chase, but he raised his head with a welcoming whinny as Cairn approached, and Cairn mounted, urging him forward.

Duncan's landscaping bled into oak and willow stands, and Nuit strained on the bit, pulling his martingale taut. He wanted a run, and Cairn agreed. Their bodies soon moved in practiced unison, the undulations of Nuit's long muscles offset by Cairn's skillful balance.

They cantered for over a mile, then stopped at a pond for a draught of cold water. But no sooner had Nuit lowered his muzzle into the pool's cool green than he jerked back up, his ears perked warily.

Cairn heard it, too. It was another horse's call, but this whinny was no demand for more rein. The animal was seized by terror. Both Cairn and Nuit knew instantly, and, with one mind, the two shot toward the increasingly loud neighing.

As they rounded a thick oak stand, Cairn saw the cry's shocking source. There, at the copse's edge, was Duncan's chestnut gelding Cabochon, his blazed head jerking upward in frenzied snaps. His nostrils flared and snorted, and his black hooves danced feverishly on the grassy sod. His terror was echoed in his wild, dark eyes. On his back was Alysanna.

At first Cairn could think only of Maude and the disastrous tumble she had taken that day. *Dear God*, he prayed silently, *not again*.

Alysanna clutched Cabochon's reins desperately, pinning them to his shivering withers in a struggle to counter his threat to rear. Yet still his twitching hooves rose higher with each vault, each leap widening and flooding the horse's eyes with more fear.

Cairn began to call, then, in horror, saw the cause of the animal's terror. Less than ten yards away, with all but its thick head concealed by a cluster of bracken, was a huge, snorting, wild boar.

Its plug of a head lifted and nodded, as if to square its angry sights on the panicked horse. The pig's wiry coat stood rigid in fury, and its dark eyes were squinty and feral, drained of anything save some devilish mission. With alternate cloven hooves, it pawed the dry turf, the dull scratching sound of its feet nearly swallowed by the grunts drumming from its puffed belly.

Cairn had seen a boar once charge a stallion, and the sight was bloodcurdling. The horse, frozen stupid with fear, had not known it could outrun it, and had foolishly tried to rush past its predator, only to have its hocks badly shredded by the pig's sharp tusks.

If Cabochon could not be made to retreat, the boar would attack. Cairn's heart froze at the image of Alysanna pitched into the beast's charging path. She had not yet seen Cairn. Her every fiber was trained on the pig's coal eyes and the sound of its guttural grunt, echoed by Cabochon's trembling whinny.

"Alysanna," Cairn almost whispered, knowing any loud noise might prompt an assault.

Alysanna threw her head in a quick snap sideways, then restruck her wide-eyed vigil on the pig, now lowering its head ominously.

"Cairn!" she said through clenched teeth, her voice soaked with fear. "He's going to take the gelding!"

Cairn knew it was impossible to dismount and sweep Alysanna to safety. The boar would beat him to her, and any movement could force a charge.

"Have you a kerchief?"

"I'm not going to faint!" she snapped, half under her breath.

"Put it over Cabochon's eyes. Back him up."

Alysanna loosened one shaking hand and searched the pocket of her riding coat, where she found a white kerchief.

"I can't tie it," she answered.

"Just lay it over his eyes."

Alysanna did so, then threw Cairn another questioning glance.

"Pull him backwards, gently and steadily. Use the reins as you normally would."

Afraid to countermand Cairn, Alysanna delivered several short, even tugs on the leather straps. In response, the gelding began a cautious retreat. Slowly, but surely, he backed away. To Alysanna's amazement, the snarling boar continued to stand still.

For an instant her heart soared with the hope of rescue, but the pig's burning eyes narrowed, and it stopped pawing. Its squat muscles tightened as it gathered its strength. Then, with one final snort, the boar's thick form hurled forward on her like a fired missile.

"Hoaaa!" Cairn's loud shout drew off the animal, but did nothing to diminish its thundering speed. Now the boar trained its livid sights on Nuit, and, as it roared toward him, Alysanna screamed.

"Cairn!" She leaned so far out on Cabochon's neck that her shout made the horse rear back in fear. Alysanna yanked the reins down to lower his head, but her eyes clung only on Cairn, who cocked the pistol he had loaded moments ago and trained it unflinchingly at his galloping target.

With calm purpose, he squeezed the trigger. The force of the leaden shot exploded Nuit backwards. Alysanna choked on her breath, and a deep terror swept through her. Let Cairn live! she prayed.

At first the animal's frenzied assault continued, and Alysanna feared Cairn had missed his mark. Then, less than two feet short of a rearing, screaming Nuit, the boar dropped to its knees, then slammed its thick head, mouth foaming, into the sod. Only then did Alysanna see the bloody tear in its chest oozing into the yellow grass, giving full testimony to Cairn's fine marksmanship.

Cairn did not move but studied his prey, half suspecting the animal would yet rise. He was clearly a beast of strength—he had run far even after the shot's blow. Alysanna dismounted, then, not knowing what else to do, threw her arms about Cabochon's neck and buried her face in his hot, moist coat.

Tears came in a fast, drowning wave, and she could not say if they were for Cabochon, Cairn, or herself. She burrowed into the gelding's throatlatch, her ragged breath nearly matching his own. The warmth of the horse's silky coat comforted her, but only when she felt Cairn's hands close about her shaking shoulders did Alysanna know what solace she longed for.

"What were you doing here?" Cairn's eyes searched hers as he spun her around.

Alysanna tried to answer, but her words flew out haltingly, pierced by sobs of relief that racked her chest painfully. "Lily had gone for some flowers, and I managed permission for a ride. We were fine, and then that . . ." Alysanna pointed accusingly toward the still-warm boar, who looked only slightly less menacing for its lack of movement. "He came from the thicket. I didn't see him. Cabochon froze, and then you came."

"Thank God." Cairn pulled Alysanna's head to his chest as if he could still her pitched breathing with his own pounding heart. "Are you all right?"

Alysanna nodded and clung to him, her fingers digging into his shoulders' ridge with desperate need.

"Thank you," she whispered, slowly straightening her head and tilting it upwards. "If you hadn't come . . ." Her composure dissolved beneath his riveting stare. Cairn's grey eyes bore into her, and, without thinking, she pushed onto tiptoe to close the distance between them.

Cairn's hands wove through her chestnut curls and tightened, canting her head back as he raised her chin. He leaned closer and breathed her name. She had heard it spoken a thousand times, but never like this. It was too sweet a summons.

One moment they were a breath apart; the next, their searching lips galvanized in a warm, moist spark. Cairn cinched her body closer, and his tongue poured like honey across her breath. Alysanna moaned a gasp of delight, then raked her nails over his back as she arched her breasts against his chest.

Her heart catapulted to her ears, and suddenly Alysanna felt as though she had been struck by a brilliant, burning star. Her flesh was no longer cold with the terror, but hot and molten. Her bones surrendered as if stripped away, her only support Cairn's strong embrace. Suddenly, even that fell free, and, though she knew not how it happened, Alysanna felt their melded form sink to the dry, fragrant rushes.

Cairn lay alongside her, and, though they barely touched, Alysanna sensed they were bound together with gossamer ropes. Cairn's hand traced her still-damp cheek, then unknotted the ties of her white riding cravat.

Her chest jumped as his fingertips feathered down her throat to the swell of her breast. A small voice deep inside her decried his liberties, but Alysanna stilled it.

She vanquished all reasoning. What she longed for was so

primal, so overwhelming, that it demanded the death of all conscious thought. A hurricane had risen in her soul, and Alysanna had neither the strength nor the desire to rail against it.

Cairn brushed his thumb over the peak of her breast, teasing it maddeningly through her dress's soft linen. Alysanna granted her permission with a small moan and closed her eyes, struggling not to drown in the storm of sensations. Cairn's head nuzzled against her cheek, then his tongue touched her like wet lightning, slipping toward her ear and pushing her beyond control.

"Alysanna. God, I nearly lost you. I thought it was Dauphin all over again."

Alysanna was barely aware of Cairn's words. Why was he speaking? All she wanted was more of the frothy pleasure he was lathering over her aching flesh.

"Dauphin?"

Cairn lifted his hand and drew back.

"I'm here because the hunt was called off. Dauphin threw Maude. She was not badly hurt, but we had to put the animal down."

Alysanna's eyes crackled with shock, then rage. Suddenly, with such force it landed Cairn half on his back in the grass, she rolled free of him.

"Maude! You choose this moment to speak to me about Maude!"

Instantly, Cairn knew he had made a mistake. He scrambled to sit, hoping to correct his error, but Alysanna was already standing.

"It is of no import. Please." Cairn extended his hand, inviting her back.

"You must think me daft!" Alysanna considered what had nearly just happened and wondered if the indictment were true. "That." she gestured toward the spot of ground where they had lain, "was madness. And it will not happen again. If you think to have your sport with me, then dance your serious attentions on the likes of Maude Delamere. . . let me correct you. Governess or no, I am no round-heeled doxy here to serve your base needs!''.

Cairn's fist hit the ground in exasperation. If he had made a mess of things, Alysanna was doing nothing to undo it.

"Maude is my friend—that is all."

"Yes." Alysanna nodded her head in quick little jolts as she laughed, disbelieving. "And what then am I to you?"

Cairn paused, then a solemnity swept over him. His eyes glazed with hard, glassy purpose, and an almost frightening transcendence suffused his face. Alysanna stared at him quizzically, wondering if he were ill. "I want you to be my wife."

Alysanna's balance crumbled away. Fearing she would reel backwards, she shot her hand out sideways, steadying herself against Cabochon's bulk. The other hand flew in shock to her mouth.

"What did you say?" She was sure she had misunderstood.

"I asked you to marry me," Cairn answered calmly.

Alysanna suppressed her urge to sputter some flustered answer. Surely this was yet another misguided attempt at humor.

"Why would you want me?" she asked, refusing his bait.

"It seems obvious that I love you. I would think you know that by now."

Alysanna's green eyes lit at the dumbfounding realization. He was serious. "But, I thought . . ."

"Yes, I know. That's something I still mean to have from you. But I want more than your flesh. Have I your answer?"

Every fiber of Alysanna screamed her joy, but logic silenced her. Even if she could believe that he wanted her honorably, as his wife, there were mammoth problems. She could not confess the truth of her identity, and a marriage between a man of his class and a governess was preposterous.

"I hope your silence is not a refusal."

"I don't understand."

"The question?"

"Your intention. Surely you are well aware that you and I come from different backgrounds."

Cairn smiled patiently. "I know you are Duncan's governess."

"That doesn't trouble you?"

"It seems to trouble you a great deal more."

Alysanna could hardly believe she was arguing against the proposal she'd longed for, dreamed of. But she could never agree until she knew what dared Cairn to this madness. "You would be outcast to make such a low match."

"I think it unlikely. At the risk of sounding immodest, the Chathams have been a formidable presence in this county for many generations. I doubt we would be dismissed simply for my wedding of you. But, even were that to happen, it would be of little import."

Cairn's cavalier indifference stunned her. He seemed willing to toss away all she even now struggled to recover. "Little import to lose your friends, the only life you know and value?"

"No true friends would desert me. And what I value most is your love." Cairn's brow furrowed an entreaty, and he reached toward her. "Won't you stand closer? To look at you, one would guess I'd just launched an insult, not a marriage proposal."

Alysanna was speechless. Cairn Chatham was everything she wanted. Before she had met him, she owned no words for the desire he now swelled within her. Surely the fiery passion she would know as Cairn's wife could easily outmatch what she'd dreamed of with Hadley.

But she was still engaged! The thought struck her like a tight, angry fist. Whatever her heart begged, there was no answer to give while still bound to another. Her promise to Hadley was a painful, heavy weight.

She had just written him again, and still had received no word. Until she had news of Julia's assailant, she was wholly dependent on Hadley's good will. She dared not anger him by ending their betrothal.

"Have you nothing to say?" Confusion drifted through Alysanna's clouded eyes, and Cairn leaned closer, as if in study.

"I can't."

"You can't marry me?"

"Yes or no, I cannot say."

"What is this game, Alysanna?"

"I need time. You must trust me."

"I trusted that you returned my love. Perhaps I was mis-guided," Cairn snapped impatiently. His words twisted like a blade in her heart. More than anything, Alysanna wanted him, too.

"I'm sorry," she blurted, tears filling her eyes. She was sure if she stood one more moment under the burn of Cairn's puzzled stare, her heart would explode in grief.

Alysanna sprang onto Cabochon and clucked loudly, tapping her heels hard on his sides. He began at a trot, but she pulled him up and wrenched backwards.

"Cairn?"

"Yes?"

"I do love you." A shower of light glittered down from the sky, bathing the clearing in a halcyon calm. Then, just as quickly, its aura vaporized, and Alysanna, not knowing what else to do, issued a loud "Hoay," hurling herself and Cabochon across the grassy meadow, soon far from Cairn Chatham.

CHAPTER
12

❦

"Ten shillings! Me company alone's worth mor'n that! I'll not leave wi' a penny less'n twelve!" Molly cinched up the dangling laces of her corset, stuffing one overflowing breast back into its cup.

"Come, love, surely the pleasure wasn't all mine?" Hadley leaned against Molly's warm back and reached around her, one sticky hand pressing flat against her belly while the other traced a suggestive trail down her neck to her bosom's swell. "Let's not quibble over a few shillings when we've had such a fine romp."

"Fine's a new frock when I've a mind ta one. The devil's wage ye pay me as chambermaid 'ardly allows that. The least ye can do is keep to our bargain."

Hadley snatched back his embrace and reached for Molly's worn loden gown. He hurled it at her head, forcing her to duck. He glowered angrily, all vestiges of the past hour's passion gone.

"What we agreed upon was ten. Here." Disdainfully, he tossed the silver pieces with a clink atop the scarred wooden bureau and finished threading his breeches' buttons through their holes. "What makes you think you can pinch me for more?"

"'Haps I'm better than I was when we first agreed on such a sum."

"All that's improved is your ambition. That exceeds your talents."

"Ye seemed pleased 'nuff."

"I paid you for what pleasure I got. Our accounts are settled."

Molly wove a broken-toothed comb through the twisted strands of her dark blond hair, struggling to unknot the tangles wrought by Hadley's lust. All the while she grumbled a string of complaints he barely heard half of. "And in me own room yet. I'll lave to wash them bed covers!"

Hadley straightened his jacket hurriedly, eager to be free of Molly's whining grievances. But before he could leave, the knob turned, and the low door parted with a creak on Roberta's scowl.

"A little downstairs sport?"

"It's none of your business if I so choose." He reddened, embarrassed to be caught in his vulgar tryst.

"If Alysanna learns you're filling her serving maids' beds, she'll fly home faster than that tart can disrobe." Roberta nodded haughtily toward Molly, who stood, mouth open and hands cocked on her hips.

"Well, ain't ye somethin', with yer fine manners and yer fault-findin' eyes," Molly screeched. "I's good 'nuff for 'is lordship, I is."

The room's full width parted them, but Roberta recoiled from Molly's hoyden call, looking as though some foul wind chased her. "Hadley, really! Can't you at least find a trollop with a bit more manners? At least a more discreet one—perhaps outside your own roof?"

"As if it's any of your business," Hadley countered, his reply making Molly smile smugly at what she believed was his defense of her.

"*This* is my business," Roberta snapped, shoving a folded paper against Hadley's chest with such force it nearly unbalanced him. With a vise grip on his elbow, she dragged him from the room and into the hall. "A love note from your fiancée. You remember her?" Roberta hauled him upstairs, slamming the parlor door with a crash. She gave the letter another push. "It's from Alysanna."

"How would you know?"

"I ran into the mail coach en route here. At first I thought only to save the driver a trip. But when I recognized Alysanna's hand, I thought it was in my best interests to break the seal."

"You have no right!" Hadley screamed, looking so agitated that Roberta wondered if his head would begin to spurt steam.

She shot him a look of impatience. "Hush up and listen."

"I suppose I might as well," he conceded sarcastically, "since you obviously intend to lecture me before I can read the note."

Roberta snorted like an angry bull and punched her finger accusingly against the paper's center. "It seems Alysanna's more desperate than ever to see you. Now, how would that happen if you'd spoken to her as you swore?"

Hadley felt a hot blush fire his cheeks. He hadn't wanted to go to London in the first place—chasing Alysanna all the way to Donegal had been too much to ask. Roberta was wrong—Alysanna was content enough to stay away, even without news of the warrant. There'd been no harm in lying to Roberta, telling her he'd seen Alysanna as promised—until now.

"All right. I didn't find her after all."

"Stupid!" Roberta slammed her fist onto a nearby table, and a crystal vase arced and crashed to the floor. "Why in the hell not?"

"I went, as we agreed, but Alysanna had left for the country. I planned to write. Following her seemed unnecessary."

"Apparently you were wrong." Roberta still held the letter, and the paper shook with her rage.

"Well, then, tell me what in God's name she wants." Hadley demanded impatiently.

"Sit down," Roberta snapped, pointing to a chair as if Hadley were a child to be lectured. "It seems your sloth has made her more desperate. She's not sure you've received her letters, and she's threatening to come home. What a pretty mess that would be."

"So, I'll take the damned warrant to Donegal. I'll go Tuesday next."

"You'll go sooner than that. She wants to see you day after tomorrow. Your inattention has made her frantic. She's asked to meet you near some outskirt called Mowbry. I assume it's close to the Granvilles'."

"Does she say what she wants?" Hadley's heart jumped to his throat at the possibilities. Had Mrs. Spooner jabbered to Alysanna about his strange visit? Worse yet, had Alysanna learned something she should not have from Cairn Chatham? Hadley's palms grew hot and moist, and he ground them against his breeches' soft leather to hide his distress.

He had not mentioned Cairn to Roberta. If she knew, it would only make her more insistent on his intervention. It had been bad enough, being caught in one lie; he was not about to invite Roberta's fury by confessing another.

"Hadley, you're pale as snow. Don't think you can avoid this task by feigning illness."

Hadley had not meant to display his distress, and he turned away, dragging one still-moist hand down the length of his tired face. "Thank you for your concern, but I think it better spent on Alysanna. What shall I tell her?"

"What we had planned before you ignored my instructions. Take the warrant, and put the fear of God in Alysanna. If you needed to make it stick before, you'd best be twice as convincing this time."

"But I don't know what she wants."

"I'm no mind reader. Meet her and find out. What else would you do?"

Hadley nodded nervously. This new request from Alysanna made him squirm. He'd pushed her off as long as he could, and now his inattention had drawn her fire. Perhaps she already suspected something.

How much simpler it had all been before Julia. Marrying Alysanna was hardly his heart's passion, yet her fat inheritance and far-reaching privileges would have been quittance enough for the temperance a wife would have forced on him. If he could only resurrect their wedding plans. . . . Just now the thought seemed possible, and Hadley wondered if he could persuade Roberta to drop her suit and return to their original agreement.

"It needn't be such a disaster if she came back, you know."

Roberta took a slow, studious step toward Hadley, craning her neck sideways as if he were some rare specimen. "Is there only air between your ears?"

"You needn't insult me. I'm tired of the endless time and

effort this takes. In the end, we'll only earn a stay of execution. Alysanna will come home.''

"By then, Briarhurst will be mine."

"She'll protest your claim."

"You'll support it by swearing to her abandonment. The will is immutable. Six months and she has no recourse, providing you keep your mouth closed. Now, enough of your bellyaches. You'd better start packing."

Roberta's scheme was precariously balanced, likely to be upended by any small slip. Hadley was not sure he was up to the task. "If I marry Alysanna, one-third of Briarhurst will still fill your purse—that's a great improvement on nothing at all, which is what we might come to if things go awry."

Roberta reeled back as if she were going to pitch something, then smacked her open hand loudly across Hadley's cheek. The blow threw him painfully against the pianoforte's curved side.

"You've made a mistake!" he shouted, his hand balling into a fist that longed for Roberta's chin.

"Be still! Don't dare try to force me! Why should I settle for part of Briarhurst when I can have it all? I warn you, more antics like these, and I'll find a way to end your bloodsucking drain of my accounts, as well. Your fortune rests as much in my hands as mine in yours. I know Alysanna's heart, Hadley Seaham, and I can assure you that she'll have no patience for a mountebank who traded her love on his greed."

Hadley was unsure if he or Roberta had won the melee. She had as much leverage on him as he her, and the uneasy stalemate infuriated him.

"All right!" he shouted. "I'll go to Alysanna and market our lies." Hadley strode to the sideboard and poured himself a stiff draught of whiskey. He sensed he was going to need it.

* * *

Alysanna hoped to God that Maude was in a good mood. She urged Cabochon down the dusty road leading to Totten-Hoo and silently mouthed the story she would tender there.

Yet no matter how convincingly Alysanna spoke the words, they did not quite ring true. Like a marksman missing against a distant target, Alysanna tried and failed, then took a deep breath to steady herself and tried again. Her plan must work if she were to have any future with Cairn.

For whatever unfathomable reason, he wanted her as his wife. That knowledge set her heart beating out her need for him so loudly, so unalterably, that she could not hear anything else. If she had to lose Briarhurst, so be it. The hallmarks of everything she had valued such a short time past—name, heritage, even the estate itself, were trifles she would gladly cast off if their loss would gain her Cairn in return.

Alysanna shook her head at her indulgent reverie. Whether she confessed her ruse to Cairn or kept her secret, she could not risk the high profile of becoming Cairn's duchess. She was still in flight from the law and Julia's killer. To set herself among the glittering ton, so easy to find, was to beg for disaster.

The best she could hope for was that Hadley had made progress. Tomorrow, God and the mail coach willing, she would meet with him. But he had not once written her, and she could only pray he had received her last letter.

Alysanna had done nothing to betray him, at least in deed, yet the thought of Hadley's face made her heart flush with shame. How could she stand before him, knowing she loved another? Perhaps he had news that would let her right her disgraceful silence.

Totten-Hoo's black gates loomed before her, and Alysanna shuddered at the task at hand. Before Hadley, there was

Maude, whose loud suspicions could altogether undo her. Alysanna's past was too easy to uncover. Once Maude caught her scent, she would be off like a hound, and there would be no buying her silence. Maude's doubts must be quelled. As Alysanna deeded Cabochon's reins to the Delamere groom, she crossed her fingers hopefully, praying that the lie she had spent most of last night fashioning would work today.

Her mouth gaped at the huge front door, its center emblazoned with the Delamere crest of griffins locked in fierce combat. Their thick tails choked each other's necks. The image hardly calmed Alysanna. For a brief moment, her confidence faltered. Then, driven by some instinct beyond logic, her hand rang the bell. When the Delamere footman led her to the library, Alysanna steeled her courage—she was here, and a change of course was now idle wishing.

More quickly than Alysanna expected, Maude popped through the door. She was as beautiful as ever, even in her redingote and traveling hat, and she wore a look of guarded surprise. Alysanna had heard the tap of her heels down the marble stairs, yet Maude was obviously on her way out.

"Miss Walker. I hardly anticipated the pleasure of seeing you here. What is it you want?"

Maude's gloved hands gripped a rust-colored riding crop, and as she spoke she tested its bow, giving the impression that she was about to snap it in half. The light manner Alysanna had often seen her wear was heavier now, making Alysanna wonder if her problem was less convincing Maude of her revised past than staying an eviction long enough to ensure that she heard it.

"I wish to speak with you."

"Obviously," Maude snapped. "Do so quickly—I've business today." Alysanna stiffened, wondering if Maude's business dealt with her.

"I can see you don't mince words, Miss Delamere. Neither will I. I wish to discuss your suspicions of me."

"Really?" Maude cocked one brow skeptically. "I can't imagine what you have to say, unless you are here to repeat your zealous—and useless—denials of them."

"I am here to tell you I've lied." Alysanna paused, anticipating the shock that flew across Maude's delicate features.

"Pardon me?"

"Regrettably, I have not told you the truth. Or Lord Granville. But I wish to set those impressions straight, if you will so allow."

"Allow? I can't imagine what could be more entertaining." Maude plopped onto a padded hassock.

"I know you have found much about me—inconsistent—with my tale of coming from humble means." Maude tipped her head forward, deigning Alysanna to continue. "In fact, I'm sure my behavior has been odd—perhaps because it does not fit a governess. My actions are more in keeping with a woman of your station."

The comparison made Maude's impatience boil; she stiffened and rose. "Of all the impudent . . ."

"Please," Alysanna entreated. "Let me finish. Then you have full license to say what you will." Maude looked calmed, if not placated, and she lowered herself again on the footstool's satin.

"Very well."

"As I said, my family was not unlike yours—at least until recently, when my wastrel father made our fortune grist for London's gaming halls. Just last winter I too sat at fine tables and toured on the Continent, taking life's luxuries as my entitlement.

"But suddenly, though I must think my father had some

inkling, the pounds disappeared. Hundreds upon thousands of them were gone, lost to foolish wagers, each larger than the last in an old man's struggle to recoup his losses. Father ruined both his legacy and my portion—and the burden was too great for him. In his agony, he loaded his pistol and took his life. Our estate fell to his carrion creditors and I to my own devices.''

Maude clapped her hands in a burst of applause. ''A nice tale, Miss Walker. Not unreasonable—and it would certainly explain your fine skills and lack of characters. But I do not yet understand your subterfuge. Many governesses are daughters of ruined fathers. Why mount such a bold lie?''

''It was—shame,'' Alysanna answered softly, closing her eyes in the hopeful appearance of anguish. ''I took no pride in my sad tale. To confess my father was not only a gambler but a bad one, and, ultimately, a man whose heart beat faster for the dice than his own daughter's fate—it was a great degradation. Knowing I must work for my keep, it seemed less painful to choose a new life.''

''Will you tell me that pretending yourself a governess, with all its discomforts, rode easier than the truth?''

''I would have suffered such discomforts in any event. It was simpler not to dwell on what I had lost by laying claim to it.''

''Perhaps,'' Maude droned, resting her crop's leather fringe on her chin. ''But it strikes me that whatever compelled you, it is of little consequence in light of your future—as Cairn's duchess.''

A cough bounded to Alysanna's throat, and, though she could not suppress it, she imagined that anything she could have said in response to Maude's accusation would have been worse.

''You seem unwound, Miss Walker.''

"I did not hear your comment," Alysanna answered, stalling.

"You claim to come in the interest of truth. If that is so, don't degrade your assertions by pleading ignorance of Cairn's intentions." Maude still didn't know just what those were or even if Cairn had proclaimed them to Alysanna, but she sensed both answers could be had.

"Intentions?"

"Miss Walker, surely you know that he means to marry you?"

"How would you know such a thing?" The blush burning over Alysanna's face rewarded Maude's fishing.

"He told me."

Alysanna stood in silent, breathless confusion. Why had Cairn confided such a thing, and to Maude, of all people? She hadn't time to consider it now.

"Did you hear what I said? Cairn told me he wishes to marry you."

"I see," Alysanna droned emotionlessly, lacking a clue what to reply.

"Then you do not deny it."

"There would be no point."

"Good. Then, with all this deceit stripped away, we can admit this new story of yours but another lie."

"You still doubt me?"

"What I don't doubt is your commitment to wind your way into Cairn's trusting heart. Miss Walker, if you believe your fancifully dressed confession in any way ends my suspicions, think again. I would not see a man of Cairn's fine mettle married to either a governess or a liar. Nothing you have said today in any way assuages my fears for his fate at your hands. In fact, I have done what I can to warn him off you."

"Pardon me?"

"I spoke with him only last week and confessed my fears. God knows how you've blinded him, what sorcery you've worked, but you succeeded to the extent that he paid me scant heed. Nevertheless, if Cairn will not protect himself, I shall take the task to heart."

"What does that mean?"

"Simply that you can change your story as often and as outrageously as you like. Your wax honey holds no sway with me."

"Then I might as well go."

"I assume you can show yourself out. I should not wish to inconvenience our footman. Unless, of course, you cannot be trusted to the door."

Alysanna's nails dug painfully into her palms, and she fought back the urge to snatch Maude's riding crop and whip her rudeness out of her. If the blond twit thought her some lower-class moll, why not play the role to the hilt? Yet reason prevailed, and Alysanna began toward the door, then stopped.

"Does it occur to you that Cairn may judge me more fairly than you?" she asked tersely.

"Cairn is misguided, but I'll see to correcting his course."

Wishing no more of Maude's pinched, smug face, Alysanna shot past her, giving her elbow a stiff, angry brush in her race for the door.

Her furious behest drew Cabochon from the groom. Free of his tether, the animal threw his head as if he too wanted to flee the Delameres.

Ignoring the groom's laced hands, Alysanna pitched herself unaided onto Cabochon's great height—a feat that, lacking her current rage, would normally have been impossible. Uncaring of her imbalanced seat, she tapped her heels hard against his side, and the two of them blew hard down the oak alley, away from Totten-Hoo.

For miles they raced until white froth dripped from Cabochon's mouth, and even Alysanna's own chest heaved in hard, swelling gasps for air. They slowed their way into a quiet clearing and were suddenly still, the only sound their struggle for fresh wind. Alysanna leaned her face into Cabochon's soft mane.

She had never thought her meeting with Maude would lack fireworks. Yet the display moments ago had exceeded her worst fears. Maude had not only refused the altered tale of her past, but her fury had leapt to new heights with Cairn's proposal. Alysanna could hardly imagine him confessing something so private, yet how else would Maude know?

Her hand flew to her brow as she realized Maude's trickery. She had not known, but was only guessing—until Alysanna had confirmed her fears. Damn! Things were bad enough without her worsening them.

Alysanna didn't doubt Maude's resolve to expose her for a moment. Her hard-set chin and feline eyes spoke more eloquently than any assertions.

Slowly, painfully, as the depths of Maude's commitment to ruin her became clear, Alysanna found the most horrifying realization: there would be no future with Cairn unless she confessed the full, shameful truth. A shudder of fear wound up her spine, making her cold, despite the ride's heat.

She had no choice—she must tell Cairn everything. But would he still love her until she was free? Would he even believe that she was not a murderess? A hot tide of tears rose in her eyes. It was a terrifying gamble—and never in her life had Alysanna had so very much to lose.

CHAPTER
13

Jenny burst from Lily's room and ran down the corridor, her hands clapped over her mouth to stifle a gathering sob. Lily's question had been innocent enough; she had only asked of Jenny's family. How could the girl know that last Monday Jenny had heard that Liam had been killed?

Even now, a week after her mother's letter, it seemed impossible that her only brother was gone. Liam's roguish spirit, shot through with mischief and as flaming as his mop of red hair, could not be cold and dead while he was still so vitally alive in her heart. To believe that he was no more and that his passing had been caused by a senseless carriage accident—it was surely only a nightmare.

Perhaps if Jenny had been able to attend the burial and mourn Liam properly, the truth might have seemed more real. As it was, she had gotten word too late, though had she known in time, the journey still would have been untenable.

Even aboard the fastest coach, it was a three-day trip one way on the turnpike. That doubled, with time to comfort her grieving mother, was a luxury her working schedule disallowed.

She had done well this past year, but only because her handiwork was fast. The ton wanted their gowns when promised—a delayed order would sully her reputation. Grief, Jenny knew, was no perquisite of her social class.

When the mail had brought Duncan's summons two days past, Jenny believed she could manage the appointment at Donegal. It was a day out from London, a night at the Mowbry Inn, and the same journey back. But with Liam's smiling memory shattering her composure, the distance seemed to stretch on forever. Now her hired hackney waited outside, and Jenny took a deep, stiff breath, bracing herself for the trip back to London. It was useless—a surge of agony filled her, and Jenny crumbled in surrender against an alcove in the corridor wall.

The raised gold pargeting pressed against her cheek, and she ground her face against its contours, uncaring of the pain. A tortured moan escaped her throat.

"Jenny?" She whirled to face the voice. It was Duncan.

She looked so fragile, so overwhelmed, that for a moment he thought she would topple forward. He reached out to brace her. "What's wrong?"

Jenny clenched her teeth hard, trying to still her quivering chin. For a moment she was too anguished to answer. Then she managed enough composure to speak. "It's nothing. I'm fine."

Duncan studied her face. "I think not," he pronounced. "Whatever has distressed you, this is no place to discuss it. Come." Still supporting her, Duncan steered Jenny to the hallway's end, then through a door she had not before seen.

Once inside, she realized why—it was Duncan's antechamber, adjacent to his bedroom.

Such apartments were often used as private receiving parlors, but a quick glance around the paneled perimeter revealed closets and mirrors—all the appointments of a dressing room. This place, with its dark walnut walls and personal effects, was too private, too intimate. Jenny felt intensely uncomfortable.

"I must go," she protested, pulling away.

"Jenny, please." Duncan urged her toward a grey settee. Something stilled her urge to flee, and, knowing she was too weak to fight, she sat.

"Now, tell me what's caused this misery."

"It is a family matter," Jenny answered softly, still unsure she could speak without sobbing.

"You family—they are in. . . ." Duncan paused, realizing he had never before asked.

"Northumbria. Near Whithorn. My mother is there. And my brother—" Jenny's hand flew to cover her mouth.

"Here." Duncan offered her a shot of brandy.

Jenny shook her head vehemently, confused. "I can't," she sputtered. For all her need to be near him, Duncan's curt dismissals made clear she was an employee, never a guest. Why now, of all times, was he torturing her with his kindness?

"Drink it." The words came first as a command, then a plea. "It will help."

Jenny caught his eyes, then obliged with an audible gulp of the fiery liquid. Slowly, she lowered the snifter and laced her fingers desperately around it, looking as if she feared its amber bowl would fly out from her hand.

"Better?" Jenny nodded silently. "Now, tell me what's happened."

Jenny cleared her throat and slowly began, hoping that if

she measured her words, her anguish would follow suit. "My brother Liam was killed last month. I just received news."

"Here?" Duncan wondered if she'd heard while at Donegal.

"No, in London. It came up—it was Lily. Not that she meant to, but she asked of him, and . . ." Jenny was sure she'd suffocate if she continued.

Duncan cupped his chin in thought. He'd never asked of Jenny's family, though Lily obviously had. He wondered if his oversight had offended her. "You loved him deeply?"

"Yes," she whispered. "Oh, yes!" Jenny's chest jumped with a sob, upending the snifter in a seeping stain on her grey serge skirt. Her control unraveled, and the crystal glass crashed to the floor. Abandoning any hope of composure, Jenny threw herself backwards across the settee and burrowed her head in the crook of her arm. She did not hear him move, but Duncan was suddenly next to her, his long arms drawing her shaking shoulders close.

"There," he soothed, stroking her sunset hair with an uneasy hand. "It will be all right."

Duncan felt prisoner of his own clumsiness, and he ached for words to assuage Jenny's pain, but her closeness rattled him. Unable to manage anything better, he repeated the litany that all would be well, knowing he had no assurance the promise was true.

He hoped his sympathy might stop Jenny's sobbing, but instead it only increased it, as if in caring, he granted permission for her grief. Jenny's cries tore at his heart, and without thinking, some instinct in Duncan drew her face toward him as he pressed his cheek against her warm, wet flesh.

"Shhhh . . ." he whispered against her ear. Jenny's breath

eased slightly, and Duncan brushed a tiny, almost reverent kiss on her temple. Gently at first, then with increasing need, his lips pressed against her again and again until, in a feverish path, his mouth slid from her cheekbone toward her lips.

He pulled back for an instant, his blue gaze searching Jenny's tear-glistened eyes. Then, driven by a taskmaster too great to challenge, Duncan's lips claimed hers with desperate abandon.

Jenny could hardly fathom what was happening, and she had no wish to. Her grief for Liam had crumbled away, as if it were a facade for her passion, which now swept through her like a wild, angry fire. Instead of anguish, she overflowed with a bittersweet vortex of gratitude and desire. Jenny allowed its force full rein, and her hands clung to Duncan with urgent need.

He wrapped her in his arms, snapping her close against him until she could feel his heart thud against her aching breasts. She felt he had scooped out her soul, then poured it full again with love. Jenny twisted hungrily against him, begging whatever he willed.

Duncan's tongue dared wild, delicious intrusions into her warm mouth, and her fingers wove greedily through his thatch of grey-blond hair. But suddenly he jerked cruelly backwards, severing their kiss and recoiling his embrace. Duncan stared at his palms as if he could scarcely believe what they had just dared.

He cleared his throat with a loud "Harummmph" and stepped backwards, as if Jenny were some dangerous, witchy thing.

"I'm sorry," he mumbled, straightening his coat. "That was . . . entirely improper."

Jenny sat stunned, her lips still warm with the sting of his kiss. What was this fine torment? Moments ago she could scarcely believe that he offered his love, and now it was gone?

"It was—I thought it was what we wanted." It was as close to an accusation as Jenny would get. If Duncan meant to deny their passion, she would not challenge his lie.

"I meant only to comfort you."

"You did," Jenny answered softly, her huge eyes staring at him hopefully.

"Not in that way." Duncan's tone, his stance, everything about him rigidly dismissed her, and Jenny knew that if he could wave his hand and make her vanish, he would do so. "I hope your grief for your brother does not prove too overwhelming. I know it was a great loss."

"I think it was not all I lost," Jenny fired defiantly, straightening her gown as she flew across the room. The door to the foyer slammed thunderously. Peeling off his stiff propriety, Duncan stood dumbfounded, shaking his head.

What had happened? The last moment was such an embarrassing tangle he could hardly remember the single events that comprised it. He had kissed Jenny—that he knew. What in God's name had possessed him? Whatever it was, he would never, never allow it again.

The stage's rear wheel dropped hard in a turnpike rut, bouncing a painful jolt up Alysanna's spine. To her amazement, for the open-benched wagon was the most miserable transport she had ever endured, Alysanna alone seemed to notice. The rest of the Granville servants, oblivious to their hardship, chattered excitedly about their imminent arrival at the Mowbry fair.

Duncan and Lily had left earlier in the calash, and, though Alysanna had briefly hoped that she might keep them company, it was not to be. Duncan dispelled the notion in a cloud of dust, his carriage thundering away as Alysanna stared dejectedly out from the Donegal portico.

Delia, Bridget, John, and the rest of the merry entourage hardly wasted their time longing for a finer conveyance. They were thrilled to have been given the day off for the Whitsun ale, and they sang and played children's finger games to wile away the five-mile ride.

John, who was fond of sport, had talked with boyish glee of last year's skittles in the Nag's Head, but Bridget, with her cook's palate, longed only for a taste from the sweetmeat stall. Delia prayed that the music would be spirited and would draw a good crowd, rife with eligibles "a notch over the laboring poor."

A century past, the Whitsun ale had been sponsored by the church to levy funds for charities. It had done so by mining the locals' personal charity—liquor. But now it had become little more than excuse for a frolic—a day free of the fields' yoke and the manor houses' drudgery. For all who came, though, whether by wagon, coach, or in brightly ribboned farm carts, it was excuse enough.

Gentlemen and their feather-hatted ladies, most of whom had hurled past their lessers' wagons in stylish calashes, sought rustic counterpoint to their high-toned assemblies. For the abject poor—those who worked dawn to dusk days as field villeins to their lords—the games, revelry, and feasting on the green were a respite from a life of hard, relentless toil. For the shopocrats, the ale and the crowds it drew might well have been a business boon, but instead, they became a fine excuse to close their own doors and sample the summer's ribald pleasures.

Alysanna wished that she could share the gaiety. Perhaps, if Hadley came with good news to tell, she yet might. But his failure to answer her letters gave her small hope. She had no assurance that he had even received them, and she half suspected Roberta's treachery.

Alysanna banished the thought; she could not afford such pessimism. Hadley would come and, moreover, with the words she longed to hear.

Her heart pounded wildly at the prospect of reclaiming her freedom, then thudded painfully as she thought of Hadley. Marrying him now, so full of the feelings Cairn stirred in her, would be a shameful lie. Once she was no longer dependent on Hadley's goodwill, she must break their engagement.

The thought filled her with disgrace. Leaving Hadley would be awkward, in any event; waiting until he helped reclaim her identity was downright manipulative. Unlike Roberta, Alysanna was not easy with using others, but what choice had she? Once she was no more a fugitive, she would handle this honorably. For now, she would be lucky to hide the deceit in her eyes.

Alysanna didn't know if the turnpike even crossed here from Wodeby, but she hoped that Hadley could find his way. When she first heard of the ale, it seemed an ideal meeting place. Duncan's tight eye allowed her scant private time, and to set an assignation near Donegal would court disaster. The happy disorder of the Mowbry crowds and the solitude of the parish church would be perfect.

As the Granville wagon thundered and creaked toward town, Alysanna hiked her head out and peered forward. Much of the dirt road from Donegal had been serpentine, its contortion nearly making her stomach pitch. But finally, the dusty highway straightened into a long lime alley, and Alysanna saw the dark stone spire of the Mowbry church rising like a saluting glance on the horizon.

The riders' prattle grew louder once they were inside the town boundaries, then peaked as the lumbering stage pulled close against the mullioned windows of a small stone and thatch cottage. Alysanna saw the ivy bush sign over the door and realized that this must be the Nag's Head Inn. Without so much as a quick good-bye, the Granville servants jumped eagerly into the throes of the mob, their cries of greeting blending with the din.

Alysanna knew Mowbry was small, its craftsmen and field workers counting less than one hundred, men and women both. Yet today the crowd that packed its narrow streets several times exceeded that meager number.

The horde teemed with life and was so tightly wedged that at first Alysanna could see naught but a sea of chip hats and Sunday-best tricornes rolling at an alderman's pace down several main alleys. It was only when she joined the crowd's thick flow that she angled close enough to the stalls for a glimpse of the wares and tasty delicacies a hard-earned wage would buy.

As he had done with the rest of the staff, Duncan had given Alysanna a special shilling allowance for her day out, and as she passed the vendors' bulkheads, she chose, then chose again, how best to spend her small capital. There were mead bowls and caudle cups, a splendid array of laces and ribbons, and, for those wishing a sugary lunch, brandy balls, gingerbread, and ample beer and cider to quench their pastry-fired thirst.

Alysanna pondered her choice, then turned at the sound of a gay laugh to see a young ploughman purchase his sweetheart a gingerbread fairing. He held it teasingly in front of her lips, then claimed a kiss as toll before raising the biscuit to her mouth. The girl, who looked no more than sixteen, took a dulcet bite, then playfully grabbed the boy's hand and dragged him, laughing, into the throng's midst. Alysanna's heart gave a little lurch; such fine, simple pleasures were but memories to her.

Alysanna pushed with determination through the packed mass, her eye wandering to the contests forming in a side clearing. For a prize of snuff, a cadre of wizened dams tested their tolerance for scalding tea, and, in youthful juxtaposition, a legion of long-haired girls doffed their shoes for a foot race, the winner to be awarded a new white smock. Just beyond, the village men dueled at cudgeling and backsword, and, in the adjacent meadow, Alysanna could see several village dandies grooming their mounts for a race she had heard announced for later.

Alysanna often went to such fairs when they came near Briarhurst, and she rued that she was not free to enjoy today's distractions. Yet even if she could not partake, the festivities served her, for they lessened the chance that some penitent would seek out the church and discover her with Hadley.

Finally free of the boisterous crowd, Alysanna raised her eyes to the church spire that loomed like a stony spinster. She straightened her ruffled handkerchief, which had been scraped askew with the horde's jostle, and looked down begrudgingly. She now dressed the governess part well, her modest wine muslin smart enough for a day of celebration, but hardly the eye-catching finery her heart preferred.

Her new style, or lack thereof, made her feel like nothing so much as a practical little mud hen, and as a private, satisfying concession to offset the dowdiness, Alysanna still wore the silk drawers and lace garters no governess could hope to afford. The artifice pleased her, particularly since would-bes like Delia were wont to display what small wealth they pos-

sessed. Smug with her secret, Alysanna considered that, if
her finery were hidden, at least it was genuine.

She mounted the Barnack stone steps to the church's north
porch and pulled on the oak door's twisted handle. Its huge
panel swung wide with a whining creak, offering up a darkness that seemed to refuse her entry.

Alysanna wanted to turn back, but she reminded herself
that the church's shadowy seclusion served her needs. She
stepped into the arch-framed nave, and was relieved to see
that the clerestory's stained windows lit the interior better
than on first impression. She nodded toward the altar and slid
silently into the polished hollow of a nearby pew.

Hadley was nowhere to be seen, and for a moment Alysanna's heart sank on her solitude. If, for whatever reason,
he did not come today, she would be forced to arrange another
assignation, and each effort to reach him jeopardized her
safety. Hoping he was only late, Alysanna tried to collect
herself, praying she could endure her deceit.

The pew backs facing the chancel suddenly shone with a
blast of light, and Alysanna spun fearfully toward the door.
There was no reason for alarm, she assured herself; she was
doing no more than sitting in the church. Whomever her
intruder, she would plead her presence to a moment of devotion. Alysanna squinted at the corona of light, then leaned
sideways over the pew's curved end. Thank God—it was
Hadley.

"Alysanna?" His deep voice echoed through the dank grey
air, and he swept his head from side to side, his eyes not yet
catching her in the dim light.

"Here." She whispered, mindful that others might follow
him in and question their purpose. Hadley stepped toward
her, and Alysanna rose.

"My dear Alysanna." He reached out in what was less inclination than duty. Obligingly, Alysanna allowed his embrace, then recoiled. He smelled of liquor—lots of it.

"Have you been drinking?" she asked, incredulous.

"Only a touch. I could not find you when I first arrived, so I bided my time at the Nag's Head. I had only one," he lied. "A clumsy sot upended his tankard on me."

Alysanna nodded in understanding, then drew Hadley to a remote side pew. His hand felt odd, but it was more than the unfamiliarity borne of their separation. With the false pledge between them, one Alysanna longed to break, their touch struck her as dishonest and improper.

"I'm glad you came," she answered, trying to still her uneasy breath.

Alysanna was anxious to hear news of his search, but Hadley drew back, taking in her full length. "You look . . ."

"A governess," Alysanna finished, not wishing to endure his shocked review of her humble apparel. Hadley stared open-mouthed, and, for a moment, Alysanna felt a tiny bite of anger nip at her heart. It was hardly her fault she was forced to this guise. "Hadley, must you gawk?"

"I'm sorry." He shook his head to stop his staring, but remained surprised. Alysanna had always been a woman of taste and means. He had never seen her so plain, so unadorned. Such modest clothing on others would have lessened the overall impression, yet Alysanna's impassioned beauty was strangely showcased by the simple outfit. "I am merely unaccustomed to seeing you so. I don't know what I expected."

"It is a far cry from my former attire, and this is the least of it. But I cannot bear one more moment without knowing —have you news of Julia's murderer?"

Hadley drew her hands between his and patted them sympathetically. "I have spent my days on little else. There is not a serving maid or footman in all the shire whose wits I haven't plumbed. Yet my heart aches to tell you that thus far, I have found nothing."

"Oh, Hadley!" Alysanna covered her face, pressing her fingertips against her eyelids, as if they could abate her incipient tears.

"There is more," he added.

"More?" She jerked her head up in alarm. "What could be worse?"

"The constable has issued a warrant." Hadley pulled the crinkled paper from his coat pocket and held it out for Alysanna to examine, but she turned away and closed her eyes in refusal.

"For me? You cannot mean there is a warrant for my arrest."

"He is convinced of your guilt, despite my protests. There was too much talk of your fight with Julia. Then, when you disappeared. . . ."

"But I had no choice!" Alysanna protested loudly. "You and Roberta said—"

"I know. If you had stayed. . . ." Hadley's voice drifted off. "I think it would have been a worse fate than that you now endure."

"Yes." Alysanna stifled a lurch of a breath. "But why do you have the warrant? Don't tell me you've succumbed to their suspicions as well!"

"The constable left it with Roberta. I stole it, thinking that the longer it was out of her hands, the safer you'd be. She'll discover it missing, of course, but by then I'll be back."

"Roberta!" Alysanna's eyes crackled with rage. "Of course! 'Twas she who bent the constable's ear. Warrant or no, I'll not trust my fate to her one more minute. I'm going home!''

"No!" Hadley scrambled for an answer, and one popped up obligingly. "It is not only Roberta. There are many who suspect you—your friends, as well. They watch me closely, as if they expect I will come to you. It was risky for me to ride here today."

Alysanna's eyes drifted in panic. "Then, what shall I do?"

"I will continue my search. But 'twould be a lie to say I hold out much hope. As it is, I can't promise when you can return—if at all."

"Hadley, what is it you mean?"

"I can hardly bear to speak the words, and yet I must. Your future lies no more with Briarhurst. It would be unfair to you—for me to hold you to our betrothal."

"What?" Alysanna shook her head, confused.

"We have no choice but to break our engagement, to allow you to pursue a new life."

Alysanna's thoughts fluttered like leaves in a wind gust, too scattered to land. Breaking off their engagement was what she had wanted, even planned for, yet she had never considered that the idea would come from Hadley.

His logic was sound, but Alysanna wondered if his reasoning ran deeper than he disclosed. Was it her well-being he thought of—or was her cause so lost that he thought her an encumbrance? If that were true, she could not count on his aid.

"I have been a problem to you, I know."

"Darling, please." Hadley pressed his head into her palm and sighed heavily. "Do not doubt my affections for you. You have been no burden, only a joy. It is because of that that my conscience will not let me tie your hands by holding you to your promise.

"I swear to move heaven and earth to clear your name and bring you home. Once I do, we can begin again. But if, God forbid, I am unable, I cannot bear knowing I have forced you to a life alone. Promise you won't shackle me with such a shame?"

Hadley popped open one eye, hoping to read Alysanna's mood. This idea had only come to him moments ago, but it was perfect. If he could not have her money, he was best rid of her. And the plan would make clear to Alysanna that she must forget returning. It would all work well—providing his story rang true.

Alysanna grew silent and serious, as if she were debating his pronouncement, though she knew their parting was a fait accompli. It wasn't that he had wounded her heart, but that he had threatened her future by severing their bond. Still, she could hardly hold Hadley to a vow he would break. And he had promised to keep searching. That was what she needed most—that and Cairn's love. Perhaps this turn would work out after all.

"Very well. If you feel we must . . ."

"There is no other choice."

"Yes." Alysanna worked so hard to affect the proper distress that she completely missed Hadley's efforts to do the same.

"Do you think there's any hope of finding him?" Alysanna turned her face hopefully to Hadley as they walked the church's main aisle.

"You are still in my heart, if not my life," he assured her, taking her hand, pleased that his account had been so well received. "I promise I will not rest until all is right."

Alysanna's face softened at Hadley's largesse. Without her promise to marry him, he had no duty toward her. If he lacked Cairn's passion, at least Hadley matched his generosity.

"How can I thank you?" Alysanna jumped to her toes and kissed her heartfelt gratitude against Hadley's cheek. The huge church door suddenly banged inward. A towering silhouette was outlined by a blast of golden light. Alysanna recoiled in fear, then shock. It was Cairn.

"Alysanna?" Her name echoed though the nave like an accusation. Alysanna didn't need to ask if he had seen the kiss; his voice mirrored her guilt.

"Yes." She brushed down the folds of her muslin skirt nervously, as if correcting their disorder could do like for her mind.

"We were just leaving," she chirped, praying Hadley would keep still.

"I can see. A fond farewell?"

The tension strung between them was so thick and oppressive that Alysanna felt she was stuck to the floor. She longed to explain, but willed herself silent, knowing that embroidering the tale would worsen her fate.

"What are you doing here?" she asked cheerfully, hoping her light mood could divert Cairn.

"I might ask you the same," he snapped curtly, crossing his arms as he studied Alysanna's blanched face.

"I came for a moment of quiet."

"Assignation?"

"Cairn!" Alysanna dropped her chin in shame and anger and glowered at him from beneath her brows. "It was entirely chance that I met my friend."

"And who exactly is your friend?" Cairn coated the word with derision. He trained his scrutiny on Hadley, who, for lack of a better notion, stared blankly back.

"This is—" Alysanna struggled to choose between lie or truth. "Hadley Seaham," she finished, unable to decide.

"Viscount Seaham," Hadley corrected, bringing an embarrassing flush to Alysanna's taut face. He reached forward to shake Cairn's hand.

"My pleasure." Cairn leaned his head sideways in study. "I must confess, my lord, that you look familiar. Have we met before? I am Cairn Chatham, duke of Lyddon."

Alysanna bit down painfully into her lower lip. Hadley knew nothing of her involvement with Cairn, and their introduction should not have distressed her. Yet there was something about the way they stared at each other that made her feel she was shrinking. Suddenly, Alysanna wished nothing so much as to sink through the church's planked floor.

"I do not think our paths have crossed," Hadley answered, his voice pulled and strange. Alysanna turned toward him, squinting in expectation of his fists readying for attack. Instead, he only dipped a courteous bow and shot his eyes sideways.

"Do you live nearby, Lord Seaham?"

"I am . . ." Hadley looked likely to finish with the truth, but Alysanna's stern cough stopped him. Apparently, she wished to guard the facts. "I am from another shire."

"Indeed? I'd no idea the Mowbry ale was of such repute."

"It was happenstance that I was nearby. I knew of Alysanna's—Miss Walker's—work here and stopped in the hopes of seeing her."

"Then you should be well pleased since you found her —and, judging from what I saw, in a most affectionate mood."

A small vein in Cairn's neck popped out tensely. Alysanna

had never before seen him quite like this, and his dark mien frightened her.

"We must be going," Alysanna announced. Cairn's choler was palpable. Hadley's mouth parted at Cairn's insinuation, then he took in his rival's imposing height and thought better of a challenge. He preferred Cairn's indignities to a cracked jaw. Unthinkingly, he offered Alysanna his arm, and the gesture made Cairn's eyes burn even hotter.

"Leaving together?" His voice strained under tight rein.

"No!" Alysanna and Hadley resounded in unison, their zealous denial firing more of Cairn's suspicions.

"I mean, Lord Seaham has business nearby. Unfortunately, he cannot stay." Alysanna's eyes implored Hadley to leave.

"Business nearby," Hadley mumbled. "Lord Chatham." He nodded perfunctorily and slid into the din of the fair outside.

Hadley wished only to resume his drinking—beyond Cairn Chatham's balled fist. But his feet froze as he saw the animal pawing the ground at the stone stairs' base. Nuit raised his head on Hadley's approach, his eyes glistening and widening into a frightened, glassy glare.

"You!" Hadley breathed low, then rushed to hide in the boisterous merriment.

Alysanna faced Cairn silently in the clerestory's crimson shadows.

"Well?" His brows twisted in accusation as he scowled at her. He expected an answer.

"What?"

"Do you think I will settle for that terse lie you wove?"

"Exactly what is it you wish to know?" Alysanna was still unnerved by his behavior of moments ago, though now it seemed to soften, as if it were Hadley, not she, who had driven Cairn's ire.

"Why were you kissing him?" Cairn leaned against the pew railing, crossing his arms impatiently.

"I only kissed his cheek." It was true, and moreover, the kiss was given in gratitude, not passion. Alysanna felt her defense was justified.

"It was close enough," Cairn growled.

"You are making too much of this. Hadley is an old friend, that is all."

Cairn rushed toward her, pinching her arms almost painfully. "Then I will allow no such friendships. Make no mistake, as much as I want you, I will not tolerate your dalliances, however innocent you plead them to be. If you are to be my woman—"

"I have not yet said." Alysanna wanted desperately to be Cairn's wife, but she bridled at his foregone conclusion. This possessive hulking was not what she'd bargained for. "You claim rights I have not given you."

Cairn's mouth swept down on hers with demonic need. His arms captured her back, crushing her breasts against him and squeezing a gasp of breath from her throat. As if he were starving and she his sustenance, Cairn cupped her head in his huge hands and tipped it sideways to deepen his kiss.

Alysanna thought she would perish for lack of breath, but she did not resist, content to surrender her fate to his strength. Finally, pulling back slowly, Cairn stared at her, his eyes scorching her with demand.

"You are mine," he whispered. "No one else's. Now, tell me—who is Hadley Seaham?"

Alysanna's breath bolted from her chest, and her eyes glazed under the weight of his stare.

"My fiancé," she gasped, then flung her hands to her face.

CHAPTER
14

❧

"What did you say?" Cairn's question squeezed through clenched teeth, and Alysanna could see a muscle on his jawline twitch.

Now Alysanna was free to wed whom she chose, but, fearing the scene with Hadley had driven Cairn away, her voice was bereft of sound. She searched Cairn's face for exoneration, but he was all stone.

Unable to face him, she fled to the chancel. She scurried behind its protective iron railing and braced her hands on the smooth top bar, as if readying herself for defense.

"I asked you a question." Cairn's voice was controlled, but soaked with impatience.

"Hadley is my fiancé. Was," she quickly corrected, raising her palms up like a shield. "He asked to end our betrothal."

Alysanna's eyes pleaded for understanding, but Cairn's offered only more questions. "I should imagine that would distress you."

"No. I mean . . . yes, I am distressed, but not by that."
Cairn stared back implacably. Clearly, nothing less than a
full confession would do. Alysanna collected her thoughts as
she walked toward the altar. This moment was premature;
she had not thought to spill her secrets so precipitously. But
again fate had forced her hand, and Alysanna knew she must
bend to its will.

Cairn's voice shot at her from behind. It was steady, so
strangely even that Alysanna feared her battle lost from the
start. "I think you'd better tell me the whole story."

Alysanna nodded silently. She tried to begin, but a tight,
painful band constricted her chest, crushing her reply. How
could she expect his understanding? What balm of words
could heal her raw, ugly past?

Even if she had not killed Julia, she had still intended to
murder the stranger. Was poor aim a legitimate defense? Her
heart was that of an assassin; did Cairn love her enough to
forgive?

"Alysanna?"

"I'll tell you everything." She spun to face him. Cairn
stood at the nave's front pew, and Alysanna was glad for the
distance between them. It made her confession easier, as if
her words would soften before they struck him.

"I am not who you think," she spoke.

"So I gathered." Cairn nodded toward the spot where he
had seen her kiss Hadley.

"No, not that, though I suppose it's reason enough for
your indictment of me." Alysanna leaned against a waist-
high crypt adjacent to the choir stall and pressed her hands
against its cold effigy.

"My name is not Alysanna Walker. It's Wilhaven—Lady
Alysanna Wilhaven. My family—what little remains of it—

lives east of here, near Bedford. It was there, at our estate of Briarhurst, that my stepsister Julia was killed this spring.'' The memory made her eyes ice with fear, and Alysanna's voice trembled.

"There was a ball that night. Julia and I fought in public over foolish matters. When I returned home to make amends . . .'' Alysanna choked on the words, burying her face in her hands. Her flesh felt wintry, like the crypt.

She had not recounted the tale in its entirety since her flight from Briarhurst. Telling it now made her shudder, as if a ghost wind whistled through her. A sob began in her belly, then swelled upward. Whether it was Julia, Hadley, or Briarhurst she mourned, Alysanna didn't know. Her legs threatened to crumble and she feared she would collapse on the floor's hard stone.

Yet a small voice rallied her. *Nothing is lost—not yet.* While Cairn stood before her, still listening, there was hope he would understand, even forgive her. Alysanna cleared her throat and drove her head upward.

"Julia had been murdered. The man was still there. I shot him.'' Fearing the sight of Cairn's face would silence her, Alysanna pressed on like an animal, fleeing in terror, not knowing where, only sure she must run.

"He was not killed. Not that I didn't wish it—but my mark was off. When he stirred, I fled. Unfortunately, so did he. As he rode away, I thought I'd escaped.

"Only later did I realize I'd have no freedom as long as he lived. I was witness to his crime, and I became his new quarry. I left Briarhurst to flee both him and my stepmother.'' Alysanna broke to catch her breath, longing for a word from Cairn to mark his mood. There was only silence.

"My stepmother, Roberta, coveted my inheritance. She

threatened to accuse me as Julia's killer, hoping I would leave
and make Briarhurst hers alone. I thought it was idle blus-
tering, until Hadley came today with a warrant for my arrest.

"Now . . ." Alysanna's voice broke like shattered crystal.
"There is almost no chance to return. If the murderer doesn't
find me, the constable will, and I shall be hanged. Only
Hadley's kindness parts me and my fate. If he can locate
Julia's killer, then perhaps. . . . If not. . . ."

Alysanna threw herself atop the crypt's folds, her head
bowing over its cold, hard marble. She pressed into its eerie
effigy, her frame racked with long, aching sobs.

She was too frightened to rise—afraid to see that Cairn
had fled, disgusted with her sordid tale. What reason did he
have to want her now? At worst, he would think her a murderess; at best, a liar. Who would want either in a wife?

His arms wrapped around her, turning and lifting her crumpled form. Incredibly, he neither struck nor reprimanded her,
only pressed his head close against her ear. "Shhhh." Alysanna had thought her misery at full vent, but now she shook
with even greater force, her voice stretched into paper-thin
wails. *Why is he doing this?* She could not bear his pity.

She wrenched back, her hands balling into fists as she shook
them. "Have you nothing to say?"

Cairn's inscrutable expression heightened her fury. *What
is the matter with him? Why doesn't he answer?*

"Cairn!" The lonely darkness of the shadowy aisle all but
swallowed her voice.

"What do you want me to say?"

"Surely the shame I've confided shocks you."

Cairn cocked one brow at her, and lifted his hand to stroke
her tears. "Indeed. I am shocked that you seem to think all
this should make some difference."

"It doesn't?" she sputtered.

"Alysanna." He smiled, shaking his head. "When I found you with Hadley, I was wildly jealous. Seeing another man hold you was like a thorn in my heart. But now, knowing the odyssey that delivered you here, how can I do else but love you more?"

"You forgive me?" Alysanna was incredulous.

"For being a victim of fate? There is no need."

"But I have lied to you."

"You seem overly eager to dissuade me. Is this an effort to refuse my suit?"

"No," she hurried, resting her palms flat against his chest. "It is only that . . ."

"Yes?"

"I thought you would cast me out when you knew the truth. A liar, perhaps a murderess—surely this is not what you bargained for."

"I bargained for you with all your twists and turns. It would disappoint me to find you less."

"Then you would have me still?"

"Any way I can."

"But the warrant—" Alysanna shook her head quickly, as if Cairn had failed to comprehend her full confession. "They want to arrest me. If Hadley is unable to find the murderer, I will be a fugitive, perhaps convicted and condemned."

Cairn took her chin in his hands, his eyes dark and grave. "Don't you think I can protect you?"

At that instant Alysanna felt they were indeed invincible —that no force, human or otherwise, could wrest them apart. She leaped to her toes and pressed her cheek in desperate gratitude against his neck. "My darling," she murmured, sure it was no less than an act of God's mercy that Cairn could forgive her transgressions. But the memory of Maude drained her happiness.

Alysanna let go a small moan, and Cairn cupped her face. "More?"

Alysanna nodded tearfully. "There is Maude."

"Maude? What in God's name has she to do with this?"

"She means to expose me. Surely you knew?"

"I know she believes she has my best interests at heart and that her efforts are misguided."

"Misguided or no, they may prove my undoing. If I am to stay hidden, she must be stopped. The trail to Briarhurst is all too easy. 'Twould not be difficult to learn that the authorities want me."

"I'll handle Maude."

"But how?"

"Trust me. And say that you'll marry me."

"I can't."

"Alysanna."

"Think on it. How can I hide as duchess to you? It would make me all too easy to find—the constable, Julia's killer. . . ."

"The constable will not journey from his shire, and the rest is perfect. We'll wed quickly and draw out your dark murderer. Then all this can be put to proper rest. But until then, I want your promise that you won't leave."

"Above all else, I couldn't bear to go on without you!" Alysanna clung to him hungrily.

"Come." Cairn offered his hand.

Alysanna answered with questioning eyes, but she obeyed, walking forward. A crimson cloth spilled from the altar, and, as they reached it, Cairn turned Alysanna, encircling her hands.

"Soon, we will seal this properly. Until then, this will do." He took a breath, then trained his gaze on her lovingly. The church's stone was cold and dark, but suddenly Alysanna felt bright and warm, as if bathed by a radiant light.

"I take you, Alysanna, as my wife. To my house, to my bed—to the innermost places inside my heart. I promise with my body and being to cherish you, protect you against all evil—even past this earthly struggle."

Alysanna's eyes glistened with joy. Cairn seemed everywhere—on her flesh, in her soul, coursing through her blood. His words were no deacon's liturgy, etched in law, but they bound her to him more irrevocably and surely than any ceremony.

Whatever befell her would now be bearable if she were his. Cairn looked down in expectation, but the tide of emotion swelling inside Alysanna stole her breath.

"Alysanna?"

"Yes," she whispered, "oh, yes," then pressed her lips to his.

"Your services are no longer needed." Duncan ripped a note from his yellow ledger and shoved it at Jenny, who stood as still as if her feet were bolted to the floor.

"I'm sorry?" Her face was blank. Surely she had misheard.

"I said your services as Lily's mantua-maker are no longer required. This should cover your expenses." Again he thrust out the paper, and it shook in his hand. "I have included the cost of all gowns ordered but not yet delivered. There is also a severance bonus."

"Lord Granville, I still don't understand."

Duncan's face caught fire with embarrassment. He had

hoped Jenny would take the money and leave. Apparently, he had to be more forceful.

"Good grief, woman, will you make me say it? You're dismissed! I have engaged another seamstress to manage Lily's gowns."

Jenny looked as if he had struck her. "What have I done? Lily has always been pleased with my work."

Duncan slammed the check angrily atop his desk and locked his arms behind him, striding away. "Lily is a child—hardly fit to make decisions as to proper attire."

"Are you suggesting my gowns were improper?"

"Yes," Duncan, blurted, relieved she had spoken the accusation. "Yes, indeed. Too—suggestive for a child Lily's age."

Jenny's mind inventoried each dress she had made, but not one suited Duncan's charge. "What specifically? Too low in the front? Too tight? Too garish? Whatever your cause, it is fair that I know."

"Miss O'Malley, I have no interest—or obligation, for that matter—in discussing the particulars. As your employer, it is enough that I have been displeased with your work. Now, take your payment and leave!"

Duncan's trumped-up ruse suddenly came clear to her, and Jenny narrowed her eyes in fury. "How dare you!"

He spun about sharply, glowering. "What did you say?"

"How dare you dismiss me with such an excuse! No work I have done displeases you. It is another matter, I think, that has your dander high."

"Is it necessary to have you shown out?"

"Not if you give me the truth. Which is, I believe, that it was our—incident—that now makes you wish me gone, not some ridiculous neckline."

"That," Duncan sputtered, shifting his eyes nervously,

"was a mistake. I will offer you the courtesy of an apology, but the error does not mitigate our current situation."

Jenny had tried, but had been unable to surrender the hope that Duncan might come to look favorably on their kiss. Yet she never imagined he would twist his passion as cause for her dismissal.

"How can you deny it? We both know that what happened between us is the issue. Whatever you think me guilty of, there was no crime in taking pleasure in your arms—even if you now claim it a mistake."

Jenny could hardly believe her bold words. But if Duncan were committed to dismissing her, she could only leave knowing she had spoken the truth. "I thought it was something we both wanted."

"It was . . . a base desire." Duncan rued his choice of words, but could think of no other way to dismiss her query.

Jenny's choler rose at his insulting description. "Well, a pitiful sampling of that, then. If you think me wanton, then why did you stop?"

"Miss O'Malley, please!"

"Please what? I've nothing to lose now, have I? Not my employ, nor sweet Lily—not even your fine opinion of me, which seems to have decayed into sad disdain."

"Very well. If candor is to be our stock in trade, I too will speak honestly. If I wanted you, surely I would not have checked my attentions. I had a change of heart."

"Yes. But not of what you wanted—only of what your strict honor would allow."

"And what is that to mean?"

Jenny took a breath, and a miserable vertigo swept through her, as if one incautious step could send her tumbling off a high cliff.

"I think your feelings for me are in keeping with my own."

She marshaled more courage, then exploded. "I never thought I could speak it out loud, but I love you. And since honesty comes so hard to your heart, I'll tell you that I think you might feel the same for me—were I other than a humble mantua-maker."

"You have pushed my patience too far!"

"Hardly far enough. You are a narrow-minded, starched snob. I know our match is unsuitable. I was born poor and won't die much better. But you are worse than a parvenu— you are a liar. To my heart and to your own."

"Enough of your prattle. Get out—now!"

Jenny was shocked how little fear Duncan raised in her. Last month, even yesterday, such a harsh tone would have sent her scurrying like a frightened cat. Now, Duncan's rage unshackled her chains, and, despite the splitting pain cleaving her heart, she felt freer and better than she had since she'd started catering to the mighty ton.

"If you wish me gone, I'll gladly go. But I warn you, I won't return."

"That will be in keeping with my wishes. Take your payment. I should not wish to have any accounts owing."

Jenny squinted furiously, disbelieving his insult. "There is no debt between us that pounds can settle."

"You act as if one indiscretion were a promise!"

"Here's a promise for you—you won't ever see me again." Jenny whipped away so quickly that her serge skirt snapped. She dashed like a deer from Duncan's parlor, the door booming to its jamb behind her.

Duncan stared at the note on his desk. How much easier it would have been had she at least taken the money. He could not bear a debt to her, yet somehow he knew that even were the paper in her purse, he'd still feel their score unsettled.

Now Duncan realized how naive he had been in hoping

this would go easily. He knew Jenny was attached to Lily. What he had not registered was the apparent affection she held for him—a fact that might not have escaped his attention, had he not been so busy curtailing his own desires.

It was only lust, he assured himself, nothing more that drew him to her. What else was possible in such an ignominious pairing? Yet were this so, why did his heart cry out in anguish, all life drained from its core?

If Jenny were only higher born. If she had been. . . . Duncan snapped his head sideways. What was this indulgent reverie? He had behaved properly, according to what was expected of him. No woman was worth repeating his grandfather's penance. And there was not only his own fate to consider—there was Lily's, as well. A stepmother of such rough stock—it was unthinkable.

He had done the right thing—he knew it. He would repeat it until it rang true.

Jenny was beyond tears. She leaned silently against Donegal's stone, as if its cold pores could soak out her ache. Her eyes were benumbed and vacant, and, as Cairn's carriage pulled against the portico, he froze at her otherworldly expression.

"Jenny?" Her eyes rose to meet him, but without greeting. Didn't she recognize him?

"Jenny, come with me." Whatever was wrong, Cairn couldn't leave her here. With a bracing arm, he drew her inside, then to the gallery. But no sooner had he seated her than she sprang to her feet, bolting toward the door.

"I can't stay!"

"Wait!" Cairn caught her wrist and forced her back gently. "Whatever's happened, you're in no state to leave. Now tell me what's wrong."

The gallery's door flung wide with a bang. Alysanna, apparently expecting Cairn, smiled fleetingly, then saw Jenny. Something about the strange tableau smacked of disaster, and Alysanna closed the door, then rushed toward her.

"What goes on?"

"Would that I knew." Cairn shrugged.

The sight of Alysanna jolted Jenny back to earth, and she jumped up, nearly toppling her friend with a tight, desperate hug. Jenny mumbled something, but her sobs ate the words, and Alysanna could make out nothing save Duncan's name. It was enough. Surely the lout had insulted her again.

"What did he do?"

"I must find my carriage!" Jenny sobbed, trying to pull free.

"Why? What has happened?"

"He ordered me from the house—I have been dismissed."

Alysanna cradled Jenny's trembling head and lovingly stroked her red twist of hair. If what Jenny said were true, this time Duncan had outdone even his own worst manners. Alysanna's lips parted in shock, then she smothered her reaction, not wanting to upset Jenny more. One of them had to stay calm.

"You must sit."

"But, if he finds me here. . . ."

"He will answer to me," Cairn assured her.

"How did this happen?" Alysanna snuggled next to Jenny and pulled her close.

Jenny wiped her soaked cheek with the back of one shaking hand and looked up. "He claims my work was inferior."

Alysanna couldn't suppress her astonishment, and she canted Jenny's chin up to see her eyes. "What? That's preposterous! Lily has always had the finest gowns."

"No," Jenny gasped, shaking her head, "it was not that. That was merely an excuse for. . . ." She stopped, her eyes jerking toward Cairn.

"Yes?" Alysanna urged.

"I cannot say."

"You can speak safely with Lord Chatham."

"I will not repeat what you tell me," Cairn assured her.

Jenny drew a ragged breath and began as best she could. "Lord Granville kissed me."

Both Alysanna's and Cairn's eyes widened at the disclosure.

"Then, why are you crying? Wasn't this what you wanted?" Alysanna asked.

"He claimed it a terrible mistake. Then he dismissed me."

Alysanna threw Cairn a look that spoke her disgust. She knew she could not stand another moment under the vile man's roof.

"He discharged you because of his own indiscretion?"

"It was hardly indiscreet," Jenny answered, unable to bridle her candor. "It seemed that we both enjoyed it very much."

Alysanna shook her head incredulously. "So you were right, after all."

"What conspiracy is this?" Duncan demanded furiously. Hearing voices from the foyer, he stormed the gallery like a battle chieftain. Sensing the siege, Jenny wrenched herself free and rushed past him, nearly knocking Duncan over as she fled.

"I want you gone!" He hurled the words at her.

His dictum echoed unanswered down the wall lined with tight-faced Granvilles and, with no more Jenny to absorb his wrath, Duncan stood pink-faced and blustery, seeking another target.

"What's this?" he asked, waving his arms wildly at Cairn and Alysanna, who stood close together.

"Jenny says you dismissed her. Is this true?" Alysanna stood with arms akimbo.

Fury dropped like a curtain over Duncan's taut face. How dare a governess address him so! He stepped forward, stalking her.

"To your room at once," he yelled. "I will not reward such impertinence with an answer!"

"Neither will you insult my fiancée!"

Duncan whirled toward Cairn, his mouth opening more in stupid than shocked effect. "Fiancée?" Duncan looked as though a gentle push would tip him.

"Alysanna and I are to be married. Save your abuse for those who will tolerate it. We will not."

"Cairn, is this some foul jest?"

"Hardly. I should think you, of all people, Duncan, would not be surprised. You seemed to entertain the notion even before us. You might even claim credit. Your obstacles may have prompted our rise to the challenge."

Duncan shuddered visibly at the thought. God forbid that, in any small way, he might have encouraged this unfitting match.

"We had hoped to tell you under calmer circumstances. As it is, your outlandish behavior made that impossible."

Alysanna bit her lip to keep still. How she longed to give Duncan a piece of her mind, but it would be better to let Cairn handle this.

"I . . . I . . ." Duncan sputtered like a hot teakettle.

"Alysanna." Cairn pulled her close, then planted a gentle kiss on the crown of her head. "If you will excuse us, Duncan and I have matters of our own to discuss. I shall see you later?"

"I'll be in the garden." Alysanna smiled, then threw Duncan a prickly stare. "Assuming I am not sent packing." Given Duncan's wild mood, Alysanna half expected he would follow her upstairs and fling her possessions into the courtyard.

Duncan flicked his hand toward the door, uselessly dismissing Alysanna after she'd gone. He collapsed wearily onto Jenny's bench.

"Cairn—have you gone mad?"

"Only mad with love. I don't imagine that's something you understand."

"I understand lust well enough. But marriage, Cairn! Good lord, she's a governess. I tell you, if you must have her, fine. But don't muddle this up with a wedding."

"Not everyone, Duncan, shares your morals. I would ask no such thing of Alysanna without my promise in return."

"So, nothing I say can change your mind?" Duncan wore an incredulous expression, which only deepened at Cairn's silence. "And this has all happened under my roof. I feel downright cuckolded."

Cairn realized the faults he'd so long overlooked were no longer bearable in a man pretending his friendship. He would not stand one more hypocritical moment at Donegal.

"Save your distress. Alysanna and I will leave tonight."

Just now understanding the damage he had wrought, Duncan struggled to soften his hasty words. "Come, man, that's unnecessary. It's just. . . . well, anyway, your quarters at Foxhall aren't finished. Where would you go?"

"Is it so shocking that I'd prefer a cold room to your cold company?"

"Cairn! You speak as if we're through!"

"We're close enough, though I would claim privilege to offer one parting piece of advice—on Jenny."

Duncan's face hardened. "I don't wish to discuss Jenny,"

he warned sternly. "Certainly not with you, given your own impropriety."

"However I behave, I know better than to deny my heart for some foolish set of my head. Do you think love's so easily found?"

"Love? What has that to do with Jenny?"

"Duncan, of all you are, I've never thought you unfair. You know the charges against her are false. Don't perjure yourself by denying it."

"I told you, I won't discuss it. Can I make myself more clear?"

"What's clear, from your vehement denial, is that you love her, and yet you foolishly let her go. This snobbery will cost you your heart. Jenny's no highborn lady, but neither any man's fool. Her carriage is still in the driveway. If you hurry, you can catch her."

"I'll do no such thing!" Duncan crossed his arms obstinately, looking as though a draught team couldn't wrest him free.

"Very well. Keep lonely company with your silly, high morals. Alysanna and I will start to pack."

Cairn strode from the room, allowing Duncan time to stop him, but no pace would bend his inflexibility.

Duncan sat doggedly silent, fully besieged. Cairn and Alysanna married—his best friend and his governess, gone in one fell swoop. Then there was Jenny. Duncan leaned his head into his hands and felt a small, painful pluck at his heart.

CHAPTER
15

❦

Foxhall rose like a tawny dream on the horizon. The russet stone of its tall columns glistened in the afternoon sun, like distant candles glowing at the end of the avenue that marked the estate's formal approach.

Cairn's phaeton sped past the twin borders of conical yews, standing like a line of green sentries on the boulevard's flanks, and Alysanna realized the tremendous size of the manor itself. When it had first risen at the roadway's end, she had thought it near. It was only as Cairn's team cantered on, still far from its destination, that she understood that the house had been so long visible only because of its huge dimensions. Alysanna had known Cairn to be a man of means, but had never realized he was this rich.

"It's quite large," she spoke shyly, scooting sideways on the leather seat, as if his great wealth suddenly made her uneasy.

"I'm afraid it's my mother's doing. It's quite an embarrassment, really. She is French, you know."

"I didn't."

"Perhaps there is still some mystery about me, then."

"Perhaps, indeed," Alysanna answered, considering how truly little she knew of Cairn's past.

"Mother could not shake the notion of a grand chateau, and when my father began to renovate the old estate, her taste got the better of him. It's a bit of a pastiche. The cornerstone is Roman. There is even a hillock behind the manor where a donjon stood. The original house was deeded to my great-great-grandfather, the duke, by Queen Elizabeth. To the design's detriment, the Chathams have forced their idiosyncratic improvements on it ever since."

"Your family does not live here now?"

"My father is dead—a fever he caught while shipping sugar from Jamaica. Since his death, my mother rarely returns. She says the stone holds too much of her heart. She and my sister Yvette, who is six years my junior, keep to mother's Loire chateau. It is best for them, but not for me. When Father died ten years ago, I chose to stay."

"I did not know you had a sister."

"She is twenty-three. Quite the toast of Paris, to hear Mother tell, but more French than English. Of all the living Chathams, I alone can endure the English winter."

"It is a large home for a man alone." Alysanna's eyes widened as their phaeton bounced through the portals of the tall iron gate.

"Yes. But for most of the season, I keep company in London. When that's done, I sequester myself in Foxhall's west wing. It's small enough to manage, and better suits my needs than the house's heart, with its empty rooms and echoing halls.

"It was in the western addition that a wild spark set this winter's blaze. The workmen have been attending to it, but the repairs are not nearly through. I had planned to stay at Duncan's until all was done. As it is, we'll have to choose a room elsewhere, though wherever we stay shall not want for heat." Cairn gave Alysanna's waist a gentle squeeze and leaned into her, nibbling her ear.

"Cairn, please!" Alysanna nodded toward his driver.

"Charles will not mind."

"But I will! I am not accustomed to such public displays."

Cairn squinted at her, smiling. "Has my wild governess turned suddenly proper?"

"Please, no more of that miserable ruse," she sighed. "At least, not with you."

"It's only that I liked your spirit so cloaked. Promise me our marriage won't make you grow staid."

The mention of their wedding made Alysanna stiffen. She still feared exposure once she became Cairn's duchess.

"I only hope, as your wife, I'll be allowed to grow old."

Cairn sighed in exasperation. "Surely you do not still fear for your fate?"

"I fear only the constable's warrant—and the face of a killer I still do not know."

"Only Hadley Seaham knows you're here. And if you can trust him, as you say . . ."

"I can, I'm sure."

"Then, your sleep should be sound. If Julia's killer seeks you, so much the better. I am ready to meet him—and no harm will come to you under my roof. Trust?"

Alysanna smiled her accession, but a worried look again swept across her. "Cairn! We have not even thought to the ceremony. I am at my majority, but there has been no publishing of the banns! Shall we make the ride to Scotland?"

"Hush, love," he answered, stroking her cheek. "It is taken care of. I did not think you would wish the three-day trip—or perhaps it was merely that I couldn't wait, so I dispatched word to the rector this morning. We shall be married tonight."

"But how? There has been no reading. The banns must be public to make it legal."

"We could wait to have them read, but that would mean three weeks more. Frankly, I am unsure how to properly lodge you during that time. Duncan's is no longer possible. Last night there was miserable enough. And though it would please me greatly to keep you here, there is no chaperone. Of course, you have already sullied your reputation by agreeing to wed me. You probably could not worsen it with our tongue-wagging arrangement."

Alysanna cringed at the prospect of living together unlawfully. They had broken enough rules of propriety already. "I should not wish any undue attention brought to bear on us. But what else is there?"

"The Chathams have always been patrons of the rectory. Parson Fulton has agreed to a slightly irregular ceremony."

"Irregular? Does that mean illegal?"

"Alysanna, you behave as if you doubt my intent. I wish you bound to me body and soul. It is irregular only in that the banns have been waived. The ceremony will serve. And, if it suits you, we can arrange later, in Scotland or anywhere else you choose, to repeat our vows. In fact, I rather like the idea. I shall require you to speak your obedience monthly, lest you forget your commitment."

Alysanna missed Cairn's jest—her peace of mind snagged on this new complication. Even if Cairn bought the parson, someone was still sure to question the propriety of such an arrangement. Yet she had hardly clung to convention of late—and Cairn was right that unless they wished the six-day drive to Scotland and back or an embarrassing wait for the banns, there was little to do but acquiesce. She shrugged gamely.

"I suppose, of all my sins, an irregular ceremony will be the least."

Cairn smacked a satisfied kiss on her cheek.

"Good. Then we shall wed tonight!"

A smile crossed and fled from Alysanna's face. "But I have no clothes, no proper attire. I had always thought . . ." Alysanna turned her head so Cairn could not see her tears. She had dreamed all her life of a grand, fitting ceremony. This was not to be it.

"Come love, what?"

"I had not thought my wedding to be some seedy, midnight affair." ·

Cairn's brows furrowed. He had considered only how to marry her quickly and safely. How stupid that he had not considered the cost to her maidenly dreams.

"You shall have exactly what you wish. Will you trust me?"

"But, if the ceremony is to be tonight, how is it possible to. . . ."

Cairn pressed his finger in silence against her lips, then touched a slow, warm kiss to Alysanna's mouth. "Trust me?" She could not argue with him when he came so close. Alysanna nodded her agreement, then jerked her head upwards as the horses' hooves clattered over the cobblestones of the arched stone bridge that spilled into Foxhall's main courtyard.

Now the house loomed impossibly tall, its myriad columns giving more the appearance of an ancient Roman temple than a Georgian manor house. A knotted parterre, which Alysanna knew to be French in design, lay in the main portico's lap. In the center of a low box hedge stood a three-tiered fountain, its center giving rise to an heraldic angel.

The house lay like a frosted cake before her, and its great breadth made clear why Cairn chose to live only in one wing. Two huge sections stretched sideways from its core, each partitioned into smaller, though still mammoth ells. On the portico's sides, the facade curved gently, cradling a quadrant of roses and cotton lavender, these too dissected by twisting hedge knots. The design was formal, but, unlike Donegal's off-putting strictness, Foxhall's pink blossoms and laughing fountains beckoned them closer.

"Duchess?" Cairn offered his hand as Alysanna stepped from the phaeton.

"Not yet, my lord."

"Not soon enough. Come." He led Alysanna up bleached steps into the main foyer. As she entered the hall, her feet stuck in awe to the floor's parqueted marble.

Above her, a Venetian dome painted with Icarus's flight shone as if his sun were real, its brilliant colors spiraling rings of light down onto the harlequined floor. Beneath, endless marble took form in Corinthian pillars and Carrara alcoves, the niches' glossy skin spidered with black.

Gilded plaster trophy panels held sway over crimson cushioned benches, and statuary stood everywhere, some full forms, others busts atop snowy pedestals pressed with gold leaf. Alysanna had been born to the manor, but this exceeded her wildest dreams.

"A bit much, no?" Cairn smiled wryly, embarrassed by the excess.

"It is quite impressive."

"Well, do with it as you wish. Shall we tear it down for thatch and stone?"

"Cairn, please! It is only that I was not prepared for such opulence."

"All its grandeur pales against you." Alysanna tipped her head sideways. "I've made you blush!" Cairn gasped in feigned surprise, coaxing Alysanna into a smile.

"If I am to be duchess of Lyddon, I will grow accustomed enough to manage. But more than your fortune, what I long for is a bath and a meal."

Cairn laughed and led Alysanna up one split of the double staircase to the quarters above. At the hallway's end, he pushed a mahogany door in on an exquisite china blue bedchamber.

"My mother's. Yours until our wing is restored. I think her closet might hold suitable garb. If memory serves, you are close in size. Her gowns are the second door down. First to your left is the bath. I'll call Mildred to draw some water. If Father were still with us, he'd smile to know mother's special plunge bath will see some use. He thought it an outrageous extravagance."

Alysanna felt much the meek governess again. She had heard of such huge baths, but had never seen one.

"The bath—one steps in entirely?"

"Altogether. It is large enough for us both, should you prefer."

"I can manage." Alysanna shot back a playful smile, then cocked her head questioningly.

"Take your leisure. I'll await you and our man of the cloth downstairs. Dinner will be sent up so you can prepare. We'll stay supper 'til after our vows."

"Yes," Alysanna agreed softly.

"After that, we'll set about each appetite in turn." Cairn brushed a soft kiss against her lips, then laid Alysanna's traveling bag on a nearby bench before he left.

Alone in the huge room, Alysanna spun around giddily, then collapsed on the bed's brocaded cover, her heart feeling as if it would burst with joy.

At first Alysanna was loath to enter the bath at all. It was rumored that such total immersion was not to one's health, and the stone tub was so large that it looked more like a pool than a proper bathing appliance.

Still, once Mildred left, Alysanna slipped bravely into the steaming center and soon found herself not only at ease, but in fact quite pleased with the bath's vast size. She could stand nearly upright and still stay immersed, and the tub's length allowed her to actually glide from end to end. Like a frolicking child, Alysanna kicked and dipped, floating her auburn hair like a rush atop the water's bubbly froth.

By all rights, the hot soak should have enervated her. But her heart still fluttered thinking of the ceremony to come, and, when she was done, Alysanna bounded energetically from the bath's sunken stone. Her hearth was lit and supper laid temptingly near the fire's edge.

She pulled on a linen sack gown that had been set out for her and settled with a contented sigh into a niche by the hearth. The food platter bore a cold haunch of venison, flour pudding, and, for dessert, fresh gooseberries and nectarines. A goblet to the tray's right glistened with ruby claret, and Alysanna silently thanked whatever housemaid prepared it for the help in calming her jangled nerves.

She took a drink, and, as she set down the glass, something clinked in its bowl. Alysanna lifted the cup against the light. There, floating in the claret's well, was a huge, glistening ruby.

She fished it free, then, using her napkin to wipe the stone clean, raised its oval in front of her eyes. The ring was dazzling in size and beauty, but the fortune it would fetch meant nothing to her. It mattered only that it was a gift from Cairn—his first true present to her. Alysanna choked back a swell of surging emotion and settled the heavy stone slowly on her finger.

Her appetite, which had been hearty moments ago, now fled. When she finally forced herself back to the meal, sure she would not last the evening lacking sustenance, Alysanna found a second, then third surprise.

Peeking flirtatiously from under the Wedgwood lay a matching pair of earrings, their round ruby clips dripping huge, tear-shaped diamonds. On the plate's far side, a fiery necklace curled under the bone china's edge. The choker echoed the earrings' pattern, its ring of cerise stones circled by diamond suns that dangled their own sparkling pear-shaped fruit.

Alysanna abandoned all thought of food and rushed to the pier glass mirror. The gems caught the candlelight and arced it back to the mirror, making her flesh luminous. She had never seen herself look like this, yet she knew it was not jewels, but Cairn's love that made her glow.

"Is she ready?" Cairn studied Mildred with the seriousness of a man about to risk all he owned on one throw of the dice.

"As ready as she'll be, milord. Oh, 'tis a pity the dowager duchess isn't here to see her only son wed." Mildred's plump face eased into a motherly smile.

"I'm sure you can remember all the details to tell." He laughed and patted her back.

Cairn straightened his black velvet waistcoat nervously, and his rattled demeanor drew Mildred's eye. "It's easy as shellin' peas—you'll see. My John and me, we did it wi' nary a glitch."

"I'm sure, Mildred. It's just that this is my first wedding, and I very much intend it to be my last."

Mildred's laugh bounced over the foyer, then fell at the vision on the stairs' uppermost landing. Cairn lifted his gaze, and Alysanna filled his mind.

She looked less mortal than dream. Her white gown resembled elegant spun sugar. Cairn knew the dress must be his mother's, for Alysanna had brought no such finery with her, yet the gown's curves and flounces looked molded for her shape alone.

The sweeping satin skirt was embroidered with a blaze of silk flowers and parted in front, revealing a gauze panel layered with lacy white ruche. A beribboned stomacher, matched by bow-capped sleeves, drew Cairn's approving eye, and his stare lingered on her rosy swell of bosom as it peeked just over the bodice's low neck. Gilding an already perfect lily, Lady Chatham's own wedding jewels burned like crimson fire on Alysanna's flesh, making her skin look warm and soft, molten to touch.

She stepped down the stairs slowly, her eyes locked on Cairn's and her rosebud mouth canted in a shy, nervous smile. As she reached the foyer, Alysanna brushed a kiss against Cairn's cheek, and he caught the scent of her freshly washed hair, rife with the white roses strewn through its curls.

"The jewels were made for you." Alysanna's hand flew to their warm weight on her throat. "Lady, you steal my very breath." He slid a soft kiss down her neck.

"Your lordship."

Alysanna's eyes flew to the strange, stern voice and she saw that its surpliced owner was the parson.

"Father Fulton. May I present the Lady Alysanna. Soon, with your good ministrations, the Lady Alysanna, duchess of Lyddon."

"My pleasure." The rector dipped a low bow, but could not wrest his eyes from Alysanna's radiance. "It seems Lord Chatham is even more fortunate than the circumstances of his fine birth have allowed."

Alysanna dipped her eyes appreciatively, then leaned forward and whispered. "Sir, this ceremony—it is according to law, is it not?"

Father Fulton shot Alysanna a look of surprise. "Madame, I would not suffer any act contrary to the church's canons."

Alysanna did not look appeased. "But the banns have not been read."

"True," he conceded, looking awkward with the confession. "But under special circumstances," he nodded toward Cairn, "it is possible to make allowances. Few of my parishioners hear the declarations anyway. The curate's record could reflect an earlier reading. I will not disclaim it, and God will know your hearts are true."

Alysanna drew a stiff breath and nodded. "Very well. I just didn't want to live . . . "

"In sin?" Cairn grinned wryly.

Alysanna threw him an embarrassed glance. "I've had enough impropriety lately. This, at least, I would do properly." In truth, she knew the ceremony was questionable, but it could be fixed later. At any rate, she could not marshal any disapproval in the face of Cairn's loving stare. Alysanna's lips wound back in a nervous smile, and she shrugged.

"Shall we proceed?" Cairn offered his hand, and together they followed the rector through the foyer, then down a long, cold hallway.

If she were ignorant before of Foxhall's huge expanse, Alysanna was no more. She, Cairn, and the parson, trailed by an entourage of Foxhall's staff, walked seemingly forever, finally entering a broad gallery of staggering length.

Alysanna could hardly guess the great number of gilt-framed portraits adorning the walls, but, as the wedding retinue pressed on, she saw faces familiar and those not so—kings and queens she knew well, and what she gathered to be a long line of Chathams whose names would soon come to have meaning for her.

More of the ubiquitous statuary was wedged between the oils. A quartet of black marble putti caught her eye. But more than the gallery's length or even its opulence, Alysanna was struck by its unearthly glow, for a blaze of candelabra lined its sides from end to end, making the hall a tunnel of sun.

"A few too many Chathams for my taste," Cairn whispered, glancing toward the walls.

"Will I meet them?" Alysanna's eyes trained on their stern expressions.

"Most are dead. But were they here to see you, I know they'd approve." Cairn squeezed her hand.

When they reached the room's end, Father Fulton's push creaked open the door to the Chatham family chapel. Moments ago the gallery's light seemed overabundant, but now, the intensity of the golden bath spilling out blinded Alysanna.

Candles and sconces flamed everywhere, mounted on walls and brass spikes, and at the altar. The beeswax's beams poured liquid apricot onto the white marble floor. The hot flames danced with the door's sudden draft, throwing strange, changing shadows on the ceiling's frescoes and filling Alysanna's nostrils with the sweet scent of cedar from the wainscot-paneled walls.

Four rows of ornately carved chairs framed the main aisle's path; behind them were plain wooden wall benches for the staff. Directly in front, a snow-white altarpiece loomed tall, its marble pediments ascending to a canopy that cradled an oval Annunciation near the structure's crest. At the base lay a crimson-draped altar, its sides flanked by single black columns. Two wine-colored cushions lay before them on the floor.

"Second thoughts?" Cairn asked, noting Alysanna's slowed pace.

"No." Her eyes beamed her joy back at him. "Merely collecting my thoughts."

"Good. I can't wait much longer for you, love."

Alysanna tugged on Cairn's hand, and the two of them stepped to the altar's base. She was vaguely aware of the shuffling behind them as their party found seats, but Alysanna did not turn to see. Her eyes held fast to Cairn's, happy prisoners of his adoring stare.

"Lord Chatham?" The rector cleared his throat for the third time.

"Yes, proceed."

"Dearly beloved," the parson began, reading the litany from a worn Book of Common Prayer. Alysanna tried hard to listen to the familiar recitals, but her mind was a jumble, whirling with joy and trepidation. Belonging to Cairn was all she wanted, yet there was still so much to be resolved, so much of her fate yet undelivered.

"I require and charge you both, as ye will answer at the dreadful day of judgment when the secrets of all hearts shall be disclosed, that if either of you know any impediment, why ye may not be lawfully joined together in matrimony, ye do now confess it. . . ." Alysanna felt her breath strangle at the parson's dire warning. Would keeping her secret send her to hell? She straightened up resolutely. No fate, earthly or eternal, would deny her what she wanted most.

"Wilt thou have this woman to thy wedded wife . . ." Alysanna lifted her eyes, and Cairn's stare burned like fire across her, hotter than the candles' heat.

"I will." Cairn's voice was deep, and its steely intonation made Alysanna wonder if he too had weighty matters on his mind.

"Wilt thou have this man. . . ." The parson droned on, but the words were unnecessary; Alysanna had pledged her heart to Cairn long ago, even before she had admitted it. Speaking that vow today only repeated her heart's solemn promise.

"I will." As Alysanna answered, Cairn's eyes danced their approval, and Alysanna took in little else 'til all was done. She heard an echo of the rector's words as Cairn placed the ruby-encrusted band on her finger, but, through the blessings and invocations—even through her own rote responses— Alysanna felt more than heard the union that fused them.

Cairn held only her hand, but it felt as though he embraced her everywhere. Only their bodies stood apart; their souls had already melded.

"You may bestow a kiss on your wife."

Cairn leaned close to Alysanna even before the parson finished, pausing only long enough to whisper against her ear. "Now you are mine, love. Always."

His lips swept down in unquestioning possession, and he crushed Alysanna wonderfully against him. The parson, the chapel, everything dropped away from her, leaving only Cairn's fiery touch and the echo of his sweet promise in her mind. Her trials were past. Now she was Cairn's.

Alysanna plumped the satin skirt of her gown for the third time, nervously arranging it across the soft seat of her chair. After the ceremony, she had planned to undress to await him, but, before Cairn had left to speak with the parson, he had begged that she leave the wedding gown on, even throughout dinner. Alysanna happily obliged. When Cairn found her, sitting alone in what would now be their shared room, she must be just as he wished.

She stared at the food platters laid on the walnut table. How did he expect her to eat when she was so excited?

Her eyes drifted across the room. As was fitting a chamber that had been his mother's, the apartment bore the mark of a woman's hand. Its azure walls and ivory accents contrasted with the dark crimson that graced most of Foxhall's interior. Even at night, the wallpaper's roses shone like springtime, a feeling echoed by the coffered ceiling, the gold and cream recesses of which looked less like plaster than sculpted icing.

The fire, which had been stirred to a blaze before Alysanna returned, threw fickle shadows on the celadon rug, then glimmered up each trough of the bed's carved pillars. Alysanna stared at the huge, satin-draped featherbed, which spread like a halcyon sea under a gold canopy. Here, moments from now, Cairn would take her.

The last week had been so wild and fast, Alysanna had not had a moment to ponder the union that, more than their ceremony, would truly make her Cairn's wife. She had come close to surrendering her virtue to him once before, the day of the boar's attack in the woods, but now, as she sat awaiting him, the notion filled her with excitement and fear.

Were she at Briarhurst, she would have ladies to advise and calm her. Here, she was mother and sister and maid to herself, left to her own devices, all of which now failed her miserably. But Cairn was the man she loved. Whatever tonight brought it would be all right.

The knock at the door made her start, and Alysanna jumped up, nearly upending a carafe of wine before she deftly caught the decanter. "Yes?"

"May I come in?" Cairn's sun-kissed tousle of hair popped around the door's edge, and his eyes gleamed as if he were a schoolboy just about to commit a delicious, forbidden prank.

Alysanna nodded her accession. She was still strangely unsettled at being alone with him, and her uneasiness embarrassed her. She reminded herself that they had been together like this before—but never with their purpose so clearly declared.

Cairn strode slowly toward her, and Alysanna realized that she had been so preoccupied with her own pounding heart, she had not yet noticed how handsome was her new husband. As was oft his custom, he wore black velvet, his waistcoat, jacket, and breeches all close-tailored jet, the jacket's revers alone flashing white lining.

A milky satin cravat was knotted under his tanned face, making his flesh look even more sun-burnished. Each step Cairn took across the marquetry echoed through the room, and, as Alysanna's eyes dipped to his black boots, she realized that he rarely wore the tights and shoes more common in men of his station.

"Your boots."

"Yes?" Cairn arched one brow questioningly.

"I had not noticed until now that you always wear them. You look as if you prepare for a trip."

"Wherever you'd take me, love." Alysanna twitched an embarrassed smile, and the Chippendale chair scraped loudly as Cairn pulled it from the table, then sat.

"I see Mildred has left our supper. Had I time, I would have asked your preference. As it is, we were forced to what the larder held. I hope it pleases you."

Alysanna studied the food laid before her. There was a mutton leg, smelling of rosemary and dotted with capers, egg custard, Cheshire cheese, and mushroom terrine, which all begged her sampling—to speak nothing of dessert. There was a colorful array of blancmange, figs, grapes, and raspberries, the last companions to a bowl of fresh cream.

"The excitement has stolen my appetite," Alysanna confessed.

"Perhaps a glass of wine will help. I should not want you to faint for lack of sustenance." Cairn's teasing smile implied she might well need her strength, and the suggestion reddened Alysanna's face. He pulled the decanter's stopper free and poured her crystal full of dark wine.

"It is French—from Bordeaux, near Mother's first home. I'm sure she would approve, though, if it is not to your taste, the cellar is amply stocked with other choices."

"No." Alysanna's eyes closed approvingly as she raised the glass to her lips. Cairn had gone to great trouble to please her, and his pampering touched her all the more for its contrast with her hardship of late.

"Wait." Cairn leaned over the table, catching her hand. "A toast—to my exquisite bride. May nothing part us— ever."

Alysanna raised the goblet, and her green eyes glistened. "And to my husband, who has restored my life." With a clink of crystal, they drank. The wine was warm and strong, and its liquid heat sailed down Alysanna's chest, loosening her breath.

"Come, try the mutton. Cook's heart will break if we send this back untouched." Cairn sliced a juicy bit from the meat's flank, then laved a dollop of sauce over it and raised the bite to Alysanna's lips.

Being fed by him felt odd, but Alysanna parted her lips at Cairn's bidding. Gently, almost reverently, he laid the meat inside her, just resting it on the tip of her tongue. Alysanna took it in slowly, savoring its thick, full taste more than she had thought to. Perhaps she could manage dinner after all.

"Is it to your liking?"

"Yes," Alysanna swallowed. "Everything is very much to my liking."

Cairn's eyes clung to hers, making her blush with their bold adoration. His attentions flustered her, and Alysanna took another sip of wine, then heard a small drop fall from the goblet's edge.

"Your mother's dress—the wine has stained!"

"It is nothing." Cairn rounded the table, brushing his napkin through her water glass and lifting Alysanna from her chair as he dabbed at the tiny red circle. " 'Tis of no concern." Alysanna nodded, but rued her clumsiness.

"There is still much food. Will you sit?"

She shook her head. "Truly, I've other matters on my mind."

"As do I." Cairn reached toward the table and dragged a raspberry through the thick white cream, then held it like a tantalizing prize in front of her.

"Perhaps we should proceed to dessert." Alysanna stared blankly back, not sure what Cairn wished, then watched as he sucked the berry between his teeth. He cupped her head and canted it toward him. The fruit's scarlet folds were achingly ripe, and, as Cairn lowered his mouth to hers, Alysanna could smell its sticky perfume.

Her lips parted in anticipation, and a flood of sweet sensations crushed against her as Cairn's flesh seared onto her own, the berry bursting into trickles of nectar as he pressed it deep inside her mouth with his tongue.

Alysanna could not tell whether it was the raspberry's juice or Cairn's kiss that made her taste of sugar. She closed her eyes, but they flew open as a wild, wet touch met her neck.

Cairn's finger trailed sweet cream across her shoulder to her bosom's swell, the liquid's velvet cold making her shudder. But it was the spark of his tongue, in his hand's wake, that brought a shocked gasp from her lips.

Almost instantly, his mouth found the valley between her breasts, and the fire of his tongue racked a chill up her spine. Cairn felt her quiver, and her obvious pleasure pleased him. He laughed low, teasingly, in response.

Now all shyness fled from Alysanna's mind, forced out by the satin burn of Cairn's touch. But her husband's deep voice, resonating against her, had an altogether unexpected effect. Alysanna struggled against it, but the fight was lost. Without warning she hunched forward, laughing as she pushed him away.

Cairn's head jerked upward, his eyes registering his amusement. "I had not thought you would find my advances humorous!"

"No, 'tis not that at all," she giggled, her hands resting on his shoulders. "I did not know I was so ticklish there."

"Neither did I." Cairn smiled broader still. "But this is a matter worth exploring. Are there other dangerous spots?"

"No, please," Alysanna pleaded, slithering free. "A moment—just a moment to set my mind—and we can begin again."

"But I can wait no longer." Like a loving predator, Cairn whirled her back to him, his mouth skimming every inch of her neck and shoulders in wet, biting nibbles.

Every touch of his lips made her giggle wildly. To worsen matters, he continued to laugh, and the vibration of his voice bore into her, completely unraveling her slim self-control. Cairn's mouth traced its torture down to her breasts, then back up, stopping only when his tongue touched her ear.

"Enough!" she begged breathlessly.

"Not nearly, love." He coiled his head around to her face until she could smell the sweet berries on his breath.

"Alysanna," Cairn whispered, lowering his lips to hers, his mood now solemn and strong. His arms cinched her tight against him, and he claimed full rights to her open mouth, his tongue plying her moistly, maddeningly.

Their playfulness fast dissolved, subsumed by urgency. Cairn drew her lower lip between his teeth, biting down softly and swelling an ache in Alysanna's belly. She moaned in response and locked her arms desperately around his back. Suddenly Alysanna felt herself lifted from the floor, wrapped in the blanket of Cairn's strong embrace.

He set her down gently on the edge of the bed, pulling back only enough to speak. "Take off the dress. I want to watch."

Alysanna could hardly believe her obedient response. No man had ever seen her naked, much less watched her disrobe. But Cairn's skilled hands had made her their slave; she knew she could refuse him nothing.

"The buttons—I need help."

Alysanna turned away from him, then felt a rush of cool air as Cairn's fingers unfastened each loop until her back lay bare. Slowly, she faced his gaze. With her eyes bound to his, Alysanna eased down the satin sleeves of the dress. With a rustle the bodice fell free and her breasts rose with quick little breaths of desire. Willed by his eyes, she stepped loose of the skirt, then her linen underclothes, until she stood naked, wearing only the fire of her glistening jewels.

Cairn's breath grew ragged as he stared at her. He had dreamed so often of taking her in love, but this devil's angel was finer than any mad reverie. He flung his coat and breeches off and stepped so close he could feel the heat of her flesh, yet he still denied himself.

His hands lifted in prayer to her face and pulled the pins loose from her hair. Alysanna shook her head gently, and her cinnamon mane tumbled down. Her auburn tendrils curled around the peaks of her swollen breasts, and at once Cairn knew his sweet torture must end.

With barely controlled languor, he slid his hands around her waist. Alysanna's breath drew in sharply at his touch, and she gasped as her eyes deeded permission. Cairn pulled her to him, the velvet feel of her belly and the rosebud kiss of her nipples making him crazed.

He pressed her back into the bed's soft folds, ripping free the satin cover as he rolled their single form beneath its warmth. Her sienna hair spilled like dark fire on the pillow, and Cairn nuzzled into its softness, breathing the heady perfume of the roses that had fallen free.

There were no words; language would have defiled their communion. Instead, Cairn's hands made eloquent his love, his fingers promising even greater passion with each pass over her breasts, his thumb teasing each pink bud to a hard, aching peak.

Alysanna arched backwards as his hand dared farther down, pausing on her flat, firm belly. Open-palmed, he pressed across the cup of her hips as if to know her outside before he knew it within. Alysanna raised herself to him, wanting their separateness to melt away.

Cairn understood, and his fingers drifted farther, stopping only as they curled around the soft flesh inside her thighs. Before this, Alysanna had no words for her wish, but now she was sure where she needed him most. Knowing, his thumb edged closer, at first only brushing against her warm center, then swelling her need as he teased her threshold in sweetest torment.

While his hand worked magic against her moist core, Cairn's mouth found its own sorcery, licking and sucking her nipples until they rose as hard as pebbles against her white flesh. Alysanna wove her fingers through the thatch of his hair, not knowing if she wished him more here or there— only that she could not bear to have him leave.

Everywhere his lips clung left a wet, tingling wake that caught cold fire as he moved farther on. Alysanna was shivering and burning, her core a torch lit with desire.

Cairn's fingers parted her, then slid easily into Alysanna's moistness, squeezing a gasp of delight from her lips. His thumb danced its torment where she felt it the most, as his fingers slipped in and out, sweetly rehearsing the fulfillment yet to come.

He pulled away, and, as she began to plead his return, Cairn swung over her, his warm weight sealing them.

"Yes," she begged, the word more breath than sound.

"I can't wait," he spoke huskily, stroking her cheek with a brush of his hand.

"Nor I. "

Cairn drove himself into her, parting Alysanna's legs and thoughts with equal ease. Gently at first, then with increasing speed, he filled her, each thrust sucking out her breath, then easily restoring it.

She had expected pain, for women had often talked of such things, but if it came, her pleasure was greater. Cairn answered her every unspoken desire, slaking her thirst with his pounding entry, feeding her hunger with his searching mouth. Alysanna knew it was Cairn against, atop, even inside her. Yet suddenly they seemed no more two, but one, bound by both law and flesh, fused with a passion destiny-born.

He rode her hard, and a misty dream of Cabochon took shape in her mind. She could see a distant fence, and, with Cairn's every thrust driving her on, Alysanna thundered toward it. In speed and force she climbed faster and higher.

Finally, she sailed off the ground on a zephyr's warm, thick wings.

Cairn lifted her up as fragrant winds rushed past like sweet currents. There was nothing beneath but glimmering light, and, in welcome surrender, Alysanna wrenched her head back, ecstatic to never more find the ground. Cairn joined her with a throaty growl, and suddenly still, the two of them lay silent, except for the rush of their doubled breaths.

Cairn pulled up after a time, smiling at Alysanna's passion-flushed face. "You are more woman than I dreamed. Did I not know better, I'd swear you'd done that before."

Alysanna scowled playfully. "Cairn! How dare you . . ."

"Shhh . . ." He pressed his thumb to her lips. "It was only a jest."

Alysanna arched her brow. "If I didn't know better, I'd think you had, too." Cairn's low laugh tickled her neck. "No, you don't!" Alysanna struggled free before she again dissolved.

"How wonderful! A weapon I can use to control you."

"Oh, so you think to control me, then?"

Cairn sobered, though still smiling. "No, only to love you. I should wish no more."

Alysanna nestled against him, nuzzling her head in the cup of his shoulder, their bodies stretched out in a long, warm seam. She trailed her toe up the length of his leg, then stopped as it hit a strange, rough welt.

"What's this?"

Cairn ignored her, stroking her cheek absentmindedly, as he stared overhead at the bed's gold canopy.

"Your leg. Are you injured?"

"'Tis nothing," He pulled the covers close. "An old wound."

"I had not thought you lame," Alysanna teased, snatching back the brocade as she sat to get a better view. "Cairn! This is a serious scar. It looks almost—as though you were shot."

Cairn pulled her back down and sighed. "Very well. It's an embarrassment, but I'll confess to my bride that I am a bad marksman. It was a duel, shortly before we met. The other fellow was much worse."

Alysanna could only think of how easily Cairn had dispensed with the charging boar. How strange that any opponent could better him. She could tell the wound was not recent, but from its size it had clearly been grave—its high crimson welt splintered sideways into several trails.

"Did the man shoot before the count? It looks like he fired too close."

"Yes, too close indeed. Now, surely we can spend our wedding night discussing matters other than my failings. Come here." Cairn slapped her rump gently and pulled Alysanna atop him, then traced the outline of her lips with a gentle finger. "Happy?"

"Yes," she breathed, wanting nothing more than to lose her thoughts in Cairn's warm, safe arms.

CHAPTER
16

❦

Alysanna rolled into the cocoon of Cairn's embrace, her nostrils full of his warm scent and the fire's nutty smell.

"Good morning." He burrowed into her soft tousle of hair. "Wife," he added. "I like the sound of that. Perhaps I shall simply call you wife from now on."

Alysanna craned her face toward him, squinting. "And what would you have me call you?"

"Master?"

"Ah!" she squealed. "So now the true terms of your love for me come clear. Did you think to get a handmaid from a governess? I fear I'll disappoint you." Alysanna twisted loose of Cairn's hold, scooting toward the far edge of the bed as she gathered the covers around her nakedness.

"No." He grabbed her wrist and tugged her gently back. "I thought only of my Alysanna, however she chooses to be."

Alysanna's eyes softened. "Then I shall not be yet another possession of the great duke, Lord Chatham?"

"Only if you promise to make me yours." Cairn pressed her back into the cloud of a pillow and lowered his mouth to hers languorously.

A crash in the hallway stopped his seduction. The bed-chamber door burst open, displaying a red-faced Duncan and Cairn's equally flustered houseman.

"Your lordship," William gushed, "my apologies. Viscount Granville insisted on seeing you—immediately. I tried to explain that you were indisposed, but he . . ."

Cairn lifted his hand to silence William's nervous explanation. "It's all right. Apparently Lord Granville has some pressing business. At least, he'd better have. You can leave us."

"Are you sure, sir?" William's brow furrowed as he stared indignantly at Duncan who, still flushed and silent, fidgeted with his jacket, which had been mussed by William's vigorous restraint.

"It's under control, William. You may go."

"I shall be nearby, your lordship." The man nodded, his curiosity as to Duncan's urgent purpose barely bridled as he shuffled backwards out the door.

Cairn's face turned stony as he stared at Duncan. "This had better be good, man. You've barged in on my honeymoon—and at this ungodly hour, yet."

"It is nigh eleven," Duncan sputtered. Then, realizing Alysanna was scrunched next to Cairn under a mountain of sheets, he threw his eyes in embarrassment to the floor.

"Cairn." Alysanna's low whisper drew Cairn's attention. She too was ruddy with pique. Cairn suspected that, had she been dressed to rise, Alysanna would have sprung up and ushered Duncan out personally.

"A moment, dear, while I finish. Scoot down—Duncan won't see anything. And I promise you, he won't be here long. Now . . ." Cairn turned back to Duncan, his patience thin and his face glowering. "What in hell is it?"

"Lily's gone."

Cairn's scowled in confusion. "To town? Where?"

"Would that I knew. I was hoping you had her."

"Of course not. Duncan, are you saying she's run off?"

"Yes, from all accounts. Delia looked everywhere this morning. Her traveling case is missing—and some clothes. My God, if anything terrible . . ."

"It seems by your account that it already has. But I'm sure that wherever she is, she's fine." Cairn rose to pull on his breeches. "You might as well sit down."

Duncan answered with questioning eyes. Given yesterday's talk with Cairn, he wasn't sure the newly married Chathams would want his company under any circumstances, notwithstanding the present crisis. He braced himself for an imminent eviction.

"Cairn's right, sit down." Alysanna sounded as exasperated as her husband. "Cairn seems willing to talk with you, and you've already seen me huddled in this sheet. Another five minutes will hardly matter."

"Thank you," Duncan mumbled, dropping his head into his hands as he sat. "I just didn't realize the strength of her attachment to Jenny."

"So that's what this all turns on," Cairn said, reaching for his boots.

"I'm afraid so. After you left yesterday, Lily learned that I had let Jenny go. We had a row. I sent her to her room, and that was the last I saw of her." Duncan stared at Cairn guiltily, like a dog who'd just laid his teeth in his master's flesh. "I know. Spare me your reprimand. I realize this all should have been handled differently."

"Then, you admit you made a mistake in dismissing her?" Cairn crossed his arms smugly over his chest, ready to hear Duncan's contrition.

"I admit no such thing!" Duncan shot to his feet, his ire rising with equal speed. "I simply meant that I should have prepared Lily better for Jenny's departure."

"You don't regret your foolish behavior?"

Duncan blew out a disbelieving snort. "I hardly came here to plead an apology."

"Your trip has been wasted," Cairn barked curtly, pulling his shirt on with a snap, as if to make clear he considered their business done.

"I thought you my friend!"

"I am—more than you know. But I can do nothing if you're hell-bent on ruining yourself. What is it you came here seeking?"

"Help in finding Lily, of course! God knows where she could be or what trouble could find her. She is but a child."

"Cairn, he may be foolish, but he's right." Alysanna cringed at the thought of poor Lily, lost and alone. "Lily should not suffer because of Lord Granville's sentiments. Surely we could help find her."

Cairn knew that the child was worth two of the father. "I'll do what I can. But once Lily's back—if I can find her at all—you're on your own to sort this out."

Duncan canted his head skeptically. "You speak as if you know where she is. Did you have some black part in arranging her flight?" His face puffed with anger, and he looked much as if he would burst.

"You push your luck with me, old friend. I don't know where Lily is. All I have is a hunch. But I will only pursue it if you swear not to follow me. Lily had her reasons for leaving, whatever they were. I won't betray her trust by leading you to her door. Are we clear?''

Yes, yes,'' Duncan sputtered impatiently. ''Just do what you can, as long as you find her.''

''I can only try. Now, as soon as I finish dressing, I'll be off. You can speed this by leaving. I'm not overly fond of an audience—except, of course, my wife.''

Duncan bristled at Cairn's brusque dismissal. Such rude treatment—and in front of that Walker woman yet! He shook his head in disbelief and marched toward the door. It would be a long time, if ever, before he'd swallow the notion of Cairn's new duchess. Duncan turned suddenly before he left.

''Thank you.'' Then, like a child sent to his room, he skulked out, slamming the bedroom door more out of habit than anger.

''Do you know where she is?'' Still clutching the covers against the morning chill, Alysanna edged close to Cairn on the end of the bed.

''I'm not certain, but I do have an idea.''

''Yes?''

''Until I know, let me handle this, please. I don't mean to keep things from you, love, but I don't want to breach any confidence. Will you trust me?'' He tipped her face lovingly toward him.

''How can I not, when it looks as though my assent may buy me another kiss?''

Cairn smiled wryly, then brushed his mouth with slow ceremony across hers.

She moaned softly. ''I suppose you must go.''

''I suppose,'' he answered, obviously displeased at the prospect of leaving her. ''But it shouldn't take long. I'll see you for supper, at the latest.''

Alysanna clutched Cairn in mock distress. "Then I am to be widowed my first full day as Lady Chatham! 'Tis a cruel, untoward fate for so fresh a bride!"

"It shall make my return to you all the sweeter." Cairn drew her close and yanked away the sheet, lowering his mouth playfully to one pert nipple. "Now," he sighed, "before I get too distracted for the task at hand, I'll take my leave. Lily's welfare can't suffer for my lust."

His compliment pleased her, and, with a contented smile, Alysanna plopped back lazily into the pillow's froth. "What shall I do while you're gone?"

"I'll have Mildred send you a tray, then you can take in the gardens. Or perhaps you'd prefer to read or simply to count all the rooms of the house. There's a full day's task."

"I fear I should be lost and never found again. But the garden—that's a splendid idea." Alysanna squinted at the blast of sunlight, unchecked by the gauzy draperies, that poured in from the window. "It seems forever since I've had a day without work."

Alysanna knew she should feel content. Still, something about Cairn's departure unsettled her.

"Cairn, be careful."

"Nothing can happen, love. You'll see me soon."

"Not soon enough." Her full lips burst wide in a smile that lingered long after Cairn had gone. She was Lady Chatham, Cairn's duchess. She had never dreamed such happiness could be hers.

The sun beat down on Alysanna's bare head, its buttery rays melting on her face. While she had worked for Duncan, she had bound her hair in a governess's bun. Now, as lady of Foxhall, Alysanna could do as she pleased, and, though it was unusual enough to draw quizzical stares from several of Cairn's staff, she let her long curls drift free in the summer wind, a style she often adopted when alone at Briarhurst.

She still felt uneasy in the rose damask gown. Though Cairn assured her his mother would gladly deed her all the closet held, Alysanna felt strange going through the woman's wardrobe, and she vowed to commission proper gowns of her own as soon as possible. Still, she could not deny the pleasure her open hands took in the damask's shiny weave, not to mention the fine fit of its waistcoat and bodice, both of which hugged her in tight counterpoint to the full flounces of the embroidered skirt.

The summer day spilled over with warmth, as if it too were brimming with love. Everything was perfect. If only. . . . Alysanna shook her head to dismiss the miserable thought. Hadley had assured her he would work for her freedom; with Cairn's efforts, they would not fail.

Alysanna breathed her relief that she was thus far undiscovered, but a duchess was that much easier to find. As her marriage became known, there would surely be questions.

She stamped her foot to ward off her fears. What good did it do to worry, anyway? Alysanna tried to envision the problem finished, and the thought raised a clean, sweet taste in her mouth, like a bite of summer peach.

She swiveled her full skirt lazily one way, then the other, as she stood on the Foxhall portico, surveying her options for a stroll. To the left, as William had said, was the orangery. Beyond, she could see several levels of terraces, the entrance to the bottommost marked with a hornbeam tunnel with a doorway that gave a slivered view of the stone benches and topiary beyond. In front of her lay the parterre she had passed on her arrival yesterday. But to Alysanna's right beckoned the most intriguing choice.

Just beyond a hyacinth bed, a massive stone portal rose

like Stonehenge, its sides bleeding into a tall hedged yew. Cairn had mentioned that his grandfather admired labyrinths and had finally commissioned one of his own. From what Alysanna could see of the front of the hedge, she guessed this was it. Longing for a diversion until Cairn returned, she skipped toward the gate.

Embedded in its left grey stone post was a tarnished brass plaque. "Ye who enter here, mind your steps. All who forget their path shall repeat it." Alysanna smiled at its dour caution. She had managed such puzzles before. She had a keen sense of direction, and not one maze had yet undone her.

She stared at the leafy wall, recalling what she knew of the history of labyrinths. In the Middle Ages, they were patterned after the minotaur's prison at Knossos, religious allegories for the pilgrim's path, sometimes even called "Chemins de Jerusalem."

Then their hedges were mown low so the traveler could see over; but the one now before her looked more recent— it had high, blind sides. This style, which Alysanna had seen at Hampton Court, was made more for entertainment than penitence.

She stepped through the maze's entry gate. The exterior, which had been clipped into a flat, green plane, now gave way to inner walls that grew unfettered in leafy waves, the yews' strange undulations lending a distorted feel to its dark green womb. The ramparts looked less grown than sculpted, and their scooped-out pockets were so uneven and irregular that they appeared the work of a madman's scythe.

A strange misgiving blew through her heart, but Alysanna shook it off. She reached out and brushed one hand against the blades, starting forward. There was only one path leading in from the gate, and, almost immediately, it began to curve smoothly. Alysanna guessed it led straight to the center, as was often the case.

Alysanna wound turn after turn, with no forks or junctures, only the tall green channel that coiled ever closer to the maze's core. Her thoughts drifted with her feet, back through Cairn's departure, to the delicious passion last night had held.

Even now she could hardly believe she was his wife. It had happened so quickly, like a wild, spring storm, its force nearly felling her. One moment she was Duncan's governess, pledged to Hadley and living a lie; the next, she was Cairn's, her life restored by the gift of his love.

She had known Cairn Chatham less than six months. It was a scandalously brief courtship, especially considering that she'd denied her feelings for him through much of it. Yet, on some unspoken, barely plumbed level, Alysanna sensed that their souls had met before, in some way she could not begin to grasp.

There was no one to see, but a blush crossed her face as she recalled last night. Cairn's lovemaking had been gentler, more exquisite than anything she could have imagined.

She had thought men's ways rough and selfish, though now Alysanna could not remember exactly how the notion had come to her. Perhaps it was Hadley, whose unskilled handling left her feeling more like bruised fruit than a woman. Whatever her expectations, they had fallen easily beneath the sword of Cairn's soft touch.

His hands were large, but not clumsy. Instead, they had teased and loved her like satin. The warm scent of him next to her, the oceanic swell that had borne them to their mutual joy. . . . Alysanna closed her eyes, happily drowning in the hazy details as she drifted down the path, allowing the wall's contours to guide her.

A sharp tug near her knee nearly tripped her, and she lurched half to the ground, then saw that a maverick yew branch had caught her skirt. The damask had not torn but was wound in a knot, and, as Alysanna twisted back to undo it, another memory washed over her, this time without pleasure.

Cairn's scar had been a serious wound—from its color and height, that much was clear. Yet something in his explanation unsettled her. Alysanna labored to remember exactly what he'd said. Cairn had attributed the welt to a duel. Such contests were common, yet not usually of such little note that he should not have mentioned it before.

It was true there was much of Cairn's past she had yet to learn, but Alysanna did know him to be a fine shot. The day in the copse, when he'd felled the boar—that was no luck of a middling marksman. How could he have failed against a man? Alysanna's mind traced the scar's raised contours. It was much too large to have come at full distance. Cairn had said his opponent shot early, yet, for such a gaping tear, the man must have fired at three or four paces. If that were true, why was the blow on Cairn's front, not his back, as it should have been were he walking away?

Cairn said he was wounded just before they met. Why had she not seen him limp? Alysanna's mind wound through their first encounter. She had met him when she was fleeing Briarhurst. There was nothing strange that day in the carriage. He had helped her into the coach, and. . . . Alysanna cocked her head sideways in thought.

No, he had not risen. Instead, he had clutched the wool throw tightly, looking, now that she reconsidered his expression, much as if he were in pain. Why had he allowed her to think him a ruffian when a simple explanation of the duel would have served? There was no shame in an honorable contest, particularly if he'd been victim to a cheat. Yet Cairn had made no mention of it.

Some inchoate uneasiness dogged her, and, as Alysanna reached the labyrinth's core, she eased onto a marble bench, her reasoning still as knotted as the path.

Why did this bother her so? Cairn had simply chosen to keep silent about the duel. Everything Alysanna knew only supported his claim that the contest occurred just before she left home, at about the time she shot. . . .

At once her throat felt dry and parched, and Alysanna's eyes began to sting. Cairn had been shot at exactly the same time she had fired on Julia's killer. And he bore a wound that looked very much like that of the stranger's, both in severity and place.

She snapped her head quickly side to side, trying to loosen the horrifying thought. It was preposterous—Cairn was her husband, not some dark murderer! The notion was only a sunstruck delusion.

Alysanna drifted toward the maze's sundial, leaning her palms into its raised face. She studied the gnomon's shadows, willing herself to a more rational mood. But the truth nagged at her like the wild yew branch, hooking her on an unthinkable fear.

So many unanswered questions now whirled through her mind. Even the wound was only the beginning. From the start Cairn had pursued her so avidly, even when he believed her no more than a governess. Now, seeing Foxhall, understanding the wealth and tradition that spawned the Chatham name, Alysanna found his risk-taking even more absurd.

Even before she had confessed her past, Cairn's easy acceptance of her had seemed too odd. Yet, wanting him so much, Alysanna had easily subscribed to his assurances. Class means nothing, he had told her, swearing to disdain what others held dear.

Even once she'd laid bare the lurid details, it hadn't mattered. Cairn had been angry to find her with Hadley, but it was only jealousy—he showed no wrath for her crime, not even for her lies to disguise it. Alysanna had thought him uncommonly generous—forgiving beyond any grace she had known in a man. Was it so uncommon as to be suspect?

A roiling nausea tossed in her stomach, and Alysanna covered her face with her hands, hoping the darkness might quell it. But instead confusion flooded her, and the voices in her head railed louder and louder, chanting the fear her lips could not speak. Dear God, had Cairn killed Julia?

The notion teetered wildly in her head. It could not be true. But even as she denied it, Alysanna's reasoning raised a more horrendous thought—had Cairn always known who she was, what she had done? And if he had, what plans did he hold in store for her now?

A wife could not witness in court against her husband. Perhaps what Alysanna had seen as Cairn's love was only his need for protection. Or—perhaps he didn't intend to keep her at all.

If what she feared were true, he had already killed once; a man could not go to the gallows twice. Why allow a witness to his crime to continue to threaten him?

Alysanna's eyes flew open in terror. The notion was too ghastly, too incredible to be possible. The coincidences could be explained. Cairn was her husband. He loved her. She had trusted him, known him intimately. How could she think him full of such evil?

Alysanna had the overpowering need to flee back to the house, back to their chamber, where her love for Cairn had been fulfilled. She could think clearly there—shake off this murky fog that confused her.

She blew like the wind toward the path that led in. But now, there was not one, but eight identical routes, each spiraling outward, each promising deliverance from the labyrinth's turns.

Foolishly, Alysanna had failed to mark her trail. Refusing her fear, she squinted at the sun, hoping its angle would orient her. The notion was sound but useless. It was nearly noon, and the perfect perpendicular of its hot rays gave no clue.

Edging toward panic, Alysanna could not still her feet, and she frantically bolted down one arcing chute, scouting the yew snag that had caught her skirt. How far down was the branch? Her recall bent like a poorly made mirror. She raced around what felt like two circles' worth, but could not find the snag and returned to the labyrinth's center to begin again. Eight times she tried; as many she failed.

Tears filled her eyes as her suspicions fired her confusion. She was lost, in every conceivable way. The more she struggled with either quandary—the labyrinth or Cairn—the more trapped she became.

Ruled more by instinct than thought, Alysanna burst like chased quarry down one more spiral, curving so fast she reeled with dizziness. Now the yew's undulations frightened her, like some artist's nightmare. Each bend revealed only more of the same, and Alysanna felt the green tunnel growing narrower with each panicked step she took.

A thick, stifling claustrophobia choked her, and she clutched her throat for air until finally, the tunnel spilled into a small grassy square. Other spokes led out from its center, but at least there was space here to breath, to rest, to think.

Gasping from her breakneck pace, Alysanna leaned, exhausted, into the yew's tangled arms. She felt like the hare in a hound's pursuit. Whether it was Cairn or her fears that hunted her, Alysanna did not know.

"Alysanna?"

Her eyes froze like glass at his call. It was Cairn, close to her, hidden behind the labyrinth's walls.

"Alysanna! Give me a shout, else I'll wander the whole afternoon looking for you."

A moment ago she had absolved him of all complicity in Julia's death. Yet now, his voice so close, so unexpected, the specter of his guilt again rose in her mind. Her heart thundered with fear, and her head ached miserably. Why had Cairn returned so soon? He'd promised to be elsewhere. Was she his prey in some twisted game?

Alysanna had no idea where she was, but Cairn surely knew the maze's forks by heart. It would be folly to try to slip past him. She could as easily crash into him as find her freedom, yet to stay still also risked discovery.

Alysanna struggled for a glimpse of her earlier faith. Cairn was her husband—she must trust him. Why then could she not answer? Alysanna opened her mouth, but there was no sound. Fear struck her like a hard, angry fist.

Time stretched and bulged like the yew's uneven planes, and the maze's eerie distortion mirrored her thinking. In near exhaustion, Alysanna collapsed on the ground of her grassy prison.

"Alysanna! I know the maze. If you can hear me, answer. I can find you!" Cairn's deep-timbred voice volleyed toward her, but the hedge's acoustics masked her sense of his place. She could at least tell his call was closer now. Alysanna scanned the yew's ramparts with frantic speed, but it was useless—the routes out looked more alike each second.

Alysanna was paralyzed. She clung desperately to the labyrinth's curved folds, as if they could protect her, and pressed
herself into the plants' hard trunks.

"Alysanna!" Now there was a hint of annoyance in Cairn's
voice, and it gave her new fear. Was what she heard pique
over a lost afternoon, or the end of patience with a wife who
knew too much?

Had there been tokens before—little signs of his plans for
her that she had been too blind with love to see? Alysanna
closed her eyes, a gush of salt tears washing her cheeks. The
rustle of foliage behind her spun Alysanna in unchecked terror.

"Darling! Why didn't you call? Surely you heard me? I've
been looking for you."

Alysanna stared blankly at him. She expected his face to
be full of menace; instead, it was creased with love and relief.
Cairn saw her consternation, then her tears.

"Oh, come, it's all right. I'm here now. No need to cry."

Cairn pulled her close, then leaned her back to look at her
as he realized she shook like a drenched kitten. "You're
frightened. I'm sorry. I'd no idea you'd start this silly labyrinth. You're not the first one this damn thing's brought to
tears. I'll have it scythed tomorrow."

"No," she answered raggedly. "It's all right. I thought
you were gone."

"I had some luck finding Lily. It went more quickly than
I'd hoped. William guessed you'd come this way—and luckily so. Having just made you my wife, I've no wish to lose
you now." Cairn cinched Alysanna tighter against his chest,
stroking her head and trailing tiny kisses along her hairline.

She could not explain how, but Alysanna's fears melted
in the warmth of Cairn's arms. Suddenly she felt safe and
calm, trusting of Cairn's every intent. He could not hold her

so lovingly, speak so gently, were he the monster of her delusions.

"Shhh . . ." he whispered. "Nothing can harm you. I'm here. I'll take us home."

Alysanna laced her arms around his back like she'd nearly drowned. His touch was all she needed to know. She swore never to question him again.

CHAPTER
17

Alysanna's head felt trapped in a vise. Her hair was too thick for the cocked hat's confines, and her vigorous efforts to stuff it into the cap had succeeded only at the expense of her comfort.

If there had been any other way to disguise herself, she would have gladly done so. As it was, she'd be lucky if her odd costume did not make her suspect, even as a man.

The blue fustian waistcoat, which was livery for Cairn's male servants, was far too fancy for the worn leather breeches she had managed to steal. Alysanna hoped the nubby cloak and half-jack boots she had pilfered from the stable hands evened out the effect. It was a peculiar mix—half gentleman, half ruffian—but the best she could do for a secret sojourn on such short notice.

It wasn't only the hat that made her miserable; it was the linen with which she had bound her breasts, and especially the false note she had left Cairn pleading attendance to some

matters at Briarhurst. The excuse was a weak one, and Alysanna knew it. Cairn would think her mad to undertake such
a dangerous trip alone. Even Alysanna herself was not un-
mindful of the risk. She'd be lucky not to be recognized,
much less delivered into the constable's hands. But there was
no choice. If she could not live with her nagging fears about
Cairn's identity, she must dispel them on her own.

Yesterday, in the hedge maze, when Cairn had held her
in his arms, Alysanna had sworn to dismiss her doubts. But
that night's lovemaking had drawn her thoughts again to his
scar, and to the specter of the wound on Julia's killer. Cairn
could not be Julia's murderer yet, until the culprit was found,
Alysanna could never trust, never know for sure.

Why had Hadley's search gone so slowly? Alysanna had
neither the luxury or the patience to wait. One more night in
Cairn's arms, torn between her love and her fears, was too
tortuous to bear. Even if Hadley failed to find Julia's killer,
Alysanna wouldn't. She couldn't if she were to return as
Cairn's loving wife.

Alysanna urged her gelding down the Wodeby road, and,
as she reached the manor house, she turned toward the west
wing, tethering the animal there to avoid Hadley's groom.
Even if her appearance served, Alysanna knew she would be
foolish to test her luck by speaking more than necessary. Her
voice was low enough to pass for a man's, but it was also
familiar to Hadley's staff.

Alysanna drew a stiff breath and rang the front bell. The
footman, Joshua, answered, his demeanor far from what she'd
seen before.

"May I help you?" He cocked one brow critically, studying Alysanna's bedraggled appearance as if he expected her
to beg food. The ride from Foxhall had taken nearly the full

day, but until this moment, Alysanna had not considered the toll the distance had wrought on her appearance.

"I would see Viscount Seaham." She pulled her voice up from her chest as she spoke, hoping it was beyond recognition.

"Indeed. Have you business with him?" Joshua made no effort to move, and Alysanna had the sense that he was about to grab her lapels and toss her headfirst off Wodeby's front stairs.

"It is why I've asked for him."

"May I know your business?"

"It is private."

"I'm sure. There has been a rash of housebreaks about lately and you look more thief than his lordship's acquaintance. Off with you!"

Joshua began to slam the door, but Alysanna's fist blocked him, though she was too dumbstruck to speak. It was bad enough that Joshua thought her a robber; on top of it, he looked unlikely to admit her.

She could not risk revealing her identity. If the search for her was as pitched as Hadley said, there was no telling who was friend and who foe. For lack of a better idea, Alysanna reached into her cloak's side pocket and withdrew a fistful of pounds. She thrust them at Joshua, thumping the crisp wad against his chest.

"Perhaps this will ease your mind. Here, take it," she barked, giving his front another hard shove. "You can see from my purse I've no need to steal. As I told you, I've business with your lord. Now, call the viscount here at once."

Joshua squinted as he stuffed the crumpled pounds into his vest. Though still cautious, he backed in slowly, allowing Alysanna passage through. She breathed her relief, astounded by the bribe's efficacy. When all else was settled, she'd make sure Hadley dismissed this scapegrace.

"You can wait in the gallery—if you don't sit down." Joshua nodded toward her breeches. Alysanna looked down and understood. The long cloak, which she had hoped would cover her, had failed miserably against the turnpike's mud, leaving her pants splattered with filth.

She nodded her agreement, and began toward the gallery door, then stopped. She must allow Joshua to lead. As a stranger, she would not know where to find the room. No foolish slip must betray her.

"I'll tell Lord Seaham that you're here." Joshua sauntered upstairs, leaving Alysanna to her peace in the long, familiar chamber. A fire blazed beneath the fireplace's hood, and she sought it eagerly, longing to shake off the deep chill of the ride.

Alysanna dispatched her gloves and lifted her hands, now chapped from the cold against the flames' rich warmth. It was late afternoon, nearing dusk, and the hearth's shadows skittered like nervous ghosts up and down the tapestried walls. The gallery looked the same as the last time she'd seen it, the morning she fled to find Beatrice in London. The memory filled her with misery, and, despite the fire's heat, a shudder wound up Alysanna's spine.

"What the . . .? Who are you?" Alysanna spun to face Hadley, and she saw her disguise had succeeded again. His look made clear he thought her a stranger. "What's your business here?" Hadley marched forward, her imminent eviction etched on his face.

"Hadley." Alysanna stretched out her reddened hands, and her slender fingers, peeking out from beneath a coachman's cloak, made him start in surprise.

"Who are you?" he repeated, this time with less anger.

"Don't you know?" Alysanna loosened the hat, and her hair spilled in an auburn tumble around her shoulders.

"Alysanna! Good God! Whatever are you doing here?" Hadley stood frozen several yards from her, his face a pasty shade of shock.

"Well, you needn't look so horrified. I've not come to rob you, though Joshua certainly thought so. I couldn't wait to hear from you. We must speak now."

"Yes, of course," Hadley sputtered, his composure returning as he drew Alysanna toward the settee.

"This must be important. Coming here was a foolish, dangerous decision."

Alysanna nodded. "I know, but my only choice. Hadley, some unsettling things have happened—events that make it more urgent that we find Julia's killer."

Hadley blushed at her words. Had she come all this way just to harangue him? "Alysanna, I'm working as fast as I can. But if a man will not be found, there is no finding him. Why is it you suddenly doubt my intent?"

"I don't," she apologized. "I know that you've done your best. It's just that some recent developments have made it harder for me to live with the uncertainty."

"Recent developments?"

Alysanna paused, wondering how best to deliver her news. There was no easy explanation; the truth would have to stand on its own. "I have married." She stopped again, correctly anticipating Hadley's shock. "A man I met in London and whom you met in Mowbry."

"Mowbry?" Hadley affected ignorance, hoping what he feared was not true.

"His name is Lord Cairn Chatham."

Hadley closed his eyes to sort out his confusion. Alysanna studied him nervously, sure the silence bespoke his fury.

"I know it seems sudden—as it was. But I swear, Hadley, on all I hold dear, that nothing improper happened while you and I were still pledged. It was only when you broke our betrothal that I agreed. You said I could not return home, that I must build a new life. My marriage to Cairn is exactly that. Please, say something!"

Alysanna knew her tale was only half true. She had behaved improperly with Cairn before she was free, but what good would it do to confess that now? Besides, though she'd longed to end her engagement to Hadley, her pride still stung from his quick undoing of it. Perhaps he had earned her lies; at the very least, they were all she could tell.

"I won't deny my surprise. I had not thought you to abandon my memory this quickly. But if you so choose, I can hardly fault you, given that it was I who ended our betrothal."

Hadley's heart hardly ached with her betrayal; it was fear for his hide that speeded his pulse. Cairn Chatham! Alysanna could not have made a more dangerous choice!

He chastised himself for not knowing. Perhaps on some level he had; there was a wild spark between them in the church that day. Hadley shook off his guilt. Even had he known, there was no way to intervene without perking Alysanna's suspicion. Now he would have to make the best of it.

"I suppose congratulations are in order." Hadley mustered a weak smile and pressed a cold kiss against her cheek.

"Yes, congratulations." Alysanna turned her head, hoping Hadley would miss her distress.

"Alysanna, what is it? You hardly look the happy bride. Did you not want to be Lady Chatham?"

"Yes, it was my fondest . . ." Alysanna stopped, reluctant to reveal how she'd longed for Cairn.

"Then, why risk it all on a trip home—a journey as likely to lead you to the gallows as to Briarhurst?"

"There is something I must confide. I hope with all my heart that it is nothing. Yet, I must know for sure—and there is no one else to tell."

"I cannot imagine what makes you so grave." Her sudden dark mood frightened him. Could the mess with Cairn Chatham be even worse?

"Cairn is wounded—on his leg. He bears a scar much like that my pistol gave Julia's attacker."

"What is it you're saying?"

"I am saying nothing." Even now, as she confessed her fears, Alysanna struggled to quash them. "Only that the wound troubles me."

"Surely your husband has an explanation."

"He claims a duel, shortly before we met."

"But you do not subscribe?"

"Oh, Hadley, I want to so badly—with every fiber of my heart and soul I long to trust him. But it's all seemed so strange—his insistence on marrying me, even when he thought me only a governess; his blasé disregard for the lies I told; and now, this scar that wounds my trust as deeply as it does his flesh."

"Alysanna, what is it you fear?"

"That Cairn has some connection to Julia's death. That he—" Alysanna dissolved into a crescendo of tears. She covered her face with her hands and scrunched forward. Her words escaped through gasping sobs. "I am afraid it was my husband who killed Julia!"

Hadley paused in shock, then drew her to him, gently patting her back. "That is quite a fear—quite a fear, indeed." Hadley held Alysanna until her tears were spent, then tilted up her chin.

"What is it you wish?"

"We must look harder for the real killer! Even if we cannot find him, I must know it was not Cairn."

"But I have done my best. How do you propose to better my efforts?"

"There were servants, tavern maids, innkeepers. Whoever committed this dark deed must have been seen."

"Alysanna," Hadley snapped impatiently, "don't you think I've already spoken with these people?"

"Yes, of course. But until now we could not describe a man we did not know. I do know Cairn. If we could ask again, see if anyone of his description. . . ."

"No." Hadley raised his finger to silence her. "That is to say, you mustn't even consider this. The constable is convinced of your guilt. He has a warrant. To stay nearby is to risk your life."

"You have done so much already," Alysanna answered, thinking that Hadley seemed not to have done much at all. "At any rate, two heads are better."

"Only as long as they both stay attached," he admonished. "You must realize that for you to come anywhere near Briarhurst is impossibly dangerous. Let me help you. I have seen Lord Chatham. I can ask again if there was a man of his description about that night."

Alysanna reconsidered and Hadley was right; it was dangerous for her to stay nearby.

"I'll start at once. But until I send word—until we have firm proof of Cairn Chatham's guilt—I want your promise to do nothing untoward."

"You mean, I mustn't go back?"

"I mean you must. To do otherwise would certainly raise his suspicions. You must not only return—I charge you to act as if nothing has happened. More than that, you must

believe it, for if you harbor doubts, your new husband will
see them proclaimed in your eyes. Promise me.''

"Hadley, I want to do as you say, but 'twas my doubts
that drove me here. To suspend them now is no simple task.''

"Alysanna, you are a woman of wit. I know you can find
a way to believe in his innocence, at least until we know
better. This all could be mere coincidence. If that were true
and you accused him otherwise, think on Cairn's response.
Would you gamble your love on a foolish delusion?''

Alysanna knew again she had panicked. Her impulsiveness
forever dogged her. Now, for her own safety and her future
with Cairn, she must still her worry and trust Hadley once
more.

"I'll try. But promise to move quickly. I don't know how
long I can beat back my fears.''

"There's a good girl. Now, I want you to go straight home.
I gather you left some excuse for your absence?''

"Of sorts, though it may take some explaining.''

"Then, all the more reason for haste. It's nigh dark out;
there's no time for return today. But first thing tomorrow,
we'll set you back on the road to your husband. No stops,
no delays—not even at Briarhurst.''

"But I thought perhaps I might see how Roberta fared. I
needn't reveal myself. It's only that it has been so long. To
see home again would give me such peace.''

"*Alysanna.*" Hadley scowled at her like a stern parent.
"Dancing yourself under Roberta's nose is the last thing you
need! Trust me in this. Straight home. Have I your promise?''

Alysanna agreed with a discouraged sigh. "Very well. First
thing tomorrow. Which room shall I take?'' An embarrassed
confusion swept over Hadley's face.

"Surely you do not intend to put me out?''

"I only want you to be safe.''

"There must be room in the back, where no one would see?"

"We could try, but I cannot guarantee anything. Even unrecognized, how can I explain an unkempt highwayman beneath my protection? Not much escapes Mrs. Gotham's eyes."

Hadley's point was well-taken but it hardly made his conclusion more palatable. Alysanna slapped her breeches angrily as she rose.

"Then, where?"

Hadley winced as he answered. "The stables?"

"You expect me to sleep in the hay?"

"I expect you to stay alive."

Alysanna struggled for a better idea, but couldn't find one. "Very well. But I swear, Hadley, I can't bear much more. Go quickly in proving Cairn's innocence—or guilt—before my impatience undoes us both."

If he had not seen Cairn stop at the stone and thatch cottage, Duncan never would have guessed that it existed. Tucked inside a large oak grove, the tiny farmhouse's roof was smothered by the overhead branches, not so much standing beneath as cuddled by its soft, leafy embrace.

Duncan tethered his mare to a nearby tree and stepped tentatively toward the door. He cupped his hand around his eyes and peered hopefully through the mullioned windows at the darkness within, struggling to make out anything familiar. From the little he could tell, a squat brick hearth fielded the room's far end, framed on either side by rough wooden benches. Overhead, a tarnished chandelier hung on a chain, its dust-powdered candles looking as though they'd gone long unlit.

A threadbare settee backed up to the window, and Duncan

craned his neck to see down its length. There wasn't a clue that made him suspect Lily was there; perhaps he had been misguided. Cairn had ridden straight here after Duncan's desperate plea, but what would Lily seek in this unkempt hermitage?

Then, at the settee's far end, a familiar satchel caught Duncan's eye. Its worn leather top parted on a tangle of ribbons. Duncan stood dumbfounded at the realization—the bag belonged to Jenny.

Had it been left at Donegal, forgotten in Jenny's angry flight, then taken by Lily for her own escape? Duncan doubted it; Delia had said Lily's traveling case was missing. Surely she would not bother with Jenny's frayed bag. What, then. . . . Duncan blew out a snort as he realized Cairn's trickery. He had known Duncan would follow him, and, with his own misguided purpose, he had led him straight to Jenny, hoping they'd reconcile.

Duncan turned to go. There was nothing more to be said between them. But just before he reached for his reins, he stopped. Peeking just around the cottage's edge, only his head visible, was Lily's pony, Alabaster. She was here after all!

Duncan rushed the house's weathered door, slamming its knocker fast and loud. He had been frantic with worry since his daughter disappeared. Lily was his only child—his whole life since his wife died—and he was desperate to mend their rift. His summons fell unanswered, and he banged again, this time louder and longer.

"I'm coming! You needn't knock it down." The voice was familiar, and, as the door cracked, Duncan realized why—it was Jenny, after all.

"Lord Granville." Her face was blank, an unpainted canvas, frozen between joy and fury. Jenny began to back in, then stopped. Duncan had insulted and dismissed her; she owed him no courtesy.

"What is it you want?"

He stepped haltingly forward, surprised when she made no effort to move. "Is Lily here?"

Jenny's lips parted, then closed, censoring her intentions.

"You needn't lie. I've seen Alabaster."

Jenny had had no role in Lily's decision to leave. She could not have been more shocked to find the girl on her doorstep. If Cairn's driver hadn't intercepted Lily en route to Cairn's and prattled indiscreetly about where Jenny hid, no one would even have known. Jenny was not responsible for Lily's flight, but neither could she ignore her need for it by aiding Duncan. She had no obligation to answer Duncan's queries, but he didn't look likely to leave.

"I assume Lily is here. May I come in?"

Jenny fired him a steely stare. "She's not. And no."

Duncan's eyes flashed angrily. Did Jenny think she could lie to him? "I told you I saw the pony."

Jenny knew the ruse was useless. "She's gone for a walk."

"I'll wait." Duncan forced brusquely past her.

Jenny swept aside with an indignant bow. "As you wish."

Duncan faced away as he studied the cottage's dark confines. The central chamber opened directly into the kitchen, and the buttery smell of fresh bread filled the room. There was one other door, which Duncan assumed led to a bedchamber. The house was humble, to say the least—hardly the sort of place he would deign to spend even one night.

"I suppose I have you to thank for my daughter's disappearance." Still he would not face her, and Jenny wondered if it was because his preposterous accusation embarrassed him.

"How dare you! Is it so hard to believe Lily would flee you of her own accord?"

"Will you tell me you didn't mastermind this?" he snapped, turning.

"Would my answer matter? You twist words and hearts to suit your selfish needs. You're not likely to believe any truth I tell."

"You must admit it does seem a strange coincidence to find you two keeping company."

"There is nothing strange about my love for your daughter."

"There is, indeed, when it interferes with my wishes."

"I owe no explanations. I don't work for you anymore."

"That, at least, I can be thankful for."

Duncan's words were flint to Jenny's tinder. Her resolution to measure her answer, to allow him no further glimpse of her heart, fell beneath her rage. With such force it made Duncan start noticeably, Jenny slammed her fist atop a trestle table.

"I will tolerate no more of your insults! You think it odd to find me here? It would not seem so if you understood for one moment the anguish you have caused. Lord Chatham, bless him, at least was not so blind. He offered me this refuge, for as long as I needed it, to recover my peace of mind. I had not thought to have my efforts to do so thwarted by your rude bullying.

"And as for Lily, I had no idea you could try her love to the point where she felt she had to flee. The notion of a child her age unable to turn to her own father! I would no more encourage a breach between you two than I would injure her. She fled quite on her own, apparently with the conviction that you neither understand her nor care to. If my presence here has offered Lily solace, I am glad for it. I won't apologize to you for the love in my heart."

Duncan stared back emptily, his calm expression belying the maelstrom in his head. Jenny looked like she was telling the truth—perhaps she *had* played no part in Lily's flight.

What was harder for him to accept was that Jenny had been so upset by his dismissal to have accepted Cairn's offer. After their row, Duncan had spent little thought on her feelings; he was too concerned with disciplining his own. He'd imagined Jenny would return to London none the worse, her anger gone and the matter forgotten.

But from the moment she left, Duncan had known that for him it would not be so simple. Yet now, as he stood facing her, thinking this might well be the last time they spoke, the fitful misery he had endured last night as he had tossed in bed paled in comparison.

An angry chorus of voices screamed in his head. It was wrong, but he wanted her. Duncan lowered his head into his hands and closed his eyes.

His odd response confused Jenny. Was he ill? "Lord Granville? Are you all right?" Thinking some sudden malady must have overcome him, Jenny leaned closer. "What is it?"

"I'm sorry," he whispered softly. His shoulders shook with an anguished sob.

A moment ago he had railed at her, accused her of frightful things; now this strange apology. Surely he meant he was sorry about what had happened with Lily. "You mean you regret the breach with your daughter?"

"Yes." Duncan lowered his hands from his face, revealing his agony. "And my behavior toward you."

Jenny searched his face frantically, desperate for a hint of his intent. He returned her tortured stare, each stumbling on the unspoken questions asked by the other's eyes.

Jenny could not bear it. She had raised her hopes on him once before. She would not risk her heart again.

"It may be some time before Lily comes back. I think you should go."

"No," he answered slowly. "That's not at all what I should do." As if a mist had lifted, Duncan suddenly understood the cost of his snobbery.

A pall fell over his features. With deliberate languor, he raised his hand slowly to Jenny's cheek, making her fear he would hit her. Instead, his fingers slid lovingly down the side of her face, bringing a soft gasp from her parted lips.

She shook her head in refusal, begging against his further teasing. Duncan's hand wound around her neck and pulled her close. Without warning, his lips were upon her, possessing her own and finding no resistance. Still disbelieving, Jenny stood frozen, afraid to touch back, lest she again be taken for a fool.

The permission of her silence gave Duncan all he needed. His arms crushed Jenny hard against his frame, and his hands wove hungrily through her hair, tipping her face to deepen their kiss.

The warmth of his mouth, his smoky scent, everything about him fired her blood. A caution of conscience warned her to stop, but Jenny wished only surrender. With welcome abandon she clung to him, her nails raking slow tracks down the back of his riding coat.

"Jenny." He whispered her name like an incantation. She had never heard it spoken with such reverence, and, almost more than his touch, the sound of it swirled a sweet ache in her belly.

"I don't know what you want from me," she pleaded, still struggling to cleave to reality.

"Forgive my foolishness. Please, don't send me away."

"Send you away?" She pulled back, her eyes brimming with surprise. "What is it you mean?"

"I have been stupid—blind to my love for you. Is it too late?"

"For what?"

"To hope you could care—that you might agree to be my wife?"

Jenny's eyes filled with tears, and a gasp of a sob rose unbidden from her chest.

"Dearest God," Duncan answered, his face contorted. "I've gambled you away, haven't I? If you won't have me, I can't blame you." He hung his shaking head.

Jenny felt weak and overwhelmed. Tears came faster and harder until she could no more see, only feel Duncan's arms around her.

"Jenny, please. I cannot bear your silence."

She swallowed hard, inching toward composure. "If you want me, I am yours. Willingly. Happily."

Duncan's face burst with joy, and he pulled Jenny tighter, smothering her tear-dampened cheeks with an explosion of kisses. "My love, my precious love," he whispered.

The front door flew open with a bang, parting them as both their heads snapped toward its burst of light.

"Father! Jenny! What is this?" Lily dropped her armful of hyacinths to the floor, and their blossoms spilled like froth at her feet.

Duncan and Jenny moved farther apart, trying to look proper, but their flushed faces made the effort useless. Duncan realized the absurdity of their pose and reached out, one hand to Jenny, one to his daughter.

"Lily, I've been a fool. But if you'll help me, I swear I'll be better. Jenny has agreed to become my wife, providing you approve."

Lily blinked incredulously, barely believing her father's words. "Approve! It's the most wonderful thing ever!" She rushed forward, the force of her impact nearly toppling all three of them. Together they stood in a warm, awkward hug, and for the first time in many, many years, Duncan knew the joy of following his heart.

Alysanna's half-jack boots squeaked with each step she took around Briarhurst's rustic, and she leaned as far forward as possible to silence the gravel's crunch. Sneaking into her own home was preposterous, yet it was all she could do, given the house steward Ryan's refusal to let her in.

"Her ladyship is resting," he had informed her, "and has requested no visitors." Alysanna didn't doubt that. Likely Roberta had been resting a bit too much lately, fat on the full coffers of Briarhurst's rents.

Alysanna had long suspected that Roberta wanted to steal the estate, but Hadley was overconcerned regarding her threat. Warrant or no, Roberta would not dare arrest her. Even if she tried, Alysanna could outride any stable hand set on her trail. Besides, the danger was immaterial—Alysanna desperately needed to know what had happened here.

In truth, she understood Ryan's refusal. Her manly disguise looked improper, to start. Now, after the ride from Foxhall, coupled with a rough night in Hadley's stable, it had worsened noticeably.

At least the houseman hadn't recognized her. There was enough risk even coming here. Revealing herself would have courted disaster.

Alysanna crouched as she hurried through the drying yard, thinking the adjacent laundry would likely be vacant this time of the morning. The kitchen was no doubt buzzing with dinner preparations, and the still room hummed all summer with the laying in of preserves and jams. But the chambermaids would already have taken their fresh linen upstairs. Perhaps Alysanna could pass unnoticed through the laundry and seek Roberta of her own accord.

The door opened with a welcoming creak. Ryan had refused to even allow her in the foyer. Now, stepping onto the laundry's sun-streaked tiles, Alysanna realized it was the first time in six months she'd touched foot to her home.

White sheets and chemises hung like linen boughs from the overhead frames, and huge wooden basins and more racks stood neatly beneath. In the room's center, the massive box mangle rose to torture wrinkles, its black wheels dark arcs in the room's blanched light. Alysanna breathed in the warm, clean smell, then scurried toward the door that led upstairs.

"Lord in heaven!" Alysanna froze, her heart in her ears. She had thought herself alone, but now she saw the alarm's source. Almost hidden behind the ringing press, just opposite where she stood, was Julia's maid, Marcy. Her eyes were huge with fear, and she looked nearly as white and lifeless as the sheets draped behind her.

"There's nothin' of value here," Marcy pleaded, her teeth chattering audibly. "The silver's next door, and my mistress is upstairs, third door from the top landing."

Alysanna almost answered, then stopped. Marcy had not yet recognized her; why tempt fate by revealing herself? Still, the maid looked apoplectic, and Alysanna knew she would not be allowed to proceed upstairs unchecked.

"Oh, my, it's not the silver ye want, is it? Have mercy, please." Marcy wrung her hands frantically.

Her fear was so ridiculous that Alysanna had to stifle a laugh. Marcy was convinced enough of Alysanna's false gender to think that she wanted her way with her. Alysanna drew in a deep breath to deepen her voice.

"I've no intention of harming you. Please, don't be frightened."

Marcy looked no less terrified for Alysanna's assurance. She arched backwards over a folding table, intending to brace herself against Alysanna's assault.

"If it isn't me you want, then what is it?"

Alysanna stretched for a plausible explanation. All she wanted was to get past, unscathed.

"I need a bite to eat. Your houseman turned me away. I believed I might beg something from the cook. I thought this was the kitchen."

Marcy ran her gaze up Alysanna's bedraggled appearance, and her expression relaxed, as if the explanation held some sway.

"Oh," she sighed. "It's next door you'll be wanting, though if Ryan said no, you'll have a hard time convincing the cook. The mistress is tight with her food, she is, like everything else around here. Didn't use to be so. But since Miss Alysanna's gone. . . ."

When Marcy had worked as Julia's lady's maid, she had always been garrulous. Alysanna had come looking to find Roberta, but perhaps Marcy was better still.

"Miss Alysanna—who is she?"

"Our mistress. Was, anyway. Oh, 'twas a terrible turn of events. I wasn't always here in this steamin' laundry. I served Miss Julia, I did. Fine gowns and everything. She was Lady Roberta's daughter, stepsister to Lady Alysanna, the manor's heir."

"You say was? What became of Julia?"

"She was murdered—shot down cold in the parlor. Ruined the carpet, it did." Marcy paused, waiting for her words to take full impact. Alysanna remembered the maid's penchant for melodrama, and was not surprised to see more than a small hint of glee in Marcy's eyes as she realized Alysanna was a captive audience for her lurid tale.

"Yes, murdered," she repeated, as if Alysanna had asked again. "That's why I'm wearing this dull gray frock. Though even if we weren't in mournin', Mistress Roberta would hardly allow me to wear my proper gowns, seeing as I have to wash these filthy clothes.

"It's been quite a tumble, since Miss Julia was killed. If you can imagine, Mistress Roberta let me go—said it was too painful; that I reminded her of her daughter and all. I can understand, but dismissing me without a spare pound—terrible! At least Master Hadley was kind. When he heard what she'd done, he gave me some traveling money. Got me to London, at least. Though, strange as it seems, I couldn't find proper work there, either. Ended up in the scullery."

"And what became of your mistress's killer?"

"They haven't found him—not yet, at least. I think it's a gentleman, to be sure, though everyone else says Miss Alysanna had some hand in it. They'd a terrible fight at the ball that night—Miss Alysanna and Miss Julia, that is. When Mistress Roberta told him, the constable got a warrant right fast."

Alysanna's fists clenched against her breeches. She had underestimated Roberta's greed.

"Have they arrested this Alysanna, then?"

"They're still looking, to hear tell. But she's gone to God knows where, none to Mistress Roberta's dismay. She's been spendin' Briarhurst's rents like her purse was real deep, though precious few pounds on the staff. Though she did come to London to bring me back, just last week. Said she realized she'd made a mistake, though I still have to slave here until her maid Sally leaves. Lord, it's hot in summer! I could swear I've died and gone straight to hell. Oh," Marcy continued, lowering her eyes, "I didn't mean to make light of Miss Julia's passing. She was a fine lady, that one, though she did have her faults.''

''Were they such that someone would wish her dead?''

''I don't think so. 'Cept maybe the father of her poor unborn babe—whoever that scoundrel was.''

Alysanna squinted incredulously. Surely she had misheard. ''Unborn babe? What is it you mean?''

''Oh,'' Marcy answered, fluffing the ribbons trailing her grey turban, ''I'm talking out of turn to say. Mistress would have my head if she thought I'd breathed a word.''

Alysanna was desperate for more explanation. ''Come, what's a bit of gossip between two hard-working souls? It's not as if I know your lady anyway. I'm only passing through.''

''Well,'' Marcy purred coyly. '' 'Spose it won't hurt. Miss Julia was carrying a babe. Told me so herself right before her accident. I woulda known anyway. Sick as an underfed cur, poor thing. Oh, it just makes me cry to think of that little unborn soul, struck down with its mama with nary a chance. Can't believe whoever attacked her would have done so if he knew.''

Marcy drew her finger against her cheek. ''Or 'haps he did. I can't help but wonder if Miss Julia got herself in that mess and the gentleman in question, if I can be so generous as to call him that, thought to dispense with his problem.''

Alysanna could have been knocked flat with a feather. Julia pregnant! She'd had no inkling. Her stepsister didn't even have a beau, much less a suitor.

''You're sure she was with child?''

Marcy stiffened indignantly. ''I'd know what my own lady confided, to be sure. Why would you doubt it?''

''I don't, of course. It's just such a wicked tale. But if you suspect the father, why haven't you told? Surely the constable should be advised.'' Alysanna was still reeling from Marcy's news, but all she could think was that if the tale were true, it might offer a lead on Julia's killer.

''I told the mistress when she came for me in London. Didn't think of it until after I first left Briarhurst, everything being so topsy-turvy. Mistress Roberta, she said she'd handle it, but I haven't heard much since. I guess the constable paid it no mind. I imagine they're still looking for Miss Alysanna.''

''And you don't have any idea who the father was?''

''If I did, I'd surely tell, but I've not a guess to make. Miss Julia was good to me, but she had her secrets, that one— nights when she sent me out, said she had business of her own to attend to. She was careful—at least 'til the end.''

''Marcy, I'd like you to. . .'' Ryan tipped his head inside the laundry room door, his face puffing into an angry glower as he spied Alysanna. ''You! I already told you we don't take beggars. Out with you, now!'' Ryan grabbed a nearby broom and raised it overhead.

Without so much as a nod to Marcy, Alysanna jumped up and bolted out the back. Running hard, she mounted her horse, then quickly spurred him to a full gallop.

The animal's rocking jolt and thundering hooves echoed her thoughts. Marcy's revelation was incredible—nearly unbelievable—yet the maid seemed convinced of its truth.

Alysanna knew one thing was clear: Roberta had done all she could to betray her. Julia's pregnancy was more than significant. Yet Alysanna knew as well as she knew Roberta's greedy heart that her stepmother had never repeated Marcy's news—particularly to the constable. If she had, Alysanna would have been absolved, the warrant rescinded.

Marcy's suspicions did not seem illogical. If Julia carried a child from any honorable entanglement, Alysanna would have had some inkling. Apparently, her relationship was more sordid. Perhaps the baby's father had wrought Julia's fate. The motive made sense. But whose was it?

The answer volleyed like a shot through Alysanna's mind, and she shook her head so hard she loosened her hat. No matter how she tried, it was no use. Cairn's visage loomed before her. Had he fathered Julia's baby and gone to Briarhurst that night to murder her?

Alysanna had come home hoping to absolve him. Instead, she overflowed with more doubt, more pain. She snapped her mount to a halt—she didn't even know where she was going. Back to Foxhall, to a man who might be a killer? She certainly couldn't stay at Briarhurst. But what other choice had she?

Like an epiphany, she suddenly knew. Hadley had no answers, and, if Roberta did, she was not about to tell. But Maude knew Cairn better than anyone. She, certainly, would know if he'd been involved with Julia.

It was a strange fate to seek. Maude had always been Alysanna's adversary. Perhaps now she could be her ally. Alysanna spurred her gelding forward with a cluck. She would go to Totten-Hoo.

CHAPTER
18

❧

Maude couldn't be dead. Alysanna stared at her sprawled form, thinking the scene some illusion conjured by her tortured thoughts. It was only a chimera of madness, brought on by fatigue.

Alysanna turned away and took a breath. When she looked again the body would be gone. Yet as she spun back, her eyes clung to the gruesome truth. Like a garish nightmare, everything looked overly crisp—too large and too vivid. Maude's ashen face, the ruby wound that had ripped through her back, turning a swath of blue carpet deepest purple, even the gold griffin-footed chair at whose base she lay—everything burned too bright, like the flash of a paper fire.

Alysanna pressed her hands hard against her temples, as if she could force the confusion from her mind. What was Maude doing at Foxhall? Only moments ago, Alysanna had returned from Briarhurst, planning to leave her disguise and ride to Totten-Hoo to ask Maude of Cairn's involvement with Julia. Instead, she faced this new disaster.

Thinking Maude's killer still might be close, Alysanna whirled in a frantic circle, searching for some sign. But there was no movement or sound, only thick silence. When she had passed the foyer moments ago, the stillness of the house had struck Alysanna only as slightly odd. There was no staff, no footman managing the door, no sound of maids rattling about in the kitchen. Yet Alysanna was so preoccupied with her fears that she'd paid it scant heed.

Now she realized how queer it was to find Foxhall abandoned. Perhaps Maude was not the killer's sole victim. Fearing she might be next, Alysanna burst toward the library, but pitched forward as her gait snagged on something on the floor. She yanked her coachman's cloak free of its tangle and froze at what she saw. It was a pistol—apparently the gun that had wrought Maude's fate.

The weapon drew her like a lodestone, and Alysanna reached for it with a trembling hand. Slowly, her fingers curled around its wooden butt. She lifted it in front of her eyes and, rotating its muzzle slowly, studied the flintlock. Something was strangely familiar. She unfurled two fingers and stared at the silver escutcheon, its engraving a familiar crest.

Alysanna sucked in a gasp of air as she flashed back to the day the boar had rushed her in the woods. It was there she had seen the escutcheon before—in Cairn's hand.

All strength to deny the truth drained out of her. The legerdemain that allowed for Cairn's innocence dissolved with the terrifying new evidence she now gripped. Cairn was not only Julia's murderer, he had killed Maude, too.

She struggled to imagine why—how could Cairn turn on Maude, his lifelong friend and confidante? What could she know? Alysanna felt the blood drain from her face as she recalled why she had gone seeking Maude. A chill racked her, so hard it nearly shook the pistol from her hands. Maude had gone to uncover Alysanna, but had also learned who killed Julia—and it was Cairn.

Alysanna slumped in grief into a chair, Cairn's pistol thudding to the floor as her hands flew to her eyes. Tears came in uncontrollable, miserable swells, squeezing in trickles though her fingers.

Conscience would have spent her sorrow on Maude or Julia. But instead, Alysanna's heart exploded with the knowledge that she had lost, forever and irrevocably, the man who owned her heart.

She felt she was spiraling downward, past the floor, into the darkness of her own tortured soul. She was swallowed, sucked like a leaf into a wind-wild void. Alysanna cried out in loud, torn wails, her lament unearthly, more banshee than mortal.

Finally, her tears were spent, and Alysanna blinked away the waters of her grief. Through a blur at first, then with increasing clarity, her eyes focused on something she had not before seen. Clutched in Maude's rigid hand, outstretched as if she meant Alysanna to have it, was what looked like a note.

Alysanna knew she must read it, yet the prospect of touching Maude's white, frosty flesh made her stomach upend. Still, some core of will rallied inside her, and, fearing she would stop if she so much as hesitated, Alysanna lunged downward, tugging hard at the paper. Maude's fingers, frozen with death, held fast.

Loathing pitched through her, yet Alysanna knew what she must do. Her trembling hand pried Maude's gray fingers free. The flesh's stony feel made her wince and shudder. Finally, the note tore loose. Wiping her palm on her cloak as if she could rub off death, Alysanna lifted the letter toward the light.

Lord Chatham:
As you did not arrive on the hour we agreed, I was forced to keep another appointment. I expect your prompt appearance within the week, and furthermore, that you will fully discharge your responsibilities toward my daughter Julia, particularly in light of the delicate condition you have forced upon her. The ceremony must be arranged quickly, before the fact that she is with child becomes common knowledge. I await your reply.

Lady Roberta Wilhaven

Alysanna read the letter again and again, until the words blurred together. There was no more confusion, no disputing the damning evidence. Cairn not only knew Roberta, he had fathered Julia's unborn babe, then murdered her to prevent a forced marriage! Everything Alysanna had feared was true, meshed like some nightmarish puzzle. It all made terrible, ghastly sense.

Her thoughts snapped to clarity. The Cairn she knew didn't exist. That man was an impostor—a ruthless killer who would commit any crime to protect himself. And Alysanna was not only his wife, she was still in his house.

She bolted toward the door, then returned for the pistol to use as defense. There was no telling when Cairn would return or what his purpose would be if he found her.

Alysanna grabbed the flintlock and dashed to the drawer where she guessed the powder and shots were kept. The first bin was empty. She tried another, then another. Finally, the bottom drawer gave up a silver powder flask and a small satchel of lead.

With efficiency belying her rattled nerves, Alysanna half-cocked the hammer, poured in the powder and tamped the lead ball down hard with the ramrod. She lifted the barrel and sighted down its cylinder. Alysanna had not fired a gun since the night at Briarhurst, but she could do it now if she had to.

She took one final look at Maude, then shuddered and began to leave. But the thunderous slam of Foxhall's oak door lurched her to a stop and choked her breath in her throat. *Don't panic*, she mouthed silently. It could be William or Mildred, though Alysanna knew neither was wont to enter from the front. She sensed her hope was futile; she knew all too well that it was Cairn.

Alysanna leaned back against the window's cold pane and fought off a sneeze at the surfeit of dust inside the curtain's velvet folds. If she held perfectly still, she could go unseen —providing she could control her galloping breath, which sped faster each moment as she listened to the dull echo of boot heels across the foyer. The sound was chillingly familiar; it had to be Cairn.

Before this moment, Alysanna had not considered why he always wore boots. Now she realized that they concealed the wound, the hallmark of his dark business with Julia—the scar she had given him.

Had he come back to dispose of Maude? Alysanna could hardly imagine why Cairn had left her there to damn him as evidence. From her color, Maude looked to have been shot some time past. Was Cairn so mad, so brazen as to commit his crimes with such leisure?

There were still pieces that could not fit, but those that did filled Alysanna with abject terror. Maude lay on the floor before her; surely the library was where Cairn was headed.

She pulled the pistol's barrel vertical, resting it against her cheek to keep it from bulging through the curtain's folds.

Alysanna would not shoot unless Cairn flushed her. But if he did, she vowed to do whatever was necessary to defend herself properly.

"Alysanna?" Cairn's voice drifted toward her, growing louder as he called again. "Darling, are you here?"

Darling! What was this grotesque charade? Did he think she could know his crimes, his evil treachery, and still suffer his mocking endearments?

The parlor door creaked with his push, and Alysanna heard his heavy boots thud across the carpet's thick warp. "Maude? My God!" Maude's taffeta skirt rustled. Surely Cairn was dragging her out to some shallow grave. But why, if he thought himself alone, did he pretend surprise?

Alysanna closed her eyes and prayed he'd leave. Then a blast of light hit her as the curtain snapped back, and she stood breathless with terror, exposed to Cairn's steely stare.

"Alysanna! What's happened here?"

Alysanna lowered the barrel to Cairn's face and narrowed her eyes into a squint.

"Get away from me."

Cairn's hand flew to her arm, but she flung it off, fully cocking the pistol's hammer and repeating her command. "I said get away, murderer."

Cairn raised his palms in surrender, backing toward Maude.

"Maude's shot." Strangely, his face registered what looked like shock.

"Don't pretend with me," she snapped. "I know all your lies."

"Lies?"

"How can you continue even now to mount them? I know

you killed her. And Julia. And that I would likely be next if I hadn't the wits to discover your deceit.''

Cairn shook his head in confusion. ''I don't know what you're saying. But for God's sake, take that pistol off me so I can get some help. I'd have already gone for the doctor if I hadn't seen William's riding boots under the curtain.''

''What twisted ruse is this? You know Maude's dead. You saw to it.''

Cairn's confounded look only hardened Alysanna's stare. She vowed not to be duped again by his lies.

''As God is my witness, I don't know what you're saying. Where the hell have you been? Why are you dressed like that? I thought some terrible fate had overcome you.''

''I'm sure you wished it. I undertook my own investigation—at Briarhurst. I know all about Julia's baby.''

''Baby?''

''Don't pretend.'' Alysanna lifted the muzzle slightly, then lowered it, resighting on Cairn, who stepped back in response.

''I know your whole sordid tale. You slept with Julia and got her with child. You should have married her—it would have been simpler.''

''You think that I fathered Julia's child?''

''God, I should have seen it all before now. If I hadn't believed you, trusted you when you promised to clear my name. If I'd taken on my own cause, then at least poor Maude would have been spared this fate.''

''You think I killed Maude, too?'' Cairn's eyes glazed with incredulity, but the urgency drained from his voice, as if he realized his pleas were useless against her frenzy.

''I suppose I was to be next?''

''Alysanna!''

"Oh, God," she breathed, tears glistening in her wide green eyes. "I gave you my trust, my love."

"Why do you persist in your belief that I betrayed you?"

Alysanna kicked Roberta's letter, which she'd dropped when the curtain parted, toward him. "Don't bother to pick it up. You know what it says."

"Indulge me. Repeat it."

"It's your letter from Roberta, insisting that you make an honest woman of Julia, having already stolen her virtue."

"Whatever this is," Cairn answered, nodding toward the floor, "I've no knowledge of it."

"You expect me to believe you?"

"I don't think you're of much mind to believe anything I say. But whatever lies fill your head, I can tell you they're no more than that."

"And I suppose you've some way to deny your scar. 'Twas I gave it to you at Briarhurst, was it not?"

Cairn's eyes searched Alysanna's, then closed in synchrony with a heavy sigh. "All right. I'll tell you. But only because my sins are not those you accuse me of. It was me you shot at Briarhurst."

Alysanna had thought she believed it before, but now the revelation, from Cairn's own lips, made her sick with misery. His confession forced all grace from her heart.

"Then, you admit killing Julia."

Cairn shook his head slowly, emphatically. "I went to Briarhurst to meet your stepmother on business about a land sale. I was late, so I hired a room at the inn, planning to stay the night. I took a horse and rode to Briarhurst. When I got there, everyone was gone. except Julia, who was as dead when I found her as when you did."

Alysanna snorted in disbelief, shaking her head.

"I know you don't believe me, and I'll admit it's an in-

credible tale. But if you ever loved me, trust me now."
Cairn's eyes implored Alysanna to reason, but he could see
his faith was ill-placed.

"Trust you? When you've kept the truth from me? If what
you say is true, why did you hide it?"

"Because I feared to lose you."

"Indeed." Alysanna nodded her head in disgust. "I should
think that confessing you're a murderer might well damage
your chances."

"I'll tell you again, I didn't kill anyone. I couldn't disclose
my involvement in Julia's murder because of exactly what's
happening now—I was afraid you'd distrust me."

"If what you say is true, why wouldn't I believe you?"

"I've been hurt by a lack of faith before. There was a
woman—Elizabeth. We were engaged. I bought a mill at
auction. It had been driven to bankruptcy by poor management. After the sale I learned that the owner had killed
himself—and that he was my fiancée's father. I trusted her
enough to tell the truth, but she couldn't believe me. So you
see, love, honesty has felled me before. This time I swore
to make it different. I would not lose you, even if my vow
drove me to lie."

Alysanna's brows tangled in confusion. God, how she
longed to believe him. Was there some hope that his sweet
words were true? If there were only a glimmer of Cairn's
innocence, there was still a breath of life in their love.

Alysanna stamped her foot, banishing the wishful thought.
It was only more of his skilled seduction.

"Can you doubt my love for you?"

"Be quiet!" she ordered, her voice rocky and frail. If she
heard any more it would shake her purpose.

"I love you."

"Enough!" Alysanna screamed.

"Alysanna." Cairn reached out his hand and took a step closer. Alysanna flew back, and the windowpane rattled with her jump.

"I'll shoot. I won't warn you again."

"Then do it," he said quietly, stepping closer. "I couldn't live without you."

Cairn edged still nearer, now only inches away. Alysanna sighted down the pistol's barrel, knowing only its lead could stop him now.

Her finger pulled against the pistol's trigger, and she tried to fire. She had the strength; where was her will? She struggled desperately, but couldn't. Cairn was a murderer, a madman guilty of heinous crimes. Yet, even at the cost of her life, she could not smother her love for him.

Cairn moved even closer, his chest nearly touching the shaking barrel. A wash of tears stung her eyes.

With an anguished moan, she hurled the weapon across the room and rushed toward the door, expecting Cairn's huge, cruel hands to close in a death grip around her throat. Yet incredibly, insanely, Cairn let her go.

CHAPTER
19

❦

The cold morning air filled Alysanna's lungs like a gulp of ice water, and each time she breathed, it summoned a dull ache that radiated out from her heart. It had been miserable enough riding all night in her flight from Foxhall. Now, the overcast sky only added to her discomfort, refusing even a glint of sunlight to slip through its grey veil.

Alysanna closed her eyes in relief as Wodeby's spires rose on the horizon. Between the cold, her fatigue, and her anguish over Cairn, she had never felt quite so wretched and overwhelmed.

She urged her gelding toward a canter, then, as they reached the manor, she slowed to soften the clop of his hooves. Alysanna headed for the southern pavilion, far from Wodeby's main entrance, in the hopes of avoiding a repeat of yesterday's confrontation with Hadley's houseman. Dismounting, she sneaked toward one of several back entrances.

Her feet ground to a halt as an angry volley boomed from the house.

"I tell you I need more—you're too fat from Briarhurst's rents anyway!" The words were slurred but unmistakably Hadley's, yet Alysanna could make no sense of them. Briarhurst—what was he ranting about?

"You're drunk, and out of luck. There'll be no more money—not a single pound, do you hear?" Alysanna pressed her cheek against Wodeby's cold stone. It sounded like Roberta. Alysanna crouched down as she scurried under the second-story gallery window. Whatever they were arguing about, she wanted to hear.

"How dare you!" A loud smack split the air. Knowing Roberta's volatile temper, Alysanna couldn't guess if she had taken or delivered the blow. "You ask for more money, after all your sins?"

"My, we're cocky. My sins have nothing to do with our arrangement. In any event, you tread dangerously. If I were you, I'd walk more carefully."

"Careful is what you should have been with Julia. I've been talking to Marcy."

"Marcy? She's gone to London."

"That's interesting—how would you know? You should have paid her better. She's back—and babbling about Julia's unborn child."

"What's this prattle of yours?"

"Don't think you can slither away by pretending you're stupid. God knows it's true enough, but your little game won't work with me."

"Have your insults a point?"

"I know Julia was pregnant when she died, and I know the baby was yours."

"Julia pregnant? And this wench Marcy claims it was me? Filthy rubbish, nothing more."

"Marcy's not smart enough to put it together, but I am. Enough to have smelled something sour and gone asking to London. All the time you and Julia spent together—what was the pretense? Polishing your rough manners to work on Alysanna?"

"Roberta, you've a mother's blindness. What if Julia and I did have our sport—what makes you think I was the only one?"

"How dare you! You were, and you know it. If Alysanna hadn't been heir, perhaps you would have chosen my daughter instead. As it was, poor Julia paid for your indiscretion."

"Drop it, Roberta."

"I'll do no such thing!" Alysanna heard the pitch of Roberta's voice rise, and she knew it meant trouble. "You foul cur! Defile my daughter's honor, then dare to deny it. Save your lying breath!"

What sounded like a fist banging wood popped Alysanna onto her toes. She could hardly believe what she heard, but instinct tabled her reaction. She sensed danger, and every fiber of her body tensed as if she would be called at any moment to meet it.

"It's hardly my fault you were dam to a trollop." The liquor slurred Hadley's speech and pushed him to an uncommon candor.

"So, you admit your involvement with her!"

"Have it as you will. Perhaps you've even earned the truth, with your nosy prodding. What if I did get Julia with child? 'Twas hardly my fault. Couldn't keep her hands off me, the hungry little bitch! Then she couldn't keep her mouth shut. I paid her for her silence, but it wasn't enough—she wanted to be my countess. Can you imagine? Obviously, I had to handle it.''

"What have you done?" Roberta had suspected him before, but now her voice pulled back in horror.

"Nothing Julia didn't deserve. It would have been quite a complication, don't you think—one sister with child and the other my bride?"

"Dear God—you did kill her!" Roberta's voice trembled with incredulity and fear, both of which coursed through Alysanna as her hand flew to cover her mouth. Could this unbelievable tale be true? She strained her head up toward the window, but could only catch the dull sounds of a scuffle muted through its pane. A loud thump, like a body hitting the floor, startled her.

"Animal!" Roberta's voice came in a gasp, as if the wind had been knocked from her. "I'll see that you hang for this."

"You'll see nothing of the sort—not if you wish to keep your Briarhurst."

"It's an idle threat. Six months have passed. It's mine—you can't change that now."

Alysanna shook her head as if she had misheard. Was Roberta talking about her father's will?

"Not even my oath to the constable that Alysanna never abandoned the estate? I'll swear she was forced off by you —driven under duress by your cruel, greedy threats."

Alysanna's mind felt as thick as a cobweb. She plumbed her memory, trying to recall what had happened at the reading of her father's will. She had been so undone she had been barely able to stand, much less think. Six months—it rang a distant bell. Was there some rule of her inheritance she had overlooked? Had Briarhurst somehow slipped from her hands?

"You wouldn't dare seek the authorities," Roberta hissed. "I could send them your head on a platter."

"That would be stupid for both of us. I should not wish a fate on the gallows, but were I so forced, I'd hardly go silently. It seems we are once again partners, are we not?"

In the ensuing silence, Alysanna could almost hear Roberta's fury. "Damn you." Her voice was heavy, soaked with anger. "All right. But I want you gone. Gone, do you hear?"

"Gladly. There is one condition. A new life, particularly the one I fancy abroad, comes dearly to the purse. I will need some funds."

"No more!"

"'Twill hardly break you, considering all your stewardship of Briarhurst will bring. One more note will do."

"How much?"

"A hundred thousand."

"Pounds!"

"Surely not guineas. I'm afraid the style to which you have accustomed me is no inexpensive matter."

Roberta stalled, grasping for any alternative. "You're a fool to think Alysanna will let this lie. She'll come back and find out both of us, then tattle her tale. Why should I pay you if I'll lose Briarhurst anyway?"

"As always, you underestimate me. A letter from me will keep you safe. Alysanna already suspects who killed Julia, and it is a suspicion I can easily confirm."

"She knows of your involvement?"

"Of course not! She thinks the man is her new husband." Hadley roared a loud, sloppy laugh and slapped his knee.

"Husband? What's this news?"

"I did mean to tell you. Our Alysanna is duchess to Lord Cairn Chatham."

"Cairn Chatham! Surely you realize . . ."

"Don't fret your greying head. She's completely convinced that Cairn fathered Julia's child, then killed her."

"Why would she think the killer him?"

"Your note—the one I forged—stated that Julia was with child, and that you expected Lord Chatham to abide by his duty."

"And what does that trickery solve? If Alysanna thinks her husband's guilty, she'll contact the authorities."

"If you'd seen her eyes when she spoke of him, you'd know better. Our girl is a woman in love, as impulsive as ever. It's a delicious mix. If she thinks he's guilty, she'll kill him—or else keep silent to protect him. Either way, our problem's gone."

"What makes you so sure she believes in his guilt?"

"Because Julia was not Cairn's only victim. He has—rather, had—a friend, the Lady Maude Delamere. 'Twas a pity, truly. She came here asking improper questions. I knew she had to be dealt with, so I followed her home. But can you imagine, she went straight to the Chathams'! I left a note drawing Cairn off so Alysanna found Maude. It was criminally simple. I shot Maude with Cairn's own pistol. Say, now, what's that puckered face? No praise for my shrewd cunning?"

"You're a beast from hell."

"You'd be well-advised to remember it. Now, fetch your carriage while I gather my things. I'll meet you later at Briarhurst. Bring the note—the full hundred thousand, not a penny less. Are we understood?"

From the slam of the door, Alysanna gathered that Roberta agreed. Afraid she'd be discovered, Alysanna pressed back tightly against the house's facade, cupping her mouth to stifle her mounting sobs. Only when Roberta's carriage pulled from sight did Alysanna allow herself tears of relief. Thank God her gelding was hidden from the front road.

But no sooner had Alysanna relaxed than her breath was choked by footsteps sounding along the window's base. A fragile, frightening pall descended, and on some instinctive level, Alysanna sensed that Hadley knew she was there. She bolted forward, praying she could reach her mount before Hadley reached her.

Alysanna ran so fast gravel flew from her boots as she raced toward her horse, but Hadley's booming "Hoay" as he bounded off the portico had scared the animal free of its tether moments too soon.

Alysanna knew she could not match him on foot, but it didn't stop her from trying. She exploded down Wodeby's drive, hoping to reach the main road for help, but Hadley's angry gait easily overtook her, and from the moment she felt his hands seize her hair, Alysanna knew that all was lost.

Hadley grabbed her arm, twisting it behind her like a painful vise. Alysanna's chest heaved as she struggled for breath, and her lips were suddenly parched and dry. A ragged "Please!" squeezed from her chest.

He pinched her chin, twisting her face into his tortured stare. "You really are too smart for your health. Julia could have used more of your wit, and you her stupidity. Now, what shall I do with you?" Hadley shoved Alysanna into the foyer. He grabbed her wrist so tightly it hurt as he dragged her back to the gallery.

"Joshua!" Alysanna screamed as loud as she could for help. Someone must be near. She could only hope Hadley's servants were not party to his dark dealings.

"Save your breath. The small staff I still keep has gone to town. It seems fate has smiled on me again."

Hadley pushed Alysanna roughly into a wing chair, then locked the gallery door. "Tell me how much you heard."

If she'd thought it would help, Alysanna would have pled ignorance, but her frantic flight from him undermined the notion. From the scowl on his face, Hadley knew she'd heard plenty.

"Enough to know you for the bastard you are. How could I have been so blind?"

Hadley circled her like a predator. "You mustn't fault yourself for the oversight. I've had practice. There were—involvements before you."

Alysanna's eyes snapped with rage and fear. "I suppose Julia was just more grist for your mill."

"Spare me the histrionics. For what it's worth, you should know that I had no mind to murder anyone. I really only wanted to marry you."

His words made Alysanna's stomach pitch, and she narrowed her eyes in disgust. "Because you loved me."

"I won't insult you with that lie. You were tolerable enough, but I had debts. And Briarhurst . . . well, that was too much to resist."

Alysanna shook her head as misery flooded her eyes. "How could I have let you into my heart?"

"You mustn't berate yourself. I had help, you know."

"Help?"

"Roberta. She was my—advisor, shall we say. Her instructions were invaluable. In exchange, of course, for my promise to return a sizable portion of your estate to her once we married. It would have been bearable enough. The sum I should have enjoyed as your husband was far greater than the hundred thousand. Though now, of course, I shall have my own purse, without some jabbering shrew to account to."

"So, that was your devil's deal. I've been living in a viper's nest." Alysanna swiped one dirt-smudged hand across her teary cheek.

"Weeping for me? I am touched."

The day's revelations came suddenly, painfully clear. Cairn was innocent. She had doubted him, and it was her lack of trust that had found her this fate. Alysanna shored up her agony, stiffening visibly. "I wouldn't give you the pleasure."

"Oh, yes, I'd forgotten your new husband. I suppose you think differently of him, now that you know his heart's so clean."

"I should have trusted my own."

"Indeed. But trust can be costly, can it not? Now I fear it will cost more than your marriage."

"What is it you want? I'll give you money—more than Roberta. Just tell me." Alysanna now fully appreciated Hadley as the demented, dangerous man he was. Her only hope was to reason with his greed.

A look of sadness flickered over his face, then vaporized. "Come, Alysanna, you know I can't let you go."

Alysanna's chest lurched as the chilling conclusion came clear—he meant to kill her. "Roberta knows, too. Surely you don't plan to finish us both?"

"My golden goose? She won't breathe a peep when I could tattle to the law. Once I'm abroad, I don't care what she does. She can talk 'til she's blue. They won't find me."

"Then, why stain your hands with even more blood? Trust me to keep silent until you're gone—by tomorrow, it won't matter."

"Would it were so simple. But you are an untidy complication. What would I do with you until I'm safe? We could hardly have you popping in at Roberta's. No, I'm afraid your damned curiosity has sealed your fate."

"Hadley, no." Alysanna shook her head imploringly, her eyes wide with terror.

"A shame. You are such a pretty thing, even in those tattered clothes."

"I'll leave. Trust me to keep silence. You owe me that after all we've been through."

Hadley released an impatient laugh. "Trust? It does not seem an overabundant trait in you. If you trusted your husband, you'd not be here now."

His sick logic made her head ache. "But you were the one made me suspect him! You indict me for the very conclusion you forced me to!"

Hadley stepped close, stroking Alysanna's wet cheek with the back of his hand. His touch felt foul, and Alysanna longed to recoil, but was frightened she'd anger him. "You have a quick mind, love. It's a fine but deadly attribute."

"So you mean to kill me, too?" Alysanna's throat tightened with fear, and she had to force the words past her lips.

He shrugged and nodded slowly. "What else can I do? But I won't make you suffer, providing you don't struggle. That debacle with Julia was such a mess—as if she thought she could flee. Maude was the same. But you're a smart girl, Alysanna—not likely to bring yourself needless pain. We'll have to go elsewhere, of course."

"Leave here?"

"It would be unwise to dispatch you in my own home. Quickly, now." Hadley hoisted her roughly from the chair and pushed her toward the door. Her mind raced wildly. Her best chance of survival was to stay at Wodeby. There might be help—perhaps Joshua, or the cook, or maybe even Roberta. Yet Hadley looked adamant. If forced, she didn't doubt he'd kill her here. If she could only stall. . . .

"Can I at least change from these sordid clothes? Allow me the dignity of a proper dress."

Hadley cocked one brow. "Good effort, but no use. Let's go." He pushed her again, and Alysanna stepped reluctantly forward, then stopped as she heard him open a drawer. She turned, hoping he was far enough back that she could outrace him. Instead, she turned face-to-face with the barrel of his pistol.

"You're going to shoot me?"

"Obviously."

She hadn't heard him load the gun. It must be a bluff. "I said, let's go." He stepped even closer, poking metal into her arm. She stood rigid, unmoving.

"It's loaded. I promise. I may be drunk, but I'm not stupid. I had this planned. Would you like me to prove it will fire?"

Alysanna shook her head quickly, lifting her hands in a plea. "Hadley, I know you don't love me, but surely there's still something decent within you. If there was ever anything between us—any friendship, any civility—I beg you, don't do this. I have a new life. I have no reason to want to steal yours."

"Well, hasn't love given you a blush? It almost makes me jealous. Truly, my dear, if there were another choice. . . . But it's you who've forced this hand." Hadley trailed the flintlock's icy barrel down her cheek, making her shudder. "Now."

She nodded wordlessly and turned, marching as slowly as she thought he'd allow.

"Where are you taking me?"

"The woods. Safe from prying eyes."

My God. That he had even thought of a place to kill her nailed down the horror of what was to happen. Panic washed over her, and, though she continued walking, Alysanna crumbled forward, her head leaning into her hands and her chest heaving with loud, explosive sobs. Hadley clapped his hand hard around her mouth.

"Shhh." Wodeby's front door creaked ominously. Hadley and Alysanna stood just outside the gallery, and, with a painful jerk, he dragged her back in, his arm around her waist like a tightly cinched belt.

Someone had entered the house. Alysanna's eyes clung to the gallery door, praying it would crack with the promise of help. Its tall panel swung inward, and the shining silver muzzle of a pistol emerged around its mahogany trim. Alysanna hadn't thought she could feel more terror—until now. It was Cairn.

Hadley jerked Alysanna back tighter as his eyes widened at the pistol's etched barrel. "Stay where you are or your wife's dead." He pressed the gun's shaft against her temple, making Alysanna twist sideways in pain. The gallery door creaked to a close.

"Cairn." Alysanna's voice was shot through with anguish. She longed to confess the error of her mistrust, but instead, Hadley's steel forced her to silence.

"Shut up, darling." Hadley pinned her wrist between her shoulder blades, making Alysanna moan.

"Let her go." Cairn's words were slow and firm, like his mask of a face.

"Give up the key to my freedom? I'm not that much of a fool."

"You're no fool. Surely you can't believe I'll let you escape?"

"You will if you value your new bride's life."

"I'll shoot you before you can fire."

Hadley nodded as he considered it. "Perhaps. It would be a wager against my reflexes. You might win. On the other hand, if you were to lose . . ." He let go Alysanna's arm, but still tipped the pistol against her head, lifting her chin in display as a prize.

Cairn began to lower his gun.

"Cairn, no!" Alysanna's cry was not for herself, but her husband. Hadley would kill her anyway. If Cairn was defenseless, he too would die. "He'll shoot me, I know it. Save yourself."

"I won't gamble with you, love." Cairn lowered the pistol until its muzzle hung against his thigh.

Tears streamed down Alysanna's face, and her chest jumped with lurching sobs. Despite Hadley's warning, she spoke anyway. "Please don't."

"I won't leave you," Cairn answered solemnly.

"A wise choice." Hadley laughed, pushing Alysanna toward the door. "But you're not quite finished. Drop the gun." Cairn paused, then laid the flintlock down. Alysanna's heart sank as he rose.

Hadley smiled. "Good. Now, if you'll go first, I think we all have an appointment to keep." He gave Alysanna another rough shove, nearly making her trip. Cairn saw the spark flash through her eyes. She slowed her gait and Hadley shouldered her forward. But this time Alysanna allowed the fall, crashing to her knees, then the floor.

Hadley grabbed her arm, trying to keep balance, but could not maintain it. With an angry shout he toppled over her, thudding to the ground as his pistol slipped free.

Cairn was instantly upon him, hurling Alysanna aside and lifting Hadley by the collar, only to slam him down on a trough of wooden floor. Their contest was no more one of weaponry; now muscle and bone struck as they rose and fell. Cairn's fists landed like dull gunfire against Hadley's torso.

It was an uneven fight, and Cairn easily pinned Hadley's smaller frame, straddling his waist in apparent triumph. Suddenly, Hadley lifted his knee into Cairn's groin, throwing him off with a thump and a moan.

Like a phoenix rising, Hadley stood slowly, his eyes now trained on Alysanna, who crouched, shaking, yards from where he stood. If she had been frozen with fear, the fury in his face loosened her, and she whirled about frantically, desperately scanning the room for a weapon. Cairn's pistol was an arm's length away. Alysanna dove for it, but she could not quite reach it.

She scrambled forward on her knees, her skirt hobbling her. She stretched her fingers out and, just barely, they closed around the pistol's butt, but shook loose as Hadley's hand pinched her neck and made her recoil. Yet almost instantly, she was once more free. Without looking to understand why, Alysanna lunged forward, grabbing the flintlock.

She turned on her knees to face him, cocking the trigger, then realized she could not shoot. Cairn had risen and was back in the melee. His fists pummeled Hadley's chest and stomach. In weak defense, Hadley grabbed him, the two of them so close they blurred one into each other. Alysanna couldn't even tell them apart, much less sight the muzzle.

Their fight seemed endless, though in fact it only took minutes. In exhaustion their battle finally slowed, and only now did Alysanna see that blood trickled from Hadley's mouth.

The two men gasped loudly for air and Hadley wobbled, barely able to stand. He looked finished; still, Cairn would not quit. He twisted Hadley's collar into a knot, then reeled back, spending a smack of a blow against Hadley's chin, sending him into final, unconscious descent to the floor.

Cairn leaned over his thighs, catching his breath, then glanced about the room. Something near the window caught his eye, and he loosened a thick curtain cord, which he used to bind Hadley's hands. Cairn turned to face Alysanna; she still trained the shaking pistol on the two of them.

"Not again," Cairn gasped, standing upright.

Alysanna looked at her hands in horror, then set back the cock and dropped the pistol with a loud thud. She wrenched her skirts up, stumbled to her feet, and rushed to Cairn's open embrace.

"Are you all right?"

Alysanna nodded wordlessly, her voice swallowed by a surge of emotion.

"Alysanna." Cairn pulled her closer, feathering kisses on her temples and cheeks. With urgent need his mouth descended, taking her lips in a hunger that seemed to have grown with the threat of her loss. She melted against him, not sure if she was more grateful for his safety or his touch.

Suddenly Alysanna pulled back, her eyes full of incredulity. "My God, you forgive me. I tried to kill you!"

"More than once." Cairn smiled wryly, stroking the top of her head with his hand.

"You tease me when my heart's so full of shame? I failed to trust you! How can you dismiss this?"

Cairn's face sobered. "Perhaps because I too am guilty. If I'd told you the truth to start, this wouldn't have happened. That day in the carriage—the day you fled Briarhurst—I knew what had happened."

Alysanna's eyes mirrored her confusion. "How could you know?"

"The portrait at Briarhurst. I could never forget such a

lovely face, though when I next saw it, you did look much the worse for the mud.''

Alysanna snapped free of his hold. He had known her dire straits, yet he had let her endure them? ''Then why did you allow me to go on suffering? My work as a governess, the misery with Duncan, the denial of my very birthright. . . . Why, you . . .'' She raised her hand to slap him, but he caught her wrist.

''What would you have had me do? I knew only that neither you nor I had murdered Julia. How could I go to the authorities without another name? I couldn't prove your innocence without serving up my own. Only, when I began to suspect Hadley . . .''

Her eyes flashed white-hot. ''You knew! And yet you didn't tell me?''

Cairn admonished her with a stern look. ''Credit me with more devotion than that. I only became suspicious after our introduction at Mowbry. Hadley's jacket that day had unusual gold buttons. They looked familiar, and as he left, I realized where I had seen the design—an identical button was in Julia's hand the night she was killed. In fact, I was loosening it from her grip when you shot me.

''If you hadn't fired, I'd have held on to it and shown the constable. As it was, the only evidence I had left was my word. Until last night, when the pistol that had been stolen from my horse at Mowbry reappeared next to Maude. Then I knew Hadley had killed her. And Julia. And that you would be next if I didn't find you in time. Thank God I guessed right, thinking you here.'' Cairn stroked her cheek gently.

Tears of shame streamed down Alysanna's face. ''You came to save me, knowing I tried to kill you?''

He smiled lovingly. ''Had you succeeded, I daresay you would have been left to your own devices. I am curious—

why didn't you shoot me at Foxhall? You thought me a murderer, yet you let me go.''

Alysanna blinked away her tears to see him more clearly. "I couldn't kill the part of me that was most alive."

Cairn pulled her head tight against his chest, closing his eyes and breathing in the sweet smell of her unbound hair.

"I should have trusted you," she whispered softly.

"And I you," he answered. "But there's still time." Alysanna withdrew slightly, her eyes huge with gratitude. "You'll still have me?"

"Life would be too dull, otherwise."

Alysanna dissolved in a mixture of laughter and tears, savoring the feel of his arms about her.

GET
LOVESTRUCK!

AND GET STRIKING ROMANCES FROM POPULAR LIBRARY'S BELOVED AUTHORS

Watch for these exciting romances in the months to come:

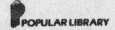

POPULAR LIBRARY

413